SUBMERGED

DANCE OF THE ELEMENTS
BOOK II

A.M. DEESE

This is a work of fiction. All characters and events portrayed in this novel are either products of the author's imagination or are used fictitiously.

SUBMERGED
DANCE OF THE ELEMENTS, #2

Maps by Tiphaine Leard
Cover design by Little Forest Cat Designs
Formatting by Kingsman Editing Services

Printed in the United States of America
Second Edition April 2022
ISBN: 978-1-957412-02-3

www.amdeese.com

This book is dedicated to the Jurado family,
for their endless love and support.

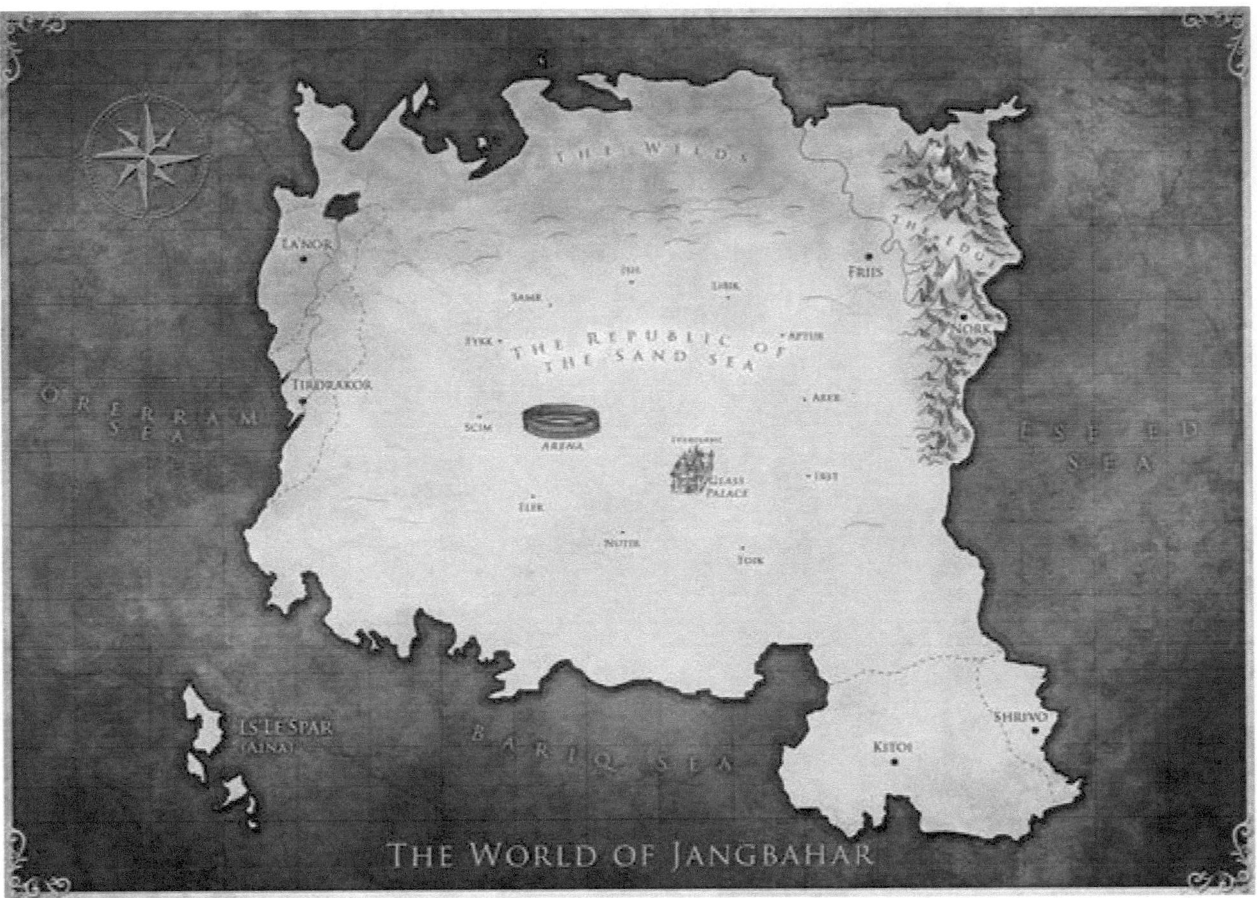
THE WILDS
THE EDGE
ESE EED SEA
FRIIS
NORK
LA'NOR
ISIL
SIRIK
SAMR
TYKK
THE REPUBLIC OF
THE SAND SEA
AFTUR
TIRDRAKOR
ORERRAM SEA
AREK
SCIM
ARENA
EVERSTORM
GLASS PALACE
IRIT
ELER
NUTIR
TORK
ISLE SPAR
(AINA)
BARIQ SEA
KETOI
SHRIVO
THE WORLD OF JANGBAHAR

JURA

CHAPTER ONE

Jura didn't tell anyone how different she felt. The first few days of travel had been a sandstorm of activity with little food or sleep, and she told herself that she only felt strange because she was tired. Except she didn't feel tired. For the first time in a long time Jura felt alive.

On the fourth night, Jura was bit by a scorpion. The pain was intense. But when she didn't succumb to its poison, she wouldn't let Tylak make a thing of it. But how could she not? What kind of person suddenly learned how to fight five men at once? Could survive the sting of a deadly desert scorpion? Her body was changing. Everflame help her, but she was becoming someone or something else.

It seemed her heart would forever be in a state of panic. It beat wildly in her rib cage, as fierce as a dragon trapped in the arena. Jura feared she would never grow accustomed to the panic. It ate at her, clawing at her insides. Now it was nearly three weeks later and they were no closer to Kitoi. The endless desert stretched out around them, and the only sound was the steady breathing of the men beside her.

They traveled during the day. Tylak made them all invisible, pulling light from their portable source of the Everflame and bending it around them. Every morning they set off and trudged across the desert, pushing themselves until Tylak collapsed and the Samur helped Jura make camp for the night. Tylak usually awakened an hour or so later, just in time to eat dinner and provide first watch. It was a tiresome schedule for him. It was a tiresome schedule for them all. He never complained. Jura appreciated that about him. Throughout this entire journey Tylak had done nothing but offer his services as bodyguard, as friend. *But everyone wants something in return.* It wasn't that long ago Tylak had needed her help to recover his birthstone. What did he want from her now?

She adjusted the heavy pack on her shoulders and bit back another disgruntled sigh. Tylak had warned her not to make her pack heavy with books. She'd laughed in his face. They needed the books, and if she had had her way, her entire library would have found its way into their packs.

He was right, though. I shouldn't have brought all these books. She would never admit it out loud, so she bit the inside of her cheek to have a different pain to focus on and readjusted her pack on her aching shoulders.

According to the maps they would be arriving at the road to the Golden City any day now. She hoped the map was accurate. There was no way of telling. The landscape was just as empty now as it had been the week before. Jura frowned at the stretch of barren land, unmarked save for two or three tiny trees struggling for life. They couldn't afford for the map to be wrong. Over a thousand years ago this land had once been lush with abundant life. That was before the Everflame had walked the earth, destroying everything in its path. A memory nagged at the edge of her subconscious, an old text she'd read from an annotated translation of the Doctrine of the Flame. Something about the Everflame walking the earth once again. She sighed. Yet another subject that required more research. But the Everflame had to wait, she had to focus everything on Amira. Her lost friend had so few people still fighting for her.

It was just the four of them at the moment. She and Tylak and the Samur. Peppik was out there, somewhere. He often scouted ahead or behind. He was an odd man. He had shown up the first night they made camp, simply walked up and sat beside her. She'd screamed and Tylak had to tackle the Samur to the ground to stop them from slicing the old man in half. He'd been a member of the group ever since. Jura didn't mind, she appreciated the extra help. They needed all they could get.

Once she found Amira, she would find the person responsible for everything. The *altta'wam* was working with someone in Kitoi, the mastermind behind it all. She only hoped she wasn't too late. She had to get a message to the Sea King as well. She wanted to fill him in on all she'd discovered. It was clear someone was trying to start a war within the Tri-Alliance, and there was no way of knowing what this faceless enemy would do next. Once she arrived in Kitoi, she would be able to speak with the ambassador for the sea people or at the very least hire a private messenger.

She felt someone's eye on her and slanted her vision toward Tylak's steely silver gaze. His stare sent an inexplicable shiver down her spine and she tightened her grip on her pack. It was hard to believe she was thinking of anyone romantically when so much else was at stake, but Jura couldn't deny the tug of attraction she felt toward the former Shadow Dancer. He seemed to fill the void left in the wake of Markhim's disappearance and Amira's capture. He felt something too, didn't he?

"Are you ready to stop?" The fading sunlight shone on his face, and Jura once again wondered at the origins of his scar.

"Hmm? Stop what?"

"Stop here. For the night." He raised his eyebrows.

Jura looked around. Here was as good a place as any. She nodded and let her heavy pack fall to the sand beside her, shoulders sagging in silent relief. The Samur men, Ichiro and Jiro, moved off to the side and scanned the horizon. Jura had a difficult time telling the two apart. They were both massive men with oily, shaved heads and dark brown eyes. Jura suspected they were brothers, but when she'd voiced the thought out loud the two men had only smiled as though sharing a secret.

The two liked to recite prayers at dusk and dawn. They seemed to worship the sun, or perhaps the moon. It was difficult to follow and neither man seemed inclined to answer any of her questions. Jura got the impression the Samur didn't like her and merely tolerated her because they were following the bidding of their true master: Beshar, Ninth of the Thirteen.

Thoughts of Beshar led to thoughts of home, and Jura caught her bottom lip between her teeth, nibbling as she worried. What would her father think now that she was missing? Could he think clearly? She still didn't quite understand what it meant to be ensnared by a blood chain. Was her father even aware of her actions? Was he forced to watch as someone else controlled his body? Was he worried for her? She shook her head and turned her attention back to setting up camp.

Tylak had begun to prepare a hare for roasting. Good thing too, he'd been traveling with the poor thing for nearly an hour. The frantic hare had run directly into their path and Tylak had stopped it with one quick flick of his dagger. The take down itself had been impressive, but Jura hated watching what came after. She hated the process, despite the fact she was a voracious meat eater.

"Won't be much longer now," he muttered. He must have felt her watching him though he didn't look up from his work.

Jura nodded. He'd removed the head and all its fur and was in the process of shoving a long stick down the length of its body.

She swallowed and began digging in her pack for something to read. She needed the distraction.

Tylak began to hum as he worked. He kept the roasting stick with their pack as well as a single torch lit by the Everflame. Jura recognized the tune but she couldn't say from where. Knowing Tylak, the song probably contained words that shouldn't be repeated in polite society anyway.

She watched as he stuck the torch deep into the stand so that only its flames were apparent as he held the hare over the heat. The flames licked at the hare and in moments the intoxicating smell of roasting meat sent her stomach into a fit of rumbling.

"When I was little, we never had our own Everflame." He still didn't look up at her, his attention focused on turning the hare over his makeshift spit.

She picked her way through the sand and sat down beside where he squatted. She'd picked a book at random and sat it on her lap.

"How did you pray?" she asked, leaning forward. She skimmed through the book, Lanfer's *A History of Kitoi: The Golden City*. Perfect, she needed to finish this one before their arrival.

He snorted. "I was always too busy trying to stay alive. Never had time for prayers. My mother did though. Every morning she went to the flame in the city square and burned a prayer."

Jura imagined making a daily trek into the city square simply to see the shared flame. The Everflame, pure and whole, was caged in the glass palace, just a stone's throw from where Jura had grown up. She had never had to leave the palace for anything

Tylak seemed to have taken up the nightly duty of cooking, and Jura wondered if this was a hobby he'd enjoyed back home.

"Did you have a Torch for cooking your meals?" she asked.

Tylak still didn't take his eyes from the flame. "When we had something to cook we went to the pits."

When they ate. Jura had never missed a meal in her life. It was a wonder her belly remained so flat. What would it be like to wonder when she would have her next meal? Even here on the road she was never truly hungry. They'd packed plenty of dried fruit, and between Tylak and the Samur she had never wanted for fresh meat.

"I-I'm sorry," she finished lamely, not quite sure how to respond. She fell back to her safe spot and began reciting recent facts she'd learned about Kitoi. "A recent census reports less than thirty percent of the population follows the Everflame. I don't expect we'll see as many pits."

Tylak didn't answer, so she continued on. "I've heard the city is lighted by the splendor of its stones. In fact, the stones are the basis of the primary religion. The theocracy believe that emotions are what separate us from a true union with the gods. Each emotion is assigned a specific leader and each leader a specific gem that is amplified by that emotion. The people are governed by the cabochon—each leader corresponds to their own emotion."

Tylak grunted. "Sounds confusing."

"Not really," Jura shrugged. "It's color coded and there are forms."

"Forms?" Tylak wrinkled his nose.

"Yes. The people of Kitoi like their forms and their rules. It's all very organized."

"You got all this from that book?"

Jura blushed. "Well, partly. I suppose there were some generalizations made. I do know to expect things to be different there." She lifted her chin. "The people of Kitoi have a very forgiving attitude when it comes to slavery. With the right paperwork, citizens can purchase anyone they wish." Jura shuddered. "That's why it's so important to find Amira as quickly as possible."

If he answered she didn't hear him, lost in her thoughts about Amira. She watched Tylak's survey of the roasting hare, watched its slow rotation over the flames and stood up. A wave of dizziness rushed through her, she placed a hand to her temple and reached at her side for her skin of water. She was careful to take only the tiniest of sips, aware of her dwindling supply. They were all running low on water. It shouldn't be much longer before they arrived in Kitoi. Jura stared at their piece of the Everflame and sent a silent prayer for their safe arrival. Slowly, she sank down to her knees back to the warm sand. She opened her book and began reading at random, her thoughts as wild as her beating heart.

The capital city of Kitoi was quite large, how would they find just one person? Jura wasn't even entirely sure Amira was still in the Golden City. It was possible her captor had moved her outside the capital to some lesser known city. She nibbled on her lip and worried.

Tylak brought her a portion of the hare and sat beside her while she ate. He was later joined by Peppik and the three sat in companionable silence until Jura unrolled her sleeping mat and succumbed to exhaustion.

Tylak's body covered her own and jerked her from her dreams. She squirmed beneath him.

"What's happening?"

He straddled her at the waist, pushing her hips into the soft sand. He'd pulled a cloak up around their heads and it shuddered violently.

"Sandstorm," he shouted, but his words were unnecessary as the wind howled around them.

Jura was grateful Tylak concentrated on holding the cloak tight and secure around them. She was acutely aware of the fact that his hips pressed into hers, that his face was mere inches from her own. She bit her bottom lip and closed her eyes. It had been years since Jura was caught in a true sandstorm. Even now she felt no true danger, despite the howling wind and sharp bites of sand. Besides, how could she worry over the sands when Tylak's face was so close to her own?

"It's just a haboob. Shouldn't last much longer." His words were soothing, as though he meant to calm a frightened child. She nodded weakly and tried to keep as still as possible. Minutes later Tylak stood up. He gripped her arm just above her elbow and hauled her to her feet as well. The two Samur stood just off to the side, shaking dust and sand from their robes. There was no sign of Peppik.

"My books!" Jura exclaimed, rushing forward. The heavy wind had torn open one of her packs and the resulting chaos had ripped apart more than one volume. She picked up the remains of the *History of Kitoi* and let out a dramatic sigh. What pages were left were now torn and ruined.

To his credit, Tylak merely patted her on the arm.

"What a disaster," she frowned at the misshapen mess.

"We lost a bactrian, either ran off or buried," he noted, no doubt trying to bring her back to more pressing issues than a damaged book. The loss of the giant camel would hurt. They'd purchased two of the beasts from a caravan traveling to the Republic. At least they'd had the foresight to divide their food and water supply between the two. One of the Samur, Ichiro perhaps, calmed the remaining pack animal. The bactrian had the ability to seal its nostrils during sand storms, but that hadn't stopped the younger beast from running in search of shelter. With any luck they would find the creature up ahead on the dusty road. And there was a road, Jura realized. Though the city wasn't apparent, Jura was confident that the appearance of the road meant that it wouldn't be long before the group found themselves at their destination. *Finally.* Once in the city Jura could reach out to the Sea King, find Amira, and get information on the politics of the Republic.

Tylak gave the signal and the group huddled tight as he once again made them invisible. The sun hadn't yet made its appearance over the horizon but there was no sleep after the attack from the wild sands. Today they would reach the Golden City. Today they would find answers.

CORAL

CHAPTER TWO

It was her wedding day.

Correction. Today was *supposed* to be her wedding day. It wouldn't be, *couldn't* be, not if she had anything to say about it.

She stared up at him, the man who wanted to ruin her life, smoothing the emotion from her face. She had to appear calm, rational, nothing like the inner storm raging within her. He was foolish if he thought she would meekly follow his orders. She *never* followed orders. Not even from this man, Sto'Ne Cur'En, her people's wisest elder, their leader, Admiral of the Kombu and Grand Wave Master of the Three Oceans. The Sea King. Her father.

She placed a hand flat against his chest, silencing him as he opened his mouth to speak. Her mother she ignored. Mother always took his side in politics and would be of no help to her now. This battle was between her and her father. And she *would* win. She always did.

"I know what you're going to say, so I'll save you the trouble. I won't do it. Don't bother trying to make me."

"Save me the trouble? You've been nothing but trouble since

you came into this world squalling." Despite the stern tone to his voice, his eyes twinkled at the memory.

"This isn't the time for your jokes," Coral scowled. "I'm not doing this, and you can't make me."

"Coral, remember your responsibility t—"

"Drown my responsibilities. I don't care about the people, I care about me!"

Her father's deep green eyes darkened and his face looked murderous, but his voice was deadly soft in his reply. "All your life you've been a spoiled child. I'll admit the blame is mine because I love you too much to ever deny you anything, but in this you cannot have your way. How can you say you care nothing of your duty to your people? Your words are blasphemous. You are their future Wave Master. Like it or not, you can't change these facts, my child. You will marry the boy and you will marry him today."

Had he yelled at her and shown his fury she might have felt she could persuade him to her favor. His calm words and sad expression at his final words however were something foreign and gave her pause. Surely this couldn't be happening . . . could it? She thought she'd have more time. She thought she'd convince her father to wait, that the timing was wrong, anything to grant her more time. Instead he stood resolute, adamant that she not only wed the boy but that she do it today, within the hour. Rather than the fury she'd expected, the emotions that came were hopelessness and utter despair. How was it that in one short morning her life could be turned completely upside down?

"What happened to you over there? What did the First of the Sand Sea say to you?" She'd asked him these questions and more upon her father's return the day before, but he had brushed them aside and retired to his chambers, choosing instead to discuss matters privately with her mother and Tiburon, Commander of the First Fleet and elder sibling to her betrothed. Coral had felt slighted by the brush-off but had let the matter rest. That is, until her father had woken her this morning by sending a tiny fleet of Noori to dress her for her wedding day. A wedding that had only previously been discussed as a far off possibility and definitely not an imminent outcome. There had been three of them, elbows deep in her hair before she had even washed the sleep from her eyes. She had yelled at them then, just a bit and she wouldn't have felt bad but then one of them started to cry and why was she to blame for the fact the girl was an obvious sodden mess? In any case, she'd sent them all away from her room with summons to bring her father. His actions demanded immediate explanation, but now all she received were more orders.

Something *had* happened on her father's trip to land, something that had frightened him enough to begin war strategies, something that was now forcing her into a marriage she didn't want.

When her father didn't answer she finally turned in desperation to her mother for help.

"Why are you letting him do this to me?" She tried to keep her voice steady and soft. Her mother was a pushover, but she didn't abide whining. "Talk sense into him, please."

"Listen to your father," she replied. Her eyes shone with sympathy, but her lips pressed into a firm, thin pink line that slashed across her copper skin.

"Just tell me why." There was no keeping the whine from her voice now. On the verge of tears, it was everything she could do to keep from falling to the floor and succumbing into an all-out tantrum.

"Something happened while you were over there. Something

is *making* you do this to me! I want to know why. I demand to know why."

Her father grabbed her by her elbow and held her chin up with his other hand so that she was forced to meet his eyes.

"I will tell you nothing because you are a child. You are *my* child, and I will make the decisions that I feel are best for you. You will marry Mano. You will do it in one hour's time. And there will be no further discussion on this matter. As for what happened to me on my trip, suffice it to say that it is my business, business that I will choose to share with my child when I deem the time right. Not before."

He let her go and his face softened, but the empathy in his expression only served to fuel her anger. How dare he? How could he think to look at her now, his eyes pleading forgiveness? He sighed and looked to her as if all the weight of the world were crushing down on his broad shoulders.

"Coralynn, I only want to protect you, to protect all of us. I have to make decisions that are for the good of the people. You will marry Mano because it's the best thing for you and for all of us. I hope in time you'll come to see that."

"Then help me understand. Tell me why this has to happen *today*. Tell me what's happening."

"Enough." His hand slashed through the air across the wide expanse of his chest. "There isn't time, Coral. Do as I say or there will be consequences."

She stared at him. He'd never threatened her before. He was a massive man, towering over everyone by several inches. His tan shoulders rippled with muscle and were curtained by his flowing hair, impossible to tell which strands were white with age and which came from the Lock. Multi-colored stones danced along the bottom strands of his hair, and his green eyes flashed fire. She knew she favored after him, everyone said so. When she was younger she'd wanted nothing more than to grow up to be exactly like the man she idolized. The man who was at this moment breaking her heart. She would never forgive him.

"I hate you," she whispered.

She watched his shoulders slump, knew that she made the weight he carried that much greater. She didn't care. She was glad he was hurting. Glad because she was hurting too.

"You don't mean that." Her mother's eyes widened and her jaw slackened for a moment before she gritted her teeth. She stepped toward her but the Sea King placed a gentle hand on her mother's shoulder before pulling her away. He paused at the doorway to Coral's chambers, opening his mouth as though he would say something before giving his head a little shake.

"I'm sorry, Coralynn. Eventually you'll come to understand."

I won't. Not ever.

He shut the door behind him and Coral sank down to her bed, shoving the delicate silk wedding wrap to the floor in the process. She watched it fall to the floor in a crumpled mess and thought about her options.

She'd never directly disobeyed her father before. Disobeying his wishes meant going against the orders of her commander, and she was too much of a soldier to do that. And yet . . . he had told her she must marry Mano, but he hadn't said she had to stay put before the ceremony. She sprang to her feet and shoved away the fluttering hands of the two Noori who had lingered to help her prepare for her big day. Born without any sense of their *wei*, the Noori fulfilled any number of household positions as well as roles in medicine and education. But without a sense of their *wei* they were forbidden to become soldiers. The two women looked distraught but said nothing to stop their future Wave Mistress as Coral tip toed out of her room.

Her temporary floating home was a network of long, intricate hallways she had memorized as early as she had learned to walk, and she didn't give a thought to where she was headed as she followed the gentle rumble of her father's *wei*. All of her people had *wei*, even the Noori, and each person's had a distinct hum. Her father's, strong and staccato as a heartbeat, pulled on her own. He would most likely feel her presence, but she could hope he was distracted enough not to notice. She stopped just outside the war room, noting the *wei* of the three present inside. Her father, his captain, Tiburon, and Ailani, High Elder.

"We need to draw anchor and sail for Aina. Immediately." Tiburon's voice carried through the door. Her tone was desperate, urgent. Tiburon was Mano's older sister and had just recently been promoted to captain. Even after his marriage to Coral, Mano would still be out ranked by his older sister. The two were fiercely competitive, but it was hard to tell if his sister's rank made Mano upset or not. It was hard to tell anything about Mano. Yet another reason Coral dreaded their marriage. Being married to Mano was bound to be as mentally stimulating as a conversation with a blowfish. She just had to make her father see that.

"I see wisdom in the words of your young commander," Ailani answered. Coral could picture the sharp gaze of the steely ancient and focused her attention on her words. "There is nasty business afloat in the Sand Sea. Best to put our distance."

"Thank you, Elder," Tiburon stuttered, the surprise evident in her voice. "I can have us set to sail within the hour."

The Wave Master's response was a low whisper. He must

have felt her *wei*, yet her father didn't end the meeting. She dared closer to press her ear against the door. What sort of business was Ailani referring to? Coral knew only the basics of the Sand Sea. They were a ruthless people, although their army, if one could refer to it as that, was nothing but a group of mismanaged idiots. More of interest were stories of the Shadow Dancers, fierce land dwellers capable of besting one of their own. She wondered if her father had met with one of them during his travel to land.

"All the more reason to sail home today. Time is not our friend and there is too much to prepare for. You said yourself we should be on high alert. And after everything that's happened . . . I'll never forgive myself if I allow something to happen to Lana, to the Noori on board, the children . . ." Tiburon trailed off, grumbling to herself the way she often did when she bit her tongue in the presence of the Wave Master.

"You're right, Tiburon. We'll sail for Aina." The Wave Master's deep voice cut off Tiburon's reply, and the joy Coral felt at his words died when he continued, "After the wedding."

Coral knew that last bit of the message was meant especially for her. Her father had felt her *wei*, had probably known she stood listening just outside the door this entire time. She sighed. There was no getting out of it. She was about to become a wife. She turned on her heel and stomped back toward her room.

KAY

Chapter Three

*K*ay *was very careful not* to do any more bad things. After the incident in the practice arena and that one tiny explosion . . . well, everyone treated her differently now. The last few weeks were a hazy blur of events. There was still so much she didn't understand. But there was one thing she was completely sure of. She was exposed. People knew what she was capable of and that made her special. But being special didn't grant her what she wanted. She'd thought if she showed them how special she was it would mean big trouble. Instead, it seemed to make everyone very happy, especially Ash. He couldn't stop talking about her abilities. Kay could only understand every other word that was said, but she knew enough and could tell by his excited facial expressions that Ash was very pleased. Kay knew that telling the truth hadn't been a bad thing, but she was still trying to figure out if it was a *good* thing.

Ash signaled it was time for a water break and Kay grinned in relief. She didn't get many during the course of her training so the few moments allotted to her every few hours were beyond precious.

As always, she wished for more water. She was *so* thirsty, but Kindle explained that water was hard to come by so they each had to make do with their ration. Kay had never had to ration water before. Her family had a well on their property, and Kay could get buckets of the cool, crisp liquid whenever she'd wanted. Here in the arena, the water was always warm and left a copper aftertaste in her mouth. As nasty as it was, Kay always wanted more.

"Break's over, Cadet. Pick up your assegai." Ash's voice made her cringe. How could someone with such kind eyes be so *mean*?

Kay didn't think she could pick up the assegai. Her arms already felt like limp noodles. *Noodles,* the thought made her mouth water. She missed mama's cooking fiercely. The food here in the arena was terrible. Dried meat, flat bread, goat stews, bleh! She craved Mama's fish pasta, made with fresh fish caught from the stream, and Mama's bread . . . What would she do for just one more taste of Mama's sweet fluffy bread that always melted in her mouth and—

"Hustle, Cadet!"

She flinched. Yes, Ash was mean now. He didn't even bother to call her by her name anymore. She picked up her assegai, ignoring the groaning protest from her stiff muscles, and placed her feet in the proper position. Well, she *thought* it was proper, but Ash came behind her and re-positioned her left foot. She leaned her weight back into it like he wanted.

Next, he was tapping at her elbows, forcing her to raise them up so they became parallel to her chest and her wrists were crossed over. She knew she had to hold the position until he was satisfied, so she held very still, despite the fact that her arms trembled from the effort. She stuck out her tongue while she concentrated. If Mama saw her she would yell at her and warn her that she might accidentally bite it off. *But Mama isn't here.* Kay tasted blood and sucked her tongue back in her mouth.

Ash grunted and turned her wrists the tiniest amount. When he was finally satisfied with that position he asked for another. Again and again, Ash positioned her through the many Forms of the fire dance, muttering under his breath the entire time. By now she was used to his mumbling and she knew enough of his language to catch on: she was behind and needed practice.

Finally, after what seemed like hours, though it couldn't have been more than one or two, he announced that she could have another break before fire movement. The announcement made her smile. Fire movement was always the last skill practiced for the day. Training was halfway over. And while she was behind on the necessary stances and positions of fire dancing, she was a master at the movement of fire.

In the last week she'd quickly come to understand that not only was she good, she was the best. Gladiators often came to the practice arena when it was her turn. They all wanted to watch her Breathe in the heat and expel the flames. Apparently no one else could do that. She created her own flames and that made her *extra* special. Kay hadn't been convinced, but she also knew there was no point in arguing with adults when they thought they knew something. They could be so stubborn.

After another break that was all too short, Ash motioned for her to join him outside the ring of the fire field. At least she had water this time. She moved to stand beside him, brushing the sand off her leggings and taking tiny sips from her water skin. It wasn't her turn in the field just yet, but Ash wanting her beside him meant that she was next. Or he wanted her to watch something. She wasn't entirely sure which. Timber was in the fire field with his cadet. The gladiator was tossing lazy balls of fire in his direction, and the cadet was catching them and tossing them back into the sky. Kay watched with little interest. She and Daddy had played similar games of catch years ago, back when she had still been a baby. The slow game of fire catching was boring. Thoughts of her Daddy brought the familiar tummy ache, and she pressed her hands into her stomach to staunch the pain. It wasn't fair that she was stuck in this horrid place, that Mama and Daddy were gone forever.

She knew what it meant to die. It meant you were gone, gone forever. Kay knew she would never see her parents again, but she refused to accept she would never again see her home. She knew she was getting stronger. She felt it in her aching muscles every day. She also knew that every day she learned more of the language and history of the Republic she gained vital knowledge to her escape. She would leave the arena one day. Leave the dry sand and nasty water and return to a home with rolling green hills and wildflowers, with cool crisp springs and summer rains.

Ash's hand on her shoulder snapped her out of her daydream and back to the present. The cadet sat in the center of the ring panting. He must have done something new because his face was triumphant and Timber patted him on the back. The cadet beamed a smile into the growing crowd of onlookers as they nodded appreciatively. His smile faded when he looked at Kay.

He was older than her, Kay was pretty sure. Taller and wider too. His arms were already cut with muscle from years of practice and discipline. Kay also knew that he hated her. She could see it in his eyes every time he looked her way. She was fairly certain his dislike came from the fact that he was jealous. She didn't need to be fluent in their language to understand this particular cadet was the best. *Was* the best until Kay came along. She smiled back at him.

Timber and Ash exchanged a few words and then Ash gestured Kay into the ring. The small fire field was surrounded by a ring of torches and there were various stones set up to look like men. Kay knew they were supposed to be men because the stones wore the same dragon scale armor she sometimes saw Kindle wearing.

Kay didn't like to think of where the armor came from. She knew that in order for a gladiator to wear the scales it meant that the dragon wasn't. She doubted any dragon could live without his scales. Did the gladiators actually try to hurt one another? Was that why they wore the protective scales of the dragon?

She looked again at the targets that were set up in the fire field. It very much looked like she was practicing to hurt people. Surely Ash didn't mean for her to do that, did he? She frowned. Why was this just now occurring to her? She'd have to remember to ask Kindle about it later. She definitely didn't want to hurt anyone. She had a hard enough time wrapping her head around the fact that Kindle and the others were hurting dragons. She knew dragons were wild creatures. She'd seen firsthand the destruction an angry dragon could cause, but she'd also seen baby dragons playing with one another. She'd hand fed younglings that were imprinted to her daddy. She'd practically *ridden* Rumble.

Ash was tossing balls of flame toward her and she'd been catching them halfheartedly, caught up in her thoughts and not really interested in the game. She knew she was training because Ash and Kindle and everyone else wanted her to fight dragons. And just as she knew this to be true, she also knew there was no way she would ever willingly harm a dragon.

Suddenly angry with the thought, Kay Breathed in the flame that Ash had been ready to hurl at her. It disappeared as she sucked in its heat. She Breathed in the flames from the ring of torches too. She ignored the heat from the hot sand and from the glowing ball of fire in the sky. The torches were enough. As always, the feeling of holding so much heat was a heady experience. She tingled all over, knew she must appear to glow as bright as any sun as the heat boiled inside her. She raised her aching arms into the air, exhilarating in the fact that the heat inside her seemed to rejuvenate her, the ache in her muscles suddenly gone. She felt good all over. Her skin stinging and hot. She held the heat for as long as she could before letting it explode from her fingertips, a stream of molten fire shooting into the sky.

Her breath came out in rapid puffs and she felt just a tiny bit dizzy until she met Ash's thunderous gaze. She knew he didn't like it when she lost control, when she changed the rules of the game and did as she pleased. Yes, Ash looked angry, but also scared. What was he so frightened of? She'd been pushing fire since she could walk, and that game of tossing the flame was a bore. She'd only sucked in the heat from the existing torches. She hadn't even Breathed in everything available to her. There was nothing Ash could teach her when it came to fire movement. She knew that now. She was in complete control and no one matched her skill. She was the master of flames.

BESHAR

CHAPTER FOUR

*U*nder *ordinary circumstances, Beshar, Ninth* of the Thirteen, would have been bored. Today's circumstances, however, were anything but ordinary. He squirmed in the hard wooden seat of the Ninth and struggled to focus his thoughts on the present.

The First presided over the Session, placing judgment on the citizens who came before him. There was an increasing number of citizens getting into trouble these days. Increased water rations led to riots in the street and even the cost of *cictuss* had inflated. The plant's horrific odor was only matched by its taste, but the foul smelling plant could keep one hydrated for a day with just one of its leaves. Citizens had taken to growing the plant in small boxes outside their homes. Beshar would have thought the smell was enough to keep any robbers away, but home break-ins had more than quadrupled compared to last quarter's numbers. They needed to find a solution to this issue with the Sea King. Without his steady supply of water, the Republic was in trouble.

Amira sat tall in the seat of the Third, her attention focused and eyes rapt on the First. Beshar had a hard time taking his eyes off her. She was beautiful, calm, deadly. It was hard to envision that the beautiful young woman was actually miles away, hidden away where only the Everflame knew. Amira was not Amira at all. She was *alttaw'am*, and she would kill him if she knew he'd learned her secret.

As if sensing his eyes on her, she turned to look at him, her lips curling up in a small smile. Beshar quickly looked away. He had to remember not to bring any attention to himself, he certainly couldn't help Jura if he wound up dead. He reached for his handkerchief, breathing deeply of the calming oils. There was plenty of wine in the privacy of his new rooms. He'd moved into the apartments of the Ninth just yesterday, taking small delight in the fact that his new wine cellar was decidedly bigger in his new establishment. At least that was something to be thankful for. He could now store more wine, he was going to need it.

He'd promptly celebrated by ordering several cases of his preferred vintage be sent to him immediately.

"I believe the council is in need of more female representation," Amira smiled down the line of the council.

Denir, the new Fourth, nodded her agreement. "Well said, Third. There are too few of us here." She looked over at Fatima, the Eleventh, who nodded enthusiastically.

"I've a cousin. A widow—"

Fatima was interrupted by the soft musical voice of Amira. "Actually Fatima, I had someone else in mind. She more than meets the requirements. Excellent bloodlines. Rich in water. I nominate Ishani, daughter of Abhaya."

"The ambassador of Kitoi? What an interesting nomination." Denir turned the corners of her lips up ever so slightly.

"It's never been done before," Nasir, the Eighth frowned. "The council has always been comprised of citizens of the Republic."

Beshar kept his face neutral and reached for the thoughts of Velder, the Second, and his puppet of the last several years. Velder's own thoughts were a mere echo that Beshar pushed aside with ease as he made the Second speak up.

"That's because it shouldn't be done. Why should we give citizens of another nation a voice in our government? I vote against this."

Nasir and Geedar, the Fifth, bobbed their heads in agreement.

Beshar let loose a relieved sigh.

Amira scowled at Velder for the briefest second before smiling beautifully at the council. "The Second makes a valid statement, and in years past I would agree with him. But times are changing and the ambassador would be a welcome addition. She has grown up in politics, she speaks several languages and, as the daughter of Kitoi's finest war general, she is well versed in all matters of war. In addition to these attributes, we should welcome our allies in times of war. Ishani has served as a worthy ambassador for the last ten years and has always shown to have the best interest of not only her own nation, but that of the Republic as well. I urge the council to heed the wisdom in my words and allow this breach in government policy during these troubling times."

Denir nodded thoughtfully. Geedar too, though his eyes still looked troubled. Beshar looked to his left and noted that the lesser council members had all schooled their faces to look completely blank. Had she gotten to each of them already? Fatima studied her fingernails and Ledair, the Twelfth and newest member of the council, looked as though he wished to be anywhere else.

Beshar spoke up again as Velder, "The Third makes an

admirable argument. Truly, voting in the ambassador would be a wise decision if the Republic didn't already have so many other worthy candidates."

A few of the council members muttered their agreement, but no one was brave enough to voice their opinion out loud, not when the Third, Fourth, and Fifth already seemed to be in agreement.

Justir, the First, and Amira's own puppet, held up a halting hand that demanded attention.

"I agree with our Third. These are difficult times, and as our great Republic prepares for war, we would be wise to accept the ambassador as one of our own. We will put the matter to a vote. I will raise my vote for her." The First raised his hand higher.

Beshar forced Velder's hand to lay flat on the table, mimicking his own. He noted that Jabir also laid his hands flat. Ledair looked anguished for a moment, but then began knocking the stone table. Everyone else did too.

"Then it is decreed that Ishani is given full Rank and authority as our Thirteenth." The First looked to Velder, and Beshar had him mumble the words that called the meeting to a close.

Beshar sat in his chair for several moments after as everyone made their way from the room. He didn't hear Amira's quiet approach and jumped when she placed a soft hand over his. His hands were still laid flat on the table and he looked up at her in alarm.

"My lady Third, you startled me."

She smiled down at him, removing her hand and crossing her arms over her chest, leaning her hip against the table.

"You were very quiet in today's session," she noted.

He'd spoken up in every way he'd felt safe. He watched Velder's departing form but kept his connection to his thoughts on a tight leash. He'd thought *alttaw'am* were mindless creatures, yet this one seemed to have no problem controlling the First and maintaining the illusion of Amira. Who was she, really?

"Should I have spoken up more, my lady Third?" The feel of her eyes settling on him sent shivers down his spine.

"I find it curious that you voted against the ambassador joining the council yet you gave no voice to your objection."

Flames but she was right. He should have at least muttered along with the rest of them. He tried for a wan smile, "Trying my hand at diplomacy. I suspect I did poorly."

Her chocolate eyes held his gaze. "You're allowed your own opinion, of course."

"Of course," he inclined his head, rising from his chair. "It irks me that I must depart your lovely presence, but my duties in the arena call."

"I hear that Justir has doubled the amount of men in search of Jura."

Justir, not the First. Was she testing him? He ignored her breach in etiquette. "Did he now? That is most pleasing to hear. It pains me that she went missing as she did. Though, I suppose, my pain pales in comparison to your own sadness. You must be beside yourself with worry for your friend."

"Indeed," she said pitifully, closing her eyes as if to squeeze away the tears. She put on a good show. "When news of those bodies found in the dungeons came I feared the worst. Now, to know that she is out there, forced to follow the wishes of that monster. How is it that the slave was even able to escape the dungeons in the first place? And what does he want with our poor, sweet Jura?"

Though Jura had left with Tylak on her own free will, it was widely believed by the Republic that the Daughter of the First had been kidnapped by the former slave turned Shadow Dancer. The two were spotted by a merchant outside the city gates, but that had been nearly a week ago. There hadn't been any trace of them since. Beshar didn't believe in prayers to the Everflame, but he sent one up anyway in hopes that the group was in Kitoi by now.

"It's very sad. Jura is a fine young woman and a dear friend. I'll burn a prayer to the Everflame that she is recovered quickly."

The creature smiled. "Yes, I burn prayers daily that she is reunited with her loved ones. Funny, I never thought of you as a religious man. I've never seen you at the Everflame."

"Troubling times have a way of bringing out the religion in all of us I imagine."

Her kohl-lined eyes narrowed, "It would seem so." She pushed away from the table and shook her head, causing her thick maiden's braid to fall over her shoulder. "Look at me, carrying on with my troubles when you have more pressing matters. I won't detain you any longer, Beshar. You're dismissed."

He gritted his teeth but bowed low before turning on his heel to hurry from her presence. Several of his Samur waited outside the imposing double doors of the auditorium. He was relieved by the sight of them. For the last week he had taken to requesting the presence of all his men whenever he left his chambers. He gestured for them to fall in place around him, and he made his way through the glass halls and back to his own apartments.

"Any news?" he asked once he was sure they were out of earshot of any council members.

Kenjiro shook his head, his expression grim. "None. It seems they've vanished."

Beshar gave the head of his Samur a tight-lipped smile.

"Good, it appears they're staying away from the main roads. If you can't find them, the First won't either. Give up the search. It's a safe assumption they've made it to Kitoi by now, or at least very near its borders. I need your ears here, the First and the Third are planning something. And get me everything you can on the ambassador from Kitoi. It seems she is our new Thirteenth."

Kenjiro nodded, stepping forward to open the doors to Beshar's apartments and doing a careful sweep before allowing the Ninth to enter. Once he was given the signal that it was safe, Beshar entered his room, immediately going for his wine cellar. He'd uncork some of his private reserve tonight. He needed the alcohol content. The Shadow Dancer and his men should be capable of keeping one tiny girl alive, right? He drank deep from the bottle and hoped that it was so.

JURA

CHAPTER FIVE

Traveling *on the road was* somehow worse than their trek through the desert. The only time they saw anyone was when the group passed unnoticed by a nomadic family traveling home to Shrivo with their tiny herd of goats. The road was long and empty with only the sparse collection of trees and wild brush to break up the monotony. It was early morning by the time they arrived on the outskirts of the Golden City, sparkling and glowing in the distance with the rising sun.

Amira is here. Jura hoped she would be able to find her friend in time to put an end to the madness taking place in the Republic. She took comfort in the fact that in order for there to be an *alttaw'am* Amira had to be alive. Jura only needed to find her. She still had to come up with a plan. She couldn't very well barge into the city, banging on doors and searching houses. It was a shame she hadn't nurtured a better relationship with the Shadow Dancers. Surely they could help gain intel on Amira's capture? She shoved the thought aside, no sense on thinking of things that would never happen. Jura had a previous arrangement with the Prince of Shadows, but neither had held up their end of the deal. Jura wondered where that left things. Tylak seemed to think it meant she was a walking target.

He was probably right. If her last night in the Republic proved anything, it was that there were a number of people who wanted her dead.

"Well, do we go in now or sneak in this evening?" Tylak nudged her shoulder and snapped her back to the present.

"Now? This evening?" Her eyes widened at the thought.

"You're nervous."

"Of course I am. There's so much at stake."

"We can make camp, go in at dawn after a full night's sleep?"

Jura battled with the idea. On the one hand she didn't want to waste any more time. She needed to find Amira and contact the Sea King as soon as possible. But on the other she still had no plan.

"I think . . . we make camp?" The words crawled out of her mouth, she was unsure if she was issuing an order or asking a question.

"It's time for prayer," Jiro announced.

Tylak rolled his eyes but Jura stopped his protest with a glare. It was settled then. The Samur would pray and she would read, and at dawn tomorrow they would enter the Golden City. She had barely a day to come up with a plan.

Tylak grumbled as he sat square legged beside Peppik, who had taken to meditating alongside the Samur. If his body winking in and out of existence wasn't indication enough, the lines of concentration across his forehead told Jura that Tylak was practicing his invisibility barrier again. He was fairly capable of holding it around the group, although they were forced to huddle together tightly. After that first day of close travel, Jura had asked if he had ever tried to extend his powers. He'd scowled at her and had mumbled that she should try it, but he'd started practicing then and every night after.

The lack of sleep from the previous night's sandstorm followed by their hours of travel already had Jura holding back a tired yawn. She was glad they had stopped. She needed time to rest and to think. She forced her gaze back down to her open book and began reading.

Tylak tapped her on the shoulder and she awoke with a start. He looked worried. She must have fallen asleep reading. She shoved the book into her pack and sprang to her feet, ignoring the crick in her neck.

"Are you . . ." He cut off her whispered question with a quick nod. He was bending the light around them. They were invisible.

"Where is everyone?" she mouthed the words.

Tylak shook his head.

He didn't know or he didn't want to say? Jura gripped the holster of her whip. She'd manage to get the weapon into a steady snap and her accuracy was improving, but only marginally. She only hit the target a third of the time, and figured at that rate she should be fairly decent with it by the time they got Amira back home. Thinking of home caused a familiar wrench in her gut. Rescuing Amira from Kitoi was only the first task for getting her old life back.

Tylak's grip on her elbow tightened and she squinted into the desert around them. The road was empty and not even a breeze disturbed the sands. Her heartbeat quickened and her stomach rolled.

A muffled grunt sounded off to her right. She whipped her head toward the sound, her knuckles white around the hilt of her whip. Tylak unsheathed his dagger. She pressed the palm of her left hand into her hammering chest and tried to take a deep breath.

The masked man appeared in front of them. Tylak shoved her to the side, tackling the man to the ground. The men wrestled, rolling over one another until Tylak stopped the man with a swift crack from his elbow into the man's face.

"Is he . . ." Jura took a step forward but stopped, trembling.

"No, just unconscious. I'll want to—behind you!" Tylak slowly rose to his feet.

Jura's heart skipped a beat.

She whirled around. Another Shadow Dancer stood directly behind her, knife raised in his right hand. He stood straight and still. Jura's grabbed her whip and it flew from its holster, poised in her hand. The masked man raised his foot and leaned forward. He seemed to move with such infinitesimal slowness that Jura wondered if he was even moving at all. She didn't want to waste her opportunity so she took careful aim and snapped the whip toward his knife. The tail of her whip caught the blade and she had snatched it out of his hand before he completed his next step. His gaze slowly dropped into a register of surprise.

Jura discarded the knife into the ground and brought the whip forward with another snap of her wrist. She dropped low when the man began to topple toward her and she flicked her weapon forward, wrapping it around the man's feet. She jumped to her own and pulled the slack from the whip sharply toward her, tightening the weapon's grip around her captive. She heard Tylak's approach seconds later and she blinked up at him in surprise.

She dropped the whip and stepped back, shaking her head. Tylak lunged for the discarded tail of the weapon and placed a boot on the man's chest to prevent him from escaping.

"Jura, are you okay?"

She shook her head.

"It happened again, didn't it?"

"You were taking so long to get up," she whispered. "I knew it then, but I . . ." She trailed off, staring at her hands. "What's happening to me?" This had happened once before. Time had slowed down around her, and Jura had dispatched and killed men. She shuddered at the memory.

"I don't know. But I intend to get some answers now." Tylak glared down at the Shadow Dancer.

"Why would I share anything with you, Tylak? You're a traitor."

Tylak grinned. His scar glowed white in the late morning sun. He reminded Jura of how he looked that first day she met him. Dangerous.

"Did you hear that, Jura? I'm famous." Tylak leaned back, his boot remained planted on the Shadow Dancer's chest. "Now what does the old Prince want wi—"

"How dare you speak his name. We do not speak of the deceased."

Tylak stiffened. "When."

"The same day you and your little First disappeared. I won't fall for your lies." The Dancer squirmed beneath him. "Release me and face your death with honor."

"Honor? You were trying to murder me in my sleep." Jura snorted. She eyed the unconscious Dancer before stepping closer to Tylak and the Shadow Dancer beneath his boot.

"Actually, Greatness, the new orders are to leave you alive."

"New orders from who?" Jura narrowed her eyes.

"Release me and I'll tell you more."

Ichiro and Jiro appeared in the horizon, picking their way

through the sand.

"We've been attacked," Jiro called.

Tylak rolled his eyes. "Get behind me, Jura."

"Why?" the Shadow Dancer asked as he stood up. "I don't want to kill her."

His mask had fallen down and though his eyes glittered dangerously, his tanned features appeared almost bored. Jura recognized the look as the same one Tylak had on the day she'd sentenced him to be executed. It must be something all Shadow Dancers learned. She knew little of Tylak's past. She didn't like to push people into sharing, but she knew the man had been a member of the secret guild at one time.

"It's okay, Jura. He's unarmed and outnumbered." Tylak jerked his head at the arrival of the Samur.

"Jura." The Dancer elongated the syllables, the name stretching from his mouth and echoing across the sand sea. "So, we're on a first name basis. Perhaps you will be useful alive. I propose an Exchange."

Tylak grunted. "I accept."

"Why did you kill our Prince?" The Shadow Dancer crossed his arms over his chest.

"I wish I could take credit for that. I only learned of his death now. When did your orders for Jura change?"

The Dancer smiled, revealing a row of neat white teeth. "Just this morning." His eyes slanted down toward his companion who was now stirring into consciousness. "When he arrived with the missive. What is your business in Kitoi?"

"A rescue mission. Whose orders do you follow?"

"My Queen's, of course. How do you want to die?"

"Fifty years from now asleep in a warm bed with a belly full of food and water. What does sh—"

"What sort of interrogation is this?" Jura's question caught the attention of both men.

"It isn't an interrogation," the Shadow Dancer said.

"It's an Exchange of Information," Tylak mumbled.

Jiro and Ichiro held the other Shadow Dancer between them. He swayed on his feet during their approach.

"Would you like us to dispatch him?" Jiro sounded bored.

"That won't be necessary. Will it?" Jura looked from one Shadow Dancer to the other. She turned to Tylak, who raised his eyebrows in question. Right, she called the shots. She squared her shoulders and turned toward the Dancer. "I would like to enter this Exchange of Information."

"It isn't done." The Shadow Dancer shook his head. He tied his mask back into place.

Tylak chuckled. "It's better not to argue with her. Go ahead, Jura. Be prepared for what he'll ask. It's an Exchange of Information. You're honor bound to tell the truth."

The Shadow Dancer sneered at Tylak's words but he turned to Jura. "Ask your questions."

"Did you come out here to kill Tylak?"

"Interesting. You and Tylak both chose to use your first question in regard to each other. And to your question, I did not. What or who are you rescuing in Kitoi?"

Jura swallowed. "My friend. If you didn't come to kill Tylak or to kill me, then why did you come?"

"I said that I did not come out here to kill Tylak. I came out to assassinate *you*. But those orders changed. Tylak was just a bonus. Who is so important that you would leave the Republic and your father in danger?"

"Amira." Jura pictured her friend's beautiful face. If she didn't fight for her, who would? She ignored the nagging guilt that spiked in reaction to his question. "How did you find us?"

"The Third. So, you are on a rescue mission for the very person who provided me with the tool for which to find you. Things are not as they seem," the Shadow Dancer said.

"Was that a question?"

He smiled. "No. But that was. Is the Third responsible for your father's blood chain?"

"Yes. What tool are you talking about?"

"A blood seeker. Is the Third *alttaw'am*?"

Jura swallowed. He knew of the creature. "Yes. What is a blood seeker?"

The Shadow Dancer reached into his pocket.

Tylak growled low in his throat. "Watch your hands."

The Dancer ignored him and pulled out a small gold object. He held it out toward Jura. She squinted at the familiar gold wiring.

"My lorgnette! Amira gave it to me . . ." She trailed off, remembering the moment. The tiny gold wiring had pricked her finger and drawn blood. Was he saying her blood on the lorgnette had somehow brought him directly to her? She'd never known such magic existed.

"Why does the Queen want you alive?" The Dancer stared at her with a hard expression.

"I could ask you the same question."

"Then we have completed our Exchange."

"Not quite." Tylak held out his hand, palm upward. "We'll take that back now."

The Shadow Dancer chuckled but he handed the lorgnette over to him without protest.

"Sleep with one eye open, Tylak. Just because the missive has reached me that she is to be unharmed, I cannot guarantee word has reached all of my brethren." He bowed low but made a mockery of the motion with an exaggerated wink at Jura. "Greatness, it was a pleasure."

"They are free now?" Ichiro frowned at the departing figures.

Tylak nodded. "We're safe. For now, anyway. There's always a day's truce after an Exchange."

Jura sat down in the sand and buried her face in her hands.

"Don't worry." Tylak sat beside her, patting her on the back.

"How can I not? I don't know who I am anymore. I don't feel like myself anymore. And Amira, the real Amira . . . I just want her to be okay. She has to be, right? We know she's alive, but what does that mean, really? What have they been doing to her?"

"We'll find her." It was a promise he'd repeated often over the last week and a half.

"I still can't believe I didn't know she was in trouble. This entire time, she's been captured and enduring only the Everflame knows what . . . her entire family is gone. What will that do to her? She has no one."

"She has you." Tylak reached for her hand, interlacing her fingers with his own.

This was new. His thumb traced a path where her wrist met her hand. Jura swallowed hard in an effort to calm her racing heart and leaned toward him. "Thanks again for helping me with all this. I don't know what I'd do without you. You're a good friend."

Tylak pulled his hand free from hers to wipe it down the length of his face.

He must be exhausted. She tried not to feel slighted by the sudden departure of his hand.

"You probably have some reading to do or something. Let me know what you need me to do for your plan." He stood up abruptly, mumbling something about his pack under his breath as he walked away.

Jura watched him leave in silence. She wanted to call after him and demand an explanation, but he was right, she should be coming up with a plan.

ASH

Chapter Six

No child should be this powerful. It had only been two weeks and Kay was already the best cadet the arena had ever seen. She fell into the motions of the fire dance as though she were born to them. Her lithe, compact body seemed to float through the air, and when she danced with the flame, *her* flame, it was a thing of magic.

Ash had sent her to the edge of the field to recite her motions. It was meant as punishment, a retribution against her earlier act. She was stunning, deadly, yet she lacked control. Or perhaps she just had more control in her little pinky than even Timber at his best. Ash wasn't sure which was more terrifying.

"She's learned fast." Kindle appeared beside him, snapping the butt of her assegai at his back side.

He glared at her for the irreverent swat, but the anger faded quickly from his eyes. "Shouldn't you be resting up before your match?"

She shrugged, a mischievous gleam twinkled in her eye. "I'm rested." Her face turned serious and gave him a careful once over.

"How are you? You're the talk of the arena. You and your miraculous cadet. Is it everything you always wanted?"

Was it? He watched Kay perform a cartwheel and rise up in a series of pirouettes. As she turned, she pulled fire toward her so that she was a tiny tornado of flames. After a few furious spins the flames shot upward and disappeared into the sky. Kay stopped spinning and sent him an impish grin.

He scowled in reply and called out for her to practice her Red Form. The various Forms were named after the colors found on dragon scales. Red was the highest level of difficulty, and she was near to mastering it. It wouldn't be long before she was the best fighter in the entire arena. Better than Timber and Kindle, better than he had ever been himself. She was easily the most dangerous creature he had ever encountered. And she was only seven years old.

"I'm terrified." Ash chose simple honesty in response to Kindle's question. What would it mean for her to have such power? Surely Beshar wouldn't have her enter the arena early simply because she could. She was just a child.

A shadow loomed over them and Ash frowned as Timber made his way ever closer. He nodded to Kindle and stopped in front of Ash.

"Old man."

Ash clenched his fist. Timber had kept his distance ever since the day Ash's cadet had flattened him to the ground. Ash knew Timber's pride was bruised and it would be a long while before his smug look returned. He was surprised to find the behemoth of a man standing before him now.

"What do you want, Timber?" He kept his eyes trained just over the gladiator's shoulder. Kay was no longer stumbling through the Red Forms and was instead spinning in aimless circles and shooting fireballs into the sky. Ash's mouth twitched. He'd have to scold her later. He finally met Timber's gaze and arched his eyebrow in question.

"You're a difficult man to catch. Alone." Timber fixed Kindle with a pointed stare before adding, "Don't you have to be in the arena?"

Kindle narrowed her eyes and took a step forward, but Ash caught her shoulder with a quick gesture.

"Leave in flames and ash or come home a hero." Ash gripped her forearm and the two locked arms for a moment. She sent a warning glance at Timber before she turned and headed off toward the barracks.

The men watched her leave before Ash turned to Timber and gave him a curious expression.

"Your cadet is really something." The words sounded strangled and forced. Timber had always been cocky, but Ash hadn't expected him to react so strongly to Kay. He had years yet before she would face him in the arena, if ever.

"She is." Ash didn't give away any more than necessary. He waited for Timber to continue.

"Akil, too, has always been gifted beyond his years. He takes after his mother." Timber's dark eyes were heavy and distant.

Akil must be his son. A cadet lost the right to his own name when he began training, but a man's son would always be his son. Why, even Ash still thought of his cadet as Kay, even if he would never do her the dishonor of speaking her name aloud.

Timber's family was an anomaly. Gladiators could not have families in the conventional sense. Death was their mistress and they met her in a blaze of fire and smoke. Yet Timber had a son and, at one point, a woman. Ash had asked what had happened to her, but Timber had never explained. Ash remained silent and waited for Timber to continue. Several seconds went by, each man lost in his thoughts.

"She danced with fire."

The words startled Ash, breaking him out of his reverie. Timber regarded him with sharp, black eyes.

"When did she . . ." Ash trailed off, unsure what he was asking. It was none of his business how she passed on. He and Timber were not friends, he was closer to his enemy, but now Timber seemed soft and open. The hooded expression had left his eyes and the corners of his lips curved into a sad smile.

"It was years ago. She was a slave. Brought into the house of the Fifth. By then I had nearly enough money to purchase my freedom. I would have purchased hers too if . . ." He shook his head and stared down at the tip of his assegai. He buried the glass tip into the sand at his feet.

"She had the most beautiful smile. The boy, he takes after his mother." He jerked the assegai out of the sand and a tiny cloud of dust blossomed around his feet. "She was powerful too. A Natural, just like your cadet. They'll make an offer for her."

"Who will?" Ash wasn't sure why he bothered asking the question. He imagined anyone with funds would make the offer for one such as Kay. He didn't doubt that Beshar had already received any number of offers.

Timber shook his head and Ash followed his gaze where it rested on Kay. She drank from her water skin and fanned at her face with her hand.

"When they come for her, what will you do then, old man? She doesn't belong to you. She never will." Timber's words were more sorrowful than mocking. Ash stared at the ground.

"The councilman won't sell her, he—"

Timber let out a sound that was something between a snort and laughter. "No. He wouldn't want to sell her, but they can be very persuasive. Ask yourself, who has the power? Is it the thirteen people who stare at us from their glass castle?"

"I don't understand. The—"

"Of course you don't. No one understands." Timber raised a voice and called his cadet toward him. The young boy jogged toward them, his movements quick and measured.

"Here comes our master now, old man. Ask him. Ask him of his intentions if you're so sure. Ask him where arena dragons come from." The boy closed the distance between them, and Timber draped an arm over his shoulders. He ushered the boy close and the two began to walk away.

"Wait." Ash stumbled after him, ignoring the sharp pain that shot through his knees after his sudden pivot.

"Ash Fire Dancer," Beshar called out to him, halting Ash in his tracks. He turned toward the voice of the Ninth and watched as he waddled through the sand.

Was it true? Would Beshar sell his protege? And what did Timber know about the arena dragons? He forced a smile as the councilman came ever closer.

"Hello, Ash. Where's my wonder child?"

CORAL

CHAPTER SEVEN

Coral sat back down on her bed with a heavy sigh. The Noori had left her room and she was blessedly alone, but even that small victory didn't help her mood. How could her father betray her like this? Before his trip to land he had invited her into the war room. She was welcomed and given a chair between Tiburon and Ailani. Now after his return she was being rushed into this marriage without even an explanation as to why. Why the urgency? It didn't make sense.

And what had Ailani meant with her ominous statement? It wasn't forbidden for her people to travel to land but it was rarely done. Why travel to a sea filled with sand when their home in the ocean was surrounded by the Great Mother herself?

Thoughts of the Great Mother filled Coral with dread. She was . . . ineffable. The Great Mother connected them all through her gift of the *wei* to her chosen people. The Great Mother demanded honor and duty. No matter the reason, Coral was honor bound to follow the wishes of her father. It was her duty to follow the orders of her Wave Master. And at the moment, he demanded nothing but her marriage to Mano.

Her lip curled up as she stared down at the crumpled heap of white silk that was her wedding dress. She didn't want to put the thing on, she didn't care how pretty it was. She'd probably never owned a wrap so beautiful. And it was white . . . white dye was impossible to come by. Her people often wore hues of blue, green, and red. But white silk was something special. Her fingers itched. Perhaps she could try it on, just to see. It didn't mean that she had to like it.

She lifted it off the ground between two fingers and held it at arm's length. Though its wrinkled state was her own fault, she frowned at it and tossed it onto her bed. Her cabin was narrow, as were most of the cabins in the large vessel her people were at the moment calling home, and she paced the length of it several times before growling in frustration.

All right then, she'd put the sodden thing on.

Staring at her reflection in the mirror she had to admit that the dress was beautiful. Made in the traditional fashion of her people, the dress was a long silken stretch of fabric that wrapped around her shoulder and fell in loose silken folds down to her ankle. Hmm, it was prettier than she thought it'd be. She would have to remember to compliment her mother after a suitable time of sulking. She shrugged at her reflection and left her room in search of a distraction before the ceremony. She needed to clear her head.

Though she hadn't meant to, Coral found herself turning down the narrow hallways toward the banquet room. The room was full of workers making last minute additions to the already abundant amount of decorations. Flowers hung from fishing twine and gossamer drapes floated in the ocean breeze. It was as beautiful as her dress. She hated it.

Someone smiled and waved at her. She responded by slightly curling her lips up. The Noori who had brought her the dress this morning insisted she would feel differently in the future. That as the years passed she would eventually come to remember her wedding day as one of the happiest of her life. What a load of rotting fish heads. She walked the perimeter of the room, shoving aside the flowers that dangled overhead and scowling at the selection of food. A wide variety of fish, dried fruit, and pickled vegetables were heaped upon the table. There was even a roasted pig. When had someone gone to land for *that*?

It was really happening. She didn't want to spend another second in the room. She turned sharply on her heel, fleeing the banquet hall in a rush of silk.

KALE

CHAPTER EIGHT

The scouts reported some odd ripples in the water but that's all. Do you want me to send men to investigate?" Kale stood at a sharp attention while he reported to his future Admiral. Well, that was what everyone seemed to think in any case. And why shouldn't they? Mano was a fine Kombu, one of the Wave Master's trusted men and betrothed to his own daughter. He was the man with everything, and Kale was the man reporting "odd ripples."

Mano shook his head. "At ease, Kombu. That won't be necessary, not so close to the ceremony." He adjusted his trishula against his back and jerked his chin across the room. "See? Won't be long before it all starts."

The sight of her made Kale stutter his steps, and he reached out a hand to steady himself, grabbing ahold of Mano's shoulder.

Mano shot him a knowing grin and wriggled his eyebrows. Trust Mano to rub it in. He'd admitted to Kale that he was aware of what he called his "little crush," but he tried to assure Kale that he wasn't bothered by it. For the most part, that remained true. Except for moments like now when it seemed he delighted in reminding

Kale just who she was promised to.

"She's wearing her dress," Mano stated the obvious. "I'd heard she wasn't that receptive to the idea of marriage, but she's wearing her dress." He smiled. "Just goes to show that you can't listen to rumor."

Kale snorted, "Is that why she turned and ran at the sight of you?"

"She didn't . . ." The words died in his mouth as Mano watched her disappear from sight.

Kale raised his eyebrows. "You were saying?" Score one for himself at least.

"Pre-wedding jitters," Mano muttered.

Kale laughed. "I'd have jitters too if I had to marry your ugly face."

Mano gave him a less than friendly punch in the arm. "She'll be back." Was he telling Kale that? Or himself? Kale didn't respond. He was the supportive friend. He always would be. And that meant creating boundaries and sticking to them. Boundaries that included not pining after your friend's betrothed like some love-sick land fool. Kale sighed and turned to Mano.

"Yeah, she'll be back." They belonged together. The future Admiral and the Wave Mistress. But if she truly didn't want to marry Mano, they wouldn't force her to, right? And what if she didn't? *That still doesn't mean she wants to marry you.*

"Maybe you should go after her. Just to make sure she's okay."

"Me? Shouldn't you be the one to check on your future wife?"

"But there's still a few things I need to see to before the binding ceremony. Come on, be a friend?"

Kale gritted his teeth but gave Mano a thumbs up in response before hurrying after her.

Mano had better appreciate this. He wondered if his best friend knew just how lucky he was. Who wouldn't want to marry Coral? She was easily the most beautiful woman he'd ever seen. Even though she sometimes—well, all the time—terrified him, he knew that no other woman would ever be as captivating. It was really unfortunate that she was marrying his best friend.

Some called her a snob, but Kale saw past that, saw that she was often caught in daydreams when she should be studying. Saw that she was cocky with a trishula because she was really one of the best. She was kind. She was often spotted outside the junior training facilities coaching others and training fiercely. He adored her.

She hated him. Or it sometimes seemed that way. She was a natural athlete, but it was well known she lacked control of her *wei*. He'd tried to help her back when they had been children, but she had called him a bossy know-it-all and pushed him off his chair. He smiled at the memory. Even then she had belonged to Mano.

Kale caught up with her in the lower galley. She sat on the floor, munching on dried crackers and working the cork off a bottle of spiced rum. He stopped short before making his presence known, loathe to startle her. The tip of her tongue stuck out between her pink lips, and her nose wrinkled in concentration. Finding success, her face broke out into an impish grin and she took a swig from the bottle that would make any Kombu proud. He'd never caught her with her guard down before, and Kale suddenly felt that he was invading on a very intimate moment.

He backed away, tip toeing because he didn't want her to be alerted to his intrusion. He would make the long trip back to the upper deck alone. Mano would just have to hope that she would be willing to talk with him later. After all, they had a lifetime together for conversation.

And I'll be happy for them, he swore to himself. He was just turning the corner up to the lower deck when a call from above caused the hairs to rise on the back of his neck. Was that a call of distress? He quickened his footwork, taking the steps two at a time.

Another scream ripped into the sea air, this one echoing in his ear drums. He wished he wasn't so far below. Who was screaming so? And why hadn't anyone helped them?

Almost there. Run faster.

He tore down the hall, not even pausing long enough to grab his trishula, though his brain screamed at him for being a fool. *Hurry, just hurry.* He stumbled faster, ignoring the shiver that tickled his spine as yet another hoarse scream echoed from above. Was it a cry for help or a cry of agony? What was going on?

He burst onto the open deck and stopped short, struggling to take in the sight that greeted him. It was pandemonium. Bodies lay everywhere. The ship was in flames. Some worked to pour water on the fire while others were still locked in battle with the ship's invaders. Who were these people? The screams were now too many to isolate, though Kale hurried into the fray, hoping to help where he could. He called up his watersense and sent up a rush of water to douse the nearby flames while simultaneously tackling the closest invader. The man had a long spear and had been locked in battle with a Kombu who had lost an arm, the stump spurting blood around them. Kale snatched the trishula from the one-armed soldier and rammed it into the invader's eye.

"What's happening?" he asked the soldier, tearing cloth from his wrap and winding it around the stump. The bleeding slowed but the soldier was already swaying on his feet.

"Attack from land. They came out of nowhere. Sodden breathcatchers. An entire fleet of dhow that came out of nowhere.

There was no alarm. Kitoi, I think. Or maybe the Republic or . . . they killed . . . they're killing everyone." The soldier's face paled as he stared down at his missing arm, as if seeing it for the first time.

Kale pushed him up against the door to the lower decks. "Stay here. I'll come back for you."

"No," the soldier struggled to stand. "I'm fine. I have to defend the ship. I have—"

"Coralynn is below deck." Kale pushed the man so that his back once again slammed into the door guarding the way into the lower decks. "She's down there," he repeated.

Understanding dawned on the soldier's face. "I won't let anyone enter. On my life."

"See that you don't," Kale nodded, throwing an arm out to catch a running Kombu by the wrist. The woman shot him a startled look before dropping her trishula. She'd nearly gutted him.

"Stay with him. Help him guard the lower galley. Help him guard your future Wave Mistress." Kale shouted the words over the chaos.

The soldier nodded, thumping a fist into her chest. Great Mother help them all, but they would have to be enough to keep Coral safe.

Kale shot one last look at the bleeding Kombu and then rushed into the mass of fighting bodies.

VEX

CHAPTER NINE

ex was surprised at how easy the battle was. Battle wasn't even the right word. It was a massacre. *Yes, a massacre,* shouted the voice. *Stop it! Stop the bloodshed.*

Vex shoved the voice aside. He was Vex now, destroyer of men.

The ragged screams of the hundred or so dying people before him did little to stop the efforts of his swinging khanjar. He ignored the piteous sounds, instead focusing and finding pleasure in the resounding crunch of his bhuj axe whenever it crushed bone. Somewhere in the deep recesses of his mind the voice shouted for him to stop, that he was wrong. But that voice was weak and easily silenced.

The people on the outer deck of the sea vessel were ill prepared. It's why they planned the attack when they did. But it seemed the timing was even better than they had planned for. The sea people had been in the middle of a celebration of some sort. There was even a feast waiting for his men!

He and his two hundred men had brought their *dhows* up

along the side of the sea people's ship. Vex had had a hard time accepting that their presence would be masked, but they had seemed invisible to those keeping watch. It wasn't until his men were all aboard that the sea people had been alerted to the invaders. Those on the outer deck would have been dangerous under ordinary circumstances. Intel on the sea people told him that these folk were not gifted in the way of water. They had watersense, *wei* he believed they called it, but they lacked the ability to control their vast ocean home. He didn't know where he had learned that information. In fact, he had no memories at all. But who needed memories when there was war and death?

He lunged forward, a deep guttural cry tearing from his throat. His khanjar had swung high and connected with one of the sea people, embedded in the man's skull. His blood was hot when it sprayed into Vex's eyes. He wiped the blood away with his arm and wrenched his weapon free, turning toward his next victim.

Warning cries and alarms sounded his arrival, but by then it was too late. His men were already on board.

A soldier rushed toward him, his trishula forward and ready. The soldier was angry, blinded by the rage he felt at watching his comrade mercilessly killed. Vex sidestepped him easily, knocking the soldier on his spine with the butt of his khanjar. The soldier fell to his knees, his back arching in pain, and Vex swung his bhuj axe at his neck, severing the head from his shoulders in one mighty blow. The body fell to the ground, twitching before it even began to bleed. Vex stepped over the man and farther into the fray. This body grew tired, but Vex never grew weary. He ignored the signs of exhaustion and pushed forward.

Those with water powers were arriving. A wave rose up from the sea and pushed into several of his men, knocking them off the boat and pulling them under into the depths below.

"Fire!" Vex signaled the command as well, pleased to see that his men were already setting small fires to the ship. Let the people worry about using their water power to put out their burning ship. He swung his khanjar at another attacking soldier, splitting the trishula in two from the might of his short sword. He kept the downward momentum of his swing and severed the man's leg below the knee. The man cried out and fell to the floor. Vex implanted his khanjar into the man's chest.

More of the sea people rushed the deck from the lower levels of the ship. The voice inside his head screamed, but Vex smiled broadly. Good, let them fight. He preferred to give them a fighting chance. He didn't care for the massacre, their stealthy approach had already left a sour taste in his mouth, and he turned to the on-comers, lifting his voice in a guttural battle cry.

Some of his men fell. He watched as one of the sea people pushed water into the face of two of his men. They thrashed at the air with their hands before toppling down. Drowned. Vex tackled the water user to the ground, satisfied when his fist crushed into the man's sternum, reveling in the feel of it collapsing under his hand. He finished the job with a quick slice from his khanjar before leaping to his feet, ready for the next attacker.

He was having too much fun. He needed to remember his objective. His khanjar sliced off a man's arm and he shoved him away with a swift kick to his ribs, moving away from the man in search of the Sea King.

His orders had been clear: damage the ship, injure and kill as many as he could, take what he wanted, but kill the Sea King. The need to fulfill his objective pulled him forward, his steady pulse keeping time against the golden chain at his wrist. His sharp eyes scanned the deck, raking over the twisting bodies locked in combat, searching through the blood and gore amidst the fires and gushing water. Where was he? Surely the man wouldn't hide below deck while his people were massacred?

He stepped over a twitching body, planted his boot into the back skull of another that was trying to rise, and smiled when he found his prey. There. The Sea King stood off to the side, pushing water over the fires of the ship, drowning at least a dozen men, and fighting off two others with his twirling trishula. The man was ferocious in battle, easily the best fighter he had ever seen. Vex smiled. He ignored the screaming in his brain and focused all his attention on his objective.

He rushed toward the sea king, scarcely taking the time to behead yet another soldier that dared to attack him. His vision tunneled. Kill the Sea King. Kill him.

He was almost there. A soldier stepped up in front of him, blocking his view and preventing him from going any farther. Vex growled his frustration and faced his new foe, scowling down at him. He was a boy, maybe seventeen or eighteen. He would soon be a dead fool.

Vex planted his feet and swung his khanjar at the youth. The boy ducked and Vex's sword whistled as it cut through the air. He pivoted on his heel, using the force from his swinging weapon to turn him in the same direction, not losing momentum as he swung his khanjar at the boy. The boy raised his trishula and caught Vex's khanjar with it, effectively blocking Vex's attempt at decapitation.

The boy was strong. Vex smiled and gave the boy his full attention. The Sea King could wait.

The boy soldier swung his trishula at him. Vex parried and sliced down at him, causing the boy to jump back to avoid being cut in half. Vex choked back laughter. He would enjoy killing this one. The boy pushed his trishula toward Vex's stomach, at the same time a spray of water hit Vex in the face, pushing up his nose and into his mouth. The boy had water power too. The water pushed its way deeper, blocking his air passage. Vex focused on the beating of his heart. The key was to not panic. Break the boy's concentration, and he would lose his control of the water. Vex swung his khanjar in a sideways motion, changing its direction at the last moment so that it sliced down and into the boy's foot.

The boy yelped in pain and lost control of the water. Vex inhaled sharply, ignoring his burning lungs. Kill the boy. Kill the king. He rushed at the youth, swinging his khanjar while the boy was still distracted by his bleeding foot. Enough playtime. Vex would finish him now. He swung his khanjar down at the boy's exposed neck.

A massive wave of water knocked him back several feet. He landed on his back and blinked several times to regain focus in a world that was quickly turning black. He struggled to his feet.

The Sea King stood beside the youth.

"Where is Coralynn?"

Who was Coralynn? His wife? A daughter? There had been no orders regarding anyone but the king. Vex blinked away the dark spots that threatened to cut off his vision.

"She's safe, in the galley."

"Go to her." The Sea King turned to Vex, giving him his full attention.

Vex's grip on his khanjar tightened. Finally. The Sea King was his. *You don't have to do this!* The voice continued its useless pleas. He tuned out the noise of those around him. It was him and the king.

"Let me help you," the boy's voice was pleading. Vex grinned down at the boy's foot, blood was squirting out making the slippery decks red and sticky.

"No." The Sea King didn't look at the youth, his green eyes were focused on Vex. *Good.*

"No, go to her. Go now, this is an order. I need to know that she's safe."

With a pained look the boy hobbled off, but neither Vex nor the king turned to watch him go.

"Who's sent you? How did you get on the ship?"

Vex smiled. Worthy questions. It was a shame they would go unanswered. He leaped toward the Sea King and held his khanjar high, aiming for his chest.

The Sea King rolled out of his way, standing up behind him and pushing a wave of water at Vex's back. The water caused him to stumble, but he pushed back against it, swinging his weapon as he did so. The king changed tactics, thrusting his trishula forward while shooting water up into Vex's face. Rather than try to drown him, the water shot into Vex's eyes and obscured his vision. He wiped at his face but could not get past the steady stream of water. He swung his khanjar blindly, hoping to connect with the Sea King. He connected, but only with the Sea King's blocking trishula. He turned sharply, rolling his weapon off the king and leaping toward the king's side. Vex swung his khanjar again, and once again, the king blocked it with his trishula.

The king was strong, a worthy adversary, his finest yet. It would be a great honor to kill such a man. The king pushed water at his face yet again, and Vex dropped down to his knee, swinging at the king's feet. The Sea King jumped easily over the weapon, and Vex growled in frustration, rolling forward and coming to stand behind the king. The king turned quickly, but Vex was ready, planting his fist into the king's face.

The king was a massive man, but Vex was faster and his fist sank into the king's face, breaking bone. The king shot more water at Vex, this time with the intent of drowning him, but Vex was ready and heaved his khanjar at the king, connecting with his trishula with enough force that the weapon snapped in half. The king's concentration broke and the water fell to the deck, harmlessly spraying at Vex's feet. He punched again, landing a blow at the king's temple before bringing his knee up to the king's gut.

The king doubled over. Vex noticed the small river of blood that flowed from the king's side. When had that injury occurred? Had the king been fighting with the gash in his side the entire time? Vex kicked the king in the gaping wound and he fell to his knees as more blood pumped from his open flesh.

The king once again shot a stream of water toward him but he was growing weaker. Vex was able to sidestep the water easily. He planted a foot on the king's chest and shoved him backward. The king was weaponless but not yet defenseless. He shot more water at Vex's face.

Vex placed the blade of his khanjar at the Sea King's throat. If Vex could speak, he might have told the king how impressed he'd been at his strength and bravery, but words were now a privilege not his own. His eyes flicked back down to the mortal wound on the Sea King's side. It wouldn't be long now.

The Sea King said nothing but growled low between his teeth as the tip of Vex's boot prodded the deep wound at his side.

Vex frowned down at the king. He wished he could claim the honor of bringing down such a worthy foe. He would have to question his surviving men later, they'd known the Sea King belonged to him.

Vex dipped his fingers into the king's blood and slowly brought them to his mouth. No, it wouldn't be long now. The king's eyes widened but he spat at Vex's feet. Vex smiled and pushed away at the tiny jet of water that pushed at his face. The king's life blood pooled around him and soon, the man would draw his last breath. Vex could not kill a man in such a state.

Vex sheathed his khanjar at the strap on his back and knelt down so that he was eye level with the king.

"I will leave you now. I've accomplished what I've come here to do. Perhaps you will live long enough to tell your Coralynn good-bye."

The king watched him with hatred but made no other movement. Vex noted the gray pallor to his skin. The wound at the king's side no longer pumped blood. No, it wouldn't be long now. The voice inside his head was weeping now. He ignored that too.

He gave the signal to his men and walked back to his *dhow*, ignoring the mass of bodies that littered the deck of the ship. There were very few left living. Those who were made no move to stop him from leaving, the fight dying from their eyes as they watched the death of their king.

TYLAK

CHAPTER TEN

Tylak *knew Jura worried for* her friend, and her loyalty strengthened the tug of his own guilt, his failure at rescuing Sykk. These past few weeks, little else controlled his mind. Well, thoughts of his brother and a certain braided troublemaker. Jura was full of surprises. She was fearless, despite her tiny stature, or perhaps because of it. He'd learned she spoke five languages, though this was her first time leaving the Republic. Jura was masterfully trained in hand-to-hand combat, but she'd only learned it to please her father and hated the idea of fighting. She was willing to walk into enemy territory not merely to stop a war but to save her best friend. She was full of contradictions and burn it all if he didn't find each one of them mesmerizing. She was dangerous. Once before he'd allowed himself to become distracted by a woman, by one of the Thirteen. He gritted his teeth in reaction to the tiny tug against his heart and strengthened the walls around him. He scowled in Jura's direction but she didn't notice, absorbed in her book, *Kitoi: A Traveler's Guide to the Golden City*. He rolled his eyes. The firelight seemed to dance in front of her, the Everflame always brighter, somehow grander in her presence. Peppik announced his arrival by stomping through the Samur at prayer and kicking up the sand near Tylak's feet.

"Anything to report?" Tylak said the words out of habit, a daily question after Peppik's return from wherever he had gone. He frowned down at the puffs of dust, wondering why Peppik found them so engaging when the old man grunted a reply.

"The sands are not as tame as one would believe."

Tylak frowned. Peppik and his riddles would forever be a tiresome thorn in his side. "There was evidence enough of that from the deadly sandstorms that plague the land."

"The dunes travel." Peppik continued on as if he hadn't heard him. Perhaps he hadn't. The man seemed content enough to have his conversations with himself. "It will happen soon."

"What will?" Tylak asked, allowing his gaze to settle once again on Jura. She was exhausted, her head bobbed forward and snapped back each time she caught herself falling asleep.

"The stones are gathering. The Everflame will walk the earth."

Tylak's attention jerked back at Peppik's soft words muttered just below his chin. The man was awkwardly close, his hand stretched out for the slender blue birthstone tied to a leather cord around Tylak's neck. Tylak tucked the stone beneath his shirt and leaned back in an effort to reclaim some of his personal space.

"It flashes around your neck. You should be more careful in the Golden City."

Thieves paradise. The unspoken words drifted between them. Tylak doubted his birthstone would make a provocative target, but the old man was right, only a fool tempted thieves.

"It won't be long now," Tylak murmured, watching Jura struggle to shove her book into her already stuffed pack. He knew a part of her regretted bringing the extra weight, though she would never admit it, but to her credit she had done nothing but read whenever she had a spare moment. He hoped it would be enough.

"She is beautiful." Peppik had followed his gaze. The two watched Jura unroll her sleeping mat. She turned toward them, sensing eyes on her and sent Tylak a sheepish smile.

"A beautiful distraction," Tylak muttered, ignoring her smile and turning to find his own mat. It was just late afternoon, but Tylak knew they all needed their rest if they were going to carry out Jura's plan.

"Your brother. He lives."

Tylak stopped. Peppik did this from time to time. He seemed to withdraw inside himself drawing up secrets and half-truths from some hidden place inside him. Always in riddles. But this, this was clear and to the point.

"Do you . . . do you see him?" Tylak wasn't sure what to ask but he felt his entire body go still from the echo of his words.

"His heart is wild and bloodthirsty, savage, with leather wings beating, but his mind is an endless labyrinth. He waits for you there."

Sykk. He never allowed himself to hope for his brother's life. Had found no indication of him during his various trips to the arena. In some deep, secret place inside him was the knowledge that Sykk was dead and he was never going to see his brother again. And yet . . .

"Is . . . has he left the arena?" Tylak saved every penny for the arena games report, scouring every name for new dancers, cringing at the names of those fallen. His brother had lost his name when he'd entered the arena. What did he go by now? What sort of man had he become? He'd have lived his entire life in the arena as a gladiator. A bloodthirsty savage, Peppik called him.

But Peppik only shook his head in response, once again enchanted by the wake of sand left from the movement of his big toe. Tylak knew he had said all he wished for the moment. When they returned to the Republic, Tylak would ask Jura to take him into the arena. She was from the First family, surely she could access places he couldn't? Jura was different than Denir, wasn't she? His gut reaction said it was so, but the clear memory of that night would forever be seared in his brain, just as the scar was a constant reminder.

Be a dear and fetch my robe." Denir linked her fingers and stretched her arms above her head. She arched her back and sent him a knowing smile as he hurried to do her bidding. It seemed he was always hurrying at her request.

She slid into the black silk and settled back against her cushions, legs curled under her and neck tilted back.

"Either get into bed with me or leave, you're pacing is thinning my rug." She hadn't moved from her position on the bed, eyes half closed, chest falling softly.

"Take me to the arena." It wasn't the first time he'd whispered the request. But never with such fervor, desperation making the whispered words come out a growl.

"The arena? Why on the sands would you want to go there?"

His silence stretched out enough that she sat up and sighed. Her eyes warmed with compassion as she said, words dripping like honey, "Yes, your brother's return is vital to my happiness too, but the arena is boring on the first night of the week. There won't be anyone there." She pouted. "Why don't you just come back to bed and we can worry about going to the arena later?"

"When? Tomorrow? The day after that? When, Denir?" he demanded, cutting off her sputtered protests. It was like a small flame had been sparked atop a loaded pit. He would ignite with just one tiny flick of the flame. Sykk's small face haunted his dreams. Tylak couldn't fathom what his brother looked like all these years later. He was so close, and yet still his station denied him. "When will you take me with you to the arena?"

"It's difficult . . . my husband —"

"Burn your husband. This doesn't concern him."

"Doesn't it, though?" The cool timbre of the Fifth drifted across the room and ran Tylak's blood cold.

To her credit, Denir leapt to her feet and closed the distance between her and her husband.

"Hello, *wife*," he sneered the word but didn't look at her, his eyes locked with Tylak's. He'd seen him before, of course. Tylak was a slave in the Fifth's home, but the Fifth never bothered to really look at his slaves. He was staring now. Tylak noticed the bulge in the man's throat work its way up and down, most likely holding back whatever was being held between clenched teeth. A vein spiraled across the length of his forehead, throbbing red against purple mottled skin.

Tylak took his cue. The Fifth's face changed to one of wonder, and he spun in a tight circle. "Where is he?"

Tylak's daggers lay atop his discarded pile of clothing on the other side of the bed, beyond the Fifth. He was invisible to the man but didn't want to risk getting too close, especially when he was naked and vulnerable.

"Where is he?" he repeated, demanding an answer from the

pale faced lady of the house. The Fifth reached his wife, shaking her shoulders and shoving her toward the bed. "You disgust me. Cavorting with a slave, one marked with such unnatural power."

Denir sat up, a rod of steel down her back. "At least he has power. At least he's a real man." She seemed to stare directly at Tylak as she said the words, although he knew she couldn't see him.

The Fifth clenched his fist and took a step toward his wife. Tylak tackled him to the ground, pummeling his fist into his stomach until a swift kick to his groin had Tylak rolling onto his back in protest. Losing concentration he appeared, a rolling mess on the floor.

"Pathetic." The Fifth rose to his feet, delivering a swift kick into Tylak's rib cage. Then another. Tylak groaned but fumbled onto his knees so he could shield his face. Good thing too, because the Fifth had unsheathed his scimitar and held it suspended over his head.

"Tylak, don't do anything stupid." Denir's pleading voice sounded so very far away as she begged him to surrender, begged him not to move even as the Fifth ran his blade down the length of his face. The hot blood flowed freely, covering his face and dripping down the length of his nose and into his mouth. He searched for Denir's warm brown eyes, found them as she gave a gentle shake to her head and plunged Tylak's dagger into the Fifth's throat.

The Fifth's eyes widened, and he gurgled and clawed at his neck as he died.

Denir did not tremble as she thrust Tylak's clothing into his arms.

"Get dressed, quickly."

Tylak obeyed, wiping his face on his sleeve. He felt the blood spread across his face and winced from the searing heat of the wound.

"Leave your dagger." She pushed back the hand that had reached for his weapon. She didn't so much as spare a glance at her husband. "I'll tell them we were attacked. One of the Thirteen must have sent a Shadow Dancer after us." She nodded.

"Once they see my injuries they'll know it was self-defense. No one will blame you for killing him."

"See you?" Denir let out a wild chuckle. "Tylak, no one is going to see you. They'll execute you and see you burned."

"Execute me? For sleeping with one of the Thirteen?"

"No, for killing one of them."

Tylak blinked. "Who killed the Fifth?"

"You did, of course. That's why you have to leave right away so you aren't here when I summon my *Arbe*." She cupped her hands around her mouth and called out past the stone walls, "Guards!"

Tylak choked back a gasp. "What are you doing?" he hissed. "We haven't figured out our plan. How will I know when it's safe to come back to you? How w . . ." A sense of understanding had him trailing off. He ignored the muffled steps of the guards rushing through her halls toward her private bedroom. They would be here any moment. He turned pained eyes toward her.

"You never meant to take me to the arena. You've just been using me, waiting to get what you want . . . to get this."

The door crashed open, and Tylak seized hold of his power and twisted himself up into a cloak of shadows.

He was invisible, so it looked to the guards as though the Fifth's widow was in shock, talking to no one or perhaps sending off one last prayer for the lost flame of her beloved when she said to no one in particular, "I did care for you, in my own little way, and I will miss you, but we could never give each other what we wanted. You'll see, you're better off this way."

CORAL

CHAPTER ELEVEN

fter more than a few swigs from the bottle, the idea of marriage didn't seem so bad. The rum was warm as it made its way down her throat and into her belly. In fact, she was starting to feel warm all over. She sat heavily on the floor and examined her dress. It really was beautiful. Mother must have had it made for her in secret. It fit perfectly, and she doubted she'd ever own anything finer. So why was she sitting on the floor of the galley ruining it? She shot to her feet and ran her hands down the length of the fabric in an effort to smooth its wrinkles.

She eyed the bottle of rum, debating whether or not she needed another sip. Probably not. This was her first time drinking heavily with the stuff and the pleasant warmth in her belly was already being replaced by a disconcerting rumble. She was getting married. The idea was suddenly hilarious and she fell into a fit of giggles. She was probably already late. How long had she been hiding away? No longer than an hour, surely. But then, she had closed her eyes for a moment so she couldn't be sure. She must be late for her own wedding. Father would be furious, more so when his precious progeny showed up sauced.

The door to the narrow galley swung open and she sobered, standing as tall as her five feet and seven and a half inches would allow. Who would dare swing the door at her so? She threw back her shoulders and glared at the intruder.

When she saw that it was Kale, she let loose a shout of laughter. Trust her father and her betrothed to be so busy they couldn't even be bothered to check on her themselves. No, instead they had sent the Admiral's lackey. She fixed him with a level stare. He had nice blue eyes. Why hadn't she ever noticed before?

"Blue." Her hand flew up to her mouth to prevent any more laughter from escaping. *Blue? Bite your tongue before he realizes you're a sodden mess.*

"Coralynn—you're safe. You need to . . . are you drunk?"

Too late.

"Are you drunk?" She waved a pointed a finger at him.

"How much have you had? Never mind, that's not important. Drink some water." He thrust a glass full at her and she drank obligingly. Why was he being so bossy?

"You came to find me." She hiccuped. "Who svent you? Hmm." She smiled. "I said svent."

Kale crossed the room and reached for her arm as though to steady her, but she jerked away from him, noticing his injured foot.

"You're hurt." She stared down at the blood and felt like she might lose the contents of her stomach. She swallowed and drank more water. How had he gotten hurt?

"I can't believe you've been down here drinking."

He was angry. Why was he so angry? He'd be drinking too if he was forced to marry Mano. But then, he couldn't very well marry his commander now could he? She wanted to laugh again but she was entirely too nauseous to do so. And there was the matter of his bleeding foot. She backed away before he got blood on the hem of her dress.

"They sent you to fine me. Fine me. *Find* me." She giggled again. "You want to bring me up for the ceremony. They sent you?" There were two of him, and she was having a hard time focusing on which one to yell at. Perhaps she would feel better if she released the bitter liquid that was fighting its way up. She turned into the disposal bin to do so.

After heaving for several moments she turned toward him and took a gulp from the offered water. That was nice of him. He no longer looked angry, instead, he just seemed sad. She wiped at her mouth with the back of her hand and remembered his injury. Blood still seeped from the top of his foot and the sticky substance had covered the entire appendage. Stupid boy, he didn't even know how to properly bandage his foot. She dropped to her knee to do so.

She was wrapping his foot with a towel when he placed a gentle hand on her shoulder.

Why did he look so sad?

"Is it time for the ceremony? You won't be able to walk very well with your foot bandaged like that. You can lean on me. What was Mano thinking sending you to find me with your foot like that?" She walked toward the door but was stopped by his hand at her elbow. His hold was gentle, but he was firmly pulling her back to him.

"Let go. I'm late and the Wave Master is probably furious by now." She moved to pull away but his grip tightened. What game was he playing at? She didn't want to get married and had made no secret of the fact but now that most of the alcohol had been removed from her stomach she realized she was foolish if she believed she could continue hiding out in the bowels of the ship. Surely he wasn't trying to delay the inevitable too, was he? For what reason?

"Coral." His voice was soft as he gently tugged her around until she was facing him.

"Kale, what's going on? What happened to your foot? Why didn't my mother come to find me?" Maybe she was still somewhat tipsy, but the pieces weren't falling together.

"Tell me." She squinted up at him and noticed the lock of white hair, such a stark contrast to the ebony locks that hung over his forehead. "Your hair! You . . . is everything . . ."

When he sadly shook his head in reply she felt her heart sink into her stomach. She bolted for the door.

"Coral, wait! It's not safe up there. You have to stay hidden."

She ignored him and opened the door, making for the flight of stairs. She could hear him let loose a string of curses as he struggled to follow after her.

It was quiet, too quiet, as she made her way to the upper deck. Where was the sound of laughter, the ceremony music and excited conversation?

There were exactly one hundred and eight stairs, two hallways, and four doorways before she gained access to the upper deck. Something was wrong. Something was terribly, terribly wrong, and she'd been hiding away, drinking like a coward.

She burst through the final door and stopped short at the sight that greeted her.

Blood. There was so much blood. Bodies littered the deck, some of them still groaning, too many of them silent and still.

Where were her parents?

In a panic, she pushed her way through the bodies, ignoring the cries of those few reaching out for her. Where was Mother?

Where was Father? She had to find them. They were okay. They had to be okay.

"Mother!" The cry ripped out of her. "Father where are you?" She wouldn't look at the bodies lying face down, she couldn't do that. No, they were tending the wounded, they were helping someone more injured . . . What had happened?

There. She saw a familiar shock of white blonde hair slumped over another body. The shoulders moved. He was alive.

"Father!" She ran to him, flinging herself down to the deck beside him.

His head snapped up and he stared at her, blinking several time before his eyes could focus. His clear green eyes were milky, his face pale.

"Father?"

"Coral, my sweet baby girl."

She didn't look down at the body he cradled in his massive arms. Recognized all too well the length of auburn hair that adorned the tiny frame. Her mother was gone.

"What happened? How bad are you hurt? We have to get you to the infirmary, we have to—"

The Wave Master shook his head, gently moved aside the body he carried to reveal the terrible injury at his side. Coralynn looked down at the blood that covered the Wave Master from the waist down. The blood that pooled at his feet and stained her white dress.

It was too late.

No. She shook her head. No. There were healers. The ship had healers. She just had to find them. Or back at the island there were plenty of medicines. She could get them back to Aina and he could live. He had to.

She reached for his hand, found his cold fingers covered in hot sticky blood.

"This is all my fault." She was the lowest coward. Honor stripped. She'd been below deck, drinking and hiding away like a spoiled brat. She could have helped. They had needed her. Her father had needed her. She'd let everyone down.

"I'm so sorry." She didn't know when the tears started, but she was crying so hard by now that her nose was stuffy and she found it hard to breathe. She sucked in deep breaths between her teeth.

"Father, please, I don't hate you. I was wrong, I was so wrong. I love you more than anything in this world. And I need you, please. We can heal you. It's not too late. You can get better."

She looked around, searching for someone who could help or something that she could make a bandage out of. She tore at the bottom of her dress, pressing the fabric to his wound. All too soon it was stained red with his blood.

He reached out his hand and gently touched her face.

"You'll be fine, I promise. I'll get us back to Aina, you'll see. I love you, I love you so much. Please don't leave me, Papa."

"Coral," her name was a sigh on his lips. His eyes closed and she watched his chest heave his final breath. He was gone.

"No, no, no, no," she wailed, screamed the denial as loudly as she could. He wasn't dead. They weren't dead. This was all a dream, a terrible nightmare.

Who had done this? Who had dared attack the Wave Master on his ground? Who could be so powerful? If she hadn't been below decks, she would have shown them the true power of the waves.

She didn't notice as the wind whipped up around her or the spray of the ocean water hit her face. She would find whomever had done this. She would make them pay.

The deck rolled beneath her feet, and she ignored the tempest around her, feeding her fury to the injustice. A tidal wave rolled from the ship. Ocean life began to fly in the air around her as the water ejected them from their homes. She ignored the chaos of the waters. Someone had come to her home and attacked her family. She would find them. She would kill them all.

The ocean was roaring around her, but she didn't notice, didn't see anything except the blood at her feet.

Someone shouted her name. She ignored them and screamed her fury into the howling wind, churning the ocean water around her. She would have revenge, she would—

A sharp slap to the face snapped her back to the present and she turned wild eyes to Kale, blinking to bring him into focus.

"You'll kill us. Get control of yourself."

The ship rocked wildly against the massive waves. Fish flopped on deck, searching for a way back to water. Had she done all this?

She took a deep breath and the waters instantly began to calm. Yes, she'd nearly killed them. She and Kale, and the other survivors on the ship.

"I . . . I just—"

The words were cut off as she was wrapped in a fierce hug. As a general rule she didn't like hugs. But this was nice. She hugged him back.

"They . . . He . . . My father—"

"Shh." He smoothed her hair and held her tighter. "I'll find Mano and issue orders. We have to get to Aina. The survivors need medical attention."

Yes, he was right. They had to worry about the living. And

Mano, yes . . . she hadn't even thought to ask if he was okay. She pushed away from Kale and struggled to reclaim a sense of normalcy. She needed to be level headed if she wanted her revenge. And she could only craft a revenge plan after arriving in Aina.

Aina lay several leagues off to the west, and Kale made short work calling the sea to push them in that direction. Coral wanted to help, but when she called up her *wei* it wriggled from her grasp, slippery as an eel. Instead she focused on organizing the survivors. She broke them into groups, those who had injuries that prevented them from moving were helped by those who still had the ability to move about the ship. There were very few uninjured, only eight, and she sent those to collecting and recording the names of the deceased.

She wrapped linen around a gaping wound on Mano's thigh. Though he'd lost plenty of blood, he would survive so long as Kale got them to Aina and the medicines their home offered. Mano pushed at her hands, insisting that he could see to his own wounds.

"The Wave Master—is he?" Mano was unable to finish the sentence.

"Where were you?" she whispered the question.

"In the battle, of course. There was so much fire and smoke and they were everywhere. Coral, I—"

"No. Don't bother." She sighed. "We can discuss future plans once we arrive in Aina."

"But the wedding . . . We still have to complete the ceremony."

Surely she'd heard him wrong. "Excuse me?"

"It was important to the Wave Master to see our betrothal through. He wanted to see you safe."

Coral clenched her teeth in response. "At the moment you can barely stand and I'm . . . We will discuss this later." She turned away from him, blinking back tears. It was true, this union had been important to her father, but she still didn't know why. Now she never would.

Those on board mourned the loss of their Wave Master, but most still retained some hope for the future. It seemed to be the common reaction among the Kombu. The Wave Master had died, but his progeny and her betrothed still lived. Coral knew they were grateful she was alive, but their gratitude in the face of her departed parents was crippling. She didn't deserve to live. Her father had been their leader; she could never hope to stand in his footsteps. When she should have been fighting at her people's side, she'd been hiding, proving to everyone she had about as much bravery as crab hiding in their shell. Useless. She didn't deserve to be Wave Master, yet that's exactly what she was.

"Mistress. The acting captain sends for you." The words came from one of the uninjured Kombu. The man bowed low in front of her, and she stared at him for several moments. Mistress. The people had already taken to her new title.

"I'll be right there."

She stood up to leave but was stopped by a tug on the hem of her dress. She stared down at the ruined fabric of her wedding gown, the once sparkling white was stained red and brown.

Mano stared up at her, his face full of sympathy. "Coral, I'm . . . sorry." He seemed to know the inadequacy of his words because he immediately released her, raking his hand through his short sandy brown hair with a soft sigh.

She patted his head and caught his fingers with her own, for the briefest of moments she allowed herself to take in the sympathy of her betrothed. This was almost normal. Except she didn't love him and her family was gone. With a sigh she squared her shoulders and left in search of Kale.

Kale stood at the rudder, moving his arms as he directed the ocean beneath him. He must have sensed Coral's *wei* because he turned back to watch her approach. He was still in his bloody ceremonial armor, chest traditionally bare. She was still in her soiled dress. They were a mess.

He was doing a fine job captaining the ship. The water pushed at the ship and the wind tore through her hair as the ship continued to pick up speed.

"You were always better at this than I was," she whispered, but somehow her voice carried to him over the wind.

Kale turned toward her, careful to keep an arm out to direct the waters.

"That's because you haven't got the patience." He gestured her closer. She stood at his left side, close but not close enough that he could touch her.

"How many survivors?" he asked.

"Thirty-two. Twenty-nine that should survive for sure."

Were they really talking about survivors in the same casual tone used for discussing the weather? Coralynn swallowed several times and then frowned up at him. He stared back, eyes searching her face. She wondered if he was looking for answers, if he already saw her as his leader.

"How long until we make it to Aina?" she asked, needing something else to break the silence. Needing to speak something other than the count of the living.

"No more than an hour or so."

Faster probably if he kept at this pace. Coral wondered how he so easily gave into his *wei*, a servant to its power.

"I'll help you." She didn't wait for a response. She never did. Her heart was too demanding to have true control over her power. *Wei* was a surrender to the ocean, a vulnerability she had yet to master. She grabbed her *wei* and commanded the water to push them along. The ship lurched and gave a few violent rocks but within minutes she had the motion under control. The ship pushed along at breakneck speed.

"I wanted to talk to you about what you said earlier." Kale had to shout for his words to be heard over the thundering winds.

Her hair whipped about her face and stung her skin, but Coral didn't care, it was nice to feel something. "What's there to talk about?"

"It's not a good idea. The people need you. You're Wave Master. You can't abandon them now. You can't go running off for revenge."

"Why can't I?"

"Coral . . . Your father wouldn't want this, he wou —"

"Don't tell me what my father would want. My father would want to be here. My father would want to know his people hadn't just been massacred. Something is happening, Kale. Father knew it. It's why he forced this union between me and Mano. Something happened while he was on land. Something scared him enough to prepare for war. And then we were attacked. You can't say that these two events aren't connected. No, Father would want me to go to land. I need to go; I have to."

"But if we leave the people now —"

"We?" She twirled to look at him. As she did, her connection to the sea was severed and the boat wobbled beneath them. She seized control of her *wei* with clenched teeth and the ship once again picked up speed.

He stifled a sigh. "Of course Mano will go with you. And I want to help too. You need my help. I can identify the man who led the army."

"I don't need your pity."

"Pity?" He grabbed her arm and even though he did, he still had tight control on his watersense and the ocean didn't stutter beneath them. "This isn't out of pity. I care about our people."

Coral swallowed. Something in the intensity of his stare made her believe how much he did care.

"I'm going to help you, of course I will. I just want to make sure that you're making the right decision. That you're not rushing off into a dangerous situation because you're angry or hurt or—"

"Of course I'm angry and hurt. My parents are dead. Slaughtered. In our home. And yes, I want revenge. But this is bigger than that, can't you see? Something is happening, and I'm going to find out what. You think that I'm not worried about my people, but you're wrong. Yes, I want revenge. Yes, I will find whoever is responsible for my parent's death and I will drain them of their last breath. But if I didn't?" She threw her hand up in the air and a spray of water followed the movement. She scowled at the wave until it once again pushed against the boat. "When Father came back he called a meeting with Mother and Tiburon. He was frightened. We have to find out why."

This wasn't a decision she entered lightly, but it needed to be done. She would have her revenge.

KAY

CHAPTER TWELVE

They were finally done for the day. Ash did the same thing at the end of every practice. He looped a single finger in the air and beckoned her toward him, holding out a fresh skin of water. Her night's rations always arrived after practice and Kay usually spent her evenings studying with Kindle. Only tonight Kindle was fighting in the arena.

She snatched the water skin out of Ash's grasp and made half of it disappear within seconds and a few greedy gulps.

"Slow," he cautioned with a string of other words Kay couldn't understand. She'd learned hundreds of words already, but her grasp of the foreign language still slipped through her fingers.

"Kindle," she muttered in response. Kindle usually brought her meal at the start of her studies.

"Kindle is at the arena today. Do you want to go watch her?" At least that seemed the most likely sentence he put together, Kay wasn't entirely sure but she nodded her head in agreement.

Ash led her past the fields of sand, through the barracks, and into a long hallway. Torches lined the stone walls and their footsteps echoed in the nearly empty stone hall. Kay ignored her rumbling belly as she struggled to keep pace with Ash's long strides. She'd never been down the long twisting hallways before. She looked around with interest, though there was nothing to see. Hundreds of feet up ahead she felt the presence of a lot of warmth and assumed they were heading toward a large fire. On a whim, she Breathed in heat from one of the torches lining the wall. A warm buzzing sensation spread through her body. The fire felt different here in the arena proper. Somehow, it felt alive. She shivered before releasing the fire back to the torch and running back to Ash's side.

"I'm hungry," she whined. Ash looked down at her in confusion. Oops. She'd said the word in her own language. She searched her brain and repeated the words in his language.

"In the arena," he nodded.

Kay sighed. If they were on their way to watch Kindle fight a dragon, why would there be food? She wanted to stay strong like Mama and Daddy would have wanted, but fat tears rolled down her cheeks. She wiped them away before Ash could see her wasting water and took a deep breath. The end of the hallway was finally coming into view. Kindle and another Fire Dancer stretched out their muscles in front of two large doors.

Kay raced ahead and threw herself into Kindle's arms. The woman hugged her tight. She smelled like oil and smoke. Nothing like her Mama, but the hug was still wonderful.

"What's wrong?" Kindle smoothed the hair back from Kay's face and used the language of her people. "You're not worried for me, are you?"

"The fire here is different," Kay blurted out, because she wanted to tell Kindle she was worried for her. She was hungry and tired. She didn't want to go to the arena, and she wanted to go back home to her farm. She wanted Mama and Daddy. She swallowed hard. She couldn't tell Kindle any of that. "It felt different," she repeated, because for some reason that seemed important.

Kindle cocked her head to the side, studying her. "The flames probably feel different because they're fed from the Everflame here. We talked about the Everflame, remember?"

Kay nodded. She remembered. And even if Kindle hadn't explained it, Kay still would have felt its existence. She didn't need to see it to know there was a massive source of heat. Kay felt it every day in the Sand Sea, just as she felt the sun on her face.

"Are you sure you want to come inside the arena?" Kindle knelt down so she could stare directly into Kay's eyes. "You don't have to if you don't want. Oh hey, I almost forgot. I had too many sweet cakes today and couldn't eat this last one." Kindle pulled out a small dessert from inside her leather satchel.

Kay's eye's widened at the unexpected surprise, and she bit into it with relish, ignoring Ash and Kindle's conversation beside her. She was licking the last of it off her fingers when Kindle knelt down beside her again. "I'm going inside now, but I told Ash you might want to head back to the barracks for dinner. You let him know, okay? I'll see you after." She winked before she stood up and took her assegai back from Ash.

Kindle said something to the other Fire Dancer and slapped him on the back before they disappeared behind the twin doors.

Ash stared at her expectantly. She shrugged. "Inside." He nodded and gestured for her to follow him to the door just to the right of the twin doors. It lead to another unremarkable hallway. Kay sighed. At least this hallway was not as long as those previous. At the end, the door opened up to a large room. The seats rose up, one behind the other. They all faced the curved glass at the front of the room. With a gentle push from Ash, she stepped farther inside. They were actually only in one section of a gigantic building. It spread way up into the sky, and the glass curved around them like a bubble. People were seated all around and there at the center stood Kindle and the other Fire Dancer. Kay sat down in the first row next to a woman who sent her a disapproving glare.

The woman muttered a string of words Kay couldn't understand, so she ignored them until Ash's firm hand on her shoulder demanded attention. She tore her eyes away from Kindle and met Ash's frown.

"Ash, Fire Dancer. Hello again. Is she yours?"

"My cadet," he answered slowly and clearly for her benefit. "Here to watch her friend Kindle."

The woman's lip curled up. She turned toward Kay and said the words slowly. "Stay. Away. You, go there." She flicked her finger off to the side. Kay entertained the idea of singeing off the woman's eyebrows, but she moved over to the side and away from the woman as directed. *She must be one of the Thirteen.* Kindle had explained the importance of the Thirteen, although Kay had a hard time grasping what made these particular thirteen people important.

"Don't mind Fatima." Ash sat down beside her and between her and the woman. Kay would have continued to scowl over at her if the sound of the trumpets blaring didn't snap her attention back to the arena. At the sound of the trumpets, the two Fire Dancers turned and faced the metal gates. A hush filled the room and Kay leaned forward. The gates rolled back and a blue dragon shot into the air. *He's beautiful.* It had been weeks since she had seen a dragon. She blinked back tears, but she couldn't help but think of Mama and Daddy and their home. Everything was so different here.

The dragon landed and a great cloud of dust rose up at his

descent. Kay squinted into the glass, struggling to find Kindle's features. She had seen angry dragons before, but this one was by far the most savage. *He's hurt.* Kay noticed the scars along his belly, evidence of past battles survived. Did that mean he had killed Fire Dancers? She placed a hand on her belly to shove down the spike of alarm and found Kindle as the dust settled. The dragon turned toward the two Fire Dancers and let out a stream of molten fire. Kindle directed the fire up toward the sky while the second Fire Dancer twisted out of the way. The dragon roared, rearing on his hind legs and stretching out his gigantic leathery wings. Kindle tossed her assegai at the dragon's exposed belly but missed and had to perform a series of flips to get out of the way from the dragon's charge. The other Fire Dancer wasn't so lucky. The dragon's jaws snapped him nearly in half. Kay began to shake. She knew dragons were dangerous creatures, Daddy always said so, but she'd never seen one kill before. She'd never seen one so deadly. Now it was just the dragon and Kindle.

Ash tried to hand her some sort of bread stuffed with meat, but she shoved his hand away, eyes rapt on the arena. Kindle was sprinting across the field in an effort to recapture her assegai. She slid into the sand, her fingers snatching the weapon just before she leaped to her feet and dove to the side to miss a swing from the dragon's mighty tail. Kindle raced around the length of the dragon back toward his front, once again trying to stab him in his vulnerable belly.

Belly and eyes. That's where Daddy said you should attack when defending oneself from a dragon.

The dragon swiped at Kindle with his claws when she got too close and sliced her leg with his sharp nail. Kay flinched at the blood. Kindle didn't even have time to inspect the wound before she leaped out of the way from the dragon's fire.

This dragon seemed to have an endless supply. He began spitting the river of fire at Kindle. The young Fire Dancer tried to keep the fire rolling away from her and back up into the glass dome. The dragon slowly advanced, flapping his gigantic wings but not stopping his endless torrent of fire.

She's getting tired. Kindle's posture was weak, even Kay could tell the position of her feet was wrong. She couldn't hold out against the dragon's attack much longer. But that meant . . . Kay stood up.

Ash grabbed her hand. "Sit down. Kindle will be fine."

But Kay could hear the worried tone in his voice and in the unidentified words he mumbled after. Mama and Daddy both died because she hadn't acted sooner. Kindle needed help. *Be brave, Kay. Go now.* It was Mama's voice inside her. She snatched her hand out of Ash's grasp and ran.

Ash barely had time to react before she was back through the door and into the hallway. *Down the hallway, right into the twin doors,* she told herself, making herself run faster. She didn't have a plan for once she got inside the arena, she just knew she had to go there. She had to save Kindle. She ignored Ash's cries behind her and reached for the final door. Ash would have been slowed down by the crowd, but he would make up for it in the open hall.

Kay shoved the doors open using both hands and all her strength, and then she was in another hallway. This place was like a maze. There. The door at the end of the hall. It radiated with warmth. Kay ran for it and pushed the door open. Kindle was just feet away, breathing hard. She used both arms to push the fire away. Sweat rolled down her forehead and matted loose strands of hair to her face. Blood still oozed from the wound on her thigh.

She turned her head and her frantic eyes met Kay's.

"Kay? What are you doing down here? You have to go! Get out of here, now!"

"His eyes! Shoot the fire back into his eyes!" Kay screamed out in response.

Kindle directed the fire back into the dragon's eye. He stopped and let out a ferocious roar before shooting into the air, circling the arena and bugling in pain.

"How did you know that would work?" Kindle ripped a piece of cloth from her hair and tied it around the wound on her thigh. The dragon still circled the arena. "Well, you're a lifesaver, kiddo. Now get out of here before—" The flame hit Kindle directly in the chest. She fell back from the impact, her frightened features lit up against the flame.

"No!" Kay screamed. It was Mama all over again.

But Kindle was standing up, assegai twirling. "Get out of here, Kay."

"I can help you." Kay took a hesitant step forward, Breathing in flames from two of the nearby torches. Once again the heady experience sent her skin tingling. *Must be fire from the Everflame.*

The dragon reared on his hind legs and roared. Kindle took her chance and plunged her assegai into the dragon's exposed belly. The dragon smashed his front legs into the ground, snapping her assegai in half as he bellowed in pain. He pinned Kindle to the ground beneath his massive claws.

Kay screamed and rushed forward as the dragon sent a stream of fire down at Kindle. Kay shoved at the fire but it was too late, Kindle was already covered in flames. Kay released her own fire at the dragon, letting out a hoarse scream. Not again, please not again. The dragon reared back and Kay took her chance to shoot her flames at the dragon's belly. His roar shook the amphitheater and he fell to the sand, rolling around to cool the searing sting of his singed belly.

"You're a bad dragon. A bad dragon. She was my friend," Kay screamed at the dragon, Breathing in the heat from the surrounding torches until her skin glowed bright and she felt the heat emanating from her. She released the fire at the dragon. Most of it slid harmlessly off his scales, but he still screamed in pain. Her anger spent, Kay fell to the sand, defeated. She was too late. She was no help. Kindle was gone, a smoldering pile of ash and dragon scale armor.

"Kay. Kay, please." He was saying her name. Ash never called her by name. She blinked up at him.

The dragon lay curled in a ball at the opposite end of the arena. He eyed Kay warily. Kay turned her attention back to Ash. "Come with me," he repeated. Kay struggled to get her feet under her, so Ash scooped her up, cradling her like a baby.

"It's okay. Everything is okay," Ash whispered into her hair.

Kay didn't respond. Things would never be okay again.

JURA

CHAPTER THIRTEEN

N*one of the dozen or* more books she'd read on the subject had prepared her for her first glance at the capital city. Jura knew Kitoi was centuries older than the Republic. Her homeland had been developed after a group of merchants and warring nomadic tribes had united under her great-grandfather and revolted against the evil ruler of a would-be empire. But she hadn't expected Kitoi to look so grand. The outer buildings of the capital city were large squares with intricate carvings and grand arches. Jura realized the Republic was fashioned after Kitoi in this way, as many of their own buildings featured such domes. However, where much of the Republic's architecture featured clay homes and glass spires, Kitoi seemed to be made entirely of colored stone and gold.

"No wonder it's called the Golden City," she breathed out as Tylak let out a low whistle beside her.

They stood under massive archways made of wrought iron. And though the iron gave the implication of a gateway, the entryway to the city was open, not even a guard to block their entrance. From either side of the massive archway was a low stone wall that stretched across the perimeter of the city. The wall was carved with all manner of symbols and creatures, from etchings of bactrians and goats to armored men and dragons. Embedded within these etchings were veins of topaz and gold, as well as several colored stones in every color.

"No wonder it's known as a thieves' paradise," Tylak said in response.

Jura shot him a sideways glare. "Keep your hands to yourself. We don't want to draw attention. In fact—"

"On it." Tylak drew his eyebrows together as he concentrated on bending the light around them. It was illegal to enter the city without proper documentation, but they couldn't be stopped for questioning if they couldn't be seen. When they were suitably shielded, he nodded they could continue and took the lead. Jura and their two Samur huddled close behind him. Peppik had disappeared before dawn, slinking off into the night as he often did. They'd released their beast several miles back, and the weight of the large leather pack already weighed heavy on her aching shoulders. Jura gritted her teeth and ignored the pain, determined to enter the city proper before nightfall. The few buildings dotted beyond the stone wall all appeared deserted. Though Jura itched to enter one, she hurried behind Tylak who kept them at a solid pace. She was content to simply stare with wide eyes. If the Samur were impressed, they certainly didn't show it. Instead, they kept their gazes forward, hands ready at rest on their scimitars.

The group traveled in silence for several minutes before Tylak came to an abrupt halt, causing Jura to slam into his back. She rubbed her nose after it had nearly implanted itself between his shoulder blades. She frowned up at him and opened her mouth to demand explanation on his sudden stop, but when she caught sight of what stood before them she felt her mouth go slack from surprise.

A wide expanse of water spread around the city proper. The gate of water was several meters across and stretched across a deep trench bordering the city. Jura searched her brain for the correct word. She'd seen such a thing once before in a book, but seeing so much water in person was mesmerizing.

"What the—" Tylak began.

"It's a moat." Jura cut him off with a squeal of delight. "I've read about these. Cities use bodies of water to prevent break-ins and unwanted visitors. Where does all the water come from? There's enough water here to provide rations for all of the Republic for an entire year!"

Tylak wrinkled his nose. "I doubt the water is safe to drink, or hadn't you noticed that smell?"

"I thought that was you," she said tartly.

He grunted in response. "So, as amazing as this is, what do we do now? I don't see any way across."

Jura frowned. He was right. Even as the city came to life and the noise and call of merchants and citizens carried over the water, the city remained an impregnable fortress. How did anyone get in for trade? And how was it she had never known the city to be surrounded by water? Surely this was something that should have been included in the histories?

They couldn't very well start yelling across the moat and demand entry, could they? They needed to find a way in, but stealth was required. The four of them crouched low against the ground, hidden along a thin line of cacti and shrubbery several meters from the drop off. How did anyone get over that moat? In her illustrated dictionary there was a picture of one, but that had had a distinctive drawbridge. Jura saw no such opening here. It was simply a city on an island. She chewed her bottom lip and squeezed her toes to keep from leaping to her feet in a nervous pace. She turned to the others.

"The guard. We follow the guard and they will lead us to an entrance."

"That should work," Tylak said excitedly. "And it doesn't involve the sewers."

"Might I suggest sending myself or my brother as scout. A large party such as ours will create too much attention. We can do it."

Jura nodded in reply, but when she tried to move closer the ground rumbled at her feet and she fell forward, digging her fingers into the sand for support. The ground continued to shake. The men fell around her. She shook her head and finally found the source of the small quake. The ground in front of the Golden City stretched forward. The earth below the moat groaned as dirt shoved upward above the water to meet the stretching ground above it. As quickly as it had begun, the quake ended, dust settling around the freshly constructed bridge. Jura gaped at it. She'd never read anything like this before. Apparently they used some sort of earth magic to create a bridge, a bridge they created daily. The resources such a project must take was mind boggling. The bridge was about fifty feet wide and stretched over the narrow gap of land as if it had always been there.

"What the hell was that?" Tylak glared at the ground under his feet, daring it to move again.

Even the Samur appeared impressed, although their grips were tight around their swords. Peppik appeared looking nonplussed. His gaze downward as he intently picked each grain of sand from his cloak.

Jura had forgotten about earth magic. Movers? Diggers? What were they called? These people were paid highly for their skill with the sands. They were a rarity and celebrated as leaders in their communities. At least, that was what her studies would have her believe. Apparently the magic was common enough it was used to build a daily bridge. Interesting. Jura bit her bottom lip and studied the constructed bridge. It was wide enough for a caravan and appeared sturdy enough to hold several at a time.

"We have our way in. Let's get moving." Her thoughts fell again to Amira. She couldn't help but picture her friend tied and bound, much as Jura had held her own father. She swallowed against the guilt and squared her shoulders. "Hoods up, you two," she eyed the Samur's shiny and freshly shaven heads. "We'll stay hidden for as long as possible. If we run into any trouble, I'll do the talking. In fact, don't talk at all. There are four of you so you can all pose as my *Arbe*." She held back a smug smile. She knew their stolen *Arbe* leathers would come in handy.

Tylak groaned in response.

It's a good plan, Jura told herself as they approached the capital. It has to be a good plan. She stayed close to Tylak and kept her eyes down on the tips of her sturdy desert boots. The steady buzz of people grew louder, and Jura began to smell the scents of the city. Her stomach rumbled in response to the smoked sausage. Surely they had time for a quick sausage before—her nose smashed into Tylak's back again.

"Oomph."

"Careful," Tylak's whisper gave warning they were still invisible. "Uniforms. Just ahead."

"Let's try to get past them and to the town square. Once we find our lodging in the city, we can separate and start our search."

They shuffled forward. This time Jura was more watchful for any sudden stops from Tylak as she allowed her mind to wonder.

Her first priority remained Amira. Jura had sworn to herself that she would find her friend and return her home to safety. The problem was, home wasn't so safe anymore, and Jura knew that Kitoi had something to do with that. Well, someone from Kitoi and possibly the Queen of Shadows. There were some important players in the game and now she was one of them. The only problem was she didn't know the faces of any of the other players, and she feared she was already failing terribly.

Someone with a lot of power was behind Amira's capture. But in a city rich in gold and water, where did one find power? Jura swallowed hard. Where did she start?

Around them, the city buzzed with life. People crowded the streets in brightly colored clothing, all with long overflowing sleeves that covered their hands. Beshar said if he had to get a blood chain he would get it from Kitoi. And no wonder, Jura thought. Any one of these people could be wearing one of the dangerous bracelets.

How had they been released back into the public? Her great-grandfather had destroyed them all, hadn't he? She nibbled on her bottom lip, boots falling in step behind Tylak's, lost in thought. If even one of the chains was left behind it could have been duplicated. If anyone had mentioned this to her a few months ago she would have thought them mad. But just yesterday she had been exposed to yet another unknown magic. Her fingers stretched deep into her pockets and brushed against the golden wiring of the lorgnette, the metal warmed from its contact with her skin. Yet another frightening example of blood magic. The creature posing as Amira, it used blood magic too. Whatever else she would come to learn of this strange magic she knew one thing for certain: blood magic was evil.

Tylak turned the crew into a narrow alley and leaned back

against the stone wall of the nearest building. He panted heavily and took a long pull from his water supply, draining the skin. Jura allowed her heavy pack to fall from her shoulder, but didn't say anything, still lost in her thoughts. She'd come up with a plan, but it was risky. In fact, it was no plan at all and no one was going to like it. Especially Tylak.

She caught him staring at her and smiled. "I might have an idea, but I need to do just a tiny bit of research first. There are a number of people here involved with the corruption in the Republic. Perhaps also the Shadow Dancers. I need to find out who they are and meet with each one."

"So what's the plan? I make us invisible and . . ." Tylak trailed off as Jura shook her head.

"I have something in mind," Jura began, determined to ignore Tylak's frown or the fact that his eyebrows were already twitching in concern.

"I'm going to make them all come to me."

AMIRA

Chapter Fourteen

The cheap itchy cotton bit into her skin, but the clothing was more of a luxury than she'd had in weeks so Amira didn't mind. She fingered the ugly scars on her wrists, permanent reminders of her time spent shackled. She'd been chained to a corner of a small stone room for weeks, so many she'd lost count. She'd had little water and barely enough food to keep her alive, and the entire time no one had spoken to her.

When she'd first been taken she'd been outraged. She'd believed she'd been kidnapped for ransom and she'd furiously refused food and water, demanding to speak with her captors. She knew her father would pay the ransom, whatever it was, and that it would only be a matter of time before he and their *Arbe* came for her. As the hours passed into days she realized her father wasn't coming. She'd taken the food and water then, whenever it was offered. The visits from her jailor were infrequent, and after a few weeks of no answers from her silent captor she'd stopped asking questions. She'd simply accepted this was her life now.

Today, without explanation, she'd simply been taken from her prison and offered a bath. The water was tepid and not exactly clean, but she hadn't cared. It was water and she was allowed to wash her filthy hair and put on fresh clothing. Her own dress had long ago been reduced to a tattered, greasy cloth that hung on her diminished frame. At her home in the Republic, Amira had only been granted permission to take a submersive bath twice before—most recently on her sixteenth birthday. Amira ignored the happy memories struggling to wiggle their way back into her conscience. *Don't think about home.* After her bath, she'd eaten a full meal comprised of barley soup with goat meat and vegetables. The meat was stringy and the vegetables browned and mushy, but she hadn't cared, she felt the most pampered she'd felt in weeks.

The door opened as she scraped the last of her meal into her mouth. She leapt to her feet, holding her spoon out in front of her. As far as weapons went, it was a meager excuse, but Amira was prepared to fight her way out or die trying.

It was the same jailor as before. She flew toward him, aiming for his eyes, but the man stopped her and wrapped her in a hug, squeezing her arms against her sides. Her struggle was brief.

He bound her arms yet again and pulled her out of the room. She followed, glaring at him as he dragged her behind like some overgrown pet lizard. If she could hiss at him she would. But she was weak. No longer a daughter of the Republic. Now she was nothing. Just some starved and weak figure who probably even now marched to her own death.

She stumbled forward after another harsh pull from the stiff ropes around her wrist. She didn't fight when she was thrown into the carriage. A real carriage, with a roof and cushioned seats. She felt like she was dreaming and wished she had water, her mouth suddenly impossibly dry. And what was that buzzing in her ears?

He'd put something in her soup. Stupid girl. No daughter of the Republic would be so foolish to eat from her enemy's hand before testing for poison. But she was no daughter of the Republic. Not anymore. She blinked back tears and laid her head back against the pillow. This was a nice place to die.

He pulled her arms. She walked up stairs and on clouds and remembered how soft the cushion had been on that carriage. Colors and images swirled before her eyes. She blinked away yet another wave of nausea.

Someone else pulled her arms and there was no carriage. Just firm hands. A woman's hands. They walked and . . .

Amira brought a tentative hand to her head, feeling for injuries but no . . . it only felt as though it had been split open. She opened her eyes. She was alone in a room. It was sparsely decorated, with a single cot for a bed and a small bedside table. She was on the floor but at least she was unbound. She rubbed her wrists, now chafed raw, and drew a few deep breaths. Her chest hurt. Her entire body hurt. Most likely someone had dumped her body into this room. But who? She remembered a woman but . . . she shook her head. This pounding headache would give no purchase to her faded memory. She had been taken away and was now stored somewhere else, that much was clear. She rose to her feet, ignoring the shooting pains racing through her joints as she crossed the length of the room. The door was locked, of course it was.

She turned to examine the room when the door opened and she stumbled backward, catching herself by placing a shaking hand on the wall. An unlikely pair had entered. A young boy, no more than twelve or thirteen, and a giant of a man with a missing eye. He wore no eye patch and the empty socket folded in with skin that was baggy and several shades lighter than his dark tan. Amira swallowed at the sight of it.

"Hello. You are mine now." The young boy smiled. He was tall and thin. Amira was just barely able to meet his eyes. His long black hair was tied with a cord at the base of his neck, and he wore expensive robes in the style of the people of Kitoi. The sleeves hung well past his fingers, and the hem was bordered with the asymmetrical pattern that had been so popular in the market. Funny that she could still even notice such things.

"I am Kuruvilla. I am your master, but you may call me Kuru. This is Luxman." He gestured to the giant man beside him. "Luxman, take her."

The giant started forward, and she let out a muted scream, her throat still raw and aching. She bolted away from him, but the man caught her easily, wrapping one meaty fist around her bicep.

The boy's wide, excited grin terrified her far more than the man's empty eye socket. She struggled against the man's grasp, beating her free fist into his chest. She might as well have struck the stone wall behind her. The man gave little notice to her attack. He flung her up over his shoulder. Her long hair hung over her face, the locks clung to her damp skin and obstructed her vision.

Kuru grabbed her chin between his hands and wrenched her face around so that she faced him. "Stop struggling. You're mine now. And so long as I keep you alive, I can do whatever I want to you." He pushed her hair off her face, and his thumbs stroked at her skin, almost tender.

"Luxman, your knife."

Luxman handed Kuru a long knife. The boy held it close to Amira's face, tracing the blade against the edge of her skin.

She immediately stopped wriggling.

"There. Now, I have your attention." He pushed back another

stray lock of hair. Amira concentrated on the ground, desperate to look anywhere except the knife and Kuru's grinning face.

The tip of the knife came to a stop just under her left eye.

"You have pretty eyes. They look like melted chocolate. Have you ever had chocolate before?"

She squeezed her eyes shut in response. Kuru moved the tip of the knife from one eyelid to the other. "Answer my question," he whispered. The blade pressed into her skin.

She tried to shake her head but all she could feel was the cold steel against her hot skin. "N—nno," she moaned. Her hair fell forward again, obscuring half her face.

Kuru growled in frustration and wrapped the length of it around his fist. He began to saw it off with the knife. Amira didn't dare make a sound, but she couldn't stop the tears escaping from her tightly shut eyes.

"There. Now I can see your eyes. Open your eyes."

Amira drew in a ragged breath and met his gaze. Her hair hung in choppy segments around her face, several inches of the once shining mass littered the ground below. She'd once been vain enough to think her hair was one of her best features, but that vain person existed long ago, now there was only hunger and fear and Kuru's knife.

He laughed. "I won't take your eye, not today. If you make me angry though, I will take it." He handed the knife back to Luxman and gave Amira a harsh swat on her bottom.

"We're going to have fun. Come now, Luxman. Take my new toy back to my room."

CORAL

CHAPTER FIFTEEN

It was nearly sunset and it was quiet on the top deck. The steady roar of water grew louder as they approached the entrance to Aina. It was widely believed her people lived and traded along the coast of a network of small islands, Is'Le'Spar the breathcatchers called it. But their true home, their ancestral home, was Aina. And there was only one way in.

Only a few miles in circumference, the circular waterfall lay far into the Western Ocean, beyond where the Orreram met the Bariq Sea and farther than any land dweller would dare to travel. Even if one was unwise enough to do so, the fall would bring their death. The waterfall's origin was as old as Jangbahar itself, older even. And below the depths of the treacherous waterfall was Aina, the capital city of her people where they followed no law but their own. A place with traditions as old as the ocean, and a fierce people who all lived and died with more honor than she could ever hope to hold.

And now I'm their leader,

It was all too much. She couldn't think of her people. Not

when her parents' remains still had to be dealt with. Not when she hadn't even given herself a chance to think about what it meant for them to truly be gone. Father had been hiding something from her. Years past he had shared nearly everything with her, but in recent weeks he'd gone reclusive. Why? What changed? These burning questions propelled her forward and gave her strength.

Well, she had to arrive in Aina before she could leave it. Coral gritted her teeth and braced for the pain. It wouldn't be long now. Her *wei* was difficult to control as they drew ever closer to the waterfall. She hated entering Aina. The last time had been the most painful night of her life. It was fitting that she should have to enter again now, when she already felt her heart was ripped out and cast off into the sea. She thought of calling and asking for someone else to escort them in, anyone else, but she bit her tongue. This was her duty, her father would say. And she refused to let him down again. Never again.

She and her father had been out on a tiny dory when he had deemed her ready to enter Aina on her own. She'd barely gotten a hold of her *wei*, had felt suffocated by it, and she had managed to hit every rock on the way down the waterfall. She broke more than her arm that fateful day, she broke part of her spirit. Father's words had seemed so wise then, but it was only in recent years that she had truly come to understand them. *"Aina's Entry is the embodiment of our wei. You cannot force the tempest within."* He then swooped her into his arms and carried her all the way to the infirmary himself. He held her hand while medics set her arm and he cut stones from his hair to braid into her own. She fingered the smooth surface of one of the stones now, still lost in thought.

You can do this.

Kale took her hand. She stared down at their clasped hands

and then frowned up at him before she shoved her attention back to the approaching waterfall. She took a deep breath and tried to gain further control. *Feel the wei. Embrace it,* she heard her old instructor's raspy breath in her ear.

Sea Squid, I'm trying. She seized down on her power. The ship lurched beneath them as it rose up on a crested wave. The water continued to rise as it curved in toward her squeezed fist. She ground her teeth together and waited.

Kale squeezed her fingers.

The water softened below. She felt the slow steady current of his *wei* beside her own and struggled to match hers to his. Beside him, she was a raging river. All she could hear was the roaring water. She took a deep breath and they *fell.*

This time was different. She felt cradled by her *wei,* a steadiness that came from the man beside her. The water from the depths below rose up to meet them. The barge was held steady and they descended slowly, as if a fallen feather from a gull was making its way to alight upon the deck. She was so captivated by their slow descent that she almost forgot they were holding hands. She jerked her hand away and the water flinched beneath them.

"I'm sorry. I don't know what I was thinking."

What had he been thinking? He had overstepped his boundaries. And, was he blushing? Good. She hoped he was embarrassed.

"I need to find Mano," she said.

Kale cleared his throat and took a step back. "Of course, Mistress."

So, he was back to the stoic Kombu, a soldier married to his duty. Good. She needed soldiers, not a distraction.

"Mano and the others need medical attention. Organize those injured off the ship and into the infirmary."

There was a deep rumbling as the barge scraped stone and sand at the bottom of Aina's Entry. It was somehow always quieter here, despite the rush of water. The *wei* moved differently. It was a steady hum, a vibrancy that connected everyone to it. Even the Noori, those unable to control *wei,* could feel it here. Coral allowed herself just a moment to close her eyes and simply embrace being home. Safe. For the moment.

The moment didn't last long. How would she tell them? The emissary on the barge had been a small one. A small contingency of Kombu and personal guard. Some staff . . . Thousands of people waited inside the citadel's walls for her father's return. Thousands would be told their Wave Master of the last thirty years was gone. That their new Mistress was a scared little girl. It was now or never. She stepped off the barge.

Water moved in a connected stream of currents, propelled in shifts by workers in the citadel. Kale projected another air tunnel to allow more access for those injured. The water bent in a tight tunnel around the passengers. And despite his protest that he had it well in hand, Coral fell into step beside him, assisting the injured off the barge. Once she had organized the injured survivors into groups based on their urgency for medical care, she allowed herself to breathe a huge sigh of relief. She was grateful for the air tunnel. Though her people could all breathe underwater, an air tunnel helped to keep their bandages dry. The citadel itself was also in a giant air bubble, and the underwater fortress was impenetrable to anyone who lived above the sea. Any important ceremonies or bindings were always performed there. Her wedding should have been if her father hadn't insisted it happen as quickly as possible.

Why were you in such a hurry? She looked up to find Kale staring down at her. She scowled at him until he stopped. Her father's urgency was just one of the questions she planned to find answers to once she was able to travel to land. Once they were out of the tight confines of the tunnel, Kale sent the barge back above sea level to anchor until it was needed again.

Hundreds of soldiers blocked the view of her home. It seemed the entire navy stood at watch, ready to speak to their Wave Master. Coral gave a slight shake to her head. As one, the men fell to their knees and beat at their hearts in remorse.

Coral struggled to swallow. She blinked furiously in an effort to keep her tears at bay. Now was not the time for sacrifices to the Sea, now was the time for revenge.

Mano found his way to her side, grabbing her hand in his. She stiffened but didn't pull away. She still hadn't quite decided what to do about him. Her father had wanted this union, but now that he was gone Coral couldn't see the point. In any case, any such union would have to wait. Now she needed to organize her troops.

"Somebody find me Tiburon, I'll need . . ." She trailed off, remembering Tiburon was among the impossibly long list of fallen soldiers. Poor Mano, his sister had died and here he was offering his support to her. Perhaps she was judging him too sharply. She needed him. She needed them all. There were but two ranking officers still alive. She wasn't sure if one would make it; the other had lost the use of both of his legs. They would have to name a new captain immediately. Kale had done a fine enough job on their way back to Aina, but perhaps Mano would feel slighted if he was passed up for the promotion? She was honor bound as Mistress to name an immediate commander and yet . . . she sighed.

Kale was the natural choice. Even if their most recent interaction left her feeling awkward in his presence. Still, if she could hold off on naming anyone just yet—

"You have to speak to the Elders," Mano said, interrupting her internal struggle. He moved his hand to her waist but she stepped out of his reach.

"I have many things I have to do. That is just one more." She wished she was as confident as she sounded. She didn't honestly believe she could move forward without the blessing of the Elders, yet she worried what she would do if they denied her.

"We need to see to our men," Mano continued despite her scowl. "Kale and I need to discuss plans for possible war. Our defenses must be fortified. You can't just collect our men and race off on your quest for revenge."

"I'm not bringing the men." Why did he keep saying *our* men? The men were *hers*.

Mano's tan skin darkened to a murderous purple. "You need the men."

"I don't need anyone holding me back," Coral snarled. "*You* don't get to decide, you—"

"You're right," he said, surprising her. "I don't get to decide. This is your decision. Your parents and . . . Great Mother you have gone through so much in so short a time. You're right, you get to decide what you need to do to grieve."

"I . . . Um. Thank you."

Mano saluted in response and limped inside the infirmary to finally get his wound properly bandaged. She thought briefly of Kale and his injured foot and hoped he had found someone to mend it too.

And so she was finally alone to discover what she needed to do next. Great Mother help her.

ASH

CHAPTER SIXTEEN

H ot as dragon's breath out here," Timber grumbled beside him.

Ash nodded vaguely in response. It was hard to notice the heat, difficult to notice anything except the seven year old girl in the training ring. Her tiny chest heaved up and down under the makeshift leather armor, still too big for her, even now. Her skinny arms were uncovered but lined with muscle. It had only been a few weeks, but already the girl had doubled her strength. She held her practice assegai—it too altered to suit her tiny frame—loosely in her hand. Just like he'd shown her. She was a flaming prodigy.

He had been surprised to find Kay dressed and ready to practice this morning. He'd figure she'd need time to grieve the loss of her friend. He knew the girl had yet to accept the ways of the arena. She didn't believe Kindle had the death of a champion. She'd said little to him, although he was unsure if that was because of the language barrier or simply because she didn't wish to speak to him. Burn it all, he would miss her translator too. The thought surprised him. The length of an assegai was the only friend a Fire Dancer ever needed. No, Kindle died in a blaze of glorious flames. Kindle died the death they all longed for. Perhaps Kay accepted more of the ways than he thought.

"She looks good," Timber said, and Ash was surprised the Fire Dancer remained at his side.

"She's learned quickly." The modesty was unnecessary and didn't prevent the smirk from playing across his features. It had been a long time since Ash felt he held the upper hand.

"Quickly enough you would agree to a sparring match?"

"Hardly," Ash snorted. "She's good but she's no match for a seasoned Dancer yet."

"Not against me. My son. A match between two cadets." Timber raised his eyebrows in question. Ash noticed the man was missing half of his right eyebrow and wondered if he had lost it from Kay's dangerous tower of flame. Flames that had been meant to protect Kindle. He frowned. What would Kindle say to the proposed sparring match? She would probably argue Kay wasn't ready. Ash shook his head. Kindle's opinion shouldn't matter, but he was a flaming fool if he tried to pretend it didn't. Her final words to him echoed in his mind. He could never ask her meaning now. *"You were right to check into arena dragons. Don't let Kay back into the catacombs."* What did it mean? Such specific instructions, as if the cadet would ever have reason to enter the catacombs anyway.

"I'm not sure she's ready," Ash mumbled, he stared at the little girl practicing in the sand. She was more disciplined today. He hadn't had to stop her aimless cartwheels or capture her attention to start her drills. "But perhaps a supervised sparring match is just what she needs." He called his cadet over to him. Kay stopped her drills and trotted over. Her face was drawn and serious. He smiled at her but she didn't smile back, simply waited before him, arms held loosely at her side, feet slightly turned out.

"Timber has proposed a sparring match between you and his cadet. Do you accept?"

Kay blinked at him, her expression solemn. Swearing slightly under his breath, Ash slowly repeated himself.

"I . . . spar . . . him." Kay nodded. Her gaze slid across from her where Timber's cadet listened to final instructions from his father.

"Yes. Great. So, I'll explain the rules. It's just for practice so don't be nervous." She didn't appear nervous, aside from the deep breathing she scarcely moved at all. He wondered how much of his chatter she actually understood as he quickly explained the rules. "This is just a practice spar," he reminded her as Timber and his cadet parted. "This is an exhibition of your skills. Follow the Forms, disarm your opponent."

Kay nodded, she seemed to follow enough, and she tightened her grip on her assegai.

"Enough talk, let's see what these cadets can do." Timber whistled sharply between his teeth and his cadet attacked. Kay began the fast, twirling movements of the Blue Form, spinning easily from his grasp. Timber's cadet was forced to grasp at nothing but air. His assegai whistled sharply as it sliced through the space where Kay had just been standing. Ash flinched. If she had been hit by that blow . . . She wasn't, he reminded himself and forced the dark thoughts away. She was doing fine.

Kay lunged forward, thrusting her assegai at the boy's face. He ducked and dropped to his knees, curling his body into a tight little ball and rolling forward. He stood up behind her and swung his assegai at her head in a high sweeping arc. She fell forward, catching herself with her hands before leaping back up to her feet.

She's a natural. Ash watched her do an easy series of

pirouettes, spinning her assegai in large defensive circles around her body. Kay had taken to the Blue Forms as easily as breathing, and she made the movements look effortless. As she spun, she twirled her assegai above her head. It was easy for Ash to imagine how she would look when she was able to add the element of fire. Not only had Ash lived long enough to witness the greatest Fire Dancer to ever live, but he was instrumental in her career.

Kay kicked out her leg after a series of twisting circles and aimed for the cadet's chest.

The cadet turned sharply on his heel, pushing himself up into the air, twirling his assegai as he did so. He flipped backward, landing behind Kay and seizing the advantage.

He's mastered the Red Forms. Without the advantage of her power with fire, Kay will be destroyed.

Kay dropped low into the rolling motion of the Green Forms, but she wasn't quick enough. The cadet's assegai grazed her shoulder. She rolled to the ground with a grunt. Kay pushed to her feet, but the cadet's assegai was already sweeping at her ankles, knocking her to her backside. She scrambled to get up, but the heavy armor weighed her down and she stumbled forward, catching herself with her hands. Timber's cadet pushed her shoulders so that Kay once again fell onto her backside.

"You can't even get up." The cadet laughed, his shoulders shaking as he pointed down at her.

Kay's face darkened and she flicked out her finger toward the cadet. His assegai went up in a ribbon of flames.

With a shriek, the cadet dropped the flaming weapon into the sand and lunged for Kay, tackling her to the ground.

"You stupid girl." He straddled her, hands wrapped around her throat.

Kay shrieked something in Drakori and punched the cadet in the face.

Ash didn't realize he was running until he caught up to Timber. The two pulled the children apart.

Ash sighed. She wasn't ready for this, but that didn't mean he had to admit to it in front of Timber. He frowned down at Kay who still struggled in his arms, screaming in her mother tongue and clawing at the air in an effort to get at Timber's cadet. Ash had a nagging suspicion her episode had more to do with Kindle's departure and less to do with her loss or the boy's teasing. He pulled her into his arms, ignoring Timber's stares and let the girl cry. When her shoulders no longer shook, Ash suggested that she head to the barracks for rest. She turned and left without another word. Once again he sighed. What had he gotten himself into?

Timber still inspected his son, turning the boy's chin in his large hand. "Go and clean yourself up," Timber grunted. "Your Red Forms are much improved. We'll speak more later."

The cadet nodded, grinning despite the fact that blood flowed from his nose.

Timber shook his head as he ran off. "Your cadet nearly broke his nose."

"She—"

"I guess I should count myself lucky she didn't set my boy on fire," Timber chuckled.

Ash allowed himself to snort in response. "She constantly surprises me. I shouldn't have agreed to this spar. She isn't ready and she's—"

"Dangerous," Timber grunted. "That girl is special. I've never seen anything like it and I . . . I've seen things."

"What do you mean?"

But Timber only shook his head.

"He wants my son, you know."

"Who does?" It seemed every time he tried to have a conversation with this man it ended in either anger or confusion. So many questions.

"Our esteemed councilman. Our owner." Timber's voice dipped so low it was scarcely a whisper over the sand. "He'll be named, and I'll lose him forever."

"May his name bring home honor. And may he leave in flames and ash or come home a hero."

"Honor. Heroes. What do you know of either? Why are you still here?" Timber growled.

"The arena is my home—"

"The arena was your home. Now you're nothing but a pitiful old man with no family to soothe the loneliness of your final years. You're the product of the arena, and you're pathet—"

Ash closed the distance between them and had one arthritic fist around Timber's throat before he could finish.

"I would watch my words. I'd had my first arena victory before you were even born." He released Timber with a flick of his wrist. The man stumbled backwards, breathing heavily. He glared at Ash.

"I do pray my son is named. Soon we can pay off our life debts and we can have our freedom. Then we can leave here, leave the Republic and live as free men," Timber grunted. "And you should leave too. It's too late for your cadet. They'll never let her leave." He rubbed at his neck in absent circles, the tan skin already turning a deep purple from where Ash had gripped him.

"Ah, here comes the great councilman now. Just in time."

"Tell me where arena dragons come from."

Timber's smile was grim. "A worthy question. But one that cannot be answered now." He dipped into a mock bow, "Esteemed Councilman."

Ash turned back to face the Ninth who stood just behind, wrapped in voluminous purple and gold robes and flanked by a half dozen oil-slicked men.

"Ash, Timber. Did cadet training end early today?"

"A different sort of training today. The cadets sparred each other in full practice armor."

"Interesting. I would have liked to have seen that." The councilman stared from one gladiator to the other. When he was met with silence, he spread his arms and raised his brow. "Well, how did she do?"

"Akil defeated her easily, but she has potential."

"She isn't ready," Ash agreed, staring at Timber. The Fire Dancer stared intently at the ground, clenching and unclenching his fist.

"The cadets have retired for the evening, but I can call them back out if you . . ." Ash trailed off as the Ninth shook his head.

"No, there is no need. I've come to speak to you, Timber. Ash you're dismissed." The Ninth had already turned his attention to the large man beside him, so Ash trailed away, once again forgotten.

CORAL

CHAPTER SEVENTEEN

The first thing she did upon arriving in her family's private wing was order a bath. She washed the blood from beneath her fingernails and threw her soiled wedding dress in the garbage. She began to order her family's funeral arrangements but decided she'd rather do it in person instead. She couldn't decide what to wear and fell into a fit of tears when a member of her staff came in and offered to braid her hair. She found her father's trishula and cleaned and oiled it lovingly. She sent the rest of the staff home and dressed herself in sensible seal leathers.

Just keep going. The empty wing was eerily quiet when Coral left her chambers. She ambled down the dark hallway and into her father's study. She wasn't sure what she was looking for, or if she was even looking for anything. But it smelled of him. Sea moss and storm clouds. Her fingers ran along the smooth leather bindings of his books. She smiled. Such a breathcatcher thing, owning books. Her people passed down knowledge orally in classrooms and training fields. Who had need for books in a world filled with a deep and endless water and dangerous currents? Her father had insisted she learn to read early on, and he'd forced her to read a large number of the volumes adorning his shelves. She detested reading, it was much better to experience something rather than read about it. But now . . . well, the books didn't seem so silly now.

She sat down in the large chair behind his desk.

He was gone.

She began opening drawers at random, pulling papers out blindly and pulling them on the floor. She screamed, but it was okay because she had sent everyone home. So she screamed louder. Then she found the locked drawer.

Coral gave the drawer another stubborn pull but no, it was definitely locked shut. She wiped at her face and wondered where she might find a key. But then she decided not to waste any time looking and kicked the drawer off its hinges until the contents spilled onto the floor. Useless stuff mostly. Ink pens, a ring of keys, old papers . . . one in particular stood out and she picked it up with trembling hands.

> I am still unable to find the source of these disappearances, but I believe I am growing closer to the truth. To date, the current number of missing citizens reaches over a hundred. The people have fled the islands—there is talk of some who would flee this ocean and its people all together. It is my belief these disappearances are of unnatural origin and probably with the assistance of one working from the inside. In short, it pains me to say with the utmost certainty that we have a traitor in our midst.

Coral threw the letter on the floor. A traitor. And over one hundred of her people missing? What did it mean? There had been stories of a few missing from recent karsh attacks but nothing of that number. Surely she would have heard of this ... wouldn't she? Unless this was just one more thing her father had kept from her?

Well, it was time to get to the bottom of things. She left her father's study and headed toward the offices of his steward. Arrangements must be made, and she needed to meet with the Elders.

She arranged for the meeting with the Elders to be held in the great hall. It was a bit unorthodox, but she was loathed to enter any place still rich with the memory of her parents. Someone had arranged for a circle of chairs to be placed in the center of the room. There were more chairs than Elders, and Coral wondered if Mano had been included in the call for a meeting? She hadn't spoken to him since his departure for the infirmary. A long banquet table was stretched out behind the chairs. The table was laden with an assortment of food, but Coral's stomach lurched at the very sight of it.

Ailani, High Elder and the oldest of the living people, entered the room. Her steely eyes sought out Coral's. When she found them her teeth snarled up in what she probably confused as a smile. Coral felt her nails bite into the palm of her hand as the Elder approached. She had been on board the barge during the attack. She was still here while her parents were not.

"Mistress."

"High Elder." Coral bobbed her head in greeting. She swallowed away the bile rising in her throat. She hadn't heard the other two, but their arrival was marked by the sharp scrape of shale against iron. She whirled around as Kapono and Bane seated themselves in their heavy iron chairs. They were soon joined by Mano and, strangely, Kale. Coral raised her eyebrows at his arrival, but Ailani seemed nonplussed. Coral sighed and took her seat between Bane and Kapono.

"I'm going to land." Coral forced her eyes to stay on Ailani's face.

The Elder narrowed her gray eyes in response. "That is not how we conduct meetings. There is tradition. Observances must be made."

Of course. But she didn't have time for all that. She needed to get to land. Immediately. She needed to find out who had written her father that letter. Coral gritted her teeth.

"What observances? Our Wave Master was murdered; our people massacred! What could be more important than righting this wrong?"

"Revenge eats at the soul and leaves one empty. It will not be made whole through vengeance."

Coral jerked her gaze away from Ailani. Mano stared at her intently and gave a slight nod. Kale sent her an encouraging smile. She was grateful for their presence, but she had to do this on her own. She lifted her chin and turned her attention back to the Elders. Kapono was slim and tall with a droopy mustache and bland eyes. The man was usually quick to give his opinion, but he said nothing, merely bounced his head in tune to a melody only he could hear. Portly and bored, Bane was the youngest of the triad and his gaze was fixed on his hands, folded on his lap.

"This is not simply some mission of revenge. This is about our safety. We were attacked and we don't even know who did it or why. I need you to tell me why Father went to land. I need to know everything you know so that I can make sure we don't lose another life of one of the people."

"You're a young pup. There will be plenty of time for revenge and the sort later. Right now the people need direction, a union—" Kapono's words were cut off by an enthusiastic Bane.

"Yes, a proper joining here in your ancestral home." Bane nearly quivered in excitement. "And a grand feast to celebrate. The people need a celebration to—"

"A celebration? Are you mad?" Surely she had heard them wrong. Coral shook her head. "There isn't any reason to celebrate. My parents are gone, nearly a hundred people are dead. My father—"

"Wanted you married to Mano," Kapono said triumphantly. "It's for the good of the people."

"Going to land is for the good of the people," Coral snarled before Ailani could add anything to the argument from the Elders. She glared at Mano, and he took the cue, nodding vigorously as he stood up.

"Coral is right. We need answers to assure the people this won't happen again. And we need to know what the Wave Master was so afraid of that he felt the need to make an unscheduled trip to land." He crossed the length of the circle to stand in front of Coral. She wasn't sure what to make of the intense look in his eyes.

"That is why I propose that immediately following the wedding, I make a trip."

"After the wedding?" Coral stiffened. "The wedding can wait. We need to get to land and find answers immediately!"

"And we will find answers." Mano placed a gentle hand on her shoulder, but she jerked away from his grasp. "We all want to help," he sighed.

"So *help* me." Why was he still advocating for their union?

What did he get out of it? She frowned at Mano, wishing the answers to her questions would somehow appear on his expressionless face.

"She's the Wave Master." Kale's voice startled her. Coral gave him her attention. Ailani, too, gave him a careful once over.

"Speak, boy." Ailani waved her fingers at him.

"I agree with our Wave Master. Our Mistress has deemed a trip to land is necessary in the investigation of her parents' death. She is honor bound to seek out the one who has killed them." His tone softened. "Just as I am honor bound to aid my Mistress. We all are."

"Thank you." Finally, someone backing her up.

"Children. You are all children with barely a Lock between you. What makes you think you can survive a trip to land? You don't know what you're asking." Kapono scoffed, his voice a low, trembling baritone.

"I know about the missing people," Coral said.

Ailani's eyes widened.

"What missing people?" Kale asked.

Coral stood up from her chair. "You have all been keeping this from me. From everyone. Over a hundred of my people! Missing. The attack must have something to do with this. Father must have known something. He went to land and, yes, what he learned there made him frightened, and he . . . I think he was killed because of it." She took a deep breath. "I'm going to land and I'll take anyone who wants to come with me, but I'm doing it with or without your blessing."

"Blasphemy!" Ailani hissed. She held up a hand to silence the muttering of the other two in the triad. "Bite your tongue, child. Your words are blasphemous. Do not forget who you speak to. I had more Locks in my hair than even your father before the Tri-Alliance was even formed. I've been to land and seen the unseen depths of evil from those living there. I've even battled one of their fire breathing beasts and brought it down with the trishula strapped to my back. Your very life is because of my blessing, and Wave Mistress or not, it would bode you well to remember that."

Ailani raised her near-transparent brows and raked a hand through her long thinning hair. Her perfectly white hair. Coral had heard the stories of Ailani in the battlefield. There was even a yearly holiday celebrated in her honor. Every child of the people learned about Ailani's every conquest before they were even in their tenth year. Coral lifted her chin.

"Child I might be, but I am still your Wave Mistress. You can tell me what you know or not, but your actions won't change my mind. I'm going to land."

Ailani sighed, somehow her aged face appeared older. She held up a halting hand.

"No, child. We won't stop you, but you should be warned. Land is harsh and unforgiving. Your power is different there. Your connection to the Mother is muted. Your *wei* will not come easy, and the foes on land are far more dangerous than any you've encountered here."

"But I—"

"You would be wise to take heed," Kapono grumbled. "The land spells disaster even to those who have killed a karsh and lived to tell the tale."

"This meeting is over. Do as you wish child. Mother knows your father never listened to me." Ailani stood from her chair, shoulders lifted in her dismissal.

"Give me an opportunity to. Tell me why you're so opposed

to me going to land?" Coral stared at the High Elder, but Ailani ignored her, making a show of adjusting the trishula strapped to her back.

"Is no one going to tell her?" Bane stood up, his heavy iron chair scraping against the floor. "It's true, land is a dangerous place, but for you, going to land ensures your dea—"

"Bane, you will cease your insolent prattle this instant," Ailani snarled.

"He will do no such thing. Why can't I go to land? Elder Bane, what is it? What do you know?" Coral asked the Elder.

Bane shook his head. He refused to meet her gaze and kept his eyes trained on the ground. "Just an old story. A warning."

"What sort of warning?" Mano's voice came from beside her. She gave a slight jump. She'd forgotten he was there.

Ailani sighed. "A warning we Elders don't usually share with a couple of young pups with barely a Lock between them."

Coral eyed Kale's single Lock. Somehow Mano had survived the massacre without taking anyone's life.

"Did my father know about this . . . this warning?"

"He did not. We did not deem it necessary information at the time. Much as he appears to have done with his knowledge of these missing people." Ailani gestured to the chairs around them. Only Kapono remained seated. "Please, everyone sit down. It's time we're forthright with one another."

"The warning is old." Ailani began so softly Coral had to strain to hear. "A cautionary tale of what might happen if the gods were released. When the eternal fire once again walked the earth, the stones will be exhumed. The Mistress will bend the knee, and the world will be made new in blood."

"So that's it? What does that even mean?" Coral leaned

forward in her chair, willing Ailani to finally start making sense.

"Just that it is not in the best interests of the people for you to go to land."

"Because some old land god might be released?" Coral shook her head. "What does that have to do with us? Do you think I'm the mistress? And so what if I am? All it says is that I will bend the knee, not that I'll die."

"Did you forget the part about world being made new in blood?" Mano asked. "That part sounds unpleasant. Nor do I like the idea of my Wave Mistress bending the knee to anyone."

"And I won't," Coral snapped. "Honestly, I can't believe we're actually giving any power to some sodden prophecy with information older than our High Elder." Mano placed a heavy palm on her shoulder, and Coral resisted the urge to shrug it off. He was trying to be comforting.

"Things are different on land. The people of the land do not follow the will of the Mother. Many do not even know of her existence. The ocean is alive and connects us, but the people on land are discordant and the land is dead," Bane said gravely.

"Is that why going to land means my death?" Perhaps the man just had some sort of fetish with the word. In any case, he had to stop throwing it around.

"The Mother is the creator of all life. From her poured the oceans and the world and we are all connected through her life source. That is why water is so valuable. And we are her chosen people. It is our duty to control the waves. We protect the land from the dangers of a wild sea. We give the people of the land fresh water, and in doing so, we open our people up to trade. Ours is not the way of the land. We follow the way of the Mother, and our hearts belong to the sea." The low timbre of Ailani's voice echoed across the chamber.

"I don't need a lesson on theology. I know of the great Mother." Coral threw her arms up, "We all do."

"You know of the Mother but you do not know everything." Ailani smiled. "But I will tell you what I can now. Your father went to land to seek out the First of the Republic. He wished aid in assembling an army to march on Kitoi. The missing people—however you came about that information, it's all true. Your father believed our people are being kidnapped and sold as slaves in Kitoi."

Coral sat back heavily and shook her head. The missing people were all slaves? How was this even possible? She asked the question out loud, but Ailani shook her head, the stormy gray of her irises cloudy with regret.

"I understand you are honor bound to seek revenge for your family's deaths. And for those of our people. You know I sometimes see things that are later found to be true. Know this, young Mistress, that warning was learned by me so that I might share it with you. If you go to Kitoi, you will find the answers you seek. You will have your revenge. This I have seen. But also know, if you go to land, you will watch your heart bleed. This I have also seen."

TYLAK

CHAPTER EIGHTEEN

There was no limit to the level of insanity that would come out of that woman's mouth. She had a plan, she said. Burn it all, he should have known he couldn't trust her plan. He didn't even try to tone down his scowl.

"So your plan is you have no plan?"

"I have a plan." She planted a fist on either hip and glared up at him.

"Where are we going to stay?"

"I haven't—"

"How are you going to question all of the cabochons, and what are you going to do once you figure out which one is responsible? You think you can just get them to fill out some sign-up sheet?" He clenched his hands together to prevent himself from stepping closer to her or punching a hole in the wall. "I can't let you just . . ." he sighed. "Jura, I don't like it. You shouldn't have to set yourself up as bait."

"I've come accustomed to it."

She smiled at him, but that only made his scowl deepen. He

felt something working in his jaw and took a deep breath. "This is already a fool's mission. We need more time."

She shook her head in response. "That's something we don't have. I know it's not much of a plan but . . . well, it's what we've got. No one will be expecting the Daughter of the First. That's what will make our villain come out of hiding. I know how to do this, Tylak. I've grown up learning the rules to this game. And in the meantime, Ichiro and Jiro can search the streets for information. We're going to find her, and this is the only way."

"This isn't a game, Jura. This is your life." He stepped forward, grabbed her shoulders, and stared at her beautiful face. Her light brown eyes appeared almost golden. "There's too much at stake. We still don't know where you stand with the Shadow Dancers or what the *alttaw'am* plans to do with your father."

"That's exactly why this search is so important. Once we find Amira we'll have tangible proof and we can get back to the Republic and get things back to normal. Then we can get your brother back. Don't you want that?"

"Of course I do." He sighed, dropping his gaze from the intense stare of her amber eyes. He crossed his arms over his chest. The Samur remained where they were, watching their exchange in silence. Peppik had yet to find the group, but Tylak figured it would only be a matter of time before the old man ambled toward them from out of nowhere. Burn it all, Jura was right. It wasn't a plan, but it was the only one they had to work with.

"So what do we do now? We've managed to get in the city without attracting any attention. We should probably take advantage of that while we can. Especially if your plan involves you drawing attention to yourself."

Jura's lips curled into a smile. "I was hoping you would say that. There's something I wanted to do before we got started."

He should have known she would drag him to the flaming library. Like the majority of the buildings in the city, the capital's library was made out of brick and stone and decorated with thousands of colorful gems. He heard Jura's tiny gasp of excitement as they approached and allowed himself to see the wonder of the building through her eyes. The stones' placement created several murals that depicted children playing, people reading, or merchants trading. The building was massive, stretching into the sky and nearly as tall as the arena.

He reached for her hand without thinking. She dragged him into the building before he had time to consider his action. It was no surprise the building was filled from floor to ceiling with books, it being a library and all, but Jura was so shocked she was actually speechless. He allowed her to pull him from shelf to shelf. She handed him a few books to hold, all titles involving the theologies and political policies of Kitoi and then finally found a quiet reading room where she ensconced herself with the books.

Tylak and the Samur were standing awkwardly outside the tiny room when Peppik found the group. He held a tiny book in his hand. The leather cover was blackened and worn around the edges. He tapped it against his leg in an odd and sporadic rhythm.

"Found some reading material, did you?" Tylak's mouth quirked up in a grin.

Peppik nodded absently, taking his post beside Tylak to guard the entry to Jura's room. He made no notice of the young woman and seemed deep in thought. But then, Peppik often seemed that way.

Tylak began to tap his foot in impatience. How long did she plan on reading, anyway? She knew they were pressed for time. She would probably argue she was doing research for their cause. Burn it all, that was probably exactly what she was doing, but they couldn't waste the entire day in the library. He'd allowed their invisibility to slip. It was exhausting enough hiding the Everflame, and he was trying to conserve his strength. Jura needed to hurry.

She'd popped out little more than an hour ago and thrust a book in his hands before disappearing back into the confines of her reading room. He studied the familiar title now, *Xao Sin: The Five Elements and Properties of Blood*. The same book they had caught the Third studying before he was attacked by the *alttaw'am*. He frowned at the leather binding. If she trusted him to hold this book out here, what was she studying in there? They needed to find a quiet place to regroup, to fine tune the plan, as it were, before it was implemented. Perhaps he should pull her out of the room now. He turned his head toward the door when he felt someone approach.

"An *Arbe* inside the capital library?" a woman's voice dripped with enthusiasm. She turned to her companion, a much shorter older woman. The first woman wore expensive clothing. The patterned silks draped about her body and hung low past her fingertips. Her tanned lips stretched into a smile.

Why hadn't he made the four of them invisible? He clenched his fists at his side.

"Who do you suppose it is?" the older woman asked. She rose to her tiptoes as though peering over Tylak's shoulder would give her access through the closed door of the reading room.

They should have changed out of their desert darks. Jura and her flaming disguise. Tylak gritted his teeth.

"Someone important, certainly. From the Republic obviously.

It must be one of the Thirteen."

The older woman gasped. "Of course. I hear they kill their own young."

"I heard they *eat* their own young." She tittered at her joke but appeared uneasy by it. "Odd that one is here now. Perhaps we're mistaken?" She frowned at Jura's door.

"I haven't heard of any tours." The older woman shrugged, growing bored with the closed door. "It's past time for luncheon and I'm starved."

"I want to stay and see who it is. It's not like this stupid lot can tell u —." The woman met Tylak's gaze and choked on her reply.

He schooled his face into the calm passive mask of a Shadow Dancer, keeping a tight leash on his anger. It didn't matter what these women thought of him. Their opinions didn't matter. But now was not the time to implement their stupid plan that wasn't a plan at all. They still needed time.

With any luck, the women would just go away.

As always, luck was never on his side. Jura opened the door.

She stepped out, eyes downcast and set on a passage from an open book. "Tylak, I think I . . ." She trailed off, realizing they had company. She met Tylak's gaze. He tried to tell her not to say a word. To go back in the room. She stiffened. Her back became an assegai, tall and straight. Her chin lifted. Her expression hardened. Her eyes changed. She became regal somehow, dangerous. She arched one delicate brow and waited for the women to speak.

"My lady . . . erhm, Councilwoman," the younger woman began, confused as to who she was addressing but now completely certain she faced one of the Thirteen.

"Normally the presence of an *Arbe* outside one's room means the one inside does not wish to be disturbed." Jura's voice was a whisper. Both women leaned forward to hear. "Of course, I can't expect such niceties to be known when traveling in a foreign country."

"Apologies, Councilwoman. We didn't know. There was no post of any tours. We were simply curious as to who was visiting our grand city?" Despite the obvious terror the woman had for the Thirteen, she was still hopeful, begging for a small tidbit of gossip. She dared to meet Jura's eyes.

Tylak opened his mouth to somehow stop Jura. To tell her this was a terrible idea, that they still had their anonymity, that they should wait. But he was supposed to be *Arbe*. Tylak bit his tongue.

"Unless my studies were mistaken, you *are* aware that one shouldn't look upon the First Family without permission?"

The woman gasped, prostrating herself before Jura and dragging the smaller woman down with her.

"A thousand apologies, Greatness. I didn't know."

Jura dismissed them with a flick of her wrist.

"You do now."

AMIRA

CHAPTER NINETEEN

Amira traced her finger against the stone floor, leaving tiny circular patterns out of dust and sand. Her room was at the end of a long hallway in what she assumed was Kuru's home. She didn't know his relation to Luxman (he appeared to be his master), and the giant man was the only adult she had seen, though she *had* seen several children.

Kuru enjoyed showing off to his friends. It seemed he was always entertaining, and part of that entertainment involved showing off his pet, a princess of the Republic. They came and they stared and Amira did as they said or she didn't eat.

She ate everything she could get her hands on, no matter how disgusting the offering. *If I eat, I'll stay strong. I am a daughter of the Republic.* She did a vigorous workout every night before bed. She had always been in shape—it was a requirement of belonging to one of the Thirteen—but now she threw herself into training, determined to gain back her strength and find her way back home. Kuru let her have free reign of her rooms. She had two chambers and a bath all to herself. But the windows were boarded up, and if

Kuru had any house staff, they were forbidden to enter for Amira never saw one. Amira didn't mind cleaning after herself, every moment was still a luxury compared to the long weeks she'd spent chained and starved. Still, she thought often of home and the life she'd left behind. She wondered idly what her family was up to, if her father still searched for her, if Jura missed her.

Kuru flung the door open and stomped inside, startling Amira out of her reverie. She jumped to her feet as Luxman quietly shut the door behind them.

There was no schedule to his visits. He came morning or night, sometimes joking and gleeful other times angry and vengeful. She tensed at his appearance, watchful of the tell-tale signs that would indicate which Kuru she would see today. His breathing came in short angry puffs and his complexion had already grown ruddy even before he raised his fists.

Today would be a bad visit.

Kuru lunged for her and Amira dropped low, cowering into a ball as he rained punches down on her neck, back, and arms. He kicked her with one final howl of rage before he turned to her bed and plunged his knife into it.

"I should slice you up right now. That will show him."

She stayed on the floor, peeking up at him from beneath her choppy hair.

"Father says I'm to give you back to him. He didn't realize who you were before, but now that he knows how important you are they want you for their own. I found you. I paid for you. You're mine!"

"Why am I so important?" Amira whispered, afraid Kuru would punish her for speaking out of turn. She slowly rose to a sitting position, breathing slowly, she didn't appear to have broken any ribs, that was good. "Is it because of my father?"

Kuru laughed. "Your father? Your father was pathetic, weaker than my own. No, it's because of you, the other you, and who you belong to."

Amira frowned. Maybe Kuru had hit her head harder than she realized because he wasn't making any sense.

"What d—"

"You know I asked my father if you were more important than his own son's happiness, and you know what he said? He said you were priceless, and I was just the product of a forgotten night with a whore. His own son, huh?"

"But that doesn't make any sense. I'm a nobody. My father is the one who—"

"Your father is dead, you stupid girl, and soon you will be too." A gong chimed in the distance, and Kuru stopped his advancement with a pained look. "*I'm* going to kill you."

Amira swallowed hard and told herself to stop trembling. She had so many questions. Was her father truly dead? What was happening in the Republic then? Had Antar become one of the Thirteen or was she now homeless, without even a home to run back to? *Focus on the here and now, Amira.* She looked back up at Kuru. "That was cruel of him to say that," she said slowly. "You didn't ask to be brought into this world."

Kuru nodded. "I didn't ask for any of this, but does he care? He doesn't even pay attention to me."

"You're right. That's not fair. No one could blame you for any resentment you might have toward him. If I was in your shoes, I'd do something about it." Amira squeezed her fingernails into the palm of her hand and prayed to the Everflame that she hadn't gone too far.

Kuru tilted his head to the side, as if considering. "No one asked you."

"You're right," she said quickly, darting a quick glance at Luxman. The massive bodyguard stood just behind Kuru, watching her with his single eye.

"You're right," she repeated. "You didn't ask for my advice. Or need it," she continued as she saw him lose interest. "I'd imagine you've already figured out exactly what your father is up to and what he wants with a daughter from the house of the Third."

"I have my suspicions. He's a *cabochon*, you know."

Amira bit the inside of her cheek and wished that information meant more to her than it did. She had never paid much attention in her studies, certainly not in the subject of their foreign neighbors. Jura would know what to do. But Jura wasn't in this situation, she was.

"He's an important man," Amira murmured.

Kuru nodded, fingering the knife he'd removed from her mattress. "Do you really kill your own parents in the Republic?"

It was rare, but it was known to happen. She struggled to show no emotion at the odd question.

"Sometimes," she answered.

"Could you . . . could you help me kill mine?"

"Kuru." Luxman's tone was disapproving but he did nothing save for utter that single word.

"We'll talk of this later," Kuru announced, turning and walking swiftly for her door. He held it open for Luxman and gave her a low exaggerated bow.

"For now you may live."

He closed the door behind him, and Amira waited for the familiar click. It didn't come. She jumped to her feet and hurried toward the door, frantic to turn the knob, terrified that she was mistaken or already out of time. She opened the door and stared into the empty hallway.

Thank the Everflame her prayers had been answered. She darted into the hall and crept along its length. A stairway was at the end of the hall and it too was blissfully empty. Another gong sounded in the distance, notifying the start of yet another service. She ignored the distant noise and raced down the stairs, taking them two at a time and half falling down some. There! The large golden doorway had to lead outside. She was almost free. Just ahead and to her right noises rose from a large room just off to the side of the home's entryway, presumably a study or office. The door was slightly ajar and the voices rising and falling from within sounded agitated. She heard a crash and some muffled cursing from within and strengthened her resolve to ignore her throbbing curiosity. *It's none of my business*, she told herself.

She crept closer to the door.

"... those are my thoughts exactly. Now you're starting to see things my way."

"All right, all right, I'm done then. But I'll need more reassurance than that. How can I be sure you have the real thing? That this isn't another one of your games?" The second voice was high, nasal, and sounded slightly familiar.

Amira shook her head and reached for the door. She was almost out of there. Now she just had to run to the ports, surely she could find one of her father's merchants and —

"The Daughter of the First has arrived in the city." Amira froze at his words. Jura was here?

"She's been missing for weeks and now she appears here? For what reason?" the nasal voice asked.

Amira turned back toward the voice, hoping to hear more information.

"It is my belief that she is a part of the great game. She's already survived several deadly encounters and she's of interest to our queen. That alone should assure you of the authenticity of my words."

Amira tiptoed even closer. Kitoi didn't have a queen as far she knew. Who were they talking about?

"Ishani has sent word—the Third has nominated her and she will be voted in as Thirteenth."

Amira grew very still. What was this about her father? Or was he truly dead and they spoke of her brother?

"It's all real. The scion stones. Everything. It's real, and I have one," the voice continued on, seizing Amira's attention.

"So why have you chosen to share this with me? Why now?" The nasal voice sounded suspicious. Amira wished she had a better memory. She'd heard of scion stones before, hadn't she? And what did these people know of the politics back home?

"Don't you see? This is all a sign. It's all happening, and the gods have found fit to place me in the middle of it. My faith wavered and then my own son . . ." the voice trailed off, ". . . better to see it. Faith can only take one so far." Amira listened as the man crossed the length of the room, heard the creak of rusty hinges and the gentle slam from an oak cabinet door.

A low gasp followed. If she was just a bit closer she could peep through the door. Although her intuition screamed at her to run in the other direction, Amira crept forward. She was careful to press the ball of her feet deep into the floor to make sure no one heard her. There was a narrow space between the door and its frame. If she positioned herself just right—she was suddenly flung backward and shoved into the golden door that just moments ago had represented freedom.

"Trying to escape?" Kuru growled in her ear. He wrapped his hand tight around her throat. "You can't escape today. Not ever." He snapped his fingers and Luxman lumbered forward. The massive man picked Amira up under her armpits and heaved her over his shoulder. She didn't struggle.

BESHAR

Beshar had sworn off wandering the streets at night. Everflame only knew why he had been convinced to do so now. He'd chosen to bring only Kenjiro. He had enough faith in his man, but the streets had been unnaturally quiet in the wake of the disappearance of the Shadow Prince. He'd heard the whispers. The Shadow Prince was dead; his people sought revenge. Beshar himself was still confused at the details surrounding the demise of the Prince, but he knew for certain the man was not coming back. And it wouldn't be long before the Shadow Dancers connected him to their Prince's disappearance. Hopefully this would be quick.

"You came." Denir's voice was a gentle purr that broke the silence of the night.

"Your message indicated it was quite urgent." He flicked her embossed missive in his hand. "And encrypted." He raised a brow. "I assume you wanted to communicate well outside the listening ears of the glass halls?"

She peered up at him, dark eyes squinting up from beneath a black hood that covered her thick hair. She'd come alone and didn't appear to carry any weapon. Denir had always appeared to be capable of taking care of herself, but it was unheard of for one of the Thirteen, a female and Fourth of the Thirteen, to go about without an *Arbe* or at least a single bodyguard.

The woman crossed her arms over her chest, ignoring his scrutiny.

"Jura. I assume you know where she is?"

He smoothed his face into one of casual indulgence. "Perhaps the wilds, or east toward the Edge." He shrugged. "This is all speculation, of course. Why would you assume I know where she is, or even care?"

Denir smiled. "I should have pegged you for a man who enjoyed games. In any case, I didn't come here to talk about the Daughter of the First. No, I have a special offer for you, all I need in return is one tiny favor."

Beshar frowned. "And why would I do that? You know my favors don't come cheap."

Denir laughed. "I'm well aware of the going cost of your favors. But, no. I have no intention of becoming one of your pets."

Beshar didn't respond. Often times the best way to get information out of someone was to remain silent. And she had yet to play her biggest card.

"They know you killed him." And there it was.

"Killed who?" He schooled his face to remain impassive, but he felt Kenjiro stiffen beside him.

Denir tsked. "You *do* enjoy a good game. Adham. Prince of Shadows. But you knew who I was talking about. Everyone knows it was you, and rumor is she's not very happy about it."

"She?" Beshar couldn't mask the curiosity from taking an edge to his question.

"You truly don't know?" A lazy smile stretched across her mouth. "Interesting." She shook her head. "The Queen of Shadows, of course. The woman behind it all."

"The Queen?" Beshar darted a quick glance at Kenjiro. His bodyguard's face remained impassive. "His mother?"

She chuckled. "No. I believe the term you meant was lover. You've killed her sweet protege, and she's going to make you pay."

"You're one of them. A Shadow Dancer."

Denir's eyes widened. "Me? Flames, no. I'm flattered. But all that disappearing and sneaking about, it really isn't me. I like the spotlight too much. I simply know things. Like you. And in exchange for the information I know, I gain certain . . . privileges. The disappearance of the Shadow Prince has stopped those privileges. I simply want the life I've grown accustomed to. So here I am, reduced to a mere messenger." Denir shrugged. "She wants to make a deal."

"I'm listening."

"You are a very interesting man. So many of your possessions are . . . quite unique. Your men, for instance." She tossed her chin in the direction of Kenjiro's still form beside him. "Having a dozen Samur sworn to you," she paused. "Impressive."

He tried to feign boredom and yawned. "My wealth nearly matches your own, I would imagine. Do get to your point."

"Your new wonder child," she began.

A bolt of panic raced through him. "What about her?"

"Her earrings. I need them."

Denir cut straight to the point. He appreciated that about her.

"Is that all?" What could she possibly want with the child's earrings? He'd noticed the trinkets, of course. He noticed everything. But he'd seen no harm in letting the girl keep them. Tiny red stones, rubies perhaps, and nearly worthless. Denir watching him with interest, so he raised his eyebrows.

"Yes," she answered. "A simple exchange. The earrings for the favor of the Queen."

"And if I don't need any favors from your queen? What happens if I refuse to deliver?"

The Fourth shook her head. "I wouldn't know. I've never known someone to refuse her. But until now, you've led quite the charmed life, have you not? How goes your conquests in the arena?"

Beshar grunted. "Are you implying the two are somehow related? That my success in the arena games is somehow related to the good grace of the Shadow Dancers?"

"I'm acquiring a new dragon. A gift from the Queen of Shadows. She can be quite rewarding." She cocked her head to the side. "Didn't you recently sell one of your cadets to the arena?"

He narrowed his eyes. The final sale happened only an hour ago. Denir was not bluffing. Her eyes were everywhere.

"I sold a boy," he admitted. "The information is no secret."

"And you don't see a connection?" Denir chuckled. "It appears we've overestimated you. Take the deal, Beshar. What do you care about some silly little girl? Take the deal and watch your wealth grow. Ignore this offer and you will find no protection. Hear me when I tell you things are changing in the Republic. You want to be sure to choose the right side."

Beshar nodded, he had had enough of this conversation. "I thank you for the offer and the, uh . . . warning? But I can take care of myself. I'll consider your queen's offer."

"See that you do." She sighed and gave her head a gentle

shake, a final reprimand before she turned back toward the darkened alley she'd come from. She was already fading into the shadows before she turned her head back to call out, "Be careful out here. The streets can be a dangerous place."

CORAL

Chapter Twenty-One

Coral *had never been to* land, but she imagined it looked like this. The earth stretched out in soft immobile waves, the color a vivid green that was both soft and stiff to the touch. Grass, the word crept up through her memories and she smiled at the sight of it. More impressive than the wide expanse of grass was the tall tree dominating the air bubble. The sapling had been brought down to Aina back when her ancestors first descended to the depths of the sea. Its growth was fueled by the rich soil beneath it, a gift from the breathcatchers centuries ago when the world was still new. The tree represented the history of the people, a family tree connecting all of them. It was the most sacred place for her people, reserved for those on pilgrimage and for remembering the dead. She had only been there once before nearly a decade ago with her parents. She only remembered feeling humbled by its majesty, dwarfed by its sheer height.

Coral stood before the massive tree, no less awed by its presence now. How was it possible to be in such a sacred place, completed surrounded by *wei* and yet still feel so lost.

"Mother . . . Great Mother of the Oceans, do you hear me?" Coral's voice echoed in the sacred meadow. She sank to her knees, raking her fingers through the thick carpet of grass.

"Mother . . . do you hear me?" Her voiced echoed in the sacred meadow.

The Mother was present in all things. She was fluid, ever changing, always flowing. If she had a home, it was here in this sacred tree. Coral took a deep breath, inhaling deeply. The air smelled different here, somehow untouched by the salty sting to which she had grown accustomed.

"I need to know if I'm wrong . . . if I'm crazy for leaving the people now." She swallowed. "Now that they need me the most. I need a sign. I need to know that I'm not doing this alone . . . I'm scared." She whispered the last bit, ashamed that anyone might hear her, terrified that someone would.

"Coral, are you—" Mano broke off, seeing her knelt in prayer. "I'm sorry—I can leave. I'll leave."

"What did you hear?" She stood up, shoulders stiff. Barnacles but he was exasperating. Must he insert himself everywhere? His face paled under her narrow eyed scrutiny.

"What? Nothing. I only noticed you in prayer. You've been through a lot, and I know what it is to lose someone. I'm angry too. And I'm here for you. I'm here to take care of you."

"No one asked you to do that." Why was he always getting in the way? Coral wanted to feel angry, she liked feeling that way, at least then she felt something.

"Well, that's where you're wrong. Our parents wanted us to be together. I'm following their wishes."

She laughed, the sound wild even to her own ears. "And what about what I want? Does anyone even care?" She shook her head.

"Yes, please. Just go away." She turned away from him and fell back to her knees, bowing her head before the tree.

It was better to be alone. She could scarcely feel her *wei*, even here in the most sacred place known to her people. Her father said she was destined to be the most powerful wave master ever, yet she had so little control of her power she couldn't even reach her *wei* here before the tree.

Coral closed her eyes and breathed in deeply through her nose. *Mother, please help me. I pray that I have the strength to lead the people, I pray—*

A gentle tap on her shoulder broke her reverie.

"What do you want?" she sighed before turning around. She expected to see Mano again or Kale, his lackey, but it was Ailani. Coral struggled not to grimace while she greeted the High Elder.

The Elder had changed into a loose wrap, the silken folds rustled around her, as if moving to an invisible wind.

"Ancient One," Coral gritted out through clenched teeth. Blessed Mother, was she to get no time for self-thought?

"I come here whenever I want a quiet moment of self-reflection. Solitude brings knowledge."

"I was just enjoying some solitude myself."

Ailani cocked her head. Her sharp silver eyes appeared mischievous. "I apologize for disturbing you." The Elder cupped her face with her hand, the grip strong despite her frail appearance. "You are strong enough, child. Mother knows you're the right person for the job."

Coral stiffened. How could she have known? Could she read her thoughts?

"We are safe here, are we not?" Ailani asked, waving a hand of dismissal before Coral could even think to object. "Oh, I know the people are far from perfect. We've paid our dues, though. Sacrifices have been made in order for us to live with the privileges we have today. Long ago, our ancestors made a deal with the Mother. They made the ultimate sacrifice so that we don't have to. Tell me, what does it mean to be Wave Master?" Ailani's expression was intense, her eyes somber.

"A Wave Master leads the people," Coral answered automatically. For what else did a leader do but lead her people?

"A Wave Master controls life as we know it." Trust Ailani to take things to their extreme.

"I hardly think the title—"

"It's more than a title, girl. The Wave Master is the most powerful of the people, and for good reason. The Wave Master controls the entire depths of the ocean. All life rests in their hands. It is the greatest responsibility and requires great sacrifice."

Coral resisted the urge to roll her eyes. She had heard this speech all her life. Hearing it yet again from the mouth of the great Ailani did not lend it any new excitement.

"Yes, Elder, responsibility. I know it well." She smiled grimly. "Do not worry. I will fulfill my duty as Wave Master. And, after I avenge my parents, I will consider—"

"There was an oath. An oath between two fathers, both passed. Is this how you would honor their memory?"

Something twisted in her insides, and she pressed her palm into her stomach. Her father had wanted this union. Would she ever understand why?

"It's more than duty that I speak of, more than a marriage that worries me. The Great Sacrifice made all this possible. Life as we know it is possible because of the sacrifices of those before us. What are you willing to sacrifice? Just remember your warning—troubled water comes in many forms. The land is dangerous. There are reasons so many chose to leave the land and never return."

Coral swallowed against the sudden onslaught of information. The Elders were secretive and aloof in their council. It was rare for any of them but especially Ailani to be so forthright. She decided to press her luck and meet Ailani's silver eyes.

"And the missing people? Am I to let that go too?" She shook her head and continued on without giving Ailani the opportunity to respond. "You can't pretend like the two aren't connected somehow. You said yourself, the Wave Master journeyed to the Republic to employ the help of their First. The Tri-Alliance is broken. Anyone can see that. I don't want to be sucked into some land war any more than you do, but I have to find out who is responsible for . . ." She trailed off, picturing her parents as she had last seen them alive and together and crowding her doorway. She blinked Ailani back into focus.

"And there's more. Something I didn't say in the meeting," Coral said.

"You still have my attention."

Coral pulled out the letter from within the recesses of folded cloth and handed it to Ailani with trembling fingers.

The High Elder said nothing of the fact that it was a written note, and she seemed to have no trouble reading it, although the sight of the letter in her bony hands was chilling. Who of the people knew how to write Jangba? Who was her father's spy?

After a moment, Ailani tsked, shaking her head. "This letter must be destroyed. Immediately. Whoever has written it is in danger. We all are."

"So you agree. I have to go to land."

Ailani nodded, but Coral took no satisfaction in her small

victory. It was no easy quest she embarked upon. Somewhere out there was the man who killed her father. She would travel to Kitoi, the Golden City, and the people Ailani said her father suspected of illegal slave trade. To think, some of her people had been forced to live in the dry scorched land, forced to live for the bidding of others. How had someone from land managed to take them all? There weren't that many tradesmen, and Aina was impenetrable to those on land . . .

Coral began to tremble. She focused on the tree and its quiet beauty. After a few moments she was able to unclench her fist and give voice to her fear. "One of our own people was behind the attack."

JURA

Chapter Twenty-Two

None of them spoke until they were out of the library and past the busy city square. They were following a winding uphill road and squinting against the setting sun when Tylak asked if she knew where she was going. She didn't, not exactly, but she had the vague idea that her destination was just ahead. That Amira was just ahead. Tylak reached for her arm, but she pulled forward, determined not to start a conversation she didn't want to finish. She knew Tylak wanted to talk about the incident at the library. She had no idea who those women were, but she had to assume news would travel quickly. It wouldn't be long before everyone knew the Daughter of the First had arrived and she was just as ruthless as any member of the Thirteen. She was happy to note the rumors still spread, fed by the majority of the population's interactions with any of the Thirteen. Her father preached they should play on those fears, had probably started the majority of the rumors himself.

I'm like him. Jura hated the thought but it echoed in time to her heartbeat.

Be brave, she reminded herself. *Be strong.*

The hill opened up to a beautiful square. The glowing stone street already beaming with light from the sun. The green opal stones sent light everywhere in the waning sunlight. The square was as clean as the Glass Halls, a wonder considering it was outside in the desert. *They must use some sort of earth magic to keep the sands away.* She frowned at the thought. It was hard to keep the frown in place when the courtyard was so stunning. The center boasted a small oasis, date palm, ferns, and other various fruit trees, all fed from what appeared to be a small body of water. Jura's mouth dropped open.

The city had its own water supply, or close to it. She staggered through what that must mean. What was the value of a water chip then? Was this why trade was down between the countries? Did this somehow explain her father's ban on contraband from Kitoi, or was that due to fear of blood chains? So many questions. After her mission here, she was determined to get back home and finally get those answers.

She felt Tylak fidgeting behind her, likely itching to say something.

It was now or never. She nodded to him. "I know. Don't say anything just yet. We're almost there, and I'm not sure yet if this will work."

"If what will work? Jura, what are you doing? What happened in the library?"

She ignored him and took a moment to look at the several townhomes that created a perimeter around the courtyard. Each home was adorned with a different color, and each color was assigned to a cabochon, one of the capital's political leaders. There were houses of every variety of stone and in more colors than Jura knew existed. She bit her bottom lip, struggling to remember which cabochon belonged to each home. She'd read what she hoped was the most current list during her time in the reading room, but that was just one more thing she couldn't be sure of. The more Jura read, the more she came to realize that books lie.

There was one detail she believed to be true, prayed to the Everflame was true. And there it was. The townhome adorned in obsidian. From this angle it was deep green with a smoky sheen like dragon oil before it was set to flame. The closer she got to it, the deeper the color appeared, changing from charcoal to black. It was beautiful.

The War Home.

Taking up residence in this home was an act of war. The person who lived in this home stayed there for as long as it took for negotiations before battle.

The last person to stay there was Gregor the Horrible. Her father would never dare. But they were already at war, and this was the best way to gain the upper hand.

Or to lose it. She still had the element of surprise. The reaction of the women at the library wasn't lost on her. Kitoians were still terrified of the Thirteen and in particular its First family. Fear made people weak; it gave her power. And yet by entering the War Home she denounced such power. Yes, inhabiting the home was an act of war but it was also meant to be a humbling experience. It made the occupant of the home an equal to the cobachons, which on the surface was a good thing. But as an equal, her Rank didn't matter. She would have to play by their many meticulous rules.

Be brave, she whispered to herself. *Be strong.* She took a deep breath and pushed open the door.

Despite the sleek and shiny exterior, the inside was surprisingly dull. The large entryway was furnished with a slim table and two tall leather chairs. An office was just off to the right; a staircase to the left. The floors were made of stone, stained dark to match the obsidian and dark leather. Straight ahead was a long hallway and presumably the kitchens.

Tylak came in after her, whistling low between his teeth. "I don't know whose house you just decided to walk into, but I hope they don't mind if I use their bed." He reached for the staircase banister, stroking the smooth obsidian with his fingertips.

"That's a good idea. We should go to bed." She felt heat rush into her cheeks. "I mean to say, we should all get some rest. It won't be long before we have visitors, and I have a busy night planned for us all."

The master bedchamber was decorated in the same dark leather furniture. Jura was poking in a closet for sheets when a throat cleared behind her. She turned to find a tall thin man, more of a boy really, with short dark hair and timid features. He wrung his hands in front of him and hunched his shoulders in order to look down and avoid her gaze, despite the fact that he towered over her.

"Greatness. It has been over a century since the War Home was last inhabited. I am your steward. I have been trained by my father and his father before him. My great-grandfather was the last to see this. My father would have liked . . ." he trailed off, his throat working up and down. "Forgive me, Greatness, he passed just a season ago." Another urgent clearing of his throat. "Please allow me to hire a full staff. I'm happy to assist you in the meantime." He crossed the length of the room to a low chest and pulled out a set of bed sheets. "Like all townhomes, the War Home is kept move-in ready. Of course, no one expected . . ." he trailed off again, busying himself with making the bed.

"Thank you. What may I call you?" Jura angled her head toward him, but the young man concentrated on tucking the corner of the sheet against the mattress.

"Her Greatness may call me whatever she wishes," he paused. "But my given name is Asim."

"It is a pleasure to meet you, Asim."

At the mention of his name, the man bowed deeply, fingertips darting from beneath voluminous sleeves to briefly touch his lips.

"Shall I draw you a bath?"

"Yes, please." The idea of a bath was a bit of a novelty. Bathing chambers in the Republic existed as steam rooms. Torches heated stones, and water was doled out sparingly. She'd heard of baths in which people submerged themselves and was eager to see the concept firsthand.

Asim instructed her on how to pull the lever to stop the flow of water, and then bowed once again. "Would you care for a coffee?"

"You're a Torch then?" Jura raised her eyebrows and forced herself not to take a cautious step back.

"No, Greatness. A simple trick of stone and hot sand. But we can procure a Torch for you if you'd like to spare your own."

No doubt he referred to Tylak, who still toted the Everflame torch about. Jura decided against correcting the man. Better for him to be a believed Torch rather than a Shadow Dancer. And Tylak would like a break from being *Arbe*.

"No, that won't be necessary. Although I will need a staff on hand for meals. I expect I'll be entertaining rather soon."

Asim nodded gravely and left the room. Jura took her first real bath.

I'll need to find a dressmaker. The thought annoyed her, but she called to mind something Amira once said: a woman's armor comes in silk. She had an important image in mind and she needed to hold to it. It was the only way. She hadn't packed much, the majority of her bags stuffed with books rather than clothing. Not that she owned many dresses. The only one hanging in her wardrobe when she'd packed a hasty bag had been Denir's. Jura sorted through her belongings now, a vague frown wrinkling her brow when she noticed the parchment on her bed.

That hadn't been there before her bath.

She reached for the paper with shaking fingers and squinted down at the paper.

Jura,

It seems you are quite different than the person the First would have the Republic believe. Do not place your trust in anyone or anything but what you see before you—and even then expect lies.

I understand why you have come to my city, but you must leave immediately.

Return to the Republic tonight, and I will see that the Daughter of the Third remains unharmed. If you do not heed my words, there will be a price to pay.

Do not tempt my favor,
The Queen of Shadows

Jura read the letter several times, frowning over the loopy handwriting and the flippant tone of the threat behind the words. Why would the Queen of Shadows choose to contact her directly? And by a hidden note left on her bed? In weeks past when she'd had an agreement with the Prince of Shadows she had come to expect random and surprise visits from Shadow Dancers in any number of places. But not this queen. No, apparently she believed in leaving notes. Cryptic ones with vague threats. Jura sighed, crumpling the parchment into a ball in her fist. It would take more than some words on paper to frighten her.

She turned at a knock on her door. She assumed it would be Asim with another coffee (startling hot despite the lack of a proper Torch), but it was Tylak wearing an awkward grin and holding a length of black silk. She raised an eyebrow, but took the garment from him.

"I hope you don't mind. That twitchy little man out there gave me an itinerary to give to you when you awoke. I figured you'd need something to wear aside from your desert garb."

"It's beautiful." And more than she expected. She pushed thoughts of the Queen of Shadows out of her mind.

"And there's something else." He gestured down to his arms. Now that she'd removed the dress, she could see the heavy volume in his hand. "*A History of Kitoi*!" She exclaimed, snatching the book from him. Her copy had been destroyed during the sandstorm. How had he remembered that?

"I can't believe you remembered. Thank you."

"It's no big deal, really. I wanted to go into town and look around anyway. The dress was easy to find, and I grabbed that on the way through the market."

"Tylak, you didn't . . ."

"I didn't steal it if that's what your implying." His tone grew defensive. "Is that really how you still see me? A thief? A slave?"

"What? No, that's not what I said at all, I just . . ." She trailed off. Hadn't she been wondering just that? Where had he gotten the money? The book alone was worth a day's ration of water. "I'm sorry. It's beautiful. I love the dress and the book." Sandstorms but she'd made a huge mess of things. Why couldn't she have simply said thank you and shut her mouth? She bit back a sigh and tried again. "It was just unexpected, I di—"

"Yeah, I get it. I shouldn't have bought them."

"No, I love them! You know how devastated I was at the loss of my book and this dress is . . ." Beautiful, a symbol of their growing friendship, the beginning of something new. ". . . just what I needed."

"Well, I should go." Tylak remained in the doorway.

"Tylak, you don't have to go. I'm grateful for the dress, I really am."

"No, I was saying I should go so you can change into it." He flashed a sardonic smile. "You got all these little things?" He reached into his pocket and handed her a fistful of tiny note cards. "We have visitors waiting downstairs." He shrugged off her stumbling questions and snapped the door shut behind him.

Jura sighed. She'd have to clear things up with him later. She had many things she needed to do later if the tiny stack of calling cards were any indication. An odd form of politics, filled with niceties and bureaucracy. Not simple like the Republic, where one could just expect everyone else to be an enemy. Without wasting more time, Jura pulled off her clothing and stepped into the dress. The long black silk stretched around her body and crossed over her chest. It left her shoulders bare but covered the lengths of her arms down beyond the tips of her fingers. It gathered at the waist and fell softly against her ankles. Jura was grateful that she appeared mostly covered despite the bare shoulders. She combed through her hair with her fingers and adjusted her braid over her shoulder. The dress suited her, and Tylak had done an excellent job in picking one that fit perfectly and was in the current fashion of Kitoi. She strapped her whip to her side and smiled at her reflection. Despite the cut of the dress, she was the spitting image of a daughter of the Republic. Or a Shadow Dancer, Jura realized. Was that why Tylak had been drawn to the black silk? Or was he simply matching her to the War House?

There was another gentle knock at her door, but this time it was an anxious Asim who notified her the number of visitors had grown to nearly a dozen. Jura took a deep breath and prepared herself to begin the first part of her plan.

KAY

CHAPTER TWENTY-THREE

*S*he didn't care for her new interpreter. He smelled. And he wasn't as nice as Kindle. No one would ever be as nice as Kindle. Kay missed her, and Mama. She missed Daddy too and Rumble. Every day was stupid. It didn't matter what she did to prove him otherwise, Ash was convinced she would be the greatest Fire Dancer who ever lived. The only problem was she didn't want to be a Fire Dancer. She didn't want any of this.

She resisted the urge to roll her eyes and went back to repeating the words after her instructor. As long as she didn't get too close he wasn't so bad, but he was hard of hearing and tended to lean toward her, hand cupped over his ear and breath reeking of dust and bitter fruit.

"You'll give me ulcers," He complained in Drakori, which only made her sad because it was something Daddy often said.

So she repeated the words back in perfect Jangba and wished again that she didn't have to learn the language. *But if you ever want to escape and travel back home, you must learn to speak the common tongue.* She didn't know if that voice inside her was Mama or not, but it sounded like something she would want. And so she practiced the language and mastered each color Form and waited for her chance at escape.

Ash refused to take her back to the arena, even though she'd asked to go on more than one occasion. Today's training session had been especially brutal so she had thought to ask again, but Ash had refused and sent her off to her studies. He was distracted by something, but Kay couldn't tell why. He had been different ever since Kindle died, but Kay could understand that. She felt different too.

"Cadet, where is your head? I asked you a question." His name was Pyre, but Kay knew that wasn't his real name. He was from another land, just like Kindle had been. Kay frowned. That meant Kindle hadn't been her true name either. Kay would never know what it was.

Without warning, tears fell from her eyes. She wiped at them quickly before Pyre could notice and punish her. In the Sand Sea, kids weren't even allowed to cry, which didn't make sense because her tears were salty like the water of the real sea. Kindle had explained it was a symbol for the Republic, that the people would do anything to prevent from wasting water. Kindle wouldn't yell at her for crying though.

He continued to stare at her expectantly, and Kay struggled to remember what they had just been talking about. He had been quizzing her on the Doctrine of the Everflame. Something Kindle had never made her do. Who cared about some silly old flame the people kept locked away in a glass tower? She was constantly aware of it, of course. Who wouldn't be? The heat it emanated was massive, the glow from it could be seen as far away as the arena. If she concentrated, Kay could almost *feel* the flame there beside her, breathing in time to her pulse.

Pyre sighed. "The Everflame is . . ." He began it for her, raising his eyebrows when she didn't immediately respond.

"Akil." Kay stood up at the entrance of the cadet. Her book fell to the floor forgotten. Though technically if the cadets had to address one another they should refer to themselves as cadet, there was no reason Kay couldn't still address him by his given name until his naming day.

The cadet frowned in response. It was a dishonor, she'd learned, to refer to one by the given name but Kay didn't see it that way. Kay was the name Mama had given her, just like Akil's mother had named him. He'd lost his mother too, she could tell. Still, Kay noticed the sneer curling his lip when the boy muttered her name.

She wasn't entirely sure why the boy still disliked her. She was better than him at flames, sure, but then she was better than everyone, even Timber. That hadn't stopped Akil from beating her at their sparring match. Her cheeks stained red as Rumble at the memory. She shouldn't have lost her temper like that. She had tried to make nice with him after Ash's encouragement, but the cadet had wanted nothing to do with her.

"Hi." She looked around her room. Akil had come alone and with nothing save his shiny new practice assegai. He always had the weapon on hand and must have immediately replaced his old one after Kay had sent it up in flames. Kay's own practice weapon lay on the far side of her room, thrown carelessly on the floor next to her discarded boots. Aside from her boots, there were a number of books and a few soiled tunics on the floor. Mama would be disappointed.

"The Everflame is life. The Everflame is death. We are born in flames. We will die in flames." Akil muttered the opening lines of the

Doctrine before dismissing her tutor with a quick flick of his hand.

"This Cadet is done with her studies for the day." Akil had a way of sounding bossy enough that even adults listened to him. Kay wished she could do that.

Pyre didn't argue and began to collect his classroom materials.

Why had Akil chosen to speak with her now? She had tried any number of times to spark up a conversation with the boy, but so far her attempts had been met with nothing but contempt. Akil had nearly mastered his colored Forms. She wondered how long she had to practice before she learned the Red Forms. She wondered if learning them made her one step closer to freedom.

"What are you?"

Kay was confused by the question. Had she translated correctly? What did he mean? She was a girl, she was a cadet, she was a slave. She shook her head and he repeated the question, slower.

"I'm a cadet."

He snorted. "No, you're not. You could have easily beaten me. Your skill with flames is . . . special."

Kay couldn't argue that. Mama and Daddy had been telling her that for as long as she could remember.

"I don't want to be special." She looked up into Akil's serious brown eyes. He seemed to understand what she meant. Seemed to understand *her*. "I'm going to go back."

He did understand. Enough not to ask her where she meant to go back to.

His silence made her brave, so she continued. "As soon as I get strong enough, I'm going to run away."

"Good. That's exactly what I came here to tell you to do."

Kay made him repeat himself a few times to be sure she understood.

"You . . . came to tell me to run away?"

"There's something they're not telling us." Akil's voice was low and his accent made it difficult to understand.

Kay bit the inside of her cheek and forced herself to concentrate. "Ash has secrets?"

Akil nodded. "I'm surprised at how quickly you've come to understand Jangba."

Kay nodded too. She didn't understand everything, but she was following so far.

"And yes, maybe Ash too. I'm not sure. But my father definitely. I thought at first it was just because he was going to purchase my freedom—"

Kay held up a halting hand. He was speaking too quickly, it was hard to follow what he was saying, but she recognized that word, had marked its importance.

"Freedom? You can . . . purchase freedom?" She breathed out the word. It was what she wanted more than anything.

"Yeah, you know, save enough winnings and you can claim your worth back from your owner. You know, be free. But now I don't think that's what's happening. Not anymore. Look, we have the same owner. You've seen him." Akil scowled when she didn't immediately respond. "Our owner?" He repeated, exaggerating each syllable. He blew out his cheeks and held his arm out on either side for good measure. "The Ninth of the Thirteen?"

Kay nodded. Yes, she remembered him. He seemed nice enough, but Mama would call him eccentric. It was Mama's way of calling someone weird in a nice way. But then, everyone in the Republic was strange.

"Right. The Ninth, my father, Ash. They all know a big secret and somehow we're involved. You especially. I heard my father and the Ninth talking, but he's not the only one. The Council came to speak with my father." He sighed. "Look, I'm only telling you this because your name came up after mine. I heard the Ninth say he'd been made an offer he couldn't refuse. If you want to run away, you better do it soon, before he sells you."

Kay struggled to translate all of his words. Pyre was long gone, already shuffling back into his room probably.

"I'm being sold?" Kay swallowed.

"I think we all are. I think my father has enough to purchase our freedom. That's why the Arena Council got involved. But I doubt Ash has money saved up to purchase your freedom. You don't belong to him and soon you won't belong to the Ninth either. I don't know what will happen to you if someone else buys you. I came here to warn you. Run away now or be stuck here forever."

BESHAR

Chapter Twenty-Four

He didn't consider himself a religious man, and yet he stood in front of the great flame, staring into its glowing center. He was alone, save for Kenjiro. The man stood at the entrance, a wary eye cast down the hall. Beshar could tell from the wrinkle in his brow that he was casting out his power, searching for anyone else using magic. He knew Jura had frequently visited the Everflame, probably still prayed to it even in Kitoi.

He wondered where Jura was now and if she would be successful in her quest? Would she find the real Amira? Was she already too late?

He'd sent the earrings to Denir's chambers and then made his way up to the Everflame. He didn't feel guilty . . . not exactly. Guilt was a foreign concept to him, and the earrings were a perfect replica of the ones his cadet wore. And yes, he would need to take them from her. Eventually. They were clearly valuable and therefore needed to be in his possession. But they were safe enough where they were for the moment.

He'd known Denir had powerful friends, but how had she

gotten the Arena Council in her pocket? Things had taken a dangerous turn in the Republic. The city's water rations had all been cut, the people were growing restless, and Ishani, their new Thirteenth, suggested they open the arena to everyone, waiving the entrance fee to the public. It seemed to be working for the moment. The arena crowds surged, people sitting on one another's laps and standing in the hallways and staircases around the dome.

"Master—"

He heard a gentle rustle behind him, parchment sliding on stone floor. Beshar nodded for Kenjiro to look for the messenger, but he knew it was a futile effort.

It was an embossed letter. The stamp unknown to him. The melted wax was so dark blue it appeared almost black, a fitting background for the crescent moon stamped into it. A part of him had known then, but he'd drawn the moment out, frightened by the possibilities of it. The Queen of Shadows had never chosen to contact him directly before. Having her direct attention was not a good thing if her reputation was to be believed.

The handwriting was flowery, girlish even, with tiny doodles on the corner as if the author had gotten bored mid-sentence and decided to draw instead. The message was simple. She thanked him for the earrings. She informed him that she had the power to destroy his life at the arena, his wonder child, his prize dragons, everything gone. He was to await further instruction.

Kenjiro returned, expression drawn in concern.

Beshar handed him the missive. There were no secrets between him and Kenjiro. The man read it quickly before giving it back with a solemn nod.

Neither man said anything as Beshar tossed the parchment into the Everflame.

Was he losing his control? He had to crack this secret at the arena, and quickly. Whatever was happening there was big. Somehow, quietly, while the Thirteen bickered in their towers, the balance of power had shifted.

It was nonsense. He nodded to Kenjiro and the man fell into step beside him. The two walked back to his private rooms long enough for Beshar to change and pour himself a large goblet of wine. He left again, calling for a team of camels rather than his normal palanquin. He was unsure what sparked the decision, but somehow he wanted to get to the arena as quickly as possible. He called for four men to accompany them. Kenjiro would drive.

As usual his guard knew where they were going without being told. He couldn't read thoughts, at least Beshar didn't believe so, but the man knew him better than anyone else and Beshar had never known a greater friend. That's why it was important to maintain a distance, to not show favoritism. Favoritism opened the window for opportunities like today, when he'd had to choose between Jura and his new cadet. Anything cherished was a weakness.

The fights had already started when Beshar arrived, but he didn't mind. None of his dragons or gladiators were on tonight's card. He took a seat next to Fatima, who sniffed at him politely. He recognized the Fire Dancer as one of hers and watched the fight with little interest, his gaze searching the crowd for something unknown. The glass spectator box reserved for the upper class was fairly empty despite the fact that the arena proper was overstuffed, people pressing into one another in a constant vibrating hum. The sound was deafening, just barely muted by the heavy glass walls.

Beshar wiped at his brow and breathed deeply of the calming oils. This was better. The Everflame was too massive, too judgmental.

This was simple, man versus beast, life or death.

That was something he could agree on with the Shadow Dancers and Denir. He should be focusing on the mystery of his little wonder child. It wouldn't be long before the child's naming day. Flames, they could do it tomorrow and she would be ready, but he didn't see any reason in rushing things. She was a natural and still so young. Beshar delighted in the potential for what she could be. If properly trained, she would easily be the most dangerous creature in the entire Republic. *Mine*. He would never sell her, no matter the pressure he received from the arena. He spotted the trio of red robes and flinched. He had jinxed himself by even thinking of them. He had no desire to have this conversation yet again. It seemed everyone was very interested in his cadets.

He waited until the men awkwardly seated themselves around him before he acknowledged their presence. Viktor, Tommon, and someone new, a woman Beshar didn't recognize. A young face for one belonging to the Arena Council.

"Councilmembers. It's a bit crowded in here, is it not?" He looked at Viktor and Tommon pointedly, the two had chosen to sandwich him between them but they made no move.

The young woman's mouth twitched.

"The Ninth is known for his humor." Viktor scowled, ruddy cheeks quivering.

"Am I? This is news to me." Beshar took another deep breath from his handkerchief.

"Is it not humorous for you to think to ignore the requests of the Arena?" Tommon asked, raising one bushy white brow.

"I seem to be ignoring more than my usual share of requests these days. What do you want now?"

"Your cadet is quite something. I watched her in practice

today." The young woman smiled at Beshar, revealing a row of perfectly straight white teeth. Her smile made her briefly stunning but it faded quickly as he saw the greed glaze over her eyes. "She will be sensational in the arena."

"Yes, she will be, won't she? If I choose to enter her into the arena." Beshar pretended to examine the sleeve of his robe.

"What do you mean to say, that she won't be entered in the arena? Are you mad? Why would you waste a natural talent like that? She could—"

Beshar cut off Viktor's ramble. "My cadet is no doubt capable of many things, but she remains mine and therefore whatever I choose to do with her is my decision. Tommon, duck your head, you're blocking all the action."

The woman made a sound that was very similar to a growl in the back of her throat. "Listen, you insolent disgusting ma—"

"Easy, Karida. No one here wants to say something they will later regret." Tommon raked a hand through his thick white hair. "The Ninth merely wishes to remind us once again that he has no intention of losing ownership of his new cadet. Am I correct?"

Beshar shrugged, struggling to appear nonchalant. This was more than just the average pursuing of a talented cadet, but then his wonder child was no average cadet. He'd heard whispers of a dragon trainer out in the western colonies, one that had a way with wild dragons and strange powers of his own. Was his wonder child from the same place? Were they somehow related? He made a mental note to look up the information on the foreign trader later, perhaps the man could provide answers if nothing else. He called for his wine to be refilled and raised his eyebrows at Tommon, the eldest of the Arena Council and the only one with any sense.

"If you know I have no intention of selling you my new cadet, then what reason do you have for this visit?" He narrowed his eyes, loathe to play this card so soon. "Did Denir send you?"

The woman, Karida, made a strangled sound in the back of her throat. "Do not say that woman's name. The very mention of it brings displeasure."

Beshar grinned. In another world, he and Karida could be friends. "Then what do you want?"

"This was never intended to turn ugly." Karida snapped her fingers and a goblet appeared in her hand moments later. She drank deeply and proceeded to ignore him, turning her attention to the fight just in time to see Fatima's gladiator get ripped in half between the dragon's massive jaws. She flinched at the splatter of gore.

"It was intended as a friendly visit, one where we remind you of how rewarding it can be when you meet us in the middle." Viktor's head bobbed in tune to her words. "As per our earlier agreement, your new dragon is scheduled to arrive tomorrow. I think you'll be quite pleased."

Beshar frowned as Viktor turned to offer condolences to Fatima at the loss of her merchandise, Embers had been a good Fire Dancer.

Had the Arena Council really chosen to visit him to make small talk? Was he being paranoid? No, this was the council, there was always an ulterior motive, he just had to find out what.

"You don't regret your decision, I hope?" Tommon cocked his head to the side, watching Beshar thoughtfully. "There's still time to change your mind . . ."

Beshar's mind worked, trying to understand everything at play. Denir had warned him of this. Things were happening in the arena, and he was entirely in the dark. "Our deal still stands?" Again the flash of unease, the quick stab at his gut that reminded him things were unwell. Guilt. Sell them his boy cadet in exchange for a dragon. By agreeing to this, the Arena Council would cease their requests to purchase his wonder child. It sounded too good to be true, it probably was, but the offer was too good to pass up.

"I sell you the boy and you won't bother me about her again?"

Viktor nodded, his ruddy cheeks deep purple in the flickering torchlight. Karida turned away from watching the dragon covering and nodded in response.

"That's right, Beshar. You sell us the boy, we give you a pretty dragon and leave your little girl alone."

It wasn't his responsibility to worry what would happen to his cadet once sold to the Arena. He pushed aside the feelings of guilt, burying them deep, burying them forever. His new cadet was worth it, wasn't she? He was doing everything in his power to keep his wonder child, he just hoped she would pay off.

TYLAK

CHAPTER TWENTY-FIVE

She looked stunning tonight. Her neck and shoulders were bare, unadorned by any jewelry. Everyone else in attendance was dressed in bright colors with gaudy stones hanging from earlobes and necklines. Jura stood out, her black silk a stark contrast in a sea of color. *She would have stood out anyway*, he thought. He was wondering why it had taken him so long to memorize the curve of her face when a gentle tap from Peppik snapped him out of his reverie. Right, he was supposed to be playing *Arbe* not some lovesick fool. He took another casual glance of the room, just as any bodyguard would do.

The downstairs living area had been thoroughly cleaned, windows thrown open allowing the gentle night breeze to creep in. A full litany of servants provided snacks and beverages to their "guests." Tylak suspected the house steward was responsible for the staff, but everything was too sudden, too rich, for his liking. Jura refused to talk about it, but she was there, she'd seen it too. The people of Kitoi, or the cabochons at least, were water rich. They must think everyone in the Republic a flaming fool with their worthless water chips. Was it fear that kept this country in check? He cast another sidelong glance at Jura. She had been surveying the room, likely wondering the same things he was. Burn it all, they should have had more opportunities to talk this all through. The dim mutter of the room began to fade as people realized Jura had entered.

"Cabochons. Shall we discuss business in my office?" Jura didn't wait for an answer, simply turned and strode off. Tylak and the rest of Jura's false *Arbe* fell into step behind her. His heartbeat quickened, and he resisted the urge to check his sheath for his dagger. Everything was going according to Jura's so-called plan.

The office was a bit crowded. Jura sat behind the large desk, an open book in front of her. There was barely enough room behind the massive desk for Tylak and the others to crowd behind her. The cabochons shuffled in one by one, each dressed entirely in one color. An elderly man was swathed in purple with golden chains hanging from his neck. A young woman wore shades of orange, complete with a tiny tiara embossed with tiny glittering orange stones. Tylak resisted the urge to roll his eyes. Each was more ridiculous than the last. How was Jura supposed to talk to these people with a straight face?

Jura had tried to explain the significance of the coloring, but it had mostly been a mess. Each color coordinated with a different emotion and each emotion a different ruler or cabochon. There were nine of them in all, or nine in the room in any case. Tylak supposed the others left outside the office were not official cabochons. Or perhaps they didn't think they would fit comfortably in the room? He turned his attention back to Jura. She studied the people before her with an intense expression.

She had warned Tylak that the people of Kitoi respected

power with their rules. She would be forced to provide a stern front. The tension in the room was palpable, and Tylak shifted uneasily. This was going to be a long night.

The older man dressed entirely in purple cleared his throat and waved a finger in the air. "Young lady, do you have any idea what you have done? The War Home is not a play thi—"

"Silence," Jura commanded, giving the man in purple a look that could cut glass. "We have not been introduced, and I have not given you permission to speak." Jura rose from her chair.

The man's skin darkened to match the deep purple of his tunic. Tylak thought the man's eyes might bulge out of their sockets. He worked his jaw up and down in an effort to remain silent.

"You've heard the rumors of the Thirteen. You know that I am Daughter of the First Family." She smiled. "As you can imagine, my family has gone through great lengths to maintain our rank. I did not enter this home lightly. Nor did I enter it with the intention of creating a war."

"That's exactly what moving in here means, you simple-minded li—"

"Cabochon, I'm going to interrupt you again. I still haven't given you permission to speak. However, I'm happy to hear all your comments after I finish, Cabochon . . . ?" She cocked her head to the side, waiting for him to answer.

"Cabochon Aja," the man mumbled.

"Cabochon Aja, Master of Histories." She inclined her head. "You will have your turn." She clasped her hands in front of her and continued on, her voice ringing out across the room, clear and authoritative. "As I was saying, I do not intend to start a war. I have always enjoyed a proclivity toward books. I find I'm most at home in a library. I visited yours." She paused and stared off into the distance, her expression softened, no doubt because she remembered how impressive the library had been. "You know, the library here in the Golden City is the most grand I've ever seen. But then, I'm not well traveled. I am, however, well read. I remembered learning of a text kept in your library, *Original Craft of Law*. Perhaps some of you have read it? We don't have a copy of it in the Republic, but it is a fascinating read, available to any patron of the library. Oddly enough, there's also a copy of it here. And inside I read something I found to be most interesting. Can you guess what it is, Cabochon Ortuna?"

The woman in question jumped, and Tylak recognized her as one of the women from the library. She wore an emerald green gown with voluminous skirts and over a dozen golden chains dangled from her neck. Bright green emeralds, bigger than Tylak's thumb, hung from her ears. "I have not read it, Greatness." She kept her eyes on the ground.

Tylak noticed the side of Jura's lip quiver as she fought back a smile.

"Perhaps any future visits to the library will be better spent exploring books rather than searching for the latest gossip. In any case, as I have said, there is a copy here. Allow me to read from it," she reached for reading glasses that weren't there and with a gentle sigh squinted down at the page.

"Entry into the War Home is also granted for ambassadors of nations crafting new laws which affect Kitoi." She stabbed her finger at the text and sent the cabochons a brilliant smile. "That's why I'm here. Things in the Republic are changing. It's time the Tri-Alliance changed too. I'm here to draft a new Tri-Alliance, a better agreement, and one that sees to the progression of our nations." She raised her voice to speak over the low murmur that had started among the cabochons. "We need to call for the Sea King and plan an allia—"

Cabochon Ortuna broke into a fit of coughing, and the room fell to muted titters and murmurs.

"What is the meaning of this interruption?"

"The Sea King is dead," Cabochon Aja, the elderly man in purple, exclaimed. His expression was almost gleeful.

Tylak stiffened. The Sea King was dead? What did that mean for Jura's plan?

"Dead?" Jura sat down heavily. Her expression fell, she no longer appeared as one of the dominating evil Thirteen. Instead, she looked to be a young woman, reeling from the sudden loss of a friend. Were they friends? Tylak wondered. Had she known the man? Either case, she was deeply impacted by the man's death.

"How did this happen?" Her voice was barely a whisper and still it echoed across the room.

When no one answered, Jura repeated the question, louder.

"We assumed you did it, Greatness. Your father . . . it's no secret he plans a war against the sea people. Cabochon Ishani sent the missive just yesterday." Cabochon Ortuna dared a glance at Jura and met Tylak's eyes. She quickly looked back down at her slippers, the soft shoes were dyed to match her dress.

Tylak found Jura staring at him. Flames, her plan had gone up in smoke before they had even started. There would be no re-drafting of the Tri-Alliance. It was shattered and it was only a matter of time before the Republic marched to sea. He wished he could take her in his arms and hold her tight. He wanted to tell her everything would be okay. He looked back down at the ground. Now was not the time to blow their cover.

"The peoples of the sea have done nothing to provoke such an attack. I can assure you that my father would never . . ." She trailed off, and Tylak thought of the First, miles away and bound by a blood chain. It was entirely possible the First *was* behind the death of the Sea King.

There was an awkward silence when Cabochon Ortuna spoke up again. "Greatness, perhaps you would be more comfortable seeking other accommodations while you continue your tour of our fine city. I would be thrilled to offer my services as host if you would like to stay in the Emerald Home."

Jura crossed her arms, clearly battling with the idea. Would she take the peace offering or was she even now scrambling to find a way for them to repair the Tri-Alliance? He saw it clearly then. This was their last opportunity, and they had failed. There would be no reparation of the Tri-Alliance now. Tylak squeezed his fist to keep from yelling in frustration.

"No," Jura whispered. Then she repeated herself, louder, her intense amber gaze sweeping across the room. "I think I'll stay. As you have said, the missive just arrived. And we are at war."

CORAL

CHAPTER TWENTY-SIX

*I*t *smelled old and rotting*, of soil and decay. Coral wrinkled her nose against the pungent odor and stared at the distant land in dismay. They had made it.

The tiny skiff bounced in the bay, the land a rip of golden white against the soft blues and greens of the ocean.

It was a small group of Kombu, the trained soldiers numbering less than a dozen including herself, Mano, and Kale. She was unsure if she was pleased or distracted by their presence. Both men had hovered around her, and their presence tugged at her *wei*, a familiarity she'd come to expect during the close quarters as they'd traveled.

"We can stay here for a few days. Send scouts. There's no—" Mano offered, sensing her hesitation.

"No sense in wasting time. We've wasted enough time as it is. It's time to face the man who killed the Wave Master," Kale answered for her. He was the only one who had seen the man who had killed her father. Something flashed in his eyes. The brilliant blue color darkened before he smoothed his face into the unreadable mask of a Kombu warrior.

Coral shook her head. It was difficult to hear her own thoughts with the opinion of those two on either shoulder. It was time. She might not feel like it, but the fact remained that the people all looked to her as their leader. It didn't matter if she still saw herself as a phony. She stiffened her back against their scrutiny and gestured off at the land in a wild gesture that sent the water trailing after her careless fingers in a restless spray.

"I'm ready." Ready to face the man who killed her parents. Ready to seek vengeance for the fallen souls of her people. Ready to learn why her people had been attacked . . .

She wasn't prepared for the pain. A searing intense heat cut into her senses and brought her to her knees. Her stomach rolled in a violent bitter protest, and she grit her teeth against the sensations of a thousand pinpricks against her skin. Great Mother, but her father had never mentioned such pain. She gasped loudly, drawing in a ragged breath and shaking her head against Mano's offered hand.

"I can do it," she muttered. She rose to her feet, digging her bare feet into the sand.

"Coral—"

"I'm fine," she snapped.

Kale too seemed to have a difficult time of it. He growled low in his throat before he snapped his fingers and brought some of the Great Mother to wrap around his bicep. The connection seemed to bring him relief, so Coral flicked her wrist in an impatient gesture and a thin rope of silvery water pulled itself from the ocean and settled around her neck. She breathed easily, feeling like herself again now that her connection to the Mother was no longer severed.

She had heard rumors of the pain before, but she had never

expected it to feel as if she was cutting herself in half and leaving part of her soul behind. No wonder her people never left their ocean home. How could they when the sensation was akin to losing one's limb? The water necklace fashioned by her *wei* would have to suffice.

The small group of Kombu stared uneasily from their position on shore. Coral was still loathe to bring them and had yet to convince the men that they should stay behind. They looked at her now, awaiting a signal from her that their presence was needed. It wasn't. Coral refused to allow any more of her people to suffer at the hands of the land. It took some convincing, but everyone finally agreed that a smaller scout party would work best. Kale was an obvious choice, as he was still the only one who could assure a positive identification of her parent's murderer. Mano was allowed by the power of their betrothal, weak as that agreement was becoming. Mano seemed intent to stay by her side, despite the fact he still nursed a slight limp from his previous injuries. The three of them would explore the ports first before making their way to the city proper.

Coral had a vague notion of foreign politics. She had always been groomed as the next Wave Mistress, so it was only natural she learn the history of her world and her place in it. However, she wished she'd paid closer attention in her studies as the trio grew increasingly closer to the tiny nation.

The Golden City was less than a day's travel from shore. Small towns outcropped the major city along the way, and they chose one at random to stop for a change of clothing. The thin silk wraps of her people were impractical against the heavy heat of the sun, and they marked their group as clear outsiders. They had enough trouble blending in without calling extra attention simply because of their clothing. Coral chose loose flowing robes in pale linen. The sleeves were long enough to cover her fingertips, and the matching scarf made short work of covering up her wild mane. Kale even talked her into wrapping her feet in leather cases, though Coral wrinkled her nose in displeasure at the footwear. Her people did not wear shoes. How could they sense the mother when they couldn't feel her? Kale reasoned that the further they drew from the Mother, the more likely the sun was to burn the already scorched lands. She took the shoes and the scarf, using the excess material to wrap around her neck and hide her water necklace. She almost fit in.

There was no hiding the Kombu. Both men were far too large, too muscular to pass for the smaller stature of men known on land. After wasting an hour or more searching for clothing large enough, Coral settled on a large head wrap that at least covered Kale's single shock of white hair. No sense in alerting the breathcatchers that they had Kombu roaming the land, even a single Kombu was enough to raise panic, more so the further they got from shore. They traded some fresh fish for goods, and after a brief lunch they headed further into the desert. Her watersense faded to a dull echo. It wasn't much longer until the memory of the pain from her initial separation from the Mother faded into a quiet buzz.

It was nearly sunset when they arrived on the outskirts of the city. The setting sun shone brilliantly against the golden walls. Coral blinked against the glaring golden light.

"Call me a karsh if that's not the most stunning thing I've ever seen."

Kale grunted. "I can think of a few. Or at least you . . ." He trailed off with a sheepish grin. "That was supposed to start as a compliment. I wasn't going to call you a karsh."

"Save it." She rolled her eyes.

Mano cleared his throat. "Let's make camp then. In the morning we'll figure out a way into the city and t—"

"No. We go now, under cover of night." Coral was surprised by the hard quality to her voice. "I'm not waiting."

"Coral, we don't even have a plan. And you've never been to this city. Crashing in, trishulas bloody, in an unknown land is not the safest course. We need time to chart a plan, a proper one, and then we can make our presence known."

"I can't." Coral shook her head. "I can't just wait here doing nothing when there's a murderer out there. You might think it's stupid or too simplistic to believe him here, but I know it to be true."

"The prophecy—"

"Said I would have my revenge."

"At the cost of your life," Mano hissed out.

"It's open to interpretation," Coral snapped, but she thought of Ailani's warning to her father. She'd told him he wouldn't survive the battle, and he hadn't. Coral didn't want to die, but she would if that's what it took to get vengeance. This would be easier if she was here alone, without Mano's words of caution or Kale's worried expression. Vengeance was not forged in partnership.

Coral sighed and dropped her pack to the ground, plopping herself into the sand beside it. The immense heat of the sands had caused her to sweat an abnormal amount. She pulled the water from her skin, separating salt and various other minerals from it until the water was pure. A clean crisp ball of hovering water. She directed the water to her mouth and sated her thirst. Skin and clothing now dry, she turned her gaze back to the Kombu. Kale stared off into the distance while Mano paced restlessly at her side.

"We don't know anything for certain. That's why we're here. For answers." She looked from one man to the other. They were both brave and stubborn. Her father had trusted them. Both of them. And yet he hadn't shared his knowledge of the missing people with them either. Who had the Wave Master trusted with that information? Would she ever find out?

"The first thing we do is find out where the majority of the slave trades are dealt."

Mano stopped his pacing. "It's a good plan. You and Kale stay put here and make camp while I—"

"What?" Coral snorted. "What did you just say? I'm not *staying put* anywhere."

Kale had the good grace to look away at Mano's scowl.

"Why is everything an argument with you? This is for more than just your own safety. Stop being selfish, Coral. The people cannot have you bend the knee, not to anyone. Ailani has never been wrong before."

"I won't bend the knee! Maybe Ailani made a mistake. It's possible. We don't know what she saw." Coral shook her head, forcing visions of her own battered and broken body away. "Besides, what would you have me do? Dive away from trouble? From vindication? Allow the murderer to continue to roam free on the mere chance I'll be injured—"

"Dead. You'll be dead. I may not have wanted a bride but, murky waters, I didn't want a dead one either."

She stiffened. "You think I want you for a husband? That I want any man? Perhaps if I hadn't been so distressed over this mockery of a union I could have learned more from my father. I wouldn't have been below decks. I could have helped him. If I hadn't been so upset about *you* my parents might still be alive. It's your fault they're dead."

"You don't believe that." Kale stopped his pacing and grabbed at her arm. His fingers slid over her wrist, but she jerked away and twirled out of his grasp.

"Stay out of this, Kale," Mano snapped. He stepped closer, glaring down at Coral. "Coral, if you had been above deck, you would have died too. And then what would the people do? The Wave Master and his progeny murdered in one day? You can barely control your *wei* on the best of days. What makes you thi—"

"Silence!" Coral shot to her feet, snatching all the moisture from Mano's mouth. She just wanted him to be quiet. She was so angry. She seized her *wei*, suffocating his with her own. She pulled more water from his body. His tongue enlarged and he choked, fingers clawing at the air.

"Coral—Coral, stop!" Kale grabbed her arm.

"Great Mother, I'm so sorry." She released her hold of his *wei* and Mano fell to his knees, staring up at her in fear.

She trembled from the release of her anger followed by the sudden spike of terror. What had she almost done? And why did she still feel like he somehow *deserved* it? She took another deep breath. Mano wasn't the problem. He was right, to a degree. She did easily lose control of her powers.

"Are you all right?" Kale asked.

"Of course I'm not," Mano seethed, scrambling to his feet. The color was slowly leaking back into his skin. How much water had she pulled from him?

Mano drew in another ragged gasp. "She tried to kill me."

"I was talking to Coral." Kale reached out his hand and helped her to her feet. She couldn't remember falling down.

"I didn't mean to. I swear." This wasn't the first time she had lost control of her power, but it was the first time she'd put someone else directly in danger.

"I know. And he's fine. And you are too. Everyone take a deep breath." Kale's voice was low and calming.

"Easy for you to say," Mano gasped.

Coral turned away, determined to keep her tears from them. No sacrifice to the Mother would take back what she had almost done. Nothing could make her forget how her loss of control had made her feel. To think what might have happened . . . she bit her tongue at the thought. Mano was fine. They both were.

"Mano, I just—"

"Give me a moment, Coral."

"But—"

"I said leave me alone!" Mano stomped away, creating distance between them.

"Coral, are you . . . do you want to talk about it?" Kale's voice was cautious. She could feel his eyes on her, but she kept her eyes on Mano's departing figure.

"I'm fine," she mumbled.

"It's your choice, of course. We'll do whatever you want. I'll follow you anywhere. All of the Kombu would."

She turned to face him, a grim smile playing on her lips. "That's the problem. I never asked for any of this. I don't need you following me. I don't need anyone."

"Of course you don't. Do you know what I thought when we first met?" Kale's dark eyes stared intensely into her own. She shivered under his stare.

"You don't remember when we first met!" She rolled her eyes, despite herself. Kale had long been a constant in her life, but she had never considered them close. He had always just sort of been around. But now, thinking back to lessons and childhood playtime, it was hard to think of a memory he wasn't in. She'd known him longer than anyone, even Mano. He had always been a better friend than she. Mano was right. She was selfish.

"I do," Kale answered, snapping her back to attention. "We were five, I believe, perhaps you so young as four. Your parents had come to dine with my family. I had been sent to stare at the wall in punishment, and that's where you found me. I told you that my father had ordered me to stare at the wall until it turned red. You argued that was stupid, it would never happen on its own."

"So I painted red on your wall," she smiled at the memory.

"In karsh blood."

"No," her hands smothered an audible gasp. She had never known that detail of the story.

"Oh, yes. Karsh blood taken from my father's study. You used every last drop of the priceless liquid."

"I just wanted you to come play with me."

He laughed. "That's how I met you. That's how I'll always remember you. Someone who sees it like it is. Someone brave enough to take action, to make change and free the innocent. I think that's how your people see you too. You're going to make a wonderful Wave Master, Coral. You'll see."

She drew in a ragged breath and searched her mind for a reply. When she didn't answer, Kale turned to his own pack and pulled out his bedroll.

"We should get some rest. Mano does this. He just needs some time to himself. He'll be fine and back in no time. You'll see."

"Do you think we should get married?"

Kale stopped unrolling his pack and stood up. He stared at her for a moment and then shrugged. "My opinion doesn't matter."

"My father trusted you." *Did he tell you any secrets?* she wondered, but Kale shook his head.

"Yes, your father wanted the union, but the only thing that matters now, Mistress, is whether or not *you* want this? Follow your heart. As I have said, the Kombu will follow you. Anywhere. As will I." He turned his attention back to his bedroll.

"Thank you." She pulled opened up her own pack and began to unroll her sleeping mat. "You think you've diffused the situation, don't you? You must be proud of yourself."

"I don't know what you mean." The corners of his mouth turned up a bit.

Coral bit back a smile of her own and finished unrolling her mat.

Mano returned less than an hour later. It had taken him longer to cool down, but what could she expect? She had nearly sucked the life from him, yet hadn't he provoked her? Coral decided she wasn't ready for a confrontation yet, so she pretended to be asleep and lay quietly until Mano's soft snoring could be heard. She rose from her bedroll and stepped over Kale, who had somehow managed to move his bedroll to her feet. He looked so peaceful when he was sleeping. His chest rose and fell in a steady rhythm. She watched him for a moment before her actions dawned on her. She shook her head. What was she doing studying this man while he was sleeping? She was wasting time. It was now or never.

She unstrapped her father's trishula and fingered the length of her knife. The trishula would have to stay behind. She didn't need the unnecessary attention, and she was good enough with a knife. Her gut screamed at her to take the extra weapon, but having it on her back would negate the purpose of her disguise. No, she was leaving it behind, final decision. She dared one last glance at the sleeping forms of her Kombu before darting into the night.

The night had brought with it a coolness she had not expected. There was no breeze that tickled her skin, instead the air was thick around her with a sharp bite that chilled. Off in the distance she felt the distant pull of the Great Mother on her *wei*. She allowed herself to give in to the pull for the barest of moments, allowed her heart to ache for just an instant. If only her father had shared his secrets with her. If only she wasn't honor bound to seek revenge. She was so close.

Her feet ate up the ground as she approached the city. The wild beating of her heart kept in time to her march. She stopped short.

The city was protected by water. *Wonderful! I wonder how the breathcatchers get across.* She grinned. The water smelled rancid, but it was an easy enough task to pull the pure water from the filth. The water was different here. Its connection to the Mother weak and quiet, yet it still bent to her will, rising up in a giant wave that carried her over to the city on the other side.

Though it was the dark of night, the city was still alive with sight and sound. Music poured out from an amphitheater and a crowd of people swayed to its beat. Food vendors stood outside selling late night snacks to the crowd. Coral didn't linger but dove deeper into the city until the amphitheater was only a dim hum in the background. The homes became larger, and Coral strode on with confidence. Whomever had been behind the attack of her people had been paid handsomely, most likely by a leader of the city. They wouldn't be living in city squalor. It stood to reason even further that this was a job one would require of his most trusted man, perhaps that of a personal guard. She was getting close, she could sense it.

The home ahead and to the left was having some sort of gathering. The entire home shone like a beacon. Emblazoned by hundreds of torches, it shone like a small sun. Coral glared against the light and moved closer. She had no clue what she would do once she arrived. She knew she couldn't simply smash the door down and demand answers. Who was to say any of these people knew anything? It was why Kale and Mano had argued that she needed a plan. Well drown their plans. She was here now and it seemed like all of the city's wealthy and privileged were at this home. She had come too far to quit now.

Before she could blast the door open, it swung open wide and people began spilling out. Coral smiled and started forward.

KAY

Chapter Twenty-Seven

It was time to activate her master plan. There was just one problem, she had no master plan. She had less than a plan. All she knew was Akil's warning. Run away now or be sold and stuck forever. Well, clearly it was time to leave. *You won't miss it here*, she reminded herself. Which was true now, considering Kindle was gone. She supposed she would miss Ash, just a bit. He was nice. It wasn't his fault she had been kidnapped. But Ash was a free man. That meant he could go anywhere and he chose to stay here in the hot sand with no water and no freedom at all. Poor Ash didn't really know the meaning of freedom. Why hadn't anyone told him?

And so she had worried all morning. Pyre had arrived two hours past dawn for her morning studies and was lecturing her in Jangba when a tiny idea began to form. *Arena dragons are kept in the catacombs.* It made sense when Kay worked it out. Dragons liked to curl up and sleep in dark places. It kept captive dragons calm, although wild dragons preferred to sprawl under the sunshine. If the dragons were kept in the catacombs, then it stood to reason that any dragon hatchlings would also be found down below. Kay figured if she could just get down there and find one, she had a good chance of imprinting a dragon to her. If a dragon imprinted, she could use the dragon to help her escape, it was probably too young to fly, but maybe she could ride it on the ground like her pony? Between her and a dragon's fire no one would be able to stop them. It was a wild escape plan but Kay knew it could work, if only she could get down to the catacombs. She answered Pyre's question on the different defense tactics found in the Red Forms when they were interrupted by Ash. The Fire Dancer had entered the room in that quiet lumbering way of his.

Kay smiled at him and rose to her feet, eager to be done with her lesson.

"No spar match today," she said with a grin, and Ash beamed at her. She hadn't said much to him since Kindle, but her new plan had her excited and looking forward to the future.

"No, no sparring match today. Not again for a while perhaps. I want to make sure you master your Red Forms before we try that again. Not that you didn't hold your own out there, but there is no reason to rush your training. Did you have a good morning? Your Jangba is much improved."

She nodded in response, struggling to keep up with the translations. "Good morning."

He laughed. "Maybe I spoke too quickly. Are you ready to practice today?"

"Practice then arena?" Kay asked.

"No, I don't think we need to go there. Grab your boots now, get them on. There's still a few hours before luncheon."

"Practice then arena," Kay repeated stubbornly. If she was going to find her way into the arena catacombs, she had to first find her way into the arena.

"We'll see," Ash grunted. "Hustle, Cadet."

She picked up her pace into a jog beside him as his long legs stretched out before her. He had a way of moving like Daddy did, a way that said: move over, I got somewhere important to be! Kay liked how Ash sometimes reminded her of Daddy. Maybe he could run away with her and the two could live in freedom on her farm? But no, maybe Ash didn't want to leave his home in the arena, and Kay didn't think Daddy would want anyone else taking over his chores. But what if she couldn't take care of the dragons and do all the chores all by herself? Kay had helped Mama make bread, but she wasn't sure she could remember how to do it on her own. If she told Ash her plans, maybe he would want to go . . . but no. What if he tried to make her stay? Ash could never know what she was planning.

They reached the practice sands, and as was her habit, Kay looked around for Akil working the Forms. She couldn't find him, so she found her place with some reluctance and began moving through the quicker more circular patterns of the Green Forms.

"Watch your toes when you kick, Cadet! You'll break a foot."

Kay scowled but flexed her toes.

"Let me see that jump again." Ash frowned and re-positioned her foot before making her complete the move three more times. Finally, he called for a water break. She finished the last of her mid-morning water ration before she took the chance to ask again about the arena.

"I want to go to arena."

"You want to go to *the* arena," Ash corrected before pushing her shoulder blades together. "Feel that? There?" He tapped her assegai. "Perfect. Hold it right there. Why do you want to go to the arena so badly?"

"Kindle." She'd been ready for this question. She figured Ash would feel bad if she brought up their friend, bad enough to let her have her way. She felt guilty for using her friend this way, but she felt like Kindle would understand if she was here.

Ash's expression softened. "I know you must miss her. But there are other places to feel her presence. Why, I bet you can feel her even now, here in the practice sands."

"Arena," Kay repeated and this made Ash chuckle.

"You're certainly as stubborn as any Fire Dancer needs to be. We'll talk about it after your practice. Now, get started on your Red Forms."

Kay tried to concentrate on the various Forms, but it was basically impossible with so many other thoughts in her head. Why were the Red Forms the most difficult? Was it because red dragons were the meanest? Rumble hadn't been mean at all. But these dragons were. She'd seen their anger firsthand. That's why Kindle was gone . . . If Kindle was still here, she could ask her the difference. She would be able to explain. Kindle could explain anything, even things that were confusing, like the Everflame.

"Why do you love Everflame?" Kay asked, surprising herself with the question. She'd meant to ask Ash a question to take his mind off her asking to go to the arena. She had wondered at the connection of course, it seemed most people in the Republic seemed to worship the giant flame. Mama and Daddy said it was important to respect nature, to respect the life of things living. But neither had ever mentioned this god made of flames.

"Well, without the Everflame there would be no fire. And without fire, w—"

"Dragons have fire. I have fire. Fire is everywhere." She performed a series of pirouettes that made Ash grin with pride.

"Where did Everflame come from?" As much as Pyre had her repeat the Doctrine of the Everflame, it never mentioned where she might find such information. The Everflame always just was. But that couldn't be right, could it?

Ash also seemed to be at a loss for words. Was he trying to figure out how to explain it to her or did he not know the answer?

"Would you rather take a trip to the Everflame? Would you like to see it in person? That might make you feel better." Ash nodded, appearing suddenly enthusiastic about the idea.

Kay shrugged, giving the idea some consideration. She was curious about the flame. Even now it called to her, its familiar ache in her chest, a flame she had always known but never given name to. It was stronger here because they were closer to it. Kay knew the people of the Republic believed it to be the source of life, that the Everflame chose its servants, marking those who should do its bidding. It was supposed to be an honor for those people. People like Ash. People like her. No, she didn't wish to see some stupid living flame, even if it did seem to call to her. Kay's power came from her Daddy and his Daddy before him. Kay's power came from the heat of the earth and flames of the sun.

"No Everflame. Arena."

Ash's face darkened, and he pointed to her assegai where it lay forgotten in the sand. She had allowed it to drop before Ash had even offered to take her to the flame, but he hadn't noticed it until now.

"Fine. But you need to tell me why. A cadet does not get to freely make demands. Why is it so important for you to honor Kindle's memory there? I would think the arena holds bad memories for you." Ash's words were slow and measured. He watched her carefully, making sure she understood every word.

"Arena." She repeated. She wished she had the words to make a better argument. "Arena dragons."

Ash inhaled and crossed the length between them until he towered over her. "The dragon? Do you want to face the dragon who killed her? Is that what this is all about?" He wiped a large hand over his face, wiping away a layer of fear and leaving only understanding. "I'll take you to the arena, Cadet, but we have no way of knowing if Inferno will be there."

"Inferno?" She stiffened at the mention of the dragon. She had gotten Ash to agree to take her to the arena, she should be more excited. Instead she felt as if the butterflies had moved out of her stomach and a bunch of angry hatchlings had taken up residence. One of them was currently trying to burn its way out of her belly. She pressed her palm tight against her stomach and clenched her teeth. Seeing that dragon again was the last thing she wanted to do. But if it was the only way she could get to the catacombs . . .

"Thank you, Ash."

"Don't thank me yet. You still have three hours of conditioning left," Ash grunted.

Kay threw herself into her exercises. She barely noticed the Ninth walk into the practice sands. Ash seemed to notice him right away. Kay remembered what Akil had said that the Ninth would sell her to the highest bidder, that he called her his wonder child. The Ninth might have plans to sell her, but Kay planned on disappearing long before then. If only she wasn't so special, then no one would care if she stayed or not. She should have never shown everyone her powers. Perhaps if the Ninth saw that she wasn't that good at Fire Dancing he would just set her free? When Kay felt the Ninth's gaze on her, she purposefully tripped.

ASH

Chapter Twenty-Eight

The man's anguished howls stopped Ash in his tracks.

Beshar's men surrounded the councilman, scimitars in hand as they stood ready against the enraged gladiator.

Ash picked up speed, kicking up little puffs of dust as he ran across the sand.

"I'll kill you. Fight me, Councilman. I'll roast you like the pig you are. I'll heat your blood until boiling and you'll scratch off your own skin to stop the pain." Timber swung his assegai wildly, slashing at the air before the men.

"Stand down, Fire Dancer. I don't want to dispatch you," the Ninth warned, frowning and seemingly displeased by the thought.

Ash stopped just outside of assegai distance in front of Timber. He held up both arms and tried to keep his voice low and reasoning. He'd seen more than one Fire Dancer brought down simply because they'd thought to speak against the wishes of their master.

"What is the meaning of this, Timber? Surely there is some misunderstanding," Ash said.

Timber spat into the sand just in front of the councilman's men. "No misunderstanding. This flaming bastard aims to steal my son. Take it back. Give me back my boy and I'll let you live."

As one, the councilman's men took an aggressive stance against Timber's threatening words. "My men won't allow you close enough to try. It's only through my grace you're even still standing. What's done is done. Accept these terms and take your anger out in the arena." The Ninth's words rang across the still practice sands.

Ash stepped closer, reaching a hesitant hand toward Timber's shoulder.

"Don't touch me." Timber flinched away, lunging forward toward the councilman.

The ground rumbled. Grains of sand shot into the air in sporadic bursts and the ground swayed beneath their feet. Timber fell to his knees, clutching at the traitorous ground to gain footing.

Ash fell forward, sharp pain slicing up from his kneecaps as he fell.

The councilman's eyes widened, but the ground near him and his men remained immobile. He stepped forward but quickly stopped himself, giving his head a gentle shake before turning away.

"I truly am sorry. It's only business." He moved away and Timber made no move to stop him, still cowering in the sand.

Once Ash was sure the ground was no longer going to move under his feet, he lumbered up and took a few shaky steps.

The Ninth eyed him warily as he and his entourage moved away.

"You'll do well to stay out of this, Ash Fire Dancer. Decisions were made, and you'll be happy to know I placed my water with you and your wonder child." He opened his mouth as though to say more but then shook his head and moved on, his men a protective shield around him.

Ash watched him walk away before turning back to Timber still trembling in the sand. He approached the man slowly, patting him absently before offering him a hand.

The Fire Dancer stared at it for several seconds before blinking back tears and lumbering to his feet.

"He's sold him," Timber whispered, disbelief making his voice tremble. "He's sold my boy." He turned to Ash, wild brown eyes appearing almost black. "I have to get him back. I won't let this happen again."

"You'll still see your boy in the practice sands. Perhaps you can even still train him. Nothing has to change simply because he has changed hands. You can still follow the plan, buy his freedo—"

"You don't understand," Timber snarled. "He was sold to the Arena. They make people disappear. I can't allow that to happen. Not again."

"Then I'll help you." Ash surprised himself. "Meet me here tonight and we'll get your boy back."

The moon was a pale light in the sky, and shadows danced from the pits as Ash made his way across the silent practice sands. He met the lone figure, nodding grimly as he tightened his grip on his assegai. It felt like it had been a lifetime since he last held it.

"Sure you want to do this, old man?" Timber's voice was whisper soft.

Ash nodded and followed Timber into the arena proper. As usual, the familiarity of entering the grand arena sent shivers of anticipation crawling down his spine. He ignored the shivers, alert to any movement or sound; but they were alone and he needn't have bothered.

Timber nodded at the thick reinforced glass gate covering the tunnel into the catacombs.

"We aim for the top corner. The glass is weakest on the edge. We'll fire there. With enough heat, the glass should shatter."

Ash frowned up at the spot Timber had indicated and noted a small flash of purple discoloration.

"How did you know it was there?"

Timber grinned, "It's always been my intention to break out of this cage."

Ash opened his mouth to respond, but Timber had already pulled a ball of fire from a nearby torch and urged Ash to do the same.

Ash drew a flame toward him, feeling awkward and out of practice.

"You'll have to bring more than that," Timber grunted. He shot out his arm and sent the full force of the tiny flame shooting toward the glitch in the glass.

Ash followed suit, gaining momentum with each toss of the flame. The two worked quickly, drawing from every torch until a final throw from Timber shattered the glass. Only one torch still flickered in the dark. Timber snatched it off the wall.

"Ready?"

Ash followed him into the abyss.

This was not his first time into the catacombs. Every cadet entered at some point, it was part of their training. He had even been gifted a glass map of them after his retirement, but that trinket was gone now. Gone like Kindle and Embers and so many before them. They all know of the catacombs, and Ash believed he knew them well. The dragons belonging to the arena all made their homes here. There were also several passages that led underneath the city and opened up into the desert. Dragon owners needed safe passage for their dragons. This was, however, the first time Ash had entered the catacombs unescorted by an owner or Arena Council member. It was forbidden for Fire Dancers to enter the catacombs without proper escort, but the rules were unknown for the limits of a free retired dancer. It was a safe bet that neither of them belonged there now, and though he would have preferred to explore them now at a more leisurely pace, it just wasn't possible. As it was, Timber kept them going fast enough to cause Ash's knees to scream in silent protest.

Ash followed him down a series of twisted stone halls, the dim light from their torch their only visibility. Ash idly wondered how Timber knew where he was going or if he was simply leading them in circles? At some point Timber had been down here enough times to explore the catacombs, enough that the man was capable of navigating through them in the dark without a map. But why? When was the man last down here?

"I followed her screams." Timber's whisper cut through the silence. Ash had the fleeting thought that he must have wondered his questions out loud, but Timber was lost in his own thoughts, pushing forward without sparing Ash a glance. "Her voice . . . it still haunts me."

There was no need to ask who Timber meant. Ash swallowed against the spike of fear that threatened to gag him.

"What do they do?" He was still having a difficult time understanding the dark underworld the arena seemed to be involved in. The questions continued to build, but here was a man who finally offered answers. "Why would the arena kill pe—"

"The arena kills all sorts of people, but that's not what they're doing here. It didn't always use to be this way, but then they learned how to do it. They call it breaking, heh," Timber laughed, the sound bitter and rotten to Ash's ears. "An apt name for it. I won't let them do it to Akil." He stopped and held the torchlight up, the flickering flame cast dark shadows against his face. Timber appeared more menacing than Ash had ever seen him.

"If things don't . . ." he sighed. His eyes searched as though he hunted for the right words. "Save my boy. Promise me, old man."

"But wait, what's a breaking? What are they doing?" Timber's words held an air of finality, and Ash had the distinct impression that this might be the last time the two ever spoke. But it was happening too fast. There were still so many questions.

"Just promise me," Timber's voice turned desperate and Ash nodded.

"I swear it."

Timber nodded. "Good. We're almost there. Whatever you do, don't interfere until I tell you to. And remember your promise."

They turned a corner. At the end of the hallway, torchlight shined in the distance. Chains rattled and a few muffled shouts had Ash tightening his grip on his assegai. Timber nodded beside him, and the two crept closer to the opening. A putrid smell assailed his nostrils as they grew near, urine and bile mixed with blood and sweat—familiar smells of the arena that rolled Ash's stomach nonetheless.

Timber tossed their torch to the ground. Ash embraced the darkness, fearful of what the torchlight would expose ahead. Timber flattened himself against the stone wall. Ash followed suit. Timber peered into the room.

"I see Akil. We still have time." He turned back to Ash. The older gladiator leaned even closer to hear Timber's whispered words, despite the fact the two were only inches apart. "I'm going to create a distraction. You grab Akil and leave the arena. Take that wonder child of yours and my son and go far far away. Afterwards, I'll find you, I—" He broke off, peering around the corner. "Flames, there's no time. We have to move now!" Timber sprinted forward, and with a mumbled curse, Ash followed.

Ash was immediately surprised by how large the room was. An amphitheater, carved out of dirt and rock. Or a holding crevice for a dragon, although there was no beast in the room. Hundreds of torches lined the walls, bathing the room in brilliant orange light. On the far side to the right of the entry way, Akil stood surrounded by hooded men. The boy was chained to the ground: massive, thick metal links circled again and again around his narrow body and clasped into a mount on the stone floor. Akil could barely stand, and he struggled under the weight of the chains. The hooded people didn't seem to notice above their heavy chanting. One hooded figure broke from the group and sliced a long silver knife against the boy's forearm. At the same moment, Timber rushed through the huddled figures and tackled the man holding the bloodied knife.

Akil screamed. Ash stumbled forward, swinging his assegai at the first man and bringing the butt of the weapon to the back of the head of another.

Akil's screams grew louder, and Ash struggled toward him. Timber rolled on the ground with one man, kicking up clouds of dust before snapping the man's neck with a violent twist.

"Akil," he roared, leaping to his feet.

The boy would not stop screaming. He didn't seem to notice the wound on his arm, though blood now drenched his entire left side.

Instead, the boy twitched and jerked, as if writhing in pain from an invisible fire.

Ash finally reached the boy, unsure how to stop his pain. He reached for the chains, dropping them instantly. They were cold to the touch, colder than anything Ash could ever imagine. Blood dripped onto the floor. The boy had a number of blood spattered, shining gemstones at his feet. Ash grit his teeth against the pain and pulled at the mighty chains. They burned his hands. His fingers turned blue against the extreme chill. He worked the long heavy chain around the twisting boy, doing his best to ignore the screams filling the cavern.

"Akil, be at peace. You're safe now." He tried to mumble reassurance, but the boy was incoherent, howling in pain and jerking beneath the chains.

Timber shoved Ash's hands away and tore at the chain. Ash stole a quick glance at the dozen or so men gutted or burned, twitching on the floor.

"We need to leave," Ash warned. There was no sign of anyone else, but he didn't want to wait around for trouble to show up.

"It hurts," the boy wailed out between his tortured screams.

"I've almost got them off you," Timber growled, snapping a link with his bare hands.

The boy moaned, gasping for breath. The air grew colder around them. The boy took several gasping breaths, his fingers clawing at his throat. He let out one last gasping cough when fire erupted from his throat in a torturous inferno. He screamed and fell to his knees.

Timber fell beside him, holding his boy close. Akil flung himself backwards, back arching against the ground. He stared down at his arm, as if noticing it for the first time. He stopped screaming.

He sat up and plunged his fingers into the wound, ripping back more skin.

Timber tackled his son to stop him from inflicting any more self-pain, but the boy shoved his father off, ripping at the hair on his head.

"Get it off," he shrieked. He bent forward in a sudden spasm, crawling forward on his knees and curling his back upwards. *Something* rippled across the boy's back.

The boy shuddered, his eyes rolled back in ecstasy or pain. He opened his eyes and stared at Timber. He took a deep breath and then breathed fire down on his body.

The acrid smell of burning flesh singed the air, and Ash choked against the rush of bile. Timber screamed but his son had stopped burning. Instead, dragon scales shone bright against the torchlight, the emerald green a perfect match to the stones scattered at their feet.

The boy hunched over, bones snapped and pierced through his skin, massive appendages broke out from his back, wings unfurling as the boy continued to grow in size. Fingers turned talons ripped at the tender skin of his face, pulling the skin back to reveal a glittering green snout.

"Run," Ash mumbled, tripping backwards as he widened the distance between him and the boy. "Run, Timber."

"No, I'm not leaving him. He's my boy—he . . ." He trailed off as he looked at the now massive creature before them.

The dragon stretched out its new wings, trumpeted in anger before blowing out a stream of fire.

"Timber, we have to go now." Ash fled toward the opening of the cavern, determined to navigate his way back through the catacombs.

"Get out of here, old man." Timber placed his assegai on the ground. "I'm staying here with my boy."

The dragon roared at Timber as the man stepped closer. Smoke curled up from his nostrils.

"Leave in flames and ash. Or come home a hero," Ash whispered. He fled into the dark catacombs, and though he heard the sound of rushing flames, there were no screams.

JURA

Chapter Twenty-Nine

This certainly wasn't the result she'd hoped for. Jura frowned at the silent room. She should have known things would be just as bad in Kitoi if not more so. Here she was, thinking herself somehow at an advantage simply because she'd been born to one of the Thirteen families. But she was just as foolish as ever, relying on books centuries older than herself only to discover people rarely do what one plans for.

She still couldn't believe the Sea King was dead. This changed everything. The Sea King had been their sole ambassador to the sea peoples. Her father would never anger the Sea King. He was their primary source of water. Couldn't the cabochons see that? Or was that precisely what they had been relying on?

"The Tri-Alliance is no more." It was more of a mumble said to oneself rather than a direct comment to anyone.

Iona Notsfar, a woman dressed in the citrine colors of the Master of Arts cleared her throat.

"Greatness, war negotiations are always on the thirteenth or the twenty-seventh day of the moon cycle. As you've missed the thirteenth, we are forced to wait seven more days before we begin."

An entire week? She felt Tylak tense beside her. He and the other three men had remained silent beside her, playing the part of *Arbe* well. She didn't like seeing him like this. It was disconcerting.

She bit her bottom lip and trailed an absent finger over the fabric covering her wrist. How easy it was to hide a blood chain here. Who was to say she wasn't wearing one now? That any one of the cabochons wasn't? Or even worse, all of them? What was the purpose of following these silly rules if people's actions were not their own? And the rules were endless. Everything in the city was done through permit, every action classified and handled by its proper coordinator. She wasn't at all surprised to find herself caught up in bureaucratic delays. She was, after all, in Kitoi.

"Then I will see you all in one week's time. I assume everyone will be in attendance this time?" She'd noted the significance of the missing cabochons, marked by the missing gemstones on the spectrum. Likely one or two was away on business, but it seemed the others had simply chosen not to come. Most likely no one had taken her seriously or perhaps had thought this entire thing some hoax.

Well, it was past time people began to take her seriously.

"Unless there was something else, you are all dismissed."

One by one the cabochons shuffled out of the office and out of her temporary home.

"Greatness, excuse me for lingering, but I would like to proceed with the necessary arrangements to have a conversation later?" a man said. His long curly hair lay in twisted coils down his back, and he was dressed in shades of pink. Amethyst if Jura's memory served her correctly.

Jura resisted the urge to smile despite the hectic day. "Shall we forgo with the formalities and converse freely now?"

The man's eyes widened, but he smiled at her. "If it pleases her Greatness, I wished to speak with you without the presence of the other Cobachon. You see, I felt it was my duty as the Master of Peace. Cobachon Abro Azaha."

Jura cocked her head to the side. "That sounds familiar. You've a niece in the Republic?"

His smile widened, the lines around his eyes deepened and the tiny black orbs seemed to fold into his brown skin.

"Indeed. Our Ambassador."

"I'm glad you lingered, Cobachon Abro. It would be wonderful to discuss further plans for peace and a redrafting of the Tri-Alliance."

The man's expression darkened. "Greatness, I apologize. But there can be no alliance between our three countries. Not an alliance of the sort you are accustomed."

Jura was taken aback. "No, perhaps I should apologize as the meaning of this meeting is lost on me. Why would you linger if not to speak of peace?" She narrowed her eyes. "Did the Queen of Shadows send you?"

Tylak tensed beside her, hands going to the daggers strapped on either hip, but the cobachon shrugged.

"Yes, I speak for peace, but it will not be manifested in this way. I speak of the peace of the gods. Please, there is a gathering tomorrow night hosted by Cobachon Nazahah. Please say you'll consider attending so that we may discuss our peace further."

"I—" She was not interested in parties and peace between gods while her country fell apart beside her. But another gathering meant another opportunity to find the answers she so desperately needed. "I'll be there."

It wasn't until she escorted Cobachon Abro out and sent Asim to dismiss the house staff that Jura finally allowed herself to fall apart. She fell back against the cool leather seat of her chair and tried to ignore Tylak's watchful eyes on her by squeezing her eyes tightly shut.

Ichiro and Jiro began muttering to themselves.

"That went better than expected," Peppik smiled broadly.

Jura cracked open an eye and glared at the older man.

"We need to form an actual plan." She nibbled on her bottom lip thoughtfully. "Ichiro, if you and Jiro don't mind, perhaps you could do some scouting tonight? I need to know where the under market slave trade takes place. You know where do they take all the unregistered and illegal slaves? If someone has Amira, I would bet they purchased her without the proper papers. Report back tomorrow after your morning prayer." She opened her mouth to issue orders to Peppik but thought better of it. The man would continue to do his own thing. There was no sense in trying to guess what that was. At the moment, he studied the palm of his left hand intently, head cocked slightly to the side as though listening to an invisible presence whispering in his ear. It was a healthy amount of paranoia, Jura told herself. Someone wasn't actually there.

"Peppik and I can head out too. I wouldn't mind getting a better feel for the city. Plus, we need to purchase a few more supplies. I want to strengthen the security of this place. I know it's only a matter of time before our friends in black find us again. I'd like to gain the upper hand if possible." Tylak raised his scarred eyebrow in question.

Jura frowned in response. "And what am I to do?" Tylak meant well, but he had to stop trying to leave her behind.

"Well, I figured you had some more reading or maybe . . ." He trailed off when Jura made a face. She'd had enough reading. It was time for action.

"I can't just sit here twiddling my thumbs while you four search for answers." She flinched at the slam from the front door as the Samur melted into the night. She gave Tylak a pointed look.

"I need to go too. I need to help."

"Jura, I'm not trying to convince you not to go, it's just that—"

"I'm not going to continue being the weak, reclusive Daughter of the First. Things are different now. I'm different."

"No one is questioning that. Of course I see that you're different. I remember the person who came to my prison cell demanding to be taught how to steal fire."

"You laughed at me."

"Only because I was taken off guard. But it wasn't stupid," he continued, rushing on when she started to protest. "It was incredibly brave. And then coming here, to save Amira, and your plans to stop this war . . . Jura, you're the bravest person I know."

She found it impossible to tear her eyes away from the intensity of his gaze. His steel gray eyes held her captivated, and she felt he was seeing her for the first time. "I don't feel very brave," she whispered, her tongue darted out to moisten her lips and she looked around for some water.

Interpreting her need, Tylak handed her the waterskin attached to his waist.

She drank deeply, using the moment to calm the erratic beating of her heart. She could still feel his eyes on her, so she lowered the skin and offered it back to him.

"Thank you."

"You're welcome." His fingers lingered on hers before he placed his water skin back at his hip. "We're going to find your friend. And you're going to end this war. I believe in you."

"I wish I had your confidence."

"I don't see why you don't. Look at all you've accomplished. By tomorrow morning, the entire city will be talking about the Daughter of the First."

"I hope that's a good thing. I need people to see me as J—"

"Jura, Daughter of the First?"

Jura jerked toward the voice. The accent was foreign yet familiar to her ears. The woman was young, close to Jura's own seventeen years and she stood in the doorway of the office with wild eyes. In her right hand she held a large dagger with practiced ease. She was dressed in the style of the people of Kitoi, although she was too tall and her eyes were too light against her tanned skin for her to pass for a true native of the country.

Her smile was more of a snarl. She looked first at Jura then to Tylak. Her light green eyes seemed to take in everything, noting the detail of Tylak before dismissing him and turning her full attention to Jura.

"Who wants to know?" Tylak slowly shifted his weight to the right more than actually taking a step to place himself in front of Jura.

Jura was grateful for the protection. There was something off about the chaotic look in the young woman's eyes.

The woman pulled back her head scarf, allowing a wild mane of riotous curls to tumble out. "They say I favor after him. That I have his eyes." She lifted her chin.

"You're his daughter. The Sea King's." Jura placed a hand on Tylak's shoulder, but he refused to budge. His hand rested on the sheath of his dagger.

"I am. Coral Cur'en. Daughter of the Wave Master. And

you're his. Daughter of the First. My father went to yours, you know. He went to your father and asked him for help. Your father refus—"

"No, that's not exactly true. It was actually me who spoke with your father."

"You?" Her green eyes narrowed. "Why would the First allow this? The Tri-Alliance states that only the rul . . ." She trailed off, shaking her head as she worked out the truth. "Why did you stand in his stead? Is the First dead? Did you . . . did you kill him? Did you kill mine?"

"No! No, that's not what happened. I respected your father. And things with the First are complicated. They—"

"He didn't just murder my father. It was a massacre. Over a hundred dead." The woman stepped closer, and Tylak raised his dagger free from its sheath.

The woman laughed. "If I wanted you dead, you would already be so. Earlier, before I came in here it looked like you were having a party. But this is the War Home, is it not? Who were those people?"

"The cabochons." Jura peeked around Tylak's shoulder. Neither he nor the woman had put away their weapons. She wriggled past Tylak. "They're the government officials for the country."

"This country has a ruling dictator."

Jura shook her head. "Not anymore, not for the last one hundred years or so. They have elected cabochons now, each for a different theology. It's actually qui—"

"I didn't come here for academics, I came for answers. Do you know who killed my father or not? And I warn you, if I find you are lying I will suck the water from your body and spill it on the desert sand."

Tylak growled low in his throat. Jura looked around the room, realizing for the first time that Peppik was nowhere to be seen. When had he snuck out?

"No," Jura said, surprised by how firmly her voice came out. "I don't know who killed your father or what provoked the attack. I only just learned of it, just moments ago. Does this . . . did you come here to claim war?"

"How can I not?" The woman visibly flinched, her hand moved up to her neck to touch something twisted around it, some sort of translucent necklace.

"Get in line," Tylak mumbled. Both women ignored him.

"I can understand why you want revenge," Jura started, unsure what to say next. She had desperately wanted to speak with the Sea King only to learn that she had been too late. This was her second chance.

"Then you won't stand in my way." The woman shoved her dagger back into her sheath with a sigh. "I came here for answers and to let the rulers of this insufferable country know that until my blade has been sated, I will destroy."

Jura swallowed against the intensity of the woman's gaze. It seemed the woman was not as cautious as her father. Jura needed to tread carefully, she needed this woman's help. "You're right. You do need answers. We both do. Someone here set this entire thing up. The attacks against my father and your father's . . . well, someone did it all with the intention of starting a war, *this* war, and now we have the opportunity to get in front of this and discover why. Together we can make them listen. We could redraft the Tri-Alliance, forge a new one even."

"Oh, no," the woman began shaking her head. "No. We're not getting involved with your breathcatcher politics. This is what got us into this mess in the first place."

"But the people of the sea—"

"*My* people. Mine." She stabbed a finger into her chest, and her lips curled up in a snarl. "Oh, I know all about your countries and our so-called mutual need for one another. This is a joke. You need us far more than we need you. My father never should have come here looking for aid. To think he asked your father when he himself knew how selfish he was, how incapable of feelings or leadership—"

"Enough." Jura's hand tightened over her whip on its own accord. She gritted her teeth in an effort to stop herself from trembling in anger. "My father may not be the best father, but he cares about me and he cares about his people, he—"

"His people?" The woman's voice had risen to a shrill octave that had Tylak wincing. "Your father cares *nothing* for his people. The only thing he cares about is power, only you're too stupid to see that. Take a look around. Haven't you noticed anything different here? Different than the Republic?" She shook her head and continued in a softer voice when Jura didn't answer.

"My father was a good man. A good leader. He tried to help the Republic, offered to double our water shipments or send a team to try and create an oasis, like we did for Kitoi." She laughed, the sound wild and high-pitched. "Your father refused."

No. Jura felt as if her body had turned into a pillar of sand, each grain fought desperately to hold onto the next. One wrong move would have her exploding into a billion tiny pieces. She swallowed, desperate for some breath to enter her lungs. No, she was wrong. This woman was wrong. Her father would never turn away water. Water was everything. It was life, it was currency, it was power . . . She shuddered against the awful truth and whispered the word out loud, but the woman was already wrapping her hair back under her colorful scarf, disgust written plainly on her face.

"It was stupid of me to come here, yes. But I do not regret this. It was . . . informative." She turned to Jura, her eyes were cold emeralds ablaze against her tan skin. "Stay out of my way, Daughter of the First. We are not allies, not anymore."

TYLAK

CHAPTER THIRTY

Can you believe her?" Jura slanted a look over at him, amber eyes widened in disbelief. She once again fell heavily against the dark leather chair. Her cheeks were stained red, but he was unsure if that was because of anger . . . or embarrassment.

"Is it true?" He whispered the words, fearing the answer, not wanting to hear it if she chose to speak. She didn't. She shook her head in response and he turned away. The implications of the Sea King's daughter were shocking. To think that the entire state of the Republic could be altered were it not for the greed of the First. And that's what it all came down to, wasn't it? The greed, the manipulations, it was to feed this man's power. Her father's. It was difficult to school his face back into the impassive glass mask of a Shadow Dancer, to repress his disgust. He reminded himself that she hadn't known, couldn't have known . . . could she?

"I didn't know," she whispered, pulling his thoughts from his head. "This could all be some lie, or part of the great game but . . . if it is true, I didn't know."

He turned back to face anguished amber eyes.

"I believe you, but Jura—"

"I know. It's a betrayal. Not just to me but to everyone. And the worst part is, it's not even hard to believe. It all somehow makes sense, you know? The ban on contraband from other countries. Why travel between our countries has always been discouraged."

"We need to do something about this. Once we get back to the Republic . . . Jura, you can't leave things like this. My mother died . . ." he trailed off, shaking his head.

Jura sighed. "That's just one more thing we'll have to deal with when we get back, and I don't even know where to start. I've already ruined things with the new Wave Master. They'll be no hope of repairing the Tri-Alliance."

"Wave Master?"

"Her Royal Highness, Daughter of the Sea King. It's what her people call the title, Wave Master, or in the case of a female, Mistress." She gestured helplessly in front of her. "I read it in this book." She scoffed. "More useless information. What does it matter what she would like to be called? The point is she's never talking to us again. Who can blame her?"

Tylak sighed, at a loss as to how to help her. She was right, of course. They would be hard-pressed to keep the Wave Mistress from murdering them in their sleep, much less change her mind into helping them.

"Then we'll do it without her."

"Without her? I don't even know if we can do it with her. Besides, I'm not giving up on her, not that easily. My great-grandfather's journal has sections filled with his diplomacy with the sea people. He trusted them, considered one, Ailani, to be one of his closest friends. But she and Josper and everyone else who crafted this alliance are long dead, and so will we if we can't get this fixed." She allowed her head to slump forward, it hit the smooth desk with a hollow thump. She brought her arms up to cover her head with a muted groan. "Maybe I'm too late. You heard the cabochons. We need to get back to the Republic as soon as possible. We need to find Amira and get back home to prepare for this war." It was hard to understand her because her words were muffled by her arms and the desk.

"So, we're back to the original plan. I'll go out—"

"We." Her head popped back up.

"We what?"

"*We'll* go out."

He couldn't help the corner of his mouth twitching in reply. "Fine, we'll go out and search the surrounding city for any clues on the underground trade. There's not much of the night left and you need some rest before tomorrow."

"I need to find a dressmaker tomorrow."

"I'm already fired as personal stylist?"

She grinned. "For the moment."

"As I was saying, the hours between now and dawn are few, so maybe it's best if we just stay in tonight and get our rest. You said yourself you have a busy day with the dressmaker."

Jura rolled her eyes. "I'm ordering a gown not a wardrobe. We're going."

"Excellent, you're ready," Peppik said, appearing in the doorway. "Which is good because now is the time to go." He was leaning casually against the doorframe. Somewhere along his escapade he'd acquired a long staff. He thumped it against the obsidian floor in a gentle rhythm.

"Time to go where?" Tylak was instantly suspicious. This

wasn't the first time the man appeared demanding Tylak accompany him to some oddly located destination simply to show him a misshaped tree.

"I went toward the docks. The men there speak of a Sharif. This Sharif, he is the one who purchased your friend."

"You found Amira?" Jura rose from the chair, stumbling forward when her skirts failed to move as smoothly as she did.

"Correction, Greatness. I found the man who originally purchased Amira. He has since sold her."

Tylak's heart clenched as her face crumpled. "Oh."

"But this man, Sharif, he will be telling us who he has sold her to. And I will take you to him."

Jura threw herself into the old man's arms, surprising them all. "Thank you! Thank you so much. This is it. Tylak, can you believe it?" She turned to him next, falling into his embrace with equal fervor. He wrapped his arms around her, pressing her close to his chest.

"It's certainly a step in the right direction."

"The right direction?" She leaned back to stare up at him but remained in his embrace, her fingers still interlaced behind his back.

"Tylak, this is a game changer. We have a lead. It's entirely possible we could bring her home. Tonight even. This is positively the best news I've had in weeks."

She looked so beautiful just then. Her eyes were shining, golden in the dim lighting of the study. Raven hair framed smooth tanned skin, and she just felt so perfect in his arms he couldn't help himself. He leaned down and brought his lips to hers.

JURA

CHAPTER THIRTY-ONE

She had not expected this. His lips were soft. Not mushy the way Beshar's had been. They were firm, gentle. She felt his hands slide up behind her neck and get caught in her hair. She had the distant thought that he would somehow muss her braid, but she pushed the thought away and pulled him closer.

A thousand butterflies tickled her skin. She felt brave and strong and beautiful. The kiss was so light, slow and sweet. It was perfect.

Too quickly he pulled away, his gray eyes wide.

"Jura—I'm sorry. That shouldn't have happened. It won't happen again." He practically shoved her out of his arms. She tumbled backward and turned her face away before he noticed her blush.

It won't happen again. His words echoed in her head. Had she been terrible at it? Did he hate the experience? What did that mean? She'd wanted it to happen, had hoped it would. Hadn't he seen that? Or had she gotten things terribly wrong? Maybe he didn't see her that way at all? Could kisses be accidents? She had certainly never accidentally kissed anyone before. Beshar didn't count.

She brought a finger up to her lips. They were still sensitive to the touch.

Peppik coughed into his arm. The moment should have been awkward, but she had never been so grateful for his presence.

"Well then, we should leave." She straightened her braid and resisted the urge to once again touch her lips. Tylak stared at her with an odd expression on his face. She turned her attention back to Peppik. "Lead the way. As Tylak said, the hour grows late."

As awe inspiring as the Golden City was during the day, it was even more so at night. Jura had read about it, the glowing streets, but seeing them was something else entirely. The stone cobbled streets were mixed with minerals that produced a phosphorescent effect. Charged by the heat of the sun during the day, the street cast a soft green glow that was strong enough to light up the city at night. There was no need for any fire pits.

The streets were quiet this late at night, the majority of the city finally asleep in those last few hours before dawn.

"This is the place. Come, Greatness. We will scout out your possible dress shop for tomorrow while Tylak gets some answers." He dipped his head, treating Jura to a glimpse of his shiny balding scalp. "This place, it's not fit for a lady."

Her lips pressed into a thin line and she stared down at her hands, which had clenched into fists at her side. When would they stop viewing her as a little girl? She might not be the most beautiful or all that desirable when it came to kissing, but she was smart and she was doing something. Had done many things to get to this point.

"No," Jura whispered. She deserved respect. "No," she repeated louder, "I don't think so. This is my friend and I'll not be escorted away like some child." She lifted her chin. "Besides, Tylak can make me invisible so no one even has to know I'm there. Wherever we're going, I can handle it."

Peppik muttered to himself, but Tylak nodded grimly. He ushered them across the street without wasting any more time. She stiffened when his palm pressed into the small of her back. He dropped his hand quickly, giving her back her space.

Jura took another healthy step away from him, allowing Peppik to wedge himself between the two of them. She studied the building, trying to understand just why Peppik had been so eager to keep her away. The building was small yet well lit, the street casting the building in an eerie green glow. The stone walls had no golden accents and less than a handful of colored gems etched into the stone. There was a peculiar smell coming from inside. It caused her nose to crinkle up and she saw Tylak scowl over at Peppik.

"Jura, it would make me feel better if you didn't come inside." Considering it was the first he'd spoken to her since he'd promised not to kiss her again, she bristled at the comment.

"You don't have a say in this. Peppik, get us inside."

She ignored the angry mutterings of both men as they made their way to the door. The sickly sweet smell grew increasingly stronger. Tylak turned himself and Jura invisible. They huddled close behind Peppik as he knocked on the door.

A tan, muscled man with a surly expression opened the door. He scoffed at Peppik's water chips and laughed at his gold, but when the older man produced a glass bottle containing an amber colored liquid the doorman finally allowed him access. Jura hurried behind the men. Inside, the odor was even stronger, a mixture of scents that were spicy like cinnamon, sweet like flowers. The air was as thick as fermented honey, and Jura could barely see or breathe through the hazy layer of smoke. Bodies littered the floor. The majority of the people in the room appeared to be asleep, save for a few who stood chatting around a long stone table.

"We better split up," Peppik said softly, an old man mumbling to his shoes. "We're looking for a man named Sharif. He is native to Kitoi and he is known for his good looks. Let's meet back here in two hours' time."

Peppik stumbled toward the group around the stone table. He was greeted with cheers when he produced another larger glass bottle filled with the same amber liquid.

"Is that . . . is that rum?" Jura's curiosity was enough to break her decision not to talk to Tylak until it was absolutely necessary.

"What's rum?" Tylak asked. Was it just her imagination or did he look relieved by her whispered question?

"An imported alcohol made by the people of the sea. They don't trade it with outsiders. Very hard to come by. I wonder how Peppik got hold of it?"

"Good question, but one you'll never get answered. I've given hope on unde—"

"You there!" A man stumbled forward, reaching for Tylak's arm. He wasn't wearing a stitch of clothing. Jura's eyes snapped to the ceiling.

"You can see me?" Tylak asked, incredulous.

"Of course I can see you, you're standing right there, aren't you?" His eyes widened as he caught sight of Jura standing just behind Tylak. "Hey, what a looker. Why'd you go and bring a pretty thing like that into a place like this? I like your hair." He reached forward but Jura stepped out of his reach. His meaty fist clutched at nothing but air. He whirled around, his bleary eyes stared right into Jura without truly seeing her.

"Hey, where did you go? Pretty lady? Scarface?" With an exaggerated shrug he sank down onto a nearby rug. Within moments he appeared to have fallen asleep.

Jura let out a nervous giggle. "What was that about? How did he see us?"

"I don't know," Tylak muttered, seemingly unsettled by the idea. "Just stay close. The sooner we get out of here, the better."

"Tylak, we need to start questioning people. We can't simply stand around hoping for some information to fall into our laps. These people are useless. They're all asleep. What's wrong with them anyway?"

"It's a *moipu* den," he sighed. "And you're right, unless we find someone early on or sober we won't be able to get anything out of these people. Chances are if Sharif is the type of man to frequent these places he won't be of much use to us either. Let's just finish looking around and get you out of here."

She frowned in response, scanning the room for the man Peppik described as "known for his looks." What did that even mean? If there was one thing she'd come to learn about attraction is that it was entirely subjective. She had been wildly attracted to Markhim, but then who wouldn't be? At the same time she couldn't deny the tug of attraction she felt toward Tylak, no matter his distaste for her, and he couldn't be more different than Markhim in looks.

Jura spotted a thin man in expensive robes. His dark hair had streaks of gray at the temple and it curled around a tanned face that sported a neatly trimmed mustache. He was handsome enough she supposed, if a bit old. He carried a long onyx box in one hand and a skin of water in the other. Nobody paid any attention to the water. It seemed the Republic truly was the only nation to worry over the worth of the life-giving substance.

"How about him?" She bit her bottom lip, considering. He seemed their best chance. Plus he was one of the only men still standing.

"Could be worth—Jura, wait!"

She darted forward, not caring that she lost her invisibility as she moved out of distance from Tylak's powers.

She stopped in front of the man. "Excuse me, sir."

"Be gone, I'm not into charity and I just . . . You don't look the sort." He narrowed his eyes at her. "Is this some sort of con? I won't give you not even a shot of my tobacco."

"Umm . . . I'm not interested in . . . I don't want any of . . . I just want some information."

The man cocked his head to the side, regarding her before he lowered himself down onto the same rug as the now unconscious naked man. He ignored the man beside him and opened his onyx box, withdrawing a long glass pipe.

"I had it made special in the Republic. Finest glass blowers in the world and just a short trip away." He eyed her suspiciously. "You have the look of someone from the Republic."

Jura sat down across from the man, careful not to allow any part of her dress to touch the naked man. "That's um, kind of you to say. I hoped I might trouble you for a moment of your time? Perhaps just ask you a few questions. Maybe you know someone by the name of Sharif—"

"Sharif? What would you want with him?" The man opened a small leather pouch and extracted some dried brown leaves. Jura recognized the earthy sweet smell as the same all around her. She drew her eyes back to his face. She had to work fast.

"I'm looking for a friend and Sharif knows where she is."

The man tsked, "Bury it, if Sharif knew about your friend she's long gone." He piled some of the leaves into the glass pipe and brought it up to his face.

"Please," Jura choked out. "I'm desperate."

"I knew it," the man chuckled. "You're all the same. Begging for another taste. Go away. Bother someone else for your next hit."

"Oh, I don't want a . . . hit. I've never even tried the stuff. I ju—"

"Never?" The man brought the pipe back down to his lap and stared up at her in wonder. "You've never even tried?" He laughed, a large guffaw that echoed across the silent room. "You must try it. Here, try it now," he said shoving the pipe forward, his lack of will to share forgotten. "You're going to love it."

Jura felt a sharp, sudden pressure on her shoulder. A warning squeeze from Tylak, invisible behind her.

"I couldn't. Thank you, but I truly just—"

"I am Sharif. You look for me because you have a missing friend, no? Smoke and I will tell you what you want to know."

Jura hesitated. She didn't wish to end up naked and unconscious on the rug, but she was willing to do whatever it took to find Amira. "Are you truly Sharif?" she asked, reaching for the pipe.

"Yes. I do not speak lies. Tell me of your friend but first inhale. Please, enjoy." He pushed the cool glass into her warm hands. The pipe was smooth, a myriad of blue, greens and gold twisted into the glass. She stared at it in her hands. What would it feel like? Would doing this cause her to end up like one of these poor souls? She sensed Tylak's presence behind her, could almost feel his disapproving glare. But she didn't care what he thought. No, more disparaging was the scene around her. Dozens of bodies littered the floor, each more destitute than the last. These had all been someone's mother, father, brother. Her roving eyes fell on one figure across the room. Something familiar pulled at her, forcing her to give the figure another glance. She could scarcely breathe as she rose to her feet to take a closer look, her hammering heart the only sound she could hear. A tall man stretched on his back, eyes languid and half closed as he reclined against several pillows. A tiny glass pipe lay forgotten in his hand. That perfect tan skin. The same lazy smile. It *was* him.

Markhim.

KAY

CHAPTER THIRTY-TWO

He'd broken his promise. Ash had promised to take her to the arena after practice, but instead he and Timber had left and not come back. There was still no sign of Akil. She'd waited for a bit, alone on the practice sands. She'd even gone through her Red Forms a bit to pass the time. When he still didn't return, she'd found Pyre. Not that she wanted to sit through a lesson, but Pyre always had snacks in his room and she was hungry. Ash usually brought her meals to her room, but he still wasn't around and Kay's belly could only wait so long. She only half listened to Pyre's lectures. He probably thought of himself as a great instructor, but the truth was he would never be as good as Kindle. A bolt of panic raced through her and she swallowed hard at the thought.

Why hadn't she realized this earlier? What if Ash was in trouble? He hadn't forgotten her at all but needed her help! What if Timber had forced him to fight? He liked to do that and he liked to show off. Kay knew that Ash could dance with fire, but he was old like Rumble. Ash was all she had left now. *I can't think of anyone because everyone is dead.*

Pyre was giving her a funny look. She blinked her eyes a few times so that no tears would drop. Her nose had even gotten a little runny.

"Are you . . ." For once, the Fire Dancer seemed at a loss for words.

"What's your name?" Kay asked, suddenly desperate to know.

"You know my name, Cadet. I am Pyre Fire Dancer.

"No," Kay slipped back into her mother tongue without realizing it. "No, what name were you born with. What's your true name?"

Pyre stiffened. "We do not speak of such things, Cadet." He snapped the words out in perfect Jangba, but Kay heard the trace of an accent in his anger. He didn't like to speak Drakori, despite the fact he was her tutor. But why? And why was it so wrong to hold on to one's name?

"My name is Kay," she said in Drakori and then repeated herself in Jangba. She stood up from where she'd been sitting cross-legged on the stone floor. "This lesson is finished."

Pyre didn't try to stop her. Akil would have been proud. She snatched her practice assegai from where it leaned in the doorway and made her grand exit, stomping her feet for good measure. She wanted to slam the door too, but Mama said it was impolite to slam doors in someone else's home. She settled on tossing her hair back with a flourish like she sometimes saw Mama do at Daddy. She pretended the fact that she would never see Mama do that again didn't bother her and started down the long stone hallway in search of Ash.

He would never approve of her walking alone through the halls. He'd told her numerous times: she must always have an escort. Ash was constantly talking to her, an endless soundtrack of rules and history on life in the arena. She probably learned more from his endless rambling than she would ever learn from Pyre. She frowned. If she was honest with herself, lessons with Pyre were helping too. She grasped the language well enough to understand, but the words still felt garbled and wrong coming out of her mouth. Well, she didn't have time to keep practicing. She needed to escape before she was sold, and before that she needed to find Ash and make sure he was okay. He was all she had left.

She reached Ash's room and entered without knocking even though she'd only been there once before. She braced for him to yell at her for barging in like she owned the place, but the room was empty and silent. She searched the room aimlessly, more out of boredom than anything else. There wasn't much to see. The room looked identical to the last time she'd entered. A cot in the corner, a table with two chairs, a fireplace, and . . . his assegai was missing from its place against the door. Ash had it with him. Ash barely ever carried his assegai. She wondered what made him do so now.

Kay hurried from the room, dragging her assegai on the stone floor behind her. She headed for what she hoped was the general direction of the arena proper. It wasn't her first time going, so she hoped she remembered the directions well enough. Daddy always said it was a good practice to watch where you were going when you went places so you could know how to get back. Daddy was full of good advice like that. If he was here, he would be able to tell her how to bust out in less time than it took Mama to roll out her dough.

Kay shook away the image of Mama making bread and concentrated on her surroundings. She turned right down the next hall, her tongue poking out in concentration. She could feel the various heat sources around her. The large one coming from what she assumed was the Everflame and the smaller dimmer ones from the various torches and fire pits. The people here very much enjoyed a good fire pit. It was an oddity. Sure, Mama used fire for cooking, but that fire was tiny and contained in her oven. The fire pits in the Republic seemed to be everywhere and hundreds of torches lined every wall. Actual torches, not to be confused with the Jangba translation of torch which could be both the object or Torch the person. Technically speaking, Kay was a Torch, but then so was Ash and any other Fire Dancer. Ash once explained that Torches were people like Fire Dancers who weren't strong enough for the arena. Still, it was odd that the arena even had Torches, especially considering nearly everyone who lived there was perfectly capable of providing their own fire source. Kay wrinkled her nose. It only cemented that the Republic was the strangest place. It seemed like they enjoyed making other people do stuff for them. Wasn't anyone capable of doing stuff on their own? Mama would be ashamed.

Kay shook her head to clear it. She shouldn't be thinking of how weird her current home was, she needed to concentrate on finding Ash. Why had he taken his assegai?

She continued forward, drawn to the separate large masses of heat. They called to her. She knew without a doubt that they were dragons. Three of them, if she was feeling correctly. She didn't often practice her power in this way. She Breathed in the fire from the nearest torch. It winked out and she felt goosebumps prickle against her skin. Yes, three dragons. The nearest didn't even feel that far away. She quickened her pace toward them, the realization that she had yet to run into anyone else dawning on her.

She was pressing her luck, Daddy would say. She didn't care. There was a possibility that Ash needed her. She sprinted forward, stopping to draw breath and smiling despite herself. She felt alive and almost happy. She Breathed in another torch, enjoying the sensation of simply holding the flames inside her. Her surroundings became familiar. She tucked her assegai under her arm to allow her to skip. She bounced down the end of the hall and turned right to the grand hall that led to the arena and was immediately knocked down.

She fell hard on her bottom, grunting from the sudden shock of pain up her spine.

Her assegai rolled down the hall in front of her and came to a stop under the toe of a woman dressed in a red robe. Kay looked up at the "wall" she had ran into. Not a wall at all but simply a large man dressed in identical red robes. Kay gasped. The people in red! They were the bosses of the arena.

"What are you doing about these halls, Cadet?" The giant man growled. Kay scrambled to her feet.

"Don't listen to him, child." The woman handed Kay her assegai and gave her a brilliant smile. "He's just a grumpy old man. Are you all right? You didn't injure yourself, did you?"

The woman's voice was crisp and clear like cold well water. She was as pretty as her Mama had been. Kay found herself smiling back. "No, I'm okay. I'm sorry I disobeyed rules. I was looking for Ash Fire Dancer." Kay stumbled over the words, somehow more worried over impressing this strange woman than she had ever been with Pyre.

The woman cocked her head to the side. "He's your trainer, isn't he? Do you like working with him?"

Kay nodded. "Ash is great. He's nice and he's really good at being a Fire Dancer. He's the greatest Fire Dancer this arena has ever known."

The woman laughed. "Well, I'm glad to hear it. It's a pleasure to meet you, Kay. I'm Karida." The woman held out her hand. Without thinking, Kay took it.

"You called me Kay."

The woman laughed again, the sound like music to Kay's ears. There was no laughter in the arena. Kay missed the sound. "That's your name, isn't it? You know, I'm so glad we got to meet in person. I've actually been hoping to run into you. Of course, it was you who ran quite literally into my friend here. Why were you looking for Ash down here?"

Kay became aware of the fact that her hand was still held by Karida's. The grip was gentle but the fingers were firm and tense. Kay was swept up in the urge to lie. Even though Mama and Daddy both agreed lying was wrong, they also said Kay should always follow her gut. At first, she had thought that meant to pay attention to when she was hungry but now she was old enough to realize what it truly meant. Sometimes your tummy could tell you when something was weird. When that happened, it was best to pay attention.

"It was a game," Kay decided to say. "A game of hide and seek." She tried to meet the woman's eyes but it was hard. Kay was almost certain the woman could tell she way lying.

"Interesting. And you believe he's hiding down here? You know, we close the arena after the night's matches. There's no reason for anyone to be out this way. And Ash Fire Dancer should have informed you that we do not allow cadets to roam the halls without proper aspect." Karida's eyes studied her carefully, but the tone of her voice was still soft and sweet. She dropped Kay's hand. "But if you think he is hiding down here then I will help you find him."

Kay gasped at the sudden eruption of fire down below. The

catacombs. There was a fourth dragon now, this one directly beneath her feet. But how had one gotten there so quickly, without her even noticing? She must have been distracted by Karida. The new dragon seemed agitated. Aside from the heat emanating from his body, Kay could feel the occasional spurt of fire as the dragon Breathed. She noticed that Karida studied her closely. She gave the woman her best smile, even going so far as to smile at the giant man beside her. It didn't appear that either of them were aware of the commotion down below. But how could they be? They weren't special like she was.

"You are right. Ash isn't down here. I will go look . . ." she trailed off, trying to remember the word.

"Don't you want my help?" Karida asked.

That was cheating, but Kay couldn't remember the word for that either. And it didn't matter because this was all a lie anyway.

"No, thank you. I go—"

"Ash." Karida's voice was startled. Her eyes were focused beyond Kay. The young girl whirled around and found Ash's panicked face.

The Fire Dancer was dressed in practice armor and still held a firm grip on his assegai. A line of sweat dotted his brow and his breathing was labored. It seemed he had cut his arm. It was covered in blood.

"Enjoying your game?" Karida arched an eyebrow and muttered something under her breath to her tall companion. She frowned when Ash failed to answer.

"I was just telling your cadet that the arena is no place for one in her position to attend without escort. Especially after the arena has closed for the evening."

"It was my idea to play," Kay blurted out. Where had Ash

been? She wanted to ask him but didn't dare say anything in front of the people in red because she didn't want to get him in trouble.

Karida gave her another smile. "Be that as it may, Ash knows better. And here he is, seeking when it was his turn to hide. Did you forget how to play, Fire Dancer?"

The woman's voice was different when she spoke to Ash. He seemed to notice it too. He sent Kay a quick glance, drawing a few ragged breaths before he finally found his voice. "She passed my hiding spot. I guess I panicked when I realized she was heading where she shouldn't be and I ran after her. I fell . . . I'm old you know, not as agile as I used to be."

He was lying. Not about his part in the game, of course that was a lie, but about the part that he fell. Unless he fell on a knife. The heat of the dragon still fizzled down below. Kay ignored it and focused on Karida.

The woman didn't seem like she believed him either, but she nodded just the same. "Well, I will let you escort your cadet back to her quarters where she belongs." She gave Kay one last brilliant smile. "I truly did enjoy meeting you. Perhaps we could speak again sometime?"

"I don't think that's a good idea," Ash answered before Kay could respond to the question. "The Ninth doesn't want her associating with anyone aside from myself and Pyre."

Karida bristled at the response but didn't press the issue. Moments later Ash was pressing the small of Kay's back and steering her in the direction of her room. She wanted to ask if that was true what the Ninth had said. She wanted to ask Ash what he had really been doing, and how a dragon could travel so quickly underground. Instead, she reminded Ash that she was hungry. With a grunt he took her to find some dinner.

CORAL

CHAPTER THIRTY-THREE

She roamed the streets with the odd glowing stones before she finally came to a rest at the docks. The ocean called to her and she almost gave in to it, but that would be foolish. She had a job to do here and now. She couldn't afford another impulsive outburst. Dawn was near. It was possible that Mano or Kale or both had already awoken in the night and found her missing. She repressed a yawn. She'd wasted her opportunity to rest and had spent the night on a wild goose chase. She'd been out of her mind with rage. The pained, final look on her father's face was engraved in her mind. She had stormed off on this manhunt, leaving behind the one man who could identify her father's killer. And the only clue she had found had been the Daughter of the First, the tiny timid thing. Coral could crush her with one hand, no *wei* necessary. Both her and her scar-faced companion. Likely they deserved to die, and she could have easily been jury and the executioner. *So why didn't you?*

"Pretty lady like you shouldn't be on the docks this time of night."

Coral smirked in response and tried to shoulder past the short man with bulging muscles. He was probably average height for the standard Kitoi, but he scarcely reached her eye level and had the audacity to ask for her purse.

He deserved to drown in his own fluid, but that seemed unnecessarily violent for a low level mugging. He didn't even have a weapon, just the cocky over-confidence of one who is used to getting his way from those he considers weak. Likely he found her weak because she was a woman. The insane ideals of this country knew no bounds. She would show him how wrong he was. She turned to face him head on, and her smirk melted into a sinister smile.

With practiced ease she dropped low, extending out her right leg and kicking at the unsuspecting man. He had expected her to drop her money and run. The sudden attack quite literally took him off balance. Coral shoved a knee into his chest and growled out that he was lucky she hadn't aimed farther south. She left him there, groaning by the docks and didn't look back. She had almost reached their campsite when she became aware of someone following her. She drew power from her necklace of water and unsheathed her dagger. There was no one in sight, yet she couldn't shake the feeling. Eyes followed her every moment, tracking invisible dots down her spine. It was nonsense to feel more fear now than she had when she had faced the mugger, but that had been different. This was the unknown. She shivered and quickened her pace. The street, earlier a vibrant emerald green, had lost some of its luster and begun to fade to muted shades of green and yellow. The gems would recharge with the sun. She would feel better under its light too.

"You're in quite the hurry."

The voice was high but whispery soft and seemed to come

from just behind her. She turned around and found no one. To calm her racing heart she began to count the various ways she could kill someone with just her dagger.

"Easy, Mistress. I did not come to fight." A woman stepped forward. She was dressed entirely in black, her dress cut much the way the Daughter of the First's had been, but her face was covered by a gold filigree mask. "Do you know who I am?"

The woman stepped closer. She had no weapon visible but it was clear she knew how to use one. One could see it in the practiced way she took her steps, in the way her eyes followed the dagger in Coral's hand.

"Should I?"

The woman smiled, her plump lips and square chin her only visible features. "No, I don't suppose you should. I am known as the Queen of Shadows."

Coral took in the regal way the woman held her head, at the air of authority around her shoulders. Yes, this woman was a leader, someone who was accustomed to giving orders and expected to see results. "I'd rather be a queen of men, shadows can't carry weapons."

"Well said." The woman's smile deepened. "You can put that away. I won't hurt you. I understand if you don't trust me, but if I step out of line I assume your *wei* is more than enough to dispatch a woman over twice your age?" She chuckled at her own words but didn't make a move to say anything else.

Coral sighed. Drown her sodden curiosity. "What do you want?"

"Only to introduce myself. Perhaps we can be friends. I can be very helpful to my friends." Though Coral couldn't see the woman's eyes, she could feel the intensity of their stare, burning into her skin.

She scratched at her neck, grateful when her hand brushed water. There was something instantly off about this offer, aside from the fact that the woman had appeared out of nowhere and called herself the Queen of Shadows. Once again Coral wished she hadn't strayed from the Kombu left at her campsite. If only she had taken her soldiers with her, or better yet was still asleep and cozy at the camp site instead of experiencing this emotional night.

"I have enough friends." Best to let this so-called Queen know up front that she had no intention of—

The woman tsked. "Don't be ridiculous. One can never have enough friends. And I can help you. You're looking for the man who killed your father, aren't you? I can give him to you. His name is Vex, and I know where to find him."

Coral stiffened. She could be lying. Or she could be Coral's path to finding revenge. She sheathed her dagger and crossed her arms over her chest to keep her hands from shaking with excitement.

"Go on."

The Queen of Shadows smiled again, delighting in her game. Coral resisted the urge to tap her foot.

"In my culture we offer an Exchange of Information. Quite simply, I ask a question and receive an answer. Then I return the favor until all questions are answered and information is gained."

Coral licked her lips, feeling impossibly dry in this long stretch of land. "What if I don't want to answer a question?"

"Then the game is complete and you are free to carry on with your night. Don't worry, that first bit of information about your father's killer was free, a gift between friends. And I do hope we can remain friends after this. Oh, and one more thing, after the Exchange there is a twenty-four hour grace period in which both parties agree not to befall harm on the other. An insurance policy if you will, for any information one might find too . . . disconcerting. Do we have an agreement?"

"If I were to say no?"

"Then I would step aside and let you get back to those delicious sleeping men of yours."

Coral masked the desire to blush beneath her scowl. She was an idiot if she agreed to such lunacy.

"It's a deal." She spit into her hand.

"How . . . interesting." The Queen spit into her own hand and the two shook.

"So, how does this work?"

"As I offered the Exchange it begins when I ask the first question."

"Oh." Coral took another anxious look around. They were just outside the city proper in that awkward stretch of land that was far enough inland it was no longer considered part of the ports yet still outside the safety of the city moat. It wouldn't be long before the early morning sky dissolved into a myriad of orange, pink, and yellow. If she could just get through this exchange.

"Did you speak to the Daughter of the First?"

The question surprised her. Coral wasn't entirely sure what she had expected but it wasn't this. How was that tiny thing mixed up with the lot of some shadow queen? She was so lost in her own thoughts she was prompted to answer when the queen gently cleared her throat.

"I did." Was that enough of an answer? Did she have to say more? "It was the first time we met." She snapped her mouth shut to stop herself from spilling out more and gave a quick thought over what to ask first.

"Where can I find Vex?" If she learned nothing else . . .

"Not far from here, I would imagine. Although it's hard to say exactly where as I haven't got any eyes on him currently."

Coral swallowed. So that was how the game was played. That wasn't much of an answer at all.

"What are her plans?" the queen asked.

Coral could only assume she meant the Daughter of the First. Why did she find her so interesting?

"She argued for peace. But she is a naive child. There can never be peace, not now." Coral gritted her teeth. "How can you be sure Vex is truly the one who killed my father? You weren't even there."

"If you're asking if I heard his confession, then yes, I know many of the gory details. Who was with her?"

"There didn't seem to be too many. A small house staff, maybe. A single scarred bodyguard." Would every question be about the Daughter of the First? "Do you . . . do you know why my people were attacked?"

"Yes." There was a long pause and Coral feared the woman wouldn't continue when she said, "It was to start this very war. Your father was a tool." She seemed to remember who she was speaking to and her head cocked to the side. "I'm sorry for your loss," the queen said, mask shining in the dim light of the moon. "Did she speak of anything specific? Mention any name?"

"That's two questions."

The Queen smiled. "Did she mention any specific names?"

"No," Coral answered quickly and then searched her memory, drudging up their unpleasant conversation. "No, we mostly spoke of her father. You said my own father was the spark with which someone ignited a war that will span the entire continent. Why?"

"Interesting. I had thought you would ask another question after your father's killer." The Queen tapped the fingers of her right hand against her hip, seemingly lost in thought.

"Very well." Her fingers stopped. "Things are unstable here. The city's population is steadily growing but there simply isn't the land available to support its expansion. Not without encroaching on the Republic's borders. Your father's demise is but one event that will lead to war. The cabochons will argue this war was started by the First himself. The man's always been power hungry. It's plausible he is unhappy with the current situation and wants to make a play for more power with force. I don't believe that to be true. I have sources that report the First is not himself. I'm surprised you haven't got your own sources. You're ill prepared, Mistress."

Coral blinked at the sudden onslaught of information. The woman was certainly forthcoming enough with information that wasn't directly related to finding her own father's killer. The Queen was most likely playing her, stringing her along with half-truths. She should take the name and be happy.

Unprovoked, the Queen once again repeated her question. "Her idea of peace? What did it involve?"

"I didn't give her much time to propose it. We're not allies and I told her as such." It was now or never.

"Where does Vex live?"

"At the time of your father's death? With his master. Who can say where he is now? Although I have my guesses. Do you believe that is truly why the Daughter of the First is here? To argue for peace?" The Queen of Shadows sounded amused.

"As that is a question, I can only assume you want my subjective answer. I'm going to say . . . yes. And further I don't care of her plans because they don't involve me. My interest is in finding my father's killer, this man Vex and his master, so I can see that they are both destroyed. Now you owe me an answer, and I demand a straight one. Who is his master?"

"Me."

Coral lunged for her but the woman disappeared, simply gone in the blink of an eye.

BESHAR

CHAPTER THIRTY-FOUR

eshar had only woken before dawn once before. It was an odd experience. He watched the sun slowly rise, casting pale pink and golden yellow in from his glass ceiling. He left the stone walls of his private chamber to watch the rest of the sun rise from the glass halls. He could have left his rooms and watched from outside, but that meant rousing his men and he was loathe to bother them during prayer. It was the only thing they asked of him. The halls were empty and blessedly quiet. He was nursing yet another hangover, a common occurrence these days. He hadn't liked delivering the news, but he had promised Timber he would be upfront about his decision. It was the least he deserved. In any case, it wasn't as if the man would never see his son again. He'd simply changed hands. There had been no reason for the dramatics.

Beshar sighed. Who was he fooling? Of course there would be dramatics. The man's son was being torn from his home. It didn't matter that he had merely sold him to the arena, the point was that he had sold him at all. He was changing. Beshar would never admit it out loud, but it seemed he was now capable of feeling remorse and it was dreadful. He was spending more and more time in the bottle. And it was no wonder, not when he had so much to feel guilty about. He grunted, noticing a lone figure heading toward him. He squinted his eyes, trying to make out features and groaned when he realized it was the Fourth. It was entirely too early to deal with Denir. He considered ducking back into his private rooms and locking the door, but that would get him nowhere. He sighed and waited for her arrival.

Today she wore a golden shade of yellow. The silken fabric shone like melted sunshine in the early morning light.

"I would say good morning," he began.

"There's nothing good about it." She folded her arms across her chest. "You stole my dragon."

"Come again?" He should have ran back inside his home when he had the chance.

"My dragon? I only just bought him. You knew that. I told you seconds after I acquired him. And now I hear that he was *given* to you instead? Sight unseen?"

"Does it matter that I haven't seen him? What's so special about this dragon anyway?" When she didn't immediately respond, he narrowed his eyes in suspicion. "Have you even seen him or are you simply upset I was gifted him right from under you?"

Denir bristled under his stare. "I'm upset because he was supposed to be mine."

"Is this a matter of your refund?" That wouldn't be a surprise. With Denir, it was always about money. "Or does this have to do with your more unsavory connections?"

She narrowed her eyes. "I'm sure I have no idea what you're talking about," she said loudly. "Listen, I just want to know why. Why did the arena choose to give him to you? What hold do you have over them?"

He couldn't stop the laughter from bubbling up, and he choked it back with a sudden fit of coughing. "I've got a hold on the arena? That's the most absurd thing I've ever heard. More like they've got a hold on me. These monthly dues are getting outrageous. And did you notice the spike in dragon entry fees?" She scowled at him until he continued with a sigh. "We made a deal and the arena was simply returning the favor. I've a reputation for gaining favors, you know."

"I know. Which is why I want to know what you're not telling me."

"I'm sure I have no idea what you're talking about," he threw her words back at her.

Her lips twitched, the hint of a smile showing. "I thought you were ignorant in the players of this game."

"I'm learning fast." Beshar wished he could wipe at his face with his handkerchief, but he knew the familiar tell would notify Denir of his nervousness.

It was Denir's turn to chuckle. "You can't pretend with me anymore. I'm making moves. You had best choose your path carefully. This is no threat, Beshar. Simply a warning between friends. I like you, despite what you must think." She dared a quick glance around. "We know of Jura's location and of her plans. I know far more than you think, Beshar. The only thing I've yet to figure out is your own role in this. Are you truly this remarkable an actor or have you truly no idea what happens in the arena?"

"Can't I be both?"

"Do yourself a favor and just stay out of this." She dropped her voice to a whisper, despite the fact the glass halls were still empty. "You're lucky there's no proof you're behind the death of her prince. Consider your role in the game finished. My dragon can be your consolation prize. I can find peace in that. Simply put, Beshar, stay out of my way."

"If you know everything then you know there's no reason to enter this war. You know about the First and . . . the *alttaw'am*." He muttered the last bit, casting another wary look down the halls. The glass halls were brilliantly lit as dawn faded into early morning. It wouldn't be long before the residents of the palace were all out of their homes and about their day.

"Your point?" Her normally lilting voice had taken on a rough edge as she spat out the words between clenched teeth.

There was no reason to stall for time. "Why? What are you getting out of this?"

"One less dragon it would seem," she sighed. "Prosperity. Money. More water and gold than I know what to do with. Do I need more reasons or is that enough for you? Look, now is your chance to pick the right side, the winning side. Jura is being taken care of. You should worry about yourself. All the pieces are falling into place and it's only a matter of time before everything changes. You've already seen how rewarding life can be when you don't cause any sandstorms. Do yourself a favor and today at the meeting vote in favor of Ishani's proposition." With those final words she brushed past him. Beshar could only watch her leave.

Denir's words resonated with him the rest of the morning. How did the Shadow Dancers fit into all of this? Did they somehow own the arena or have some sort of agreement with them? What did they have to gain? Certainly not money. It was rumored the Shadow Dancers had deep pockets that were kept lined by industrious thieves. Certainly not for any notoriety. The arena could offer fame to those who sought it but the very name Shadow Dancer gave credence to their invisibility. Power then. The Arena Council arguably had more power than the Thirteen, given the situation of course. So what did this all mean?

He hadn't realized he'd stumbled back inside and onto his chaise lounge until Kenjiro stood in front of him offering a delectable smelling breakfast, no doubt crafted seconds before by his chef, Yemekk. He attempted his hand at breakfast, fried strips of *ipga* meat and eggs, but after a few bites he pushed the plate away. He had lost his appetite, yet another piece of himself.

"You are troubled." Kenjiro's eyes, so dark a shade of brown they often appeared black, stared into his own.

"There's been no contact from her or the twins." Beshar said the words out loud though he wasn't sharing any new information. Any word sent to Beshar would first go through Kenjiro. Instead of a reply, the man took the plate from Beshar's hands and set it on his desk. He came to a seat beside the Ninth.

"I had thought the twins would send word when they arrived," Beshar continued as Kenjiro remained silent. "Maybe my part in the game really is over. There are too many secrets now."

"They are alive," Kenjiro replied solemnly.

Beshar almost smiled in response. Kenjiro was a man of few words, yet he somehow always knew what to say. Beshar allowed himself another moment of companionable silence before he pushed himself to his feet to prepare for the meeting. A message had been waiting for him when he'd arrived home last night. A simple piece of paper stating a council meeting was to be held the following morning. The wax seal was that of the First. Another lie. He sighed and dressed in his typical dark robes. His sleeves were long, similar to the style in Kitoi, but shortened considerably in an effort to fit in with the shorter style of the Republic. As was his habit, he turned for

Kenjiro to inspect and straighten before he had the men escort him to the justice dome. He nodded at Kenjiro one last time before leaving his men just outside the heavy twin doors.

Despite his best effort otherwise, Velder was one of the last council members to arrive. That was yet another worrisome topic. Beshar found himself more and more distracted as of late, he found he had to concentrate harder than usual to push aside Velder's complaints as he forced the man to hurry along for the council meeting. Years ago this had all been part of the fun, something to keep himself from fidgeting, a mental puzzle to occupy his free time. Now, Velder and the blood chain seemed like nothing but work. He called harder, a thin line of sweat dotting his upper lip when the tall man finally appeared. Velder took his spot to the right of the glass throne and stroked his thin gray mustache while Beshar breathed deeply. He noticed Denir's eyes on him. When he met her gaze, she raised her eyebrow and then looked toward Ishani. She was reminding him to vote in favor of the Thirteenth's proposition, whatever that was. He wondered why it should even matter when the majority vote already allied with the *alttaw'am.* Once everyone was seated he tugged at his invisible leash and had Velder call the meeting to order.

"I've called this meeting to discuss updates on the upcoming war," Justir started. The First was a handsome man, with a strong jawline and intense dark eyes. He too wore long sleeves, as did a few others. Beshar could assume the others were not hiding the fact they wore a blood chain, but one couldn't be too sure. Ishani, surprisingly, had bare sleeves, and her fabric was fashioned in the style of the Republic, tight waisted and loose at the ankles. Beshar forced Velder to nod along with everyone else and struggled to focus.

"I've received a missive that my daughter has arrived safely in Kitoi. Now that we have confirmed her whereabouts, it is safe for me to tell you the truth. The Daughter of the First never disappeared or ran away. I was aware of her location at all times. In fact, it was I who sent her away."

The room fell into excited murmurs and Beshar straightened. Denir caught his eye and winked.

"As you all know, the attack on my life from that of the Sea King called for an immediate retaliation. You probably also know that any act from that moment forward was to be considered an act of war. What you don't know is that I sent my daughter ahead. Jura is in Kitoi as we speak. She has taken up residence in the War Home and even now rallies for our cause. The Sea King is dead and when the Daughter of the First arrives home she shall be greeted as a hero."

What was the purpose of such a lie? Had something happened to her? A picture of Jura enslaved by a blood chain invaded his thoughts. He blinked the images away. Perhaps it was for the best that he step away from the game. Quit while he was ahead, so to speak. Velder's cries echoed in his mind, begging for release, for death even. Strange, he had learned to tune those cries out years ago. Why did he hear them now? Beshar thought for a moment that he was going to be sick. He gripped the edge of the heavy stone table until the wave of nausea passed.

"Now I give the floor to the Thirteenth, who has a proposition she would like us to hear out." The First inclined his head toward the last chair of the stone table.

Ishani stood up with a shy smile and cleared her throat a few times before saying, "A true alliance."

Velder mimicked Beshar as he leaned forward in interest.

"It is true, the Tri-Alliance has failed us. In its time it was a fine document, crafted by the greatest hero this Republic has ever known." She smiled over at the First in his glass throne. "But times have changed since then. The Republic has evolved and so should its relationships." Gaining confidence she walked around to the front of the table to pace its length as she talked. "What is your most precious resource? Come on, don't be shy, you can interrupt m—"

"Water," Denir purred. She rearranged her ebony locks so that they fell artfully over one shoulder.

"That's right. Water. But what if I were to tell you that we can change all that? That we can make this one precious commodity as easily accessible as the snap of your fingers?" Ishani demonstrated by snapping her own fingertips.

"I say sign me up." The Third smiled and Beshar once again shuddered at the eerie similarity between this creature and the real Amira.

A few of the Thirteen chuckled in response.

"Well, a world such as the one I describe is possible. We already use slaves as Torches and Fire Dancers."

"The slaves are the chosen people," Fatima began, but Ishani continued on as though she hadn't heard her.

"Why shouldn't water be just as accessible to us? Why not open up slave trade to other countries? Open up to the possibility of every resource being nothing more than a simple command away? And it's all possible with just a simple vote. Who here has traveled to Kitoi?" Ishani stopped her pacing just in front of Beshar. Though it seemed the question was directed at him, he gave no immediate response.

Beshar tugged at Velder until the man said, "It is prohibited to travel to Kitoi without the proper license and only merchants are permitted for trade travel."

"Interesting point." The Third nodded.

"Archaic rules invented by my grandfather," the First added. "Which can be addressed later. Do carry on Ishani while you still have our attention. You spoke of a new alliance?"

Ishani seemed to bristle under the direct order. "Yes, well. As I was saying, if any of you should be so fortunate as to visit my home you would see that while we live beside you in this dry and scorched land we do not thirst for water. Kitoi is the solution to all your problems. Don't you see? With the Sea King's death and the Tri-Alliance broken, we can provide you with the water rations you'll need. All we ask for in exchange is a new alliance, a stronger alliance, one forged by marriage."

Beshar clenched his teeth to keep his jaw from falling open. Surely she wasn't proposing marriage to the First? Was this their plan then? Forcing the First into a marriage and this country into a war?

"Ishani," the Third stood up, and though her voice still dripped honey, her chocolate eyes were thin narrow slits glaring at the Thirteenth. "Perhaps you overstep your bounds. In the Republic, a lady *never* proposes to a man, and certainly not to the First."

Ishani paled. "Yes, of course, my lady Third. I was simply acting in capacity as ambassador and the proposal is not my own." She darted another quick glance at the First. "My uncle, you see. It seems he was quite taken with Jura. And as one of the leading cabochons of Kitoi, he thought a betrothal woul . . ."

Her words were replaced by an odd buzzing in Beshar's ears. How did anyone stop this? He swallowed several times, forcing himself to follow what was happening. The First was speaking once again.

"An excellent suggestion. Of course I should like to meet this man later." The First smiled. "Matters such as these will be further discussed in private. In the meantime, we will put your proposition to a vote."

Beshar didn't know which matter to address first. This entire meeting was lunacy. First to lie about Jura and her motives, and then they were carrying on, hinting that she was behind the Sea King's murder and planning her future to the foreign ambassador's father. And now to put to vote this proposition, as she called it. With scarcely any explanation at all and just the empty promise of easily accessible water? He couldn't stand for it.

Beshar cleared his throat. "Some clarification, if you would? Exactly what proposition are we voting on? Your daughter's betrothal to some unknown cabochon or for permission to pillage Is'Le'Spar islands for water people to enslave?" Denir sent him a warning glance and he bit his tongue.

"Be at ease, councilman. The matter is only being put to vote. Though I for one can't imagine one such as you voting against anything that would make your life easier." The Third giggled and then turned her attention back to the First. "Shall we vote?"

The majority of the Thirteen began knocking the table. Beshar knocked too when Denir continued to glare at him, but he forced Velder to clasp his hands behind his back, indicating that he not only did not vote but he strongly disagreed with the majority.

It wasn't enough.

Ishani smiled down the length of the table. Beshar ground his teeth to keep from further fidgeting. The meeting was almost over, and Everflame help him he couldn't get out of there a moment faster.

"If there are no other matters, this meeting is called to a close." Velder unclasped his hands to stroke his thin mustache.

"Not quite." The Third stood up, Amira's face scanning the room and smiling at each in turn. "There was something else, actually. A small concern, if you will, and one that can easily be put to rest. Ishani, earlier you asked if any of us had visited Kitoi. The Second was quick to remind us that the majority of the Thirteen have no reason for such a trip and the Republic does not allow for idle travel, but that doesn't mean that people from the Republic are not frequent visitors. My father, for instance." The Third smiled. "Ahmar was quite the merchant. He came from generations of merchants and he traveled to Kitoi at least twice a year. In fact, I was allowed to accompany him on his last trip. You remember that, of course, Councilman Velder?" Although the Second stood off to the right of the Third, her eyes met and held Beshar's as though she asked him the question.

"I was aware of your travels," Beshar tugged at Velder to murmur.

"And you as well, Councilman Beshar? You have also traveled to Kitoi, have you not?"

Beshar tensed at her question. It seemed he had entered a private game with the Third, only this time he knew none of the rules. "I have." He looked at either side of the table and the Thirteen's varying states of interest. Fatima appeared bored. Ledair concerned. Denir was rapt with attention.

Beshar told himself to remain calm. She didn't know anything. And even if she did, he knew enough of her secrets to bring this entire scam down with him.

"Isn't clothing interesting, Ishani? You seem to have dressed yourself in the style of the Republic, and yet here I thought the trend now was to favor the billowing sleeves of Kitoi. I noticed everyone there had sleeves that covered even their fingertips. Did you notice that in your travels, Beshar? You must have because your own sleeves seem to mimic that style."

"Do get to your point," Velder said. Beshar tried to get Velder to sound bored and unconcerned.

"The point, Councilman, is that I don't trust you." She turned from Velder back to Beshar. "Either of you. And I have a sneaking suspicion why." The Third flung an accusing finger toward Velder. "They're working together. I noticed it at the last meeting when Beshar cast his vote but didn't voice his opinion. Show us your wrists, Velder."

Beshar's blood turned to ice. No, she wouldn't. Not when she herself also wore a master blood chain. She had to know that outing him meant outing herself.

"I'll do no such thing," Velder said. Beshar didn't have to try very hard to get Velder's voice to shake with anger. It was everything he could do to keep from trembling.

"Greatness, surely you can see such a claim is ridiculous." Beshar finally spoke up. He inclined his head toward the First, hoping the *alttaw'am* and her group would be leery of creating an unnecessary public scene.

"A foolish claim, yes. And one that is quickly put to ease if you will but show us your wrists."

Beshar hesitated, weighing his options. If he continued to refuse they would make him, of course. But the focus was currently on Velder, and that gave him an opportunity for escape. His men were just outside the double doors. They still didn't know which of the two wore the master chain. There was still a chance.

"Then show us yours." The words seemed to escape on their

own accord, but Beshar straightened up after he said them, meeting the intense stare of the First.

"I would watch your words carefully, Ninth of the Thirteen. You make a dangerous claim," the Third warned.

Denir's eyes widened and she gave a quick shake to her head as if in disbelief.

"No less dangerous than the claim made by you." Velder's thoughts screeched in his mind and Beshar shoved the voice away, sweat breaking out across his brow. "Make your claims clearly. You speak of blood chains."

To her credit, Denir gasped, as did several other members of the Thirteen. The Third was unfazed.

The First held up a steady hand, calling for silence. Then, with a casual slowness he lifted each sleeve of his robe, baring first one naked wrist and then the other. The First no longer wore his blood chain.

No, Beshar thought. *How could this be?* He had thought the First would be bullied, that he and the master of his blood chain would prevent this scenario from ever happening. But they had called his bluff. And survived.

The Third's smile was triumphant as she jerked her chin toward Beshar. "Go on then, he's shown you his."

If he did that his life was over. Everflame take him it was over the moment he'd stepped into this cursed hall. He could call for his men, run for the double doors. Kenjiro would fight for him, but there were dozens of men in assembled *Arbe.* It would be a bloodbath.

Someone screamed, probably Fatima, when he exposed the gold and silver chain at his wrist. It all began to happen so quickly. The First called for his arrest, denouncing his Rank and stripping him of all assets. Beshar listened to the words without really hearing them. He needed his handkerchief and his chaise lounge. Kenjiro needed to bring him a glass of wine.

Strong arms grabbed him on either side, forced him to remove the master blood chain from his wrist. He was shoved to his feet and he stumbled forward, noting in some distant part of him that they were not heading in the direction of his rooms.

This wasn't happening. He was one of the Thirteen. He would always be one of the Thirteen. All too quickly he was pushed down a long stone hallway and into a dark stone room. This is wrong, he wanted to shout at them, but his tongue felt too large for his mouth and his body was a traitor that could only stumble and cry in the darkness.

CORAL

CHAPTER THIRTY-FIVE

The sun had just begun to appear in the horizon by the time Coral made it back to their campsite. The men were awake, Kale pacing and Mano frantically stuffing his pack when she arrived.

"There you are! What were you thinking? Leaving like that without telling anyone? We were about to tear the city apart looking for you . . . what's wrong?" Kale stopped mid-stride, his outstretched arms falling to his sides. "What's happened?"

"I met her." The whimpered words that fell from her mouth were not her own. Coral swallowed several times, pulling the necklace of water from her throat to shape the water in her hands. She gave herself into the simple motion of the water, mimicking the movement of waves. Kale didn't press for more answers, he simply closed the distance between them. His arms wrapped around her, pulling her closer and holding her tight. The furious swell of emotions within her calmed somewhat in his familiar embrace and she became dimly aware of the fact that he wasn't wearing a shirt. His warm skin burned into her own.

Mano cleared his throat and the two broke apart.

"Is there something I'm missing?" he asked.

"No! Nothing." Coral was too angry to blush. She stepped back, wiping at the tears she hadn't known had been flowing. "She's here. This woman, *the* woman behind it all. She ordered the massacre she . . . killed my parents."

She told them everything, her encounter with the Daughter of the First, the woman's insane ideas for peace, and the threat from the Queen of Shadows. Mano studied her quietly while shooting glares at Kale.

"It seems like the Queen of Shadows was only interested in the Daughter of the First. Why do you suppose that is?" He bent down to pack away the last of their items.

"I've been asking myself that same question." Coral muttered, squatting down beside him. She opened herself up to her *wei*, calling on the water she felt hundreds of feet below ground. It took a few minutes, and then it was only a matter of removing the salt, sand, and various other unwanted minerals from the pure water. She drank deeply from the floating orb, offering some to Mano and then Kale (who politely declined after another glare from Mano) before she fashioned another necklace of water around her skin. As usual, her close contact with the element gave her a sense of peace.

"I believe I underestimated the Daughter of the First. She certainly warrants another visit." She voiced her latest thought out loud.

Kale grunted as he lifted the stuffed pack onto his shoulders. At least he'd finally put some clothes on. Sodden man. No wonder Mano scowled at him so.

"Agreed. I'd like to find out why this Queen of Shadows is so interested in what you described as . . . what was it? A miniature woman-child with as much backbone as a jellyfish?"

Coral grinned in response to Kale's imitation of her. "Something like that. She must have a spine in their somewhere." She paused. She wouldn't admit it, but having Kale along for company was the best thing that could have happened. He always seemed to know how to calm her, yet he quickly forgave any moments when she succumbed to fits of passion. "Thank you. For coming with me. Both of you." She smiled, turning back toward Mano. He smiled back, but it didn't quite reach his eyes. He had a right to feel threatened by Kale. She felt more amicable toward him than she did her betrothed, and surely Mano sensed that.

"Mano," she placed a hesitant hand on his shoulder. " Can we talk?" She sent a meaningful glance toward Kale but he was already ambling off toward the city.

"Is there something between you and Kale?" he blurted.

Coral crossed her arms over her chest, tensing for the upcoming argument. "No. And I won't say it again but," she paused, searching for the right words, "I don't think there is anything between us either."

"Coral . . . this is what your father wanted."

"And now he's gone. And what matters is what I want and . . . well, maybe I don't know exactly what that is right now but I do know this. I don't need a husband. What I need are soldiers, men and women honor bound to me and our people. What I need is a friend. And that's what I want for us. What I want from you. Can you accept that, Mano? Can we be friends?"

His eyes searched hers for a long moment. He was handsome, would probably make some future woman's heartbeat flicker. But not hers. In that moment, all she felt was relief.

"Coral I—of course. Of course, we're friends. And, as a friend I have to say I'm glad you found out what you did. A name, a face behind it all . . . but why? Why would you do something so incredibly irresponsible?"

His words shoved a rod down the length of her spine, and she lifted her chin to glare at him. "You just said you're glad I found out the information."

"And I am. But that doesn't make it any less stupid. You could have been hurt."

"That's a price I'm willing to pay."

"Your life is not your own to give!"

"Oh? And it's yours?" Coral shoved a fist into either hip and clenched her jaw in order to prevent herself from spitting on him or saying something she would be quick to regret. Just when they had been getting along so nicely too. The nerve of him. Just because they had always had a casual, *casual* betrothal was no reason for the man to start viewing her as a possession.

"In a way it is. It's also Kale's." He hurried on when she all but snarled at him. "It's also Ailani's, Konane's, and Ira's. All of us. You are our Wave Mistress. Your life belongs to your people. Your life can't be easily thrown away." He sighed and turned back toward her, allowing the large pack to once again fall into the dirt as he placed a hand on either of her shoulders. "I'm begging you, Coral, please don't do something like that again. The people need you." He fixed her with one of his intense stares. "Besides," he grinned, dropping his hands and reaching down once again for his pack. "It was a foolish move running off to execute someone you've never seen before."

It felt good to laugh at herself. "It was foolish but I still learned something."

"Are we back to liking one another?" Mano asked.

Coral snorted. "For the moment." She called ahead for Kale to wait for them. When the trio reunited, she implored him to describe the man the Queen of Shadows had named as her father's killer. The man called Vex.

Kale scratched at his head in recollection, his fingers finding the shock of white. "He had the tanned skin of one of the Republic. Tall if a native to that land. Dark curling hair. His skill with his sword and axe was . . . impressive. No distinguishing marks. He sustained some injuries but . . . he'll be difficult to find, Coral."

Coral nodded. She had known it wouldn't be easy, but she wouldn't stop until her father's trishula once again tasted the blood of his enemy. They would find him, she was sure of it, if they had to tear this city apart in her search. A part of her had secretly hoped Jura was lying, that Kale would describe her scarred companion and Coral would have a reason to destroy them all. The woman's talk of peace was laughable. Was she really so naive as to believe such a thing was possible? After all her people were responsible for? She allowed herself to get lost in thoughts of revenge, and it wasn't long before she found herself back in the depths of the Golden City. It was different during the light of day. The city streets glowed golden in the sunlight, each building covered in any assortment of sparkling jewels. She shoved her curls further back under the silken fabric and hunched her shoulders as they hurried past the main city square.

Mano seemed to have an inadvertent sense of direction for this sort of thing. He directed them down yet another side alley before stopping at what appeared to be a dead end.

Coral suppressed the urge to crack a grin. And just when she had been giving him such credit. The stone wall was tall and wide. She made a move to turn away, but Mano stopped her with a gentle tug on her hand. She looked down at their joined hands, and he released her with a sheepish grin.

"Try knocking three times," Kale offered, surprising her.

Mano thumped the stone wall three times. Seconds later the ground began to vibrate and hum. The stone wall seemed to fold away from itself and stairs carved themselves into the ground before them.

Coral couldn't stop her jaw from hanging open in surprise.

"How did you know to knock three times?" she breathed out, still staring in wonder.

"I read about it," Kale answered.

Mano pulled her down the stairs before she could ask any more questions. The stairs led to what appeared to be an underground storeroom. There were a few scattered tables, most displaying illegal glass from the Republic, chocolate from Friis, rum from the island, and other spices and fruits she didn't recognize. One vendor claimed to be selling karsh blood, but his stock proved to be fake after closer inspection. Coral left them all to their fraudulent behavior and followed close behind Mano. She was acutely aware of Kale's presence beside her. She wondered if that had to do with her recent admission to Mano.

They stopped at another vendor selling assorted jewelry. Each simple piece was exorbitantly priced. Coral couldn't fathom at their cost, despite the fact they were sold in pairs.

A couple stood surveying a bracelet. They were lost in conversation, and Coral tried not to lean closer in her attempt to overhear.

". . . course everyone is going because everyone else is going. They say the Daughter of the First will be there. I'll be sure to tell you all about it."

The woman shoved the man playfully on the arm. "As if you can stop me from attending. Do we truly need a blood chain my love? I do believe our little angel has begun to see the error of her ways."

Kale nudged her along and they left before she could hear more.

"Did you hear that?" she asked, poking Mano in the back. "Everyone is going to be at some fancy party tonight. And if it's common knowledge that the Daughter of the First is going to show up then I'm willing to bet the Queen of Shadows shows up too."

"I guess we're going to a party tonight." Kale grinned in response before pointing just ahead.

"Coral." Somehow her name sounded like a warning on his lips. She stopped short, tensing at what had caught his attention.

Mano stopped too. For some reason, he drew his trishula.

At the far side of the underground square a small cluster of people had gathered around a short podium. There was some sort of live sale going on that Kale had been able to see due to his height. She pressed forward, bumping into Mano who remained still, clutching his trishula. He had an odd look on his face. She started to ask what was wrong, but Mano swung the trishula at her head. It was so loud as it cracked against her temple. Great Mother it hurt! Everything went dark.

JURA

CHAPTER THIRTY-SIX

She couldn't stop looking at him. Markhim, here, in front of her. He had fallen unconscious as soon as they had gotten him to leave the *moipu* den. It hadn't been easy, and the task had attracted unwanted attention. Now they were out and the sun had begun its ascent into the sky. Tylak had slung the much larger man over his shoulders. He should have staggered under the weight, but he seemed to be just fine and walked on without complaint. It still didn't seem quite real. She had so many questions: Why had Markhim disappeared? What was he doing in the *moipu* den? In Kitoi, for that matter?

Markhim was covered in cuts and bruises. Jura couldn't fathom what he had been through since he left the Republic. And why did he leave the Republic? Surely not in order to become this wretched mess. She tore her eyes away from him and met Tylak's curious gaze.

"Do you still plan for us to get Amira tonight?"

Jura stiffened at his question. Sharif had given them the name of a cabochon before they left the horrid place. Ferrin Neorar, Master of Knowledge. They finally had a name and perhaps a location for Amira. Did Tylak truly believe Jura could so easily delay her friend's rescue? As though Amira could become any less important simply because they'd gotten more than they came for?

"Of course I do," Jura answered more forcefully than was probably necessary. "She's not staying a minute longer than she has to."

Tylak grunted, repositioning the unconscious man on his shoulders.

"The Samur should be back by the time we get to the War Home." She squinted up at the sky. The men had probably come back just before dawn in order to pray. "Once we get settled, we can go over the plan for tonight." She angled her head back up toward him. "Why would you ask that?"

"Ask what?"

"If I still planned to get Amira. That."

"I wasn't sure if your priorities would change."

Jura stopped walking so she could give him a proper glare. "Everflame help me but I could strangle you."

"I don't understand what you're getting so angry about," Tylak muttered.

"What don't you understand? Rescuing my best friend doesn't become any less important simply because my ex-boyfriend suddenly appears back in my life." If he hadn't been carrying Markhim Jura might have attempted to hit him. She settled for a frustrated growl. Markhim's appearance changed nothing. He hadn't even appeared in her life; she'd stumbled back into his. There was just as equal a chance he would run away from her again. She didn't voice any of that out loud.

"So that's what he was to you? Your lover back at the palace?"

"Ahem," Peppik coughed dramatically. "Pardon the interr-uption but, Tylak, it would be in our best interest if you made yourself and Jura invisible. We don't need anyone noticing her, and you carrying a semi-unconscious man is bound to catch some unwanted attention."

Jura blinked at the man, but he began to hum to himself. She turned her attention back to Tylak.

"It shouldn't matter who he is to me. He's someone I once considered a friend and I couldn't leave him there. Are you going to be okay the rest of the walk or do you want to take a break?" Jura knew he expended more energy when widening his invisibility. She couldn't imagine how much more difficult it was with the extra weight of an added person.

"I'm fine," Tylak snapped.

Jura bit her lip to prevent herself from saying anything back. He had no right to be angry with her. She didn't do anything. He was the one who went around kissing people and then—

Markhim groaned. She reached a hand out to touch the stubble of his chin. "Markhim, can you hear me?"

He rolled his head toward her but his eyes remained glazed and unfocused.

"He's going to need a bit longer to regain his senses," Tylak said. "What's his story then? Son of one of the Thirteen?"

"He was a Light Guard," Jura muttered. Markhim's distaste for the Thirteen was almost as strong as Tylak's. He would hate to be considered one. Or at least he would have. It was hard to say how this Markhim would feel on the matter. The Markhim she knew would never have allowed himself to fall down such a path. Did she even know him at all?

"A Light Guard? One of those idiots paid to watch the

Everflame all day? What's it going to do, run away?"

"It's an honorable position." Why did she feel so defensive? She frowned when Tylak rolled his eyes. "How long do you think he'll stay like . . . this?"

"Another couple hours I imagine. *Moipu* is powerful but the effects don't last for too long. Once the drug is out of his system he should be fine, unless . . ." Tylak trailed off, once again repositioning Markhim over his shoulders.

"Unless what?" Jura demanded.

"Unless he's become a slave to the drug. You saw the people in there. The majority of *moipu* users waste their lives away in places like that. Sharif was an odd sort. Most people don't use the drug recreationally, it becomes a lifestyle."

"And you think that's what Markhim was doing? That this is his life now?"

"I guess we'll find out when he wakes up."

They continued the rest of the way in silence. Once they reached the doors of the War Home Jura let out a sigh of relief. Asim had left fresh water and sheets in the room. After asking the Samur to settle Markhim down the hall, she succumbed to exhaustion and took a nap.

When she awoke, the house was silent and empty. She went to Markhim's room and found the man still sleeping soundly. She sat down on the edge of his bed and watched the gentle rise and fall of his chest. Someone had cleaned and bandaged his wounds. She took his hand in her own and marveled that even now his hand seemed foreign to her, even though she'd held it over a dozen times.

"Jura?" he croaked out.

"You're awake." She scooted forward, latching on to his other hand when he reached out for her.

"It really was you." His voice was scratchy, harsher than she remembered.

"It's me." Stupid girl. Is that really the only thing she could think to say?

He looked around them and then down at himself, no doubt taking a surveillance of his many injuries. "How did you get it off?"

"Get what off?"

He didn't answer and his eyes blinked back sleep. She couldn't allow that yet, she needed answers. There were a thousand things to ask him but only one question seemed important.

"Why did you leave?" she blurted out.

"Jura, it's complicated."

"No," she shook her head. "No, you don't get to do that. You were my best friend. I needed you. I . . ." *Loved you.* She refused to say it out loud. She took a deep breath and crossed her arms over her chest. "I deserve to know why you just left like you did."

Markhim's face softened. He raked a hand through his hair. It was in need of a cut, already much longer than the close crop worn by the palace guards. Now his dark curls hung disheveled and fell into his eyes, it reminded her of Tylak's.

"Jura, you have to know that I would never leave you, not intentionally." He took a deep breath. "It was a blood chain. A Shadow Dancer got the jump on me and put the flaming thing on."

"A blood chain," she said slowly. Her eyes immediately went to his wrists.

He held his arms back out for inspection. "The first thing I was forced to do was write you that letter. And that was only the first of the many terrible things I was forced to do. The last thing I remember was going into the *moipu* den before I woke up here. If you didn't take the chain off me, the Shadow Dancer must have removed it."

"None of that makes any sense. Why would they enslave you only to release you there?"

"I'm sure they didn't count on you being there to rescue me."

"Or maybe that's exactly what they were counting on." Jura stood up and gave his body another careful once over, going so far as to pull back the cover and check his ankles.

"There. Are you satisfied? I'm not wearing a blood chain now. I have no weapons on me, and other than my new assortment of cuts and bruises, I'm fine."

"I have so many questions," Jura started.

"Ask away. I'll tell you anything you want to know."

"What's it . . . what's it like?"

"It's terrible. Imagine hearing someone else's voice in your head, yelling over your every thought. Imagine watching your limbs move on their own accord and hearing someone else's words come out of your mouth in your voice. But it's even worse than that. Jura, you become someone, *something* else. It's like forgetting yourself . . . Jura, the things I was forced to do, some of them are unforgivable."

"I forgive you," she whispered.

He reached for her hand again but she kept them clasped firmly together in her lap.

"Jura, I need to ask. What were *you* doing in that place? Not that I'm not grateful you found me, but that sort of place is no place for someone like you. It's dangerous."

"Markhim, I—"

"In fact what are you doing in Kitoi? And where's you *Arbe*? "

"Markhim, if you would allow me to speak I can tell you everything." She started from the moment he left and told him almost everything. There was no reason to tell him about the kiss she shared with Tylak. Not that it was his business in any case.

When she was finished, Markhim fell back against his pillows and stared unblinking at the vaulted ceiling.

"And it all happens tonight. So what is this plan to rescue Amira?"

"Well, I haven't quite figured that bit out yet. There's a large social gathering tonight. It's not much of a stretch to assume Neorar will be there. And it's expected I attend."

Tylak knocked on the door frame. "Sorry to interrupt the reunion."

His scowl indicated he was angry rather than apologetic, but Jura felt too drained to care. "Markhim, this is Tylak. He's one of the men working with me to rescue Amira."

Tylak raised an eyebrow at the introduction but stepped forward and twisted his fingers in the formal greeting of the Republic. She tried to hide the surprise from registering on her face. She'd never known Tylak to be so formal.

Tylak gave Markhim a careful once over. Jura resisted the urge to blush, somehow embarrassed at being caught on a man's bed.

"Glad to see my bandages are holding."

"You did those?" Jura asked, whipping her head around to stare at Tylak.

He shrugged in response. "Yeah, someone had to clean him up."

"And I thank you for that," Markhim said, sitting up straighter and watching Tylak with interest.

"Jura, I, uh, brought someone here for you." Tylak walked back to the open door and poked his head down into the hall. Muffled whispers were heard and finally a young boy, no older than twelve or thirteen, stumbled forward.

"My Lady First Greatest." The boy bowed deeply and Jura bit back a grin.

"Jura will suffice." She stood up. "And why do I have the honor of your acquaintance?"

"The majority of the dressmakers laughed in my face when I told them I wanted to commission a gown for tonight," Tylak began. "The ones who would all backed out once they found out the dress was for you. Don't take it personal," he added. "I think they were just spooked they might lose a limb for failing to please one of the Thirteen. In any case, I found Jip here. He claims to be able to do it, so I figured we'd give him a try being as how we're pressed for time and we've had certain . . . distractions as of late. He's to be rewarded handsomely but," Tylak fixed the boy with a stern stare, "only after the job is done."

"I like a challenge." The boy said, pushing up his sleeves. "We better get started."

ASH

CHAPTER THIRTY-SEVEN

espite his somber attitude, Kay shined perfection at morning practice. The child had basically mastered the Red Forms. He couldn't concentrate on her moves, however, not when he couldn't stop thinking of Timber. He had searched for him on the sands this morning, despite knowing it was a futile effort. In his heart he knew he would never see Timber again. Timber had died in flames and ash, a hero's death, so why then did it feel so wrong?

Arena dragons come from people. They *made* them. He still had a difficult time accepting the truth of the revelation, despite the fact that he had witnessed it with his own two eyes.

They call it Breaking. Timber had told him. *Don't let Kay into the catacombs.* Kindle had warned him during their final conversation together. He would never get to ask her what she meant. He still struggled to make sense of it all. Why turn people into dragons? What purpose did this solve? Dragons are wild creatures, they lived free in the wilds . . . didn't they?

Where had the hours gone? It was nearly mid-morning. His

cadet usually begged for a break before this point, but she continued going through her Forms, fierce determination staining her features.

"Get some water, Cadet." He'd heard of the new water rations in the city. It seemed that's all anyone was gossiping about these days, but Ash hadn't noticed a change in his own water supply.

"Is my arm good?"

"Looks good," Ash responded without looking over at her. The girl noticed and asked the question again until he walked over and moved her elbow in closer to her body. "Now, get some water." He gave her a gentle push for good measure, and she scampered off to collect her water skin.

Kindle's warning continued to ring in his ears. He had to keep Kay from the catacombs at all costs. Perhaps if he spoke with the Ninth about his concerns. The man seemed honest enough for one of the Thirteen. It had been just days ago that the man had assured Ash he had no intention of selling his wonder child, as he called her. Ash frowned, no doubt if he ever lost her he would go through great lengths to retrieve her.

A bugle sounded the arrival of one the Thirteen, and the Fire Dancers all turned toward the sound ready to acknowledge their master. For the first time ever, Ash hoped it was the Ninth. He turned away when he realized it was a woman. She was familiar, but Ash couldn't recall her Rank. His cadet came to stand beside him, taking casual sips from her water skin.

"Fire motion?" she asked.

"Fire motion." He followed her across the sands.

Kay had barely begun when Ash was tapped on the shoulder. He thought for a moment he stared at the lady First, but no, this woman was much older. She was familiar still, and beautiful despite the fact that her expression was a stone mask on her face.

"Ash Fire Dancer."

"I am honored my lady . . ."

"Fourth. My name is Denir."

Ash twisted his fingers into a formal greeting and bowed as low as his knees would allow.

"No need for such niceties. Consider this an interview." The woman smiled.

"An interview?"

"Yes, for the position of trainer to my new cadet here."

"Your . . . but the Ninth . . ." Ash struggled to make sense of her words. The Ninth had sworn to him he had no intention of selling Kay. What was the meaning of this? When he saw that man again he was going to smash his fat skull.

"Yes, you see this cadet's previous owner is not long for the executioner's block, and his assets have all be reallocated. Quite fairly, in my opinion. Now, convince me to keep you on as this cadet's trainer and be quick about it." When he could only stare in response, she snapped her fingers. "Answer me you ignorant waste of flesh and stop wasting my time."

Ash swallowed. It was deadly to hit one of the Thirteen, and aside from that he didn't much like the idea of hitting one so tiny and armed with just a tiny fashion dagger at her hip.

"The cadet trusts me. She's lost a lot and she considers me a friend."

The Fourth cocked her head to the side. "A friend?" she snorted. "Trust and friendship?" She gave him a thorough once over, running her eyes down the length of his body and back up again. Her appraisal left her smirking. "I'll admit, not the answer I was expecting. Well go on then, let's see a display. I want to know what all the hype is about this new wonder child."

Ash nodded at Kay who had stood in the smallest of the practice sands' ring of torches, watching their exchange. At his gesture, she began dancing with the flames. She pulled them tight, spun them in circles around her body, in fireballs shot high into the sky. When she had gone through all the Forms, she Breathed in the flame. Her skin seemed to glow for a moment before she shot the flames back out from her fingertips, igniting all the torches once more. When she was finished, she stood panting in the ring.

The smile the Fourth wore made her appear years younger. "I knew she had this reputation but that was simply spectacular. When is her naming day scheduled?"

Ash shook his head. "Oh, it's much too early for that. She's only seven ye—"

"Too early? I know what I just saw. It's not too early. She's ready." The woman began to pace in her excitement. "If I pull a few favors, I can get her in the arena tonight."

"Tonight?" Ash reminded himself to stay put, it was not possible to shake good sense into someone. "The cadet is not ready for the arena. Certainly not tonight. You can't . . ."

The Fourth stopped pacing. "I'm certain you didn't mean to address me without first being addressed by me? And I'm certain you didn't just presume to tell me what I can and cannot do with my property? I've had slaves killed for less."

"I'm a free man," Ash said.

The Fourth sniffed. "And you are free to leave. Your services as trainer are no longer needed. You're fired."

"You're firing me? All because I'm telling you it's lunacy to make a child no older than seven fight a dragon? And another seasoned Fire Dancer? He'll have her gutted in seconds."

"Then I'll place her in a solo match. I won't defend my

decision to the likes of you." She smiled at Kay's approach. "Hello, dear. Big news for you. Today is your naming day. You'll finally get to fight in the arena."

Kay's eyes widened, surprising Ash that she had been able to grasp enough of that conversation. She looked around, no doubt looking for Beshar. Ash too wished the councilman would come back into their lives.

"I'm going to make the necessary arrangements. I'll see you tonight." She stiffened, staring at the girl's face for a moment. "What lovely earrings." She gave Kay an affectionate pat on the head before turning back to Ash. "I want you to stay away from my property. Keep your hands to yourself or I'll see them removed." She brushed past him. Ash scowled at her retreating form.

"What happens now?" Kay asked. Her wide blue eyes searched his face for answers he couldn't provide.

He couldn't allow Kay to enter the arena. A plan had to be made. He didn't know how just yet, but if it cost him his life he was going to get her out of this.

"Don't worry," he lied. "Everything will be fine. Go rest."

TYLAK

Chapter Thirty-Eight

arkhim. He didn't like the man. He certainly seemed to be making himself right at home. And what sandstorm had brought him back into their lives? Tylak sighed. If he was honest with himself, it wasn't Markhim he was angry at, it was himself. He had acted out of line when he kissed Jura. Any fool could see how that simple, stupid action had altered her perspective of him. She barely looked at him now, not that she had looked away from Markhim. If Jura had never mentioned the name before, Tylak still would have known something was going on between the two of them. Tension buzzed in the air around them, thick enough that Tylak had felt strangled. After his excursion into town to find Jip, he'd been horrified to find Markhim and Jura sitting in the bed, heads together in quiet conversation.

The two of them looked *right* together: the princess and her guard. So where did that leave Tylak? Perhaps it was for the best. Amira would be rescued within the next few hours and then his arrangement with Jura would be done once and for all. Well, after Jura held up her end of the bargain. He no longer wondered whether or not she would take him to the arena and help him find Sykk. Jura had too much honor to go back on her word. She would help him, and then they would truly be done with each other. Forever.

He flexed fingers he'd been unaware had formed into angry fists. Burn it all, *why* had he kissed her? He needed some air. He left the War Home and stood in the courtyard, mostly empty despite the fact that it was only late afternoon. The Samur approached, Ichiro lifting his arm in greeting. Always home before sunset; always awake at dawn for prayers.

"You look troubled," Jiro noted. Jiro seemed to be the more relaxed of the two, though both men stood alert and in a fighting stance, despite the fact they were alone outside their temporary home.

"I'm always troubled," Tylak replied honestly.

Ichiro nodded solemnly. "Knowledge brings trouble, does it not?"

Tylak couldn't agree more. In the Republic knowledge was power, and as a Shadow Dancer he had stolen more than his share of information. And it always brought trouble. The two Samur continued to stand with him in companionable silence. It brought him a small measure of peace, and he didn't feel quite so alone. The truth was Jura would remain his friend in any capacity for as long as she would have him. He had grown accustomed to her presence, to all of them. He realized that although they'd been companions for over two weeks, Tylak still knew very little about the two men. He studied each now, overcome with a sudden intense desire to know them.

"Tell me about your god."

Jiro smiled and nodded, as if he had somehow been expecting

the question. "Our gods are beautiful and wicked. Both nurturing and taking. Vengeful and respected. What would you like to know?"

"Sounds like your god is a female," Tylak muttered and Jiro actually chuckled.

"Our people tell a story about the moon, the sun, and the stars. You see, the moon is deeply in love with the sun. Who wouldn't be with the way it shines and brings life? But the moon cannot catch the attention of the sun no matter how hard she tries. The moon will alter her image in hopes that changing herself will alter the sun's perception of her. But it will never work, because the sun is in love with the stars. He loves them all and keeps them stashed away in his harem in the night sky. Every night, the stars twinkle and shine for the sun, hoping their display will have the sun call out for them to join him. When the sun chooses a new lover, she will fall from the night sky down to the earth so that she can bask in the sun's love during the day."

"Are you saying I'm like the moon and Jura is the sun?"

"It is simply a story told among our people." Ichiro shrugged and the two brothers exchanged a look.

He had it bad then if he was grasping at connections between him and Jura from simple stories. Peppik would get a good laugh of it. Then he would say something odd and disappear. Where was the man anyway?

"Jura and Markhim were friends before," Tylak said even as he wondered at the overshare.

"The Daughter of the First cares for you," Jiro started but Tylak interrupted him before he could finish the embarrassing thought.

"So which one do you worship then? The sun or the moon?"

"The sun, of course. We are the children of stars."

Tylak thought about that. So he truly had been inserting him and Jura into a story they had no place in. Just as he had inserted himself where he had no business. She was the Daughter of the First of the Thirteen, for flames sake.

Jip, the spindly youth, flung open the front door and stumbled forward, stopping short when he saw Tylak.

"I did it. I told you I could make a new dress from an old one in under four hours." He thrust his hand forward, and Tylak deposited the agreed upon payment. Then he doubled it, depleting the rest of his funds. The boy deserved it. With any luck, this time tomorrow the group would be on their way back to the Republic. Jip's eyes widened at the hefty sum. With another awkward bow, he was off and running down the street. Tylak shook his head at the boy's departure and hoped he hadn't been ripped off. He wasn't exactly sure why Jura felt so strongly that she needed a new dress for tonight, no doubt she already had plans for this evening. He cracked his knuckles in anticipation. It was all happening tonight.

He entered the house, trailed by the two Samur. He was surprised to see Markhim up and sitting in one of the dark leather chairs in the entryway. The brothers exchanged another look before heading up the stairs for their rooms.

Tylak took a quick moment to study the man. He was slim, although heavy with muscle, with dark skin and curly hair. He had a face most ladies would drool over. No scar to mess with his perfectly symmetrical features. The man smiled at him a bit too easily, and Tylak lifted his chin by way of response.

"You seem to be recovering quickly."

"No doubt in part to your medical attentions."

"It was just a few bandages," Tylak grunted.

"That's not all I wanted to thank you for." The man lumbered to his feet, thrusting his arm out before him. "I wasn't here for her, and you stepped in and helped her—"

"I wasn't doing anyone any favors," Tylak interrupted. To his credit, Markhim didn't step down but remained standing with his arm outstretched. With a sigh, Tylak took it, working the palm up and down. "So, I guess this means you'll be sticking around now?"

"Where she goes, I go." Markhim smiled again, and Tylak wondered how long he would smile after he punched his face in. Tylak unclenched his fist. Jura would probably get angry if he punched Markhim, and it didn't seem worth the argument.

"I'm sure Jura is glad to have you."

"I'm not so sure she is." It was Markhim's turn to sigh. He fell back into his leather chair with an exaggerated gesture. "Things are different now. Not that I can blame her. I just wish she could see that none of that was my fault. I would never have intentionally left her."

Tylak nodded, uncomfortable with the conversation. Just because he had promised himself not to hurt the man didn't mean he had to be nice.

"I should probably go upstairs and check in on her. We still need to go over the plan for tonight."

"Oh, no need. We discussed the plans for the night while that boy was taking her measurements."

Tylak stopped in his tracks at the base of the stairs, one foot still on the bottom step. "You and her already discussed strategy?" While she was being measured for a gown? Just how close were these two?

Burn it all, the man grinned at him and gave a hapless shrug. "By that I mean Jura told me the plans for tonight, and I mostly just nodded."

Tylak bit back a smirk. That sounded like her.

"In any case, she's changing now. She told me to make sure you dressed in your Shadow Dancer gear?" Markhim raised his eyebrows. "I can't say I wasn't surprised to hear of your occupation."

"Former occupation," Tylak muttered. He headed up the stairs to change his shirt and boots, and met Jura just as she was exiting her room. He stopped short to avoid stepping on her bare feet.

His eyes darted up but stopped in wonder at her dress. How in the name of the Everflame had the boy managed to do this in so short a time? The dress was . . . it wasn't Jura. He'd never seen so much of her exposed before, and he felt heat rise into his cheeks at the mere sight of so much of her skin.

The black of the bodice wrapped around her chest. Her sun-kissed shoulders and arms shined, bare and golden. The gown tightened at the waist and dropped straight to the floor, pooling at her feet. The entire dress was covered in bits of glass placed intricately to glimmer in all the right places. The result was a shimmering masterpiece that was both startling and dangerous looking.

"Is it stupid? I thought it was representative of the Republic . . . you know, because of the glass. And we were short on time, so Jip suggested we just use materials we had on hand. He altered the dress you bought me, which seemed a great idea, but now I'm not so sure and you're not saying anything . . ." She trailed off and Tylak gave his head a mental shake.

He wanted to tell her that she was stunning. That her tanned, exposed skin was doing something to his insides. That her amber eyes appeared to be golden pools that he would drown himself in if only she would ask. He swallowed.

"Sandstorms. I don't have anything to change into. I didn't have shoes for this anyway—"

"Jura!" Her name squeaked out of him. He cleared his throat, deepening his voice, "Jura, you look beautiful."

Her smile was radiant. "Thank you. It isn't . . . well, of course, it is but do you really like it?"

"I do." He finally nodded, kicking himself back into action before he spent the next few minutes staring at her like some love sick fool. "I need to go change for the plan." *For the plan you told Markhim and not me.*

"Yes. I hope you don't mind that we've to split up, but I feel like it was always the plan."

He blinked. "What was?"

"For me to distract Neorar while you rescue Amira. Assuming he'll be in attendance at Cabochon Nazahah's tonight, this is our best and probably only opportunity to get in there and steal her back right from under his nose." She cocked her head to the side. "Didn't Markhim go over this with you? I told him to tell you."

Of course she had, but knowledge was power and so Markhim had held onto it. Tylak grinned. He didn't mind a little trouble. Besides, there was a bit of stubborn pride in the fact that Jura trusted him to retrieve Amira. She might not have more than friendly feelings toward him, but what they had was mutual trust. He almost laughed out loud at the thought. Who was he kidding? It would never be enough. He squared his shoulders and went off to his room to change.

Despite the fact that he started well after her and she had been already dressed, Tylak beat Jura to the entry hall. The Samur mumbled to one another quietly and Peppik bobbed nervously, rolling on the heels of his feet.

Markhim whistled low between his teeth.

Tylak raised his eyebrows and Markhim shook his head in

response. "I'm sorry, it's just that . . . wow. You're really one of them. So what is your secret? Some sort of special training or . . ." he trailed off as Tylak disappeared from sight in front of him.

That shut him up, Tylak thought with a smirk, reappearing by the Light Guard's side.

"Flames, that was amazing," Markhim squinted at him. "That was . . . you, right? I mean, it's not something special you're wearing or i—"

"You can't be taught to do it, Markhim. It isn't possible. I've tried," Jura said.

Tylak turned toward her voice and once again caught his breath at the mere sight of her. That woman got more beautiful every time he saw her. He shook his head.

"I just have to get something and then we can be on our way," Jura said, striding toward the study.

Books? Again? He opened his mouth to protest but Jura cut him off, calling from the study, "I just want to write a quick note for Amira. So she'll know it's me. She's never met you before, and while she's more daring than I am, I don't believe she's ever had any interaction with a Shadow Dancer . . . unless it was Shadow Dancers who took her in the first place." She continued on, not giving him a chance to respond. "She's bound to be frightened at first, but she's resilient. Amira's always been more self-sufficient than me."

Jura could more than take care of herself. He'd seen it multiple times. He started to remind her of this when in the silence of her shouting across rooms he could hear the faint scratching of pen on paper. He turned to Markhim with a grunt.

"How are you involved in all this?" It was time to get some solid answers.

"I . . . what do you mean? I've known Jura for years."

"Yes, but you left the Republic and then came here. How are you involved with the Queen of Shadows?"

"Is that what you shadow people call your leader?"

Tylak's scowl must have been truly frightening because Markhim hurried on to explain. "It wasn't a Shadow Dancer who enchained me." He looked behind him toward the study, but Jura remained inside. "I lied to Jura. It was a woman, a woman in the palace. One of the Thirteen." He sighed. "I don't remember more than that, though, I swear. Look, I know you must be wondering what it's like, and I wish I could explain it to you. It was a dark time for me, you can't imagine what it's like. I know that I did things . . . awful things." Markhim's gaze focused behind Tylak, staring out into a distant past the man seemed keen to repress.

Burn it all if he didn't feel a tug of sympathy toward the man.

"Jura got me through it, you know. Through everything. I just kept thinking, everything will be okay if I can just get back to her."

"Oh," Jura said from the doorway of the study. She blushed when the men turned toward her. "We should go."

Tylak frowned but met her at the doorway. She thrust the folded letter into his hands and then stepped into his arms. A hug? Not that he was complaining. He folded his arms around her, the gesture awkward and hesitant.

"Please be careful. Get Amira and come back to me," she said.

"I'll always come back to you," he whispered but his words were muffled in her hair. If she heard him she gave no indication.

AMIRA

Chapter Thirty-Nine

"*You could poison him.*"

The voice startled her out of her reverie, and she turned sharply toward the speaker. Kuru stood before her, his usual dagger spinning between his hands in what she had come to learn was a nervous tick. The boy was persistent in his request, she had to give him that.

"I suppose you want me to do it tonight?" Amira asked, frowning at her dirty fingernails in an effort to appear nonchalant.

Kuru shook his head. "Can't do it tonight. My father is going to a party. He'll likely be gone all night." The boy gave her a wicked grin. "It will be just me and the house slaves."

Amira swallowed. Everflame save them from a household ran by Kuru. He was constantly reminding her that she was too important to lose a limb, but that he might someday change his mind. He didn't care about angering his father. He wanted to kill him, after all. So instead Amira was forced to watch as Kuru hurt others. Beating and breaking bones and slicing off pieces of any who stood in his way. Or any who didn't. There didn't seem to be any logic to his attacks. Sometimes Kuru was giving, offering double food portions or a new dress. Amira believed his sporadic attacks were likely a result of boredom, so she struggled to keep his interest whenever he engaged.

"I'm sure it pleases you, Master. What will you do with your free evening?" He liked it when she groveled and called him master. Spoiled slug. If she'd met him in the palace . . . no. As usual she sealed off all thought of home. Stay strong, stay alert, and run when you get your chance. She had no intention of dying here. She was Daughter of the Third and as soon as she was back in the safety of the Republic she would see to it that they were all made to pay. Don't think about Antar or father or Jura. Not yet, not until you're free.

She smiled at Kuru and tried to concentrate on his words.

"Did you know her?" He repeated the question. "Daughter of the First?"

Jura? What did he know about her?

"I know of her." She shrugged, keeping her face impassive. "I know of many people who make their homes in the Republic. Is . . . is the Daughter of the First really in the city?"

"She is." Kuru nodded, replacing his long knife in its sheath. "Would you like for me to bring her to you? Wouldn't that be a nice treat, a friend here for you?"

No, she would never allow it to happen. She gritted her teeth but said nothing.

Kuru smirked despite everything. "Perhaps they will take her." He was gleeful at the prospect. "When they take her, they will bring her here. That will give us something to do."

Would they? Was someone out there at this very moment plotting to kidnap Jura? What was she even doing here anyway? They wouldn't go so far, would they? She was the Daughter of the

First and yet . . . They had certainly wasted no time in stealing Amira and she was Daughter of the Third. She thought about that day, touring the market with Father and having her pick of purchases from any vendor. She was known on sight and everyone gave her royal treatment, fawning over her and throwing out gifts that would no doubt later end up on her father's line of credit. Amira hadn't minded it. She enjoyed the attention. When the woman had begun pulling at her arm, she hadn't paid it much attention at first. But the tug had gotten insistent and then the woman had bitten her. She shivered once again, staring at the ugly wound on her left shoulder. It had been weeks and the bite still hadn't fully healed. What kind of person bit another? Drank their blood? No, she wouldn't allow Jura to suffer the same fate. She snapped at herself to focus and turned back to Kuru.

"I've got something we can do. I will poison your father. Tomorrow. We can spend the evening making preparations."

It didn't take much more convincing than that. He had already dismissed the majority of the staff, keeping just Emi, Jeen, and Meli, his two favorite maids and the house chef.

He called for them now, poking his head out and yelling into the hallway.

"You still don't trust me not to run?" Amira asked. Her plan wouldn't work from within the confines of her room. He had only just allowed her to have small interactions with the staff. She suspected they were all under strict instructions to ignore her because the majority of their interactions had been one sided.

Kuru frowned in response and made no move from her doorway.

"And yet you trust me to kill your father." She continued poking. She would try every chance she got.

"What do I know of killing fathers?" he sighed. "I suppose you'll want access to the kitchens."

Amira nodded. "And we'll need to send Luxman to the market for supplies."

Kuru snorted. "Right, send my bodyguard away from me and leave me alone in the hands of one of the Thirteen. I'll send Emi." He said with a jerk of his chin.

Amira shrugged as if it didn't matter to her one way or another and began rattling off a long list of ingredients.

With a grunt, he asked her to follow him downstairs so she could write the list down.

The list was long enough that Kuru sent both the maids, leaving himself, Luxman, and the chef alone in the kitchen.

She wondered how Jura would react in her situation. She would have noticed the *orphanel* nut by now, but would she have dared to use it?

Well, Amira didn't have a choice.

"Meli doesn't have to stay," Amira dared.

Kuru lifted a brow. "What if I get hungry later? Who will fix my snack?"

"I could—"

"Hah! I would never touch something prepared by your hand." He shuddered, as if the mere thought of it was enough to give him chills.

Amira resisted the urge to roll her eyes. She had to play this carefully. "Then I suppose I'm just down here to supervise? You said yourself, you're no master at the science of poison, and unless you're willing to pe—"

"Luxman will mix the necessary components under your direction."

Amira couldn't help the small smile that escaped. She bit the inside of her cheek and smoothed her features. "You should take me into your father's study now."

"Why?" Kuru narrowed his brown eyes and frowned at her. "What do you want that's in there?"

"I don't want anything from there." She shrugged. "I just figured it would be the best place to set the trap because he spends so much time there . . ." She trailed off, Kuru was already nodding in acceptance. She shot a wary glance at Luxman, but the one-eyed giant didn't seem inclined to join their conversation.

"He hates when I go in there." He grinned. "But the opinions of dead men don't matter, do they?"

Amira swallowed and forced herself to nod in response. How could this boy speak so nonchalantly about murdering his own father? She'd grown up in the glass palace, so underhand politics were nothing new to her, but this premeditated murder of one's own father was something else entirely.

He gestured for her to follow him. She fell into step behind him, Luxman wedging her between the two. They crossed the short distance in silence, and Kuru opened the heavy wooden door without hesitation, swinging it open. There was a single torch on the wall, the majority of the light provided by lanterns stuffed with softly glowing stones. They mimicked the effect of the streets at night, although Amira could barely remember them. Her first visit to the golden city seemed another lifetime ago.

Don't think about it, she reminded herself. She focused on the room. Like the rest of the home the room was lushly decorated, only with a decidedly more masculine tone. The majority of the furniture was comprised of dark woods and smooth marble. A large desk dominated the room. Amira made a great show of measuring his desk and ruffling the papers. Behind the desk was a massive piece of wooden furniture. The top was made up of shelves, and those shelves were lined with books. The bottom half was made up of cupboards. She didn't know what was hidden in those cupboards but she knew that it was important to Neorar. And that meant she had to take it from him.

"I suppose his desk chair will have to do . . . unless . . ."

"Unless what?" Kuru sidled closer, peering at the same papers she pretended to study.

"Unless there was something else in here that you think would be better, Glorious Master? Perhaps an object of some sort that your father is accustomed to handling on a daily basis?" She blinked her eyes and hoped she wasn't overdoing it.

"There is one thing." Kuru put down the letter opener he'd been eyeing suspiciously and walked toward the cupboard. "Oh, the key! It won't open without . . ." he trailed off at Luxman's grunt of disapproval. The bodyguard clicked his tongue and gave a small but firm shake of his head.

Sandstorms. It wasn't going to be that easy then.

"You don't need to bother with nothing else, just put the poison on his chair like you said. What kind of poison are you using anyway?"

"I'm crafting a gaseous poison that he will inhale. There will be zero evidence. You won't have to convince him to digest anything. The chair is fine. Doesn't matter to me." She shrugged and walked toward the door. "We might as well get started."

"Don't we have to wait for the maids to return with the list?"

"Yes, but we can take care of quite a bit before they arrive." She paused in the doorway. "Shall we?" Without waiting for a response, she turned and stepped through the doorway, taking long strides toward the kitchen and feeling more like herself than she had in weeks.

When Amira was ten years old her mother died. She wasn't poisoned or murdered in her sleep. She didn't die in some tragic accident. She simply became sick and died. It was a silly thing, really. One day she was alive and then she was simply . . . gone. Her father was different after that. They all were. And poor Antar was so young. She hadn't wanted to speak to anyone and lessons were torturous. Who could focus on studies when everything that was good about the world was suddenly gone? Befriending Jura had made the world a bit better. Jura had understood what it was to lose someone, she had felt it too. They probably would never have become friends had her mother never gotten sick. She had nothing in common with the Daughter of the First, even less after her most recent experience, and yet she had thought of her often over the last few weeks, perhaps because Jura represented home.

Back in the kitchen Amira began mixing ingredients at random, trying to avoid Meli's suspicious glare. Every few moments she dared a quick glance at the *orphanel*. The plant remained un-noticed in the corner. This would never work with Meli in the room.

"Will we continue to live here after your father . . . has his accident?"

Kuru snapped to attention, sheathing his knife and stepping toward her. "You said we. You intend to stay then?"

"Where would I go? You're my Master, are you not?" Luxman frowned at her, and Amira reminded herself to play her hand slowly.

"I suppose we'll stay here. After you kill my father—"

A loud gasp followed by the crack of glass against wooden floorboards.

"Sandstorms," Kuru grinned. "Meli didn't know about our plan. It's okay Meli. I think we can all agree old Ferrin has it coming to him." Luxman clucked his tongue, but Kuru shushed him. "She won't say anything, will you Meli?" Before she could answer he continued. "Besides, Meli, you have to know that if you say something about this, to anyone, I'll have to kill you."

Meli let out a wail and fled across the room crying softly against the wall.

Kuru sighed. "Aww, hush woman. Your hysterics will get you nowhere. Go upstairs and clean yourself up."

"I'll take her," Amira offered but Kuru pushed her back toward her table of strewn ingredients.

"Luxman can take her. You get back to work. The girls will be back with the rest of the ingredients soon. This potion of yours better work."

"It will work," she muttered to herself and walked toward the *orphanel*. It was heavier than it looked. A small green bulb, no bigger than her fist, covered in brown fibrous layers. The fruit lay atop a glass container, but she ignored that as well as its tight fitting lid.

"What's that?" Kuru asked as she set it on the table. She was careful to wash her hands after despite the fact the thing had made it to the table with no incident.

"An *orphanel*." Amira said the word almost reverently.

"You have to be an orphanel." The young Daughter of the First had

long black hair and eyes too big for her face. She clutched a book to her chest and didn't smile.

"An orphan? My dad isn't going anywhere he—"

"Not an orphan, an *orphanel*. Potionemmortnuc, to be more precise, but that's hard to say and everyone just uses the common tongue anyway."

Amira frowned at her. What did she know about anything? And what the heck was an *orphanel*? She resolved to ignore the little girl, but she continued to stand there so Amira sighed and gave in.

"What's an *orphanel*?"

"It's this plant that only grows once a year. It has the most delicious fruit inside, but the outside is made up of this armor the plant produces itself. It's basically indestructible. You can set it on fire or smash it but it won't break open. It's impossible because it's so strong." The Daughter of the First seemed to remember herself and took a deep breath before thrusting her book out toward Amira.

Amira took a step back as if the thing had fangs. Books meant studies and Amira was having none of that. Father had told her she didn't have to think of such things . . . given the circumstances. Still, the Daughter of the First was being nice . . .

"I don't like reading," she admitted.

The girl shrugged in response. "It's not for everyone."

"I like what you said though, about the *orphanel*. My name is Amira."

"I'm Jura."

"I know. Why did you say you I have to be like some weird plant?"

"It helps," Jura whispered. "I miss my mother and sometimes, when it starts to hurt too much, I tell myself that my heart is an *orphanel* fruit. That no matter what happens to me, I will stay strong and nothing can ever really hurt me."

Amira thought about that. She wished she could turn her heart into something strong, but it was too late for her. The hurt was too deep. Still, she gestured for Jura to sit beside her and the two spent the rest of the afternoon talking about exotic plants and foreign lands.

"If it's impossible to break it open, how do you get the fruit inside?"

Amira blinked her eyes and focused on Kuru. "This is a very exotic fruit." She smiled. "But then, we knew the Neorar household has expensive tastes. It's nearly impossible to open unless you know this trick," she gestured Kuru closer. "All you have to do is b—"

"What is this thing?" Luxman returned, his eyebrows wrinkled in confusion. He placed a large palm on either side of the fruit and stared at her with his single eye.

Amira resisted the urge to shudder. Did he know? If he knew the properties of the plant, her plans were ruined, she was a dead woman, and yet . . . he didn't seem too concerned over the fruit.

"Kuru and I were just about to open it."

"I will open it." Luxman plunged his dagger into the tough fibrous shell, but it deflected off the armor and the knife slid harmlessly to the side.

Kuru laughed. "It's shell is indestructible and can only be opened by this trick." He gestured toward Amira. "Well, go on, tell us."

"You blow on it."

"Truly?" Kuru cocked his head to the side.

Amira nodded. "Go on, give it a try."

Kuru took a deep breath and so did she. He leaned forward, she stepped back.

The pressure of a gentle breeze or one's breath along the length of its armor causes the plant to open up and dispel its gas into the air, transferring spores as it does so. A perfect cloud of deadly poison.

Amira held her breath and thanked the Everflame Jura loved to read.

JURA

CHAPTER FORTY

She had probably sent Tylak off too abruptly. And all alone? What was she thinking? She caught her bottom lip between her teeth and chewed as she worried.

"You look beautiful," Markhim whispered at her right.

For some reason his comment only made her frown. "You're supposed to be *Arbe*. No talking." She needn't have bothered with the admonishment as there was no one around, but for some reason it still felt good to be angry with him. Even if it wasn't his fault he'd disappeared. He'd vanished when she needed him the most. And then he appeared now . . . now, when things were different. Sandstorms. She took a deep breath. Everflame take her emotions she needed to be strong. She couldn't afford to be distracted by petty emotions, not when her country was at the brink of a war.

She forced away the bitter scowl and tried to smile. They were here to make new friends, after all. She squared her shoulders and entered the foray.

It was both familiar and unusual at the same time. The architecture was different, of course, stone and golden lattice replaced the glass walls. But the guests were the same, cloistered in small groups, huddled and sneering at others.

The clothing was different. The Republic favored layers of fabric. Here, fabric was an afterthought to the jewels and accessories. Jura didn't feel as out of place in her dress now that she was surrounded by so many who were even more colorful and grand. A young man was swathed in silver with actual silvered strands of wire sweeping across his shoulders. An older woman with a marbled cane wore a pink gown that had sparkling pink jewels hanging from the hems. They clinked against her cane in a musical manner. One woman was completely covered in feathers that must have been dyed blue to match the sky because surely no bird in existence had a blue so vivid.

In the heavy lights of the flickering torches and sparkling gemstones, the glass on Jura's dress against the shimmering black fabric reflected every color and shined out tiny prisms of lighted rainbows whenever she turned. The effect was dazzling and eye catching and exactly what she had been hoping for. She could feel their eyes on her, stolen glances hitting her one by one. For some reason, she didn't feel shaken by them. Instead, she felt powerful. *Be brave*, Tylak had whispered to her before he left, and she had echoed his request because surely he had the more dangerous mission. Well, she would be brave now, but not just for him or Amira. She would be brave for *herself*.

She felt different here, now. Lighter somehow, as if suddenly freed from some invisible burden. She was changed and yet she didn't quite know why. But that didn't matter now. It was time to try another approach. She had tried things their way, now it was time to embrace the fact she was of the Thirteen.

Her mind spun through her character index, searching for the right face to approach. By Sharif's account, Amira was now imprisoned in the home of Ferrin Neorar, Master of Knowledge, and his color was yellow. She scanned the room but there was no one matching his description. The large room was nearing capacity. Servants bustled back and forth carrying large trays laden with food. Each servant was swathed in the deep blue of Hadiya Nazahah's colors. The deep sapphire appeared almost black, and Jura looked for the Master of Judgment. There, wearing an outfit of varying shades of dark blue and in deep conversation with a man dressed in a muted red. He had only one shade of the color and paired it with black trousers. He caught her staring at him and lifted his chin in invitation.

With a resigned sigh, Jura walked toward him. It seemed Neorar had yet to make his appearance. She couldn't worry over the implications of what that might mean for Tylak. Was he trying to steal Amira away from an empty house or was the master at home?

Jura pasted a smile on her face as she drew near.

"Daughter of the First, it is a pleasure. I'd heard rumors you would be in attendance. Allow me to welcome you to my home." The woman dipped her head and twisted her fingers into the formal greeting of the Republic. "Hopefully I didn't just insult you, dear. It's been quite some time since I've had to greet one of the Thirteen."

Jura offered her a genuine smile. "Yes, it's a pity you were unable to attend the Call of the War Home . . . I suppose party planning takes its toll."

Hadiya Nazahah, Master of Judgement, had the courtesy to blush. "I *was* sorry to hear of its outcome. I would love for us to continue to grow and flourish in peace."

Jura gritted her teeth. "Then why don't you help me fight for that? It's not too late—"

"Oh, no child, that's where you're wrong. It's much too late to change anything now. The drums of war are already beating. This is vengeance and we must follow it. To denounce my following would make me a heretic."

Jura sighed. Though a handful of the country still followed the Everflame, the majority had turned to the cabochons. It seemed they preferred to have someone in charge of their emotions rather than handling them for themselves. The religion was a total release of one's emotional freedoms. It sounded dangerous to Jura. She tried another tactic, "Is it not justice to follow through with the doctrine of historical documents? When peace is pre-established?" She was unsure if she was relieved or saddened by the fact that Cobachon Abro was also delayed in his arrival. Would he now give her the opportunity to advocate for peace?

"Your speech of the histories might gain some footing with old Aja or perhaps Ferrin when he arrives. Historical facts are out of my jurisdiction."

"Not if the history pertains to your laws. Surely your faith can distinguish the difference." Jura took a literal and figurative step back and let out a deep breath. There was no sense in entering a religious debate.

"My lady, have we sparked a curiosity for our faith?"

And it seemed she was too late. The new question came from the man in deep red. The Master of Faith himself.

Jura chose her words carefully. He would be of little use as yet another enemy. "A curiosity would be an apt word for it. I'm intrigued behind the mystery of it all, although my own faith resides in the Everflame."

"Of course." Amin Leal, Master of the Faith, had a reputation for being stubborn and quick to anger. He too had been missing in attendance during her Call of the War Home. He smiled at her now. "Please, allow me to answer any questions you might have."

"I had believed the majority of the city to be faithful to the flame."

"And many are, Lady First, but it is the responsibility of the cabochons to devote a life of teaching and learning to the children. How can we do that when we are burdened by so many emotions? We teach that once you release your emotions you become free to self-reflect on what you truly need. The release of one's emotions is the true gift we offer. In this way, we offer a selfless service to the Everflame and its children, providing the children with what they truly need."

"How do you know what you need if you can't feel anything?" Markhim muttered under his breath.

Jura agreed but instead asked another question, "Who are the children?"

"We all are. You, me, everyone. We are the children of the gods, and we should serve them freely, not cage them and force them to our will. This is why we teach that the Everflame is an abomination. It is a caged god and must be set free."

"Excuse you?" Jura struggled to keep her expression neutral, although her voice had risen several octaves higher. She cleared her throat.

"My lady, I mean no disrespect. I wish only to teach you our ways. As children of this land we have certain responsibilities to it. Some children are gifted with extraordinary powers. They are marked by the gods, and it is their duty to devote their lives to the service of that god. Is that not what you believe in service to the Everflame? Those slaves who work as Torches in the city, or your Fire Dancers. The chosen ones are marked and they must serve as protectors for the gods other more defenseless children. People who are unmarked, like you and I."

Jura fidgeted under his intense stare. It was true, her beliefs mirrored his own to a degree. But all this talk of letting the gods free . . . that would create anarchy. The apocalypse. She shook her head. He said she was unmarked . . . but was she? She had already demonstrated she was capable of bigger things than she'd ever thought possible.

"You believe it is the duty of everyone gifted to serve those who are not. Do you disagree?" He prompted when Jura remained lost in her thoughts.

"No, I suppose that is part of one's duty to the Everflame but—"

"Does it not stand to reason then that every gifted person has a duty to serve the ungifted? Should not the children of the water serve under those in need of water? Or those children in touch with the earth, should they share the richness of their power with those ungifted, those the gods found pure and left unmarked? So if every gifted person belongs to someone else, then the lands must be pillaged until they are all found and brought here to serve under us."

"No," Jura snapped, finally finding her voice. "No, that would be ma—"

"The extremists here believe it is within their right. Those still faithful to the Everflame. They covet that you house the flame, you who the gods have chosen to mark less and less." The man's eyes took on a hungry look and he stared off into the distance. "It is good that you have come here, Daughter of the First, because now you can see there is nothing we can do to stop it, to stop any of this." He gestured to the room and then turned back to her with a gentle smile. "You were brave to attempt to stop this war. I admit, I find your arguments intriguing. But the treaty is broken. War comes for us all. That is why we must free the gods, release their power into the lands."

"You believe that freeing the gods will release magic. You think you'll get powers." Jura's eyes widened as the realization sank in. "And the extremists . . . they did break the treaty. The Sea King was right, this does mean war. What have you done?" The members of her false *Arbe* exchanged nervous glances. Surely she had heard him wrong.

"My lady, I have done nothing. I am simply a teacher. I pursue knowledge because that is my access to true power. Our combined knowledge has led us to believe that we can gain powers from releasing the gods. We just need to show you that our way is right."

"So that's why you've allowed me to stay here. Granted me access to your homes. Because you wanted to convince me to release the Everflame? And Amira, the *alttaw'am*? Was that you too?"

Amin Leyal had the decency to appear shocked. "*Alttaw'am*? In the republic? My lady, that is dangerous magic. What you suggest—"

"I know what I suggest. Do you know who is behind it?"

"My Lady First—I'm afraid I don't understand your meaning?"

"Shall I repeat my question?" She clenched her hands into fists at her side and willed her body to quit trembling. She was near, she could sense it. "Who controls the *alttaw'am*?"

He licked his lips once again and shook his head violently. "Impossible. Blood magic is mostly lost, reserved for those Deserters."

"What do you know about blood magic?" Jura changed

tactics, desperate for answers.

"We only use it here at its basest degree. Blood chains, nothing more. And they're illegal, I swear it."

"Tell me what you know about blood magic," she repeated.

"It is the strongest and the purest of the magics. It is the most sacred. It is the most dangerous." His eyes glazed and stared beyond her. "Oldest Wind. Youngest Fire. Strongest Water. Softest Earth." His gaze slid back to hers. "Blood that binds."

"What does that mean?"

He smiled. "Now that is the topic of much debate. Purists believe—"

"I don't need any more of your propaganda. I need answers. Concrete answers. My friend . . ." She trailed off as her attention was caught up by the enormous aquarium against the back wall. *How did I miss that before?* She wandered forward, frowning through the murky water at the image of the two people who floated within. Amin and Hadiya trailed behind.

"Servants of the water element. Quite useful when one lives in a desert. Still somewhat of a scandal." Amin gave a pointed look at Hadiya, and she lifted her shoulder in a careless shrug.

Jura didn't answer. She was too busy gaping at the two captive water people. Was this why the Wave Master had attacked? This was a defiant breach of the Tri-Alliance. If Kitoi was kidnapping the people of the Is'Le'Spar islands there was nothing in the world that would stop a war. Perhaps that was the point.

The people in the tank barely moved, long hair hovering over their heads the only other movement aside from the steady rise and fall of their chests. So it was true. The sea people did breathe underwater. The aquarium allotted them little room to move about, a glass box just big enough for them each to turn in a full circle.

"They're caged." Jura was unable to rip her eyes away from the aquarium.

"Indeed. They are bound to this house."

"In that tiny box?" Jura's fingers itched for the whip at her side. If only she could whip some sense into these people.

"They prefer it. It's filled with ocean water. Makes them feel closer to their god."

Jura shook her head, unable to justify his flippant attitude.

"In that tiny cage," she repeated to herself, but Hadiya let out an undignified snort. "Scoff all you wish, Greatness, but how are these slaves any different from the number your house owns? How is this cage any different than the one you've constructed around your god?"

Jura ignored her and squinted at the tank. Something about the woman tugged at Jura, a sense of familiarity that had her drawing even closer. Surely she was mistaken.

No, it *was* her.

Everflame help them all, what had they done?

"Do you know who this is? What you've done? You have to release them, immediately!" The Wave Mistress and her companion continued to float, unconscious in the tank.

"I'll do no such thing. A member of the Thirteen or not, I am a cobachon and I will have respect in my home."

Jura opened her mouth to respond, but a flash of golden yellow caught her eye. Ferrin Neorar, Master of Histories, had arrived. Yet another piece of the puzzle. New plan: distract Ferrin, free the Wave Mistress, rescue Amira, return home.

"Excuse me," she mumbled, tapping both Peppik and Markhim on either side of her. He had finally arrived. Her mind was still reeling from the sudden onslaught of information. Would this all boil down to an argument of faith? She couldn't afford to be distracted now. If Neorar was here, that meant Tylak had put his plan into action. He'd promised to offer some sort of signal once the deed was complete, so she simply had to distract the man until then. She started forward, resolving to not look again at the helpless figures with vacant expressions until she had a viable rescue plan. She had to focus on Amira and the plan, she—glass exploded. Thousands of tiny shards erupted from the aquarium, shooting out in every direction and spraying the guests in a shower of glass and briny water.

CORAL

Chapter Forty-One

The sounds were muted and distant. Her head ached something fierce and she had trouble opening her eyes. It took her several long moments to realize that she was submerged, that she breathed in the Great Mother herself. Coral squeezed her eyes tight and gave herself just a moment of the Mother's embrace.

Her eyes snapped open with her last memory of Mano.

She wasn't reunited with the Great Mother, not truly. She was trapped, suspended only Mother knew where.

Kale must have woken at the same time beside her because she had to shake her wrist free from his embrace. She didn't bother trying to control her *wei*, she released it with a fury she hadn't known she held.

This aquarium couldn't contain her. No one could.

The ringing in her ears was replaced by actual screams as the partygoers were bathed in water and bits of broken glass. It was easy and terrifying to piece together the last few hours of her life. Mano had betrayed her, betrayed everyone. The room was filled with a splash of gaudy colors, and Coral struggled to make her breathing even, to focus her anger. She spared Kale a quick once over before leaping to her feet.

"Who is in charge here?" Coral demanded. She realized she's spoken the question in her native tongue and repeated it again in Jangba. When no one immediately answered, she drew the water from the shattered aquarium back up into the air.

"I'm prepared to start drowning people one by one until I get a straight answer. Who did this? Who purchased me and then *put me on display*?" Coral's breath came in rapid puffs. She tried to force herself to calm down but she felt at any moment she would explode.

Still, no one spoke. So be it. She entrapped the nearest person to her in a tomb of water. The woman immediately began to choke and gag, she didn't even have the sense to try and hold her breath.

"Don't do that." A voice, soft and strangely familiar said by her side. And then a gentle touch on her arm.

She looked down at the petite hands of the Daughter of the First.

"Don't drown this woman. She's done nothing to you. She's an innocent partygoer."

With a snort of disgust, Coral released her hold on the water, allowing it to fall back to the ground. The woman who had seconds before been struggling to live was now a sodden mess, sobbing on the floor. Coral looked away. She had almost earned her lock of white here and now. It wouldn't have been right, not this way.

"Why do you care, Daughter of the First? How are you any better?" she sneered. It felt good to be angry at her, somehow *right*.

"It's terrible, I agree."

Why did the woman keep looking to her left? What did the man in yellow have to do with anything?

Coral frowned at the man and then turned her full attention

back to the Daughter of the First. She was wearing some ridiculous concoction made up of clear beads of glass. Entirely impractical for fighting.

"Don't just agree with me, do something about it."

"I will."

"No, I mean . . ." Coral trailed off, inspecting the woman more closely. The young woman stood as tall as her frame would allow, and her back was ramrod straight. Perhaps she had a spine after all.

Perhaps Coral had been too quick to dismiss her earlier. And she *was* a person of interest to the Queen of Shadows. That certainly meant something, even if Coral wasn't sure what that was just yet. In any case, the Daughter of the First would continue to live until Coral had another chance to hear her out.

Coral narrowed her eyes. This woman still wasn't to be trusted, yet she had yet to prove herself as enemy.

"Who is responsible for my imprisonment?" Coral lifted her chin, allowing her gaze to sweep across the room, daring everyone to meet her eye.

"Cabochon Hadiya, Master of Justice, is our host this evening. I dare say she'd be delighted to explain to you how she felt *justified* in her ownership." Jura darted another glance at the man in yellow.

"Who is that?" Coral asked, jerking her head toward the man. She could notice nothing special about him. He was slightly overweight with bland features. The shades of yellow he wore were the most interesting thing about him.

"He's no one," the Daughter of the First licked her lips. Coral wondered if that was her tell. Either way, the woman was lying. She made a mental note and turned her attention to the woman in blue who was inching away from the crowd.

"Stop where you are." Coral called up a ball of water and

hurled it at the woman. It stopped just in front of her face. "I demand justice, and there will be a reckoning." She drew in a ragged breath and called the water back toward her. She cradled it in her hands and stared into its tiny depths. "But the true vengeance I seek is not through you." She released the water and turned back to the Daughter of the First. "I would have more words with you."

Kale had come to stand beside her. He placed his palm on her shoulder. The warmth of his touch steadied her and gave her strength.

To her credit, the Daughter of the First didn't even look frightened. She simply snapped her fingers and called for her *Arbe* to assemble. The men had been dispersed about the room, apparently tending to those wounded by the shrapnel of her explosion. Coral winced at the unnecessary violence, but she wouldn't feel ashamed. Instead, she noted that the Daughter of the First had sent her men to help others. Coral found that she respected that. She turned to Kale, their voices muted by the gentle hum of the room as everyone fell into conversation about what they had just seen.

"We need to get word back to the ports, warn the other Kombu of Mano's treachery and sto—"

"I'm not leaving your side. You can't say anything to convince me otherwise," Kale interrupted.

She was too exhausted to argue. Her head pounded from the distant ringing in her ears and she vaguely smelled smoke. "Fine, wait for me outside then. Once I finish with the Daughter of the First, we'll go to the port together. But know this, Mano will soon feel the wrath of my blade."

He left without further comment. Relieved, she turned back to Jura. After the excitement of her arrival the partygoers were now either gaping openly or whispering fervently about her. Coral decided they were both equally annoying.

"I believe we've overstayed our welcome," Jura murmured, as her men gradually formed a square around her.

Coral nodded. That was an understatement. If the Queen of Shadows had planned to make an appearance, she wouldn't do so now. The party was ruined and people had started going home as soon as the immediate threat of danger had passed.

But how could she simply go home after this? Mano was out there somewhere. Mano, the man her father had insisted she marry. Had he been working with the Queen of Shadows all along? And how was it that she had so easily found herself a slave? Was that all it took, one moment and one's life was lost forever?

How many more were out there in similar circumstances throughout the city? If her life had almost changed in the course of a few hours, how many more were out there now? Her people did not enter wars lightly and the Daughter of the First was determined to push for peace, but how could Coral accept a Tri-Alliance that was such a blatant lie? The Tri-Alliance didn't protect her people, it enslaved them. They were better off cutting all ties with every breathcatcher on land.

Coral eyed the men around Jura. Scarface was missing, replaced with a man who was almost as pretty as Kale. She would have smirked but for the way he watched her. His relaxed military stance told her the man was no stranger to war. Good. The Daughter of the First needed strong warriors around her. They shuffled along with the rest of the departing guests, although they were given a wide berth. Coral tried to ignore the way her heart swelled at the sight of Kale wrapping a blanket around the shoulders of a woman who shook with sobs. He was so compassionate, it was one of the many things she admired about her friend. He had many admirable qualities, but that didn't mean anything. Still, she couldn't help but feel at least a tiny bit better when Kale noticed her and lifted his arm in greeting.

She directed the group toward him, taking lead. "I was hasty in our last encounter. For that, I apologize," Coral swallowed. That had been more difficult than she thought it would be. "In the future, I will try my best to ask questions first and take actions later." Even as she said the words out loud they brought a small whisper of a smile to her lips. Mother knew a vow of simple words would never calm the tempest in her heart.

The man who was too handsome for his own good smiled at her. "I think we have all been there," he said, surprising her. Didn't the barbarians cut out the tongues of their bodyguards? Perhaps those rumors were wrong because he was talking now. He had a lovely baritone that matched his face.

"Don't worry, Jura," he continued. "I think we have our signal."

Coral wasn't sure what he meant until he gestured behind them to the distant flames. She *had* smelled smoke. He'd mentioned a signal. A signal for what? What were they planning?

She was about to demand answers for everything when Kale jogged up, catching her arm.

"That fire down there is spreading. If we let it go unhindered . . ." He trailed off, letting the implication hang. Homes would be destroyed, people injured, possibly killed. She knew the stakes. Mother, but she was exhausted. Well, she'd start calling in favors now. They didn't have *wei* but they had the strength of their own backs and at least basic medical knowledge. It was something.

"Jura and her team here are going to stick around until we get some concrete answers. I imagine you have stuff to ask of me as well?"

Jura nodded. Coral cut off any further words with a long exaggerated sigh. So be it, another long night.

"We'll need to spli—"

Kale tackled Jura's handsome bodyguard to the ground, driving his fist into his face.

"Kale! What are you doing?" She grabbed either shoulder and ripped him off the man. Kale rolled on the ground, clambering to his feet and throwing an accusatory finger at the bodyguard.

"That's him. Coral, that's him. Don't let him go anywhere!" Kale's voice was hoarse. She'd never seen him so worked up over anything.

"What is it? What's happening?" And then she knew.

Invisible beads of water trickled down her spine. No.

"He's the one who killed your father."

KAY

CHAPTER FORTY-TWO

I won't do it. Kay fidgeted under the heavy dragon scale armor and squeezed her hands into fists. Her nails dug into the palms of her hand, burning her skin. Today wasn't real. Today was a dream. It had all been a dream. Any moment now she would wake up at home with Mama and Daddy.

Ash had rambled on and on with his steady timbre, the words an unrecognized blur that rang in Kay's ears. With desperation he pressed her hands into his palms and whispered the words again.

"Wait for my signal. Run for the halls." She nodded, repeating the words over and over to herself. Wait, signal. Run halls. Somehow Ash would give her a signal. But she didn't know what that signal was. And how would she see it if she was in the arena proper? She'd asked to see Ash again, but her new owner said Ash wasn't allowed to see her anymore. She wouldn't explain why.

She didn't need a full explanation from Ash to understand what it meant to enter the arena early: it was bad.

Wait for a signal; run for the halls. That part was easy. All she had to do was follow directions. She could do that.

Someone thrust her assegai at her. She reached for it with trembling fingers. She looked up and tried to focus on the figure in red, but her eyes were starting to water. She pressed her lips together hard to stop them from trembling. If she blinked her eyes fast enough, maybe the tears would go away.

"You'll do great." Denir's voice was lifted with optimism, and she smiled sweetly at Kay.

Kay didn't even bother to pretend to smile back. She couldn't seem to stare past the assegai that rose up from her fingertips, several feet taller than her own meager height.

"This is a huge honor. The biggest honor," the Fourth cooed. "I had to pull several strings to make this happen tonight."

Kay swallowed several times and pressed her free hand into her mid-section, hoping the pressure would remind the contents of her belly to stay put. The sharp edges of the dragon scale dug into the tender lines of her stomach. They had made the armor especially for her. Kay was pretty sure she had heard her new owner bragging about it earlier. No armor had ever been made to fit one so small. She traced her fingers along the harsh lines of the red armor and shivered. The deep red sparkled and glistened in the sunlight, the color of rubies, the color of Rumble.

Horns blared in the distance. The sound normally brought a smile to Ash's face. Kay wondered if he was smiling now. Probably not. He had appeared super worried. Would she be able to find him once inside? Would she see the signal?

The person in red robes squeezed a hand onto Kay's shoulder, but she didn't feel the pressure. She knew what the horns meant; it was time.

"You'll be sensational," the Fourth said, repeating herself. "Just sensational."

"Remember your Forms," said the figure in red. Kay blinked at the man, but she had never seen him before.

I can't do this. I won't. Kay opened her mouth to once again beg the Fourth to put an end to this.

"It's time." The man in red placed his hand across her back and gave her a gentle shove.

The horns sounded again, closer because the trio had moved down the hall and now stood just outside the heavy steel doors that led to the arena. Once open, they would stay that way until the end of the battle. And past them was the halls that led to her freedom.

When had they walked closer? The Fourth was beaming. She reminded Kay of a traveling performer she'd once seen. The man's face had been painted with exaggerated features. His wide illustrated grin was almost as big as the Fourth's was now.

Heat billowed out from those doors in giant waves, the same heat from the north barn. The same heat she'd felt the day she'd lost Daddy, Mama, and Rumble.

"I d-don't want to do this," the words tumbled out. "I want to go home." She knew she sounded like a baby but she couldn't stop. She let the assegai slip from her fingers. It fell into the sand creating a soft puff of dust.

"Please, I can't—"

"Stop it right now." The Fourth bent forward so she could stare deep into Kay's eyes. Mama would do that too, whenever she believed Kay wasn't telling the truth. But Kay was telling the truth. She couldn't go through with any of this. She needed to go home. "Stop crying," the Fourth repeated in Drakori. "You're the most powerful Fire Dancer I've ever seen. Today you will be named, a name that will be known to the world for centuries."

Kay didn't care. She didn't want a new name and she hated

her new home. She wanted Daddy and Mama, fresh baked bread and cool springs.

The giant steel doors opened and Kay was shoved inside.

"Make me proud." The Fourth's command rang in her ears, but as they disappeared back down the hall, Kay was left very much alone.

When did I pick up the assegai? She stared at the tall wooden spear threaded between the fingers of her right hand. The screaming of the crowd reverberated throughout the glass arena. She turned in a quick circle, taking in the whirl of chanting onlookers, the torches lining the arena dirt, and finally the massive iron gate stretched across the black opening on the opposite side of the circle.

A tiny whimper escaped from her mouth.

Wait for a signal. Run for the halls.

The halls were right behind her. Ash would make sure she saw the signal . . . wouldn't he? She whirled in a slow circle, taking another careful look at her surroundings. She searched for Ash in the crowd but couldn't find him in the puzzle of faces.

The grounds of the arena proper stunk. It smelled like Daddy after a hard day of yard work, like chickens freshly slaughtered. Of campfires and Mama burning.

Kay blinked away the image. Soon she would be running. She was good at running. And in a way, that was following directions. That was the last thing Daddy had told her to do.

She couldn't hear the crowd, although she could clearly see their open mouths, screaming over one another. Who would they cheer for if she battled a dragon?

I won't do it. She repeated the words to herself even as the giant iron gate began to slide open.

It made a terrible noise. The metal teeth screeched against one another and hurt her ears, but instead of bringing her hands up to cover them she tightened her grip on the assegai and slid her feet into First Position. She Breathed in the heat from a few of the closer torches. She immediately felt better, calmer somehow, and she Breathed in a few more. The fire burned inside her and she held it back with clenched teeth.

She waited for several seconds that seemed to stretch a lifetime before the beast finally appeared.

Please don't let him look like Rumble.

He didn't. His scales were a deep, brilliant blue. He thundered out of the holding cell and bellowed a roar that sent shivers down her spine. Angry, silver eyes met hers and the dragon charged forward, marking his prey.

Kay leapt to the right and tucked her body into a ball, barely rolling away in time to miss the stream of molten fire directed at her. She performed a series of back handsprings. When she stopped tumbling, she stood several feet away from the dragon's monstrous snout. But where was her assegai? She'd dropped the weapon when she had been flipping for safety. She was already off to a bad start. Ash lectured that a Fire Dancer must be one with their assegai. Well, there wasn't time to worry about what she should have done. The dragon was already shooting another batch of liquid flames her way.

She caught it, staggering slightly over the feel of his flames. They felt different somehow, heavier almost. She shot the flames up into the glass dome above her and finally heard the crowd's screams. She dared a quick glance at the glass spectator box but didn't have enough time to make out anyone's features. Ash would probably give the signal from there. She needed to give him time. She spotted her assegai in the sand and made her way toward it.

She Breathed in more heat, several torches winking out as she did so, and shoved a line of liquid fire directly at the dragon's chest. The orange and red flames bounced harmlessly off his blue scales. Kay raced in the opposite direction, trying to put as much space as possible between her and the dragon. He shot into the air, circling the glass dome and waiting for the right moment to complete his aerial attack.

She hadn't wanted to know his name, believing that denying the beast's name would make this all seem less real, yet she heard it chanted on the voices of the thousands of spectators.

"Inferno! Inferno! Inferno!"

That was Beshar's dragon. She knew because this was the one dragon Ash had told her she would never have to fight. The dragon who killed Kindle. She hadn't wanted to believe it until now. Had refused to connect that this blue dragon was the same as the one that had killed her friend. She once again looked for Ash in the spectators box. She saw the familiar face of her new owner but no trace of Ash.

Inferno thudded into the sand in front of her.

He was so big, so utterly angry looking that it was impossible not to be frightened. He was nothing like Rumble. Not a beloved friend but a dangerous predator.

He blew another stream of fire directly at her. She Breathed it in by instinct and then immediately fell to her knees, gasping at the sheer intensity of his flames. This was something different entirely. She shot the flames back out, her fingertips pointed and aiming for the dragon's eyes.

He trumpeted his anger and stood up on his hind legs, roaring out another gale of smoke and flames.

Kay dived forward, tucking her compact body into a neat roll just inches from the ground. She slid in the sand, scrambling to her feet and throwing careless balls of fire behind her. She just had to distract him long enough . . . there it was! Her assegai flew up into her fingertips and she drew her hand back, prepared to strike when the beast next exposed his belly.

Wait for the signal. Run for the halls.

She couldn't wait anymore. She drew back her hand.

Inferno's eyes had once been shiny and black, now they were dull and gray but still feral and angry, but she didn't see his eyes, she saw Rumble's. Her hand faltered. *I can't do this.* The assegai slipped from her stiff fingers.

The dragon dipped down and charged forward. Kay dropped down to her knees, sinking into the soft sand of the arena floor. She could never harm a dragon. It went against everything she knew.

I miss Daddy. I miss Mama. I miss Rumble. She closed her eyes and allowed the flames to take her.

ASH

CHAPTER FORTY-THREE

Ash worried he wouldn't make it there fast enough. He couldn't quite run, his old knee injury wouldn't allow that, but he'd adapted a respectable jog which he fell into now. He had bombarded his cadet with last minute instructions. Flames only knew if the poor girl was able to translate all the information. He knew he'd gotten the basic gist through to her. Stay alive, wait for his signal, and when he gave it, run like the Everflame itself gave chase. A necessary component to his plan of course was arriving in time to get Kay out of there.

He gritted his teeth and ran faster, ignoring the ache in his knee. Once again he cursed the Ninth and his manipulations. No doubt the man had gotten himself into this mess, leaving Ash to deal with his innocent wonder child. He wished that he had never purchased her.

If it wasn't you, then someone else would have taken her. Maybe even the Arena Council. That wasn't much of a stretch. They were the very reason he was late.

He'd been approached by Kadira and her tall lackey, both in

their usual red robes. She'd been all business, asking why Denir had fired him and demanding to know what had prompted the impromptu Naming Day. Ash wished he had an answer for her, but he was just as confused as she was. More so, for at least the Fourth had to register her new property through the Arena Council so they knew about the sale before Ash did. He'd reminded her of this and had been unwilling to share anything else.

He hadn't seen the point in admitting his knowledge on the creation of arena dragons. No, the best thing to do was grab Kay and flee the arena. The arena battle horns had sounded and the stress built itself into a frenzied fire within him. It had taken far too long to excuse himself from the conversation. He had, in fact, simply left while the woman was still talking. Just because she had no intention of watching the cadet's naming day was no reason to keep him from watching it. At least, that's where he hoped her thoughts would turn after he'd simply fled the room.

He heard the second and final battle horn and drew in his breath in ragged gasps. Burn these infernal twisting hallways, he was going to be too late.

He still hadn't even had time to fully plot out his plan. He knew it involved Kay escaping the arena and the two of them leaving the arena via the catacombs. He wasn't entirely sure where they would go after, perhaps back to her home. If her parents were gone, he could step in and make a life for them there, couldn't he? He just needed to get her out of that arena. He needed a distraction, something big enough to give his cadet the time she needed to escape. An idea began to shape, he just hoped he had enough Fire Dancing left in him to pull it off. He pulled the flame from a nearby torch toward him. And then another. It was clumsy at first, maintaining his awkward gallop while pulling the flames off torches and adding it to the ever growing ball of fire. Behind him the stone hallways winked into darkness.

The dragon's screech caused the hairs on his arm to rise, despite their proximity to the now massive ball of flames trailing behind him. Ash spared a quick glance to the doors leading to the spectators box long enough to pull the flames from their torches too. Without another thought, he hurried down the length of the hallway and entered the arena proper.

Kay was in the center of the arena, kneeling in the sand. Her head was bowed. She didn't hear him call her name. With a curse, Ash stepped onto the sand, dragging his flaming ball behind him. Flames he was tired. He took a deep breath and hurled his giant ball of fire directly at the dragon's head.

For a moment, the light was staggering. He'd caught the beast right as he'd been expelling his own flames. The result was a dazzling explosion of fire and billowing black smoke. Ash took the opportunity to throw the rest of the torches toward the enormous twisting ball of fire and rushed to Kay's side. He ignored the protest from his old knees and hunkered down beside her.

"Kay, it's me. I'm here."

"Is this signal?" She opened her eyes.

He couldn't control this much fire for much longer. Already it was more than he'd ever held, and the effort to maintain it in a tight ball around the dragon's head would only last for so long.

"Kay, look. You see that big ball of fire?" There was nothing else to see. He'd collected nearly every torch in the arena. The fire rolled together in a lazy tornado of flames, a beacon of light in the now darkened arena.

"Can you . . . can you Breathe that much in?" Was he asking too much of her? But this was the only way. He was already lightheaded. "Kay, Breathe."

The arena plunged into darkness. Almost. The little girl beside him blazed as bright as the sun. Ash blinked and turned his head, blinded by the sudden absence of light when he looked away. What did it mean for her to be holding so much fire?

He thought of Timber and his belief that enough heat at the right spot would shatter the arena dome. Timber had been so sure; Ash wanted to believe too.

He grabbed the girl's hand, ignoring the searing heat that burned him at the touch of her skin.

"Look there," he pointed, wondering if Kay could even see where he pointed, the spot only vaguely outlined by the moon. There was no time to question it further.

"Shoot the flames there!"

Kay did as she was told, shooting a rush of flames at the glass dome. The dragon shot his flame at them too, but his aim was off. Ash pushed the flame further off course and into the sand.

Once again the arena darkened, only this time Ash was more easily able to adjust to the darkness. He peered up at the glass dome. It wasn't cracked. Either Timber had been wrong or they had scorched the wrong spot or the glass truly was impenetrable. Either way, the glass dome still stood. It doesn't matter, he told himself. The important thing is you have your distraction. He pulled Kay along behind him and rushed toward the exit, pulling her down the long hall that led out of the arena proper.

"Get your hands off my cadet at once."

The Fourth placed a hand on either side of her hip, but Ash

was still inclined to smash her against the wall and have her out of his way. He couldn't do that though, not when she was surrounded by members of the Arena Council. He didn't have time to count the red robes, not with Inferno still screeching behind them. The hallway was narrow but he'd heard of more than one determined beast worming himself into the narrow hall in search of his prey. For the moment, he decided to ignore the dragon.

"Let us pass, Councilmembers. Consider her forfeit."

"She was doing fine. This is her naming day and these people came to see blood." Denir jutted her chin toward the chanting crowd. They were in a frenzied state, screaming out Inferno and . . . FireShot? She'd been named. Despite it all, Ash felt a stubborn jolt of pride.

"Then I will give them blood." Ash murmured the words. "But not hers," he said loudly. "I'll fight the dragon in her stead."

"Don't be ridiculous." Tommon, an elder member of the Arena Council, shook his head. "The Fourth would never agree to that."

"Oh, I agree."

"What?" Ash's cry mimicked Tommon's.

Denir shrugged. "I agree on a few conditions. You finish this now, there will be no postponement, and you finish this with her. My cadet will complete her naming day and slay her first beast."

If she had followed their exchange, Kay gave no indication. Although if one listened carefully, they could hear her trembling in her dragon armor.

Ash rolled his shoulders and bit down on his tongue to think of something aside from his aching knees. He had wanted another chance in the arena against a dragon as formidable as Inferno. There was no time to go back for his assegai, so Kay's smaller one would have to do. She reached up and took his hand.

"I'm sorry we have to go back in there, but I promise not to let anything happen to you."

She nodded. "Signal . . . run."

"That's right, no matter what happens you run. You get out of here and you run home, do you hear me? Do whatever it takes."

Her grip on his hand tightened. He carried on, determined to keep talking even if she couldn't understand everything, as long as she understood the *tone*. He once again warned her about the dangers of the catacombs, told her to turn left when she left the arena, that that would lead her home. He told her he was proud of her, that she'd given his life new meaning.

Inferno waited for them with snapping jaws.

"Are you ready?" There were no torches for him to pull flame from. He'd used them all up earlier.

Kay nodded and with a deep Breath brought a tiny flame forth to dance across her fingertips. She tossed the flame to Ash and he caught it in wonder. This child would never cease to amaze him.

It seemed Inferno was even more angry now. But Kay was a thing of wonder. With Ash there to call the Forms out to her, she blended from one to the next, darting and twisting between Inferno's attacks in the most beautiful dance Ash had ever seen. It was marvelous dancing with her. She watched him carefully, tossing him fireballs whenever he needed help in his attack and distracting the dragon so he could get close enough to reclaim her assegai. He spun it now between deft fingers, waiting for the right moment to plunge it into the dragon's belly.

Kay spun around him, dancing with a ribbon of flames that shot up into the air and tickled the dragon's nose.

Now was his chance. Ash lunged forward, prepared to deliver

the killing blow into the tender skin of Inferno's belly, a blow he'd delivered countless times before, a move that was as natural as breathing. So natural that he'd forgotten the pressure the move took on his back leg. His knee crumpled underneath him, there was no other way to describe it, and he fell to the sands in a heap of tired bones and singed flesh. The slender wood of the assegai snapped between his fingers as he fell. Or was that his finger? Something broke. Desperately his eyes sought Kay, still dancing, an endless pirouette of flames. She was so fiercely powerful, her movements so magnificent that in those wild seconds he entertained the thought that he could live in this moment forever, just watching her dance with fire.

The dragon crashed down in front of him. The moment was lost.

No, ignore it. Ignore the searing hot pain in your knee. Your entire leg burns as if it is on fire but get up. You can still do this. *His fingers once again sought the assegai. It was broken, but the top half still held its wicked blade.* Ignore everything and throw the blade.

Ash struggled to climb to his feet. He hurled the broken assegai at the same time Inferno released a stream of molten fire directly into his chest.

When delivering the killing blow, the Fire Dancer exposes his chest to flames. A necessary disadvantage to get the power needed to rip open a dragon's stomach, which is why a Fire Dancer wears dragon scaled armor. Ash wore no armor.

His throw was effortless. Perfect. Ash watched with a satisfied grin as it slid into the beast's gut before he was thrown to his back, an overwhelming heat scorching him down to his insides. He thought of Kay. He hoped she knew his death was beautiful, that she would remember he had died in flames and ash, a hero.

TYLAK

Chapter Forty-Four

Tylak enjoyed the night. The streets of the Golden City were silent compared those surrounding the Glass Palace, although not as silent as the dangerous quiet he had grown up with on the streets of Ish. He didn't often think of the early years, the wandering years after he lost Sykk and before he got mixed up with the Shadow Dancers. Odd that he would choose to think of it now. He supposed it was better than thinking of Jura . . . And now he was thinking about Jura.

He deserved a swift kick in the . . . Burn it all. It didn't matter if he tried to think about her or not, until Sykk was found and safe at home he would remain in her life. He quickened his pace, eager to finish his rescue mission and get back to her. She was more than capable of taking care of herself but, well, she was his friend and it was only natural for him to worry. He'd remained invisible for the majority of his journey, slipping in and out of shadows as he made his way across the city. He didn't need the Everflame torch to twist the light, but he'd brought it anyway, accustomed to its presence after these weeks. The adventure had started with the flame, it only seemed fitting he should finish with it. And Amira would soon be in sight.

It didn't take long, mere minutes really before he arrived at the large home imprisoning the Daughter of the former Third. There was a lazy guard at the gate but no one else patrolled the lawn.

Tylak stayed invisible as he crept across the lawn and around the back of the home. It was always better to sneak in from the back or even better a basement or an upstairs window. None of those options were available so Tylak entered through the kitchen door and slipped into the house.

A low hum sounded from across the house. The melody was sporadic and jarring. He heard the noise before he noticed the bodies.

A large man lay face down, blood pooled around him but had already begun to dry on the wooden floor. A smaller body was draped across the table just in front of a strange plant Tylak had never seen before.

The humming stopped.

He looked up to find a young woman in tattered clothing. Her choppy hair fell around her face at awkward angles as though someone had hacked it away with a knife. Perhaps someone had. There appeared to be some sort of wound on her shoulder, but otherwise she was unharmed.

"Amira?" He tried to make his voice as calm as possible. Though he'd worn his darks, he'd intentionally left the mask behind. No sense in shouting out he was a Shadow Dancer.

It seemed she had clear ideas of him already. "I won't go back. You'll never take me!" She screamed and threw her knife at him.

He turned invisible by instinct, but the knife still glanced off his shoulder, slicing through fabric and into tender skin. He bit back a muffled curse and moved to the other side of the room before she thought to throw another dagger where he had stood.

"I'm here to . . ." he trailed off. Was he rescuing her? From what exactly? "I'm here to bring you to Jura." There. It had a nice directness to it. He ducked at the porcelain vase that flew toward his head. Could she see him? Flames that woman had accuracy.

"How do I know this isn't a trick?"

"If you stop throwing things I can give you a letter from Jura."

"You have a letter from Jura?" she squealed in an unexpected nasal tone that seemed unlikely coming from her tall slender frame. "Give it to me."

He reappeared beside her out stretched fingers. To her credit, she didn't flinch at his sudden appearance. She twiddled her fingers and he produced the letter. She eyed it warily for a moment before she snatched it open with practiced fingers. She seemed to read it several times but finally she burst into rich laughter.

"She's truly here?"

Tylak nodded.

"And she's employed the Shadow Dancers to save me?"

"Uh, just the one, although technically I can't call myself a Shadow—"

"Then what is she doing here?" Amira pointed behind him where the kitchen door hung open. A woman dressed entirely in black with a gold filigree mask stood in the doorway.

Tylak jerked his head toward the front entrance of the house. "Go on, get out of here. I'll hold her back while you run."

The woman in black laughed. Amira stared at them both for a moment before she snatched a knife strapped to the side of the dead body on the table and ran down the hall. He heard a door slam and sighed. The flaming woman hadn't even run out the front door.

Locking herself in a room would never protect her from the attack of an experienced Shadow Dancer.

He gave his new adversary his full attention. "What are your orders?" Shadow Dancers didn't leave without primary objectives. Steal the information, plant the lie. Commands were clear, concise.

The woman shrugged, moving forward slowly. She appeared to carry no weapons, but Tylak felt threatened all the same. He resisted the urge to reach for his daggers.

"I have no orders."

That was impossible, everyone had orders. Unless . . . "It's you."

He imagined the woman smiling beneath her mask though he could only guess at her features.

"It's me."

"I demand an Exchange of Information."

"And I refuse."

Tylak gaped at her. A refusal simply wasn't done. Unless one was the Queen of Shadows. Then one could do anything they wanted.

"Did you come here to stop Amira from leaving with me?" He could hear her in the room down the hall and wondered what she was doing to create such a racket. What was so important that she didn't immediately run?

"The Third family is important to me, and her disappearance would be unfortunate."

"Because you need her to control the First?"

"The First is no longer enchained. I'm not doing this with you, Tylak."

"Then what? You want to fight?" He stalked across the length of the kitchen, crossing back and forth with angry strides and stopping just before the dead body every time.

"I didn't come to fight. I thought we could chat. I want you to answer a few questions."

Of course she did. But he'd be a flaming fool if he thought he could trust her for even a moment. She was the Queen of Shadows. Secrets.

"Why would I do that without an Exchange? Why would I do anything for you?"

The Queen shrugged, throwing up a careless hand. Even her hands were encased in black gloves. There was no indication of how old or how young she might be except for what he could see of her eyes. They were a light brown and they stared at him intently.

"You will do it," she said. "You will answer my questions because these questions will gain you insight into what I'm truly after."

Burn it all she was right. He needed to know her questions. He sighed. "What do you want to know?"

"You were looking for me not so long ago. Why?"

That's what she wanted to ask? The question caught him off guard. He'd assumed she had heard he was looking for her. A common soldier like himself didn't go provoking the attention of the Queen without expecting certain repercussions, but he never thought she cared enough to wonder why. Well, it seemed he had her attention now. Once he'd sought her out at the urging of Denir. Then again, he'd searched for her after with the crazy hope of asking for her favor. For her assistance in finding Sykk. That seemed so long ago now, though it had only been a few weeks. How was any of this connected to Jura? He decided to answer with honesty.

"I thought to find you to beg for a favor. I'd heard you sometimes granted favors if—"

"You still want your brother back." The woman stepped closer.

"Yes," he whispered. How did she know?

"Done. Return to us, Tylak. You and the girl leave with me now and I'll get your brother. I'll return him back to you by tomorrow."

"I . . ." Was she telling him the truth? There was no one more powerful than the First family yet the Queen of Shadows had her hands in everything. This was true power. She could return Sykk to him. But at what cost? What did that mean for Jura? She needed him. He pushed aside thoughts of Markhim. Burn it all, Jura did want him around. He was sure of it. And she was willing to help find Sykk, no strings attached.

"I can't do that." He shook his head and reached for his dagger.

"Because of the Daughter of the First? You have worked out some sort of deal where you assist her in exchange for her connections in the arena. And you have developed feelings for the child." It wasn't a question. The woman nodded to herself. Tylak flinched as yet another thump sounded from the room down the hall. This time the sound was accompanied by breaking wood. They both looked down the hall toward the sound.

"I have to take her with me," Tylak warned.

"I'll have to try to stop you." The woman continued to stare toward the distant banging down the hall. "I'll also want whatever she's working so hard to retrieve. If it's what I think it is, the Daughter of the Third has once again proven her immeasurable worth."

Tylak thought about his options. He wouldn't consider returning to Jura without Amira, but the Queen of Shadows seemed determined to prevent him from reaching his goal. "It isn't possible to stop us. There are two of us and only one of you."

"Is that so?" The Queen of Shadows had every reason to sound amused. No sooner had the words left her mouth than Tylak realized how foolish he sounded. He was talking to the Queen of Shadows Dancers. For all he knew he was surrounded by her invisible spies. All right then, time to resort to plan B.

He still carried the torch of the Everflame. It was a ready source of power, portable light and heat he was able to bend to his will. With a resigned sigh, he hurled the torch toward the back kitchen door. It sailed over the Queen's shoulder. He once again wished she hadn't been wearing a mask because he very much would have liked to see her expression.

The pantry immediately erupted into flames.

"What have you done?" she hissed.

The Queen shoved past him, making for the hallway. He tackled her to the ground. For a moment the two rolled around on the floor, neither gaining purchase over the other. Then Tylak suffered a sharp blow to his groin. He sucked in a deep breath, for one moment unable to even so much as hold in the breath before the chills subsided. He released her and groaned on the floor before he pulled himself to his feet and stumbled toward her, but the wall directly beside him ignited in flames and he was forced to step back from the fire.

"You stupid boy," the Queen admonished him. "I could have helped you." She stared at him for one agonized moment and then ran out of the home, leaving him in the pile of smoldering wreckage.

"Amira," he shouted.

The door down the hall swung open and Amira peeked out. "What's happening?" she asked.

He gestured around at the obvious, because clearly the growing flames and smoke weren't enough. Amira nodded, distracted. "Just another moment. I just have to get one thing." Her words echoed back to him despite the fact she'd already disappeared back inside the room. Tylak groaned but darted down the hall, determined to get her out of the house, even if it meant throwing her over his shoulder and carrying her out.

The room was in shambles. The desk was turned upside down. The rugs were thrown back. The bookshelves destroyed. Everything lay ripped open and exposed. He couldn't help it, he whistled low between his teeth.

What's going on in here? He didn't get a chance to voice his question out loud before Amira exclaimed in delight. She bounced to her feet, raising a brass key in his general direction before stabbing the tiny instrument into the appropriate cupboard. He wasn't disturbed by the lack of fanfare, there was a raging fire, after all, fueled by the Everflame, so when Amira produced the shining blue stone he let out a satisfied grunt before pulling her and it out of the burning home. He half expected the Queen of Shadows or one of her minions to be waiting for him, but the street was entirely quiet except for his own labored breathing and that of the woman beside him.

CORAL

The entire world had dissolved into a red fog. The only sound was the rush of the falls in Aina. It roared in her ears.

For some reason, Jura's face was the first she saw. The Daughter of the First had wide amber eyes. She shook her head and tried to deny Kale's accusation.

"Did you know?" Coral interrupted her.

"It's not true. It ca—" Coral refused to allow her to finish. She cut off Jura's words by shoving water down her throat. Then she lunged at her father's killer.

He was ready for the attack and kept his footing despite the low tackle. She grunted. It was like running into a pole. She reached for the dagger strapped at her side and sliced at his face. He dropped low, sweeping at her legs. She tumbled to the ground but used the opportunity to shove water in his eyes. It was the last of her holding supply. This time he wasn't ready for her tackle and crumpled easily after her blow.

Before this moment, the rest of their party had stood off to the side, giving her, Jura, and her bodyguard their space. They rushed forward now, Kale leaped forward to greet them. The oldest man, (Much too old to still be Arbe. Why hadn't anyone noticed?) placed gentle but firm hands on her shoulders and heaved her off her father's killer.

She turned quickly, catching the man's fist and flipping him to the ground directly atop the fallen bodyguard.

"Stop it!" Jura repeated her cry.

Coral barely spared her a glance. She had probably known about this the entire time, thinking to play her as the fool. Well, it wouldn't happen, not today. Kale had the other two occupied. Perfect. She shoved her elbow into the face of the older man and then kneed the younger in the gut. She scrambled to her feet and called for her *wei* to bring up water from deep underground.

Both of the men clambered to their feet. She was ready. If she had to kill them all, so be it. She drew the trishula strapped at her back. Her father's weapon. It was time for retribution. She drew back her arm.

A sharp burning sting caught her around the wrist. She blinked in confusion at the leather strap.

Jura pulled the whip and sent her sprawling. *So, the jellyfish had barbs.* Coral grinned, leaping to her feet. She kicked the handsome bodyguard in his jaw and used that same momentum to throw a punch at the old man who, to her surprise, ducked the blow.

She whirled around just in time to catch Jura's whip with her spare hand. She pulled hard enough for the young woman to fall face first in the sand. Coral wrenched the whip from her grasp, discarding it in the dirt behind her. Kale was still entertaining the other two. They were an angry mass of clashing steel and spinning water. She turned her attention back to her two greatest foes, but the older man had disappeared. She kept a wary eye out for him as she advanced toward the handsome one, her parent's killer.

"You have to pay for what you did," she told him.

"Let me explain. The Queen of Shadows—"

"Will also taste my blade." She drew back her arm and was shoved roughly on her side.

The Daughter of the First had a good tackle for one so tiny. Coral fell hard, twisting her left arm under her at an awkward angle. Searing pain tore through her shoulder.

"Stop this, please! We have to—"

"Get off of me," Coral shoved the wisp of a girl back but she refused to move. She tried another tactic, drawing an orb of floating water to cover her face. Confident the Daughter of the First would now be distracted, she jumped to her feet, trishula ready.

Jura wasn't drowning.

Impossible. *What is she?* Not one of the people and—*oomph.* She kicked hard too. Coral grunted. She caught Jura's ankle, still marveling at the orb which would have killed any normal breathcatcher yet here she was . . . *Don't get distracted,* she *doesn't matter.* With a frustrated growl Coral retracted her orb of water and shot it all directly into Jura's eyes. She turned back to the bodyguard and sent him a wicked smile. He'd drawn a scimitar from somewhere. Good.

"What did she give you? Hmm? Was it money? Land?! Access to *her?*"

"I don't . . ." he blocked a blow from her trishula, breathing hard. ". . . know what . . ." Another deep breath. A wide sweeping blow from his scimitar, easily dodged. ". . . you're talking about."

"Don't play stupid. You killed my father. Kale saw you."

"I . . ." He leaped to the right, narrowly missing getting

speared in the gut. "I can explain."

What a load of rotting fish heads. There was nothing to explain. There were no excuses. There were only true and simple facts. Her parents were dead, hundreds of people were dead, and he had started it.

"Please, just listen. We can stop—" Jura started.

Coral tuned her out. She didn't want to listen to her whining. Didn't want to hear Kale cautioning her to stop. Didn't care about the fact that Jura's scar-faced bodyguard had returned with some other girl in tow. None of that mattered.

"I'm tired of listening." She turned and threw her trishula directly at the bodyguard.

TYLAK

The flames ate up the home in a matter of minutes. They didn't stick around to watch it happen. Amira allowed Tylak to pull her along as they ran down the streets and back toward Jura. He'd never seen the Everflame released before and didn't quite know what it meant. It was inextinguishable in its true form, but surely this fire could be put out? He didn't like thinking about what would happen if that wasn't the case.

It was a dumb move, he chided himself, pulling Amira behind him. She was tiring but was keeping pace. She was strong. He'd noticed the scars on her wrists, the hollow circles around her eyes. She was a survivor. It was time to find Jura and leave Kitoi as fast as they could. That had always been the plan. Rescue Amira and return to the Republic with visible proof of the Thirteen's deceit. Well, they had that now. Hopefully Jura had managed to stay out of any trouble at the party. Maybe they would have an opportunity to talk during the trip home. They needed to talk. He was finally ready to talk, and he felt she was ready too. Thinking of Jura only made him push them harder. They arrived at the party minutes later.

It was pandemonium. Here on the slightly raised hill he could see the fire still raging behind them. Growing.

The party had spilled out into the lawn, and Jura was at the very center of it. Only it wasn't a party at all. The princess of the sea or whoever she was fought Markhim with a fervor he'd never seen. Another tall man fought the twins, his long spear twirling with the grace of a Fire Dancer.

"About time you showed up," Peppik mumbled at his side. The old man was breathing hard as if he had just finished running.

"What's happening?" Tylak asked, drawing his daggers and stalking forward. The sea princess needed to be put down.

"Hold on," Peppik warned, grabbing at his arm. "She's more powerful than you realize."

Tylak didn't care. His friends were out there. Jura had some sort of strange ball of water attached to her face but she didn't appear to be drowning.

"Jura!" Amira chose that moment to scream by his side.

They caught the attention of the sea princess. Markhim and Jura too. They were all left wide open. Tylak lunged forward, crashing into Markhim and tackling the man to the ground seconds before the woman's trishula speared him in the chest. Instead, it flew directly behind him and embedded itself into the abdomen of the taller man. He sank to his knees, surprise registering on his face.

The scream that followed was feral. The sea princess rushed to catch her falling companion, already his skin grew ashen and his wound sprayed blood.

"Stay back," she ordered, slashing out with her arm. The ground slashed open and water tumbled out.

Markhim stepped forward anyways. He held his hands up before him and took slow cautious steps toward her. "It's a bad wound. He'll need to be bandaged and quickly, I can—"

"Stop it. Don't come any closer." The water rose up in front of her.

The Samur began chanting, the deep rumble of their voices echoed into the night. She ignored the rumbled of the ground, her hand shoved into her companion's wound.

"Please don't die. Don't you dare die on me, do you hear?" The sea princess stared at the wound with desperate eyes.

"He won't die," Jura said, falling to her knees beside the sea princess. "I won't let him." Jura tore at the sea princesses wrap, muttering prayers to the Everflame under her breath. "We need to stop the bleeding," Jura said, pressing the cloth into his stomach with all her strength. "Help me. Use your magic."

"I can't!" The sea princess screamed her denial and storm clouds gathered above her.

"Do something!" Jura screeched. A streak of light shot across the sky and the ground rumbled. For a brief moment, Jura shone as bright as a thousand suns.

Seconds later the man opened his eyes, blinking up at the sea princess.

"You didn't want me to die." He shot the sea princess a brilliant smile before he fainted.

Tylak blinked. All the blood was gone. There was no sign of injury. *Had Jura done that?*

The sea princess shot to her feet.

"Do you know what would have happened if he'd died?" the woman shrieked.

Jura stepped forward to meet her. "I won't apologize for your own actions. Nor will I allow you to attack my men again. Markhim would never do something so horrendous on his own accord." She took a deep breath. "Please. Let me help you. I don't want to fight anymore . . ." Her voice trailed off and for a moment Tylak thought she was finished. But then she looked up again. Her face was that of a changed woman. She was terrifying, an angry goddess. Her amber eyes were golden infernos, her long hair rippled down her back, pulled by an invisible breeze. The ground rumbled at her feet and when she spoke, the deep rumble of her voice echoed in the now silent night. "But if you again lay a hand on me or any of my men, I will see you drown in a pool of your own making."

Just as suddenly, Jura was herself again. She shot Tylak a terrified glance and he wondered if the wonder on her face mirrored his own.

The only person who seemed unfazed was the sea princess, who cocked her head. "Explain. This time I will listen."

BESHAR

CHAPTER FORTY-SEVEN

The room was silent and cool but dry of wine or any other baser comforts. There was a bucket in the corner. No one had come to offer food or even water, and Beshar began to suspect that no one might show up at all. Tomorrow was his execution. What did his jailors' care if their traitor died hungry? He tried to recover the path that had led him here, but his mind was sluggish due to hunger and fatigue and lack of drink. Jura was still out there. Perhaps she had succeeded down in Kitoi, perhaps even now she was coming back with proof of the treachery that had befallen the house of the Third. He smiled at the prospect. But Kitoi was miles away and the city was dangerous. It was just as likely the Daughter of the First would fail, that she had already failed. He leaned forward, but it was impossible to get his head to rest comfortably on his knees. He gave up and rose to once again pace the short length of his cell.

He was still pacing when the creature posing as Amira arrived. He wondered what her true name was, because surely the creature had a name. It was not some mindless puppet, as he once believed. He eyed her warily.

She was a perfect replica of Amira, right down to the way the Daughter of the Third carried her shoulders, wrought with confidence and the arrogance of youth. He wondered of the real Amira and if she still carried herself the same way.

"Beshar."

"I would greet you in kind, but I don't know what to call you."

"Amira will do." She pursed her lips into what some might call a seductive pout. Beshar once again ached for a cask of wine, but he said nothing, waiting for her to go on. They were silent for several moments, her breathing light and steady and the only sound in the eerily quiet dungeon. Where were all the other prisoners? If anything, the prison should be fuller with all the recent arrests. The people were angry over the new water rations and there was even a shortage on the cictuss. Prices surged in the black market and the people were turning violent. His side of the prison however remained silent and empty, like a tomb.

"You are frightened."

"You're frightening." He stopped his pacing to frown at her. "Who do you work for? Is it Denir? No ... bigger. The Queen of Shadows? How does the arena tie into all this?"

She smiled. "The Queen is nothing but a pawn herself. You ask the right questions. I respect you."

"Enough to release me?"

Her smile widened. "Wouldn't that be fun? But no. No, tomorrow morning you will die, as scheduled."

"So then why did you come down here? To gloat? I would expect that from the likes of Denir but—"

"The Fourth is quite busy at the arena. She is debuting that wonder child of yours. Fighting her against Inferno, if memory serves. I would wager that's a fight you never thought you'd see."

Beads of sweat began to trickle down the length of his spine, but despite that a chill shook his shoulders. "She's too young still for that . . ." He trailed off, thinking about the Arena Councils' interest in the child. The fact that she had been acquired through means of an illegal slave auction. She was caught up in this somehow. *Everflame help him, what did it all mean?*

He swallowed hard and sucked on his tongue. He would give all his possessions for just one more glass of wine. Except, he didn't have any more possessions. Everything had been seized in the name of the Republic.

"You've replaced him too. The First." He stated the realization out loud.

"Blood chains grow inefficient. This is cleaner." Her eyes had widened, but she seemed otherwise unimpressed at his sudden clarity.

"Where is he?"

"Back in his wine cellar. As the Daughter of the First has shown us, it works out quite well."

"It's a foolish plan."

She laughed. The sound was deep and throaty and her shoulders shook with mirth. "Foolish? My plan is a complete success. Everything has worked exactly as I envisioned. I sent the Daughter into action as the First Interim. I killed the family of the Third. Slowly the Thirteen have turned to my side, to *my* plan."

"Why then? You say you act on your own accord, so tell me why? *Who* are you?"

"That's none of your business." She straightened her shoulders and frowned. "I own the Republic now."

Beshar thought of all her recent changes implemented to the government and had to agree. Lately, the Third had had her hands in everything. She controlled over half the council, if for no other reason than the other members were terrified of her. And within reason, she was allegedly single-handedly bringing down the entire Republic.

In the shadows, a figure moved and his heart leapt for a moment at the thought that it might be Kenjiro, finally come to rescue him. But he was the son of the stars, and Beshar knew of only one sort of creature who slithered in the shadows.

"And the Queen of Shadows? What of her?" Beshar had always been a gambling man.

"Why do you continue to bring her up? She is not my master. I'm the one who planned everything. I'm the one who had to infiltrate the Thirteen. She's nothing without me, a worm. I wouldn't be surprised if sh—"

A low gurgling noise replaced her rant and blood bubbled from the slash across her throat.

"My Queen sends her regards," the Shadow Dancer murmured as the *alttaw'am* sank to the floor. As the blood poured out from the body, the creature underneath became evident until there was no evidence of Amira at all. Beshar pulled back against the door of the cage despite himself.

The man was masked, of course. The black silk stretched across his face but his eyes were black and sharp, seeking Beshar in the dark cell.

"I don't know anything if that's why she's sent you," Beshar said, eyeing the gray creature on the stone floor.

"Of course not. If you knew anything at all, you wouldn't be alive." The man's voice held a faint southern accent, most likely from the ports of Kitoi. So that's where the Queen considered home these days. Beshar had to give the man his point. He had not an inkling of the Queen's ulterior motives, except now he knew the arena and his wonder child were somehow involved.

"I suppose the question is, were you sent here to kill me . . . or her?"

"Neither, actually." The man laughed. It was a nice sound, almost musical. "No, I don't suppose my Queen will be too happy with my decision here," he gestured toward the dead body. "The Shadow Dancers do not tolerate dissent among their ranks. This was within my right, but blood magic is no easy feat to come by." His sigh sounded regretful but his dark eyes flickered menacingly in the distant torchlight. He shrugged. "What's done is done. No, the Queen wants you set free. She is giving you another chance. She says you're to find the Daughter of the First and wait for plans from her there. Your man waits for you now. I'll escort you to him." The Shadow Dancer started forward and began to work on the lock, but Beshar could only stare and blink at him from the corner. It took the Shadow Dancer swinging the door open wide and holding his arms out in a harmless gesture before Beshar trusted him enough to leave his cell. Why would the Queen of Shadows care if he was alive or not? And how did she know of his involvement with Jura? He didn't have an opportunity to ask any questions before the Shadow Dancer shoved him into a jog.

The Shadow Dancer pulled him along at an alarming pace, and Beshar had the regrettable thought that he still hadn't been given any sort of dinner. Then the smell grew rancid and Beshar was grateful he held nothing in his stomach to retch up.

KAY

CHAPTER FORTY-EIGHT

It was easy dancing with Ash. She was doing a good job, she could tell, but still she turned to face him to hear reassurance. The flame around her sputtered out. No. Ash was on the ground. She ran toward him but something stopped her from going any further. There was no heat coming from Ash. Already his body turned cold.

She didn't like to think of Mama, but she thought of her now. Kay recognized that smell. She glared at the dragon. He was Rumble's opposite in every way, but now, curled in on himself, he reminded her of her friend. Twin lines of smoke drifted up from his nostrils and he eyed her warily. She noticed the immense heat he carried inside himself. Much more than her own. Ash had said to wait for his signal, turn left, run home . . . there wouldn't be a signal now. The crowd began to jeer, calling for blood. There was heat out there in the thousands of bodies. Kay could feel each individual source. She could pull the heat from them. It would be easy.

But what would Mama say? Mama would be horrified and it would make Daddy sad. All of this would. Kay turned toward the glass spectator box and her eyes met the Fourth. The woman was angry. Her brown eyes narrow and her pretty face slashed into a frown. She was mad because Kay hadn't finished the fight.

Why did this keep happening to her? *Everyone I love dies.*

The crowd continued to scream. Ash, the Greatest Fire Dancer the world had ever known, was dead. She couldn't understand what they were saying but she grew angry all the same. It was their fault too. She suddenly hated the people of the arena, but not as much as she hated that woman who had forced her into the arena. Kay Breathed.

"I'm sorry, Daddy," Kay whispered and blew her flames toward the glass spectator booth, aiming for the Fourth. This had to stop. She was a bad guy. The arena was full of bad guys, and Kay had to put them all down. She searched for more heat, seeking to build her fire. She was so angry all she could think of was adding to the flames. People screamed, but they were nothing to her flames. She Breathed in their body heat, turning it against them. More, she needed more. Kay Breathed in all she could, shooting the flames at the dome. The dragon rose beside her, he too shot out flames at the crowd, ignoring her for the most part.

Kay Breathed in his flames and shot them at the arena dome too. It wasn't enough. All around her the arena was in flames. She had no shortage of heat to Breathe in and yet none of it was hot enough to set her free. She screamed in frustration, Breathing in as much as she dared, more. And still, it wasn't enough. It would never be enough. She needed more.

Yes, there. *That.* In the distance she felt the silent massive hum of the Everflame, the great fire in the capital of the Republic. It was exactly what she needed.

Kay Breathed that in too.

The world plunged into darkness in an instant. Kay was ablaze, brighter than any sun. She felt a million tiny bee stings all at once. It was terrifying and painful, burning and powerful. She quickly learned several things at once. This heat source was unlike any she'd ever held before, a thousand times more powerful than dragon's breath and yet somehow as manageable to her now as her own. She was stronger than she had ever been, stronger than Daddy even. And no one could stop her from leaving now. No one could ever hurt her again.

Turn left, run home. She raised her arm and pure hot fire streamed from her fingertips and into the arena dome. It shattered. Millions of glass pieces fell to the ground around her, slicing at her arms and legs. She didn't care. She was finally and completely free. The warmth of the flame rolled inside her, hotter than her anger. She turned once again to the dragon, Inferno. He dipped his head toward her. It was then Kay noticed the broken assegai embedded in his stomach.

She walked toward him. If circumstances were different, someone might have stopped her. But everyone was gone now, taken from her or burning and at the moment nothing else mattered except for her, the dragon, and the burning fire roaring within her.

She pulled the assegai from him and set the wound on fire. She didn't know what made her do it, she simply knew that it was right. The dragon didn't seem to mind. He stood quietly as she administered to his wounds, watching her with careful eyes.

She was suddenly very tired. *Turn left, run home.*

Home was so very far away. *Don't run, fly.*

Kay walked closer to the dragon, placing her hands along the width of his neck. Inferno sank to the ground. She scrambled on top, wrapping her arms around his neck and digging her fingernails into his scales for support. Kay wasn't frightened. She was hot and alive. She was free.

Turn left, she told the dragon, somehow knowing that he understood. *Fly home.*

JURA

Amira was here. She was real. Tylak had brought her back safe. Was it all finally over? Everything seemed to happen at once. First Markhim, stumbling over himself in his effort to explain the horrors he'd been forced to commit while under the influence of the blood chain. Amira would not be dismissed and demanded answers despite her recent capture. The fire, which had been an imminent threat, had suddenly disappeared along with a distant rumble from the north. Jura felt herself pulled in at least a dozen different directions but one thing remained at the core: the Queen of Shadows needed to be brought down.

Jura turned toward Coral, determined to make a final stand for peace between herself and the Wave Mistress.

"The Queen of Shadows is behind all of this. I aim to find out why. You have my word. My people need yours, I'll admit it. But we can help you too."

"Your father would want to keep the peace. He fought for the Tri- Alliance." Her companion, Kale, she'd heard the Wave Mistress call him, murmured the words at her side but they all heard them.

"My father died in his blindness," Coral snapped in response but she turned back to Jura with raised eyebrows. "I accept your proposal and we will join you here in your quest—"

"We're not staying here. We're going back to the Republic. Something is happening there."

The Wave Mistress laughed, the sound an unpleasant cackle. "Again, the selfishness of the Republic. Already you seek to leave the Queen of Shadows to go back to your home? Please explain why the safety of your own people somehow trumps my own?"

Jura gritted her teeth. Would nothing be easy with this woman?

"Of course I'm not suggesting that. But we need to find out why the Queen of Shadows has taken such an interest in the affairs of the Thirteen."

"Why would we leave now when we know exactly where she is?" The Wave Mistress stabbed her trishula into the earth with a grunt. "I say we attack her now. We'll outnumber her. Surely we can take her. You're scrappy."

Scrappy? Jura swallowed back a sharp retort. "It's more than just outnumbering a single woman. She has an unknown number of Shadow Dancers at her disposal, an entire army of them. And she's working with dark magic," her voice dropped to a dramatic whisper. "Blood magic."

Jura had the satisfaction of seeing surprise bloom across Coral's face. "Is that what you used just now? When you saved Kale?"

Jura shook her head. "When I saved Kale? That was you, your magic."

"My magic? I've heard I'm powerful, but I don't know of any *wei* that can do that. Besides, I didn't *do* anything. That was all you."

Jura refused to believe her, couldn't believe her words to be true. Because if what the Wave Mistress said was true, that meant Jura was discovering yet another frightening side to her strange abilities. It was time to get to the bottom of her powers, to discover just what she was capable of.

"No, we develop a better plan after some more research." She felt Tylak shift beside her and turned to give him a careful once over. He was still bleeding from a shallow cut on his arm but otherwise he appeared uninjured. They needed to talk. She turned to her other side to find Markhim studying her intently. He was going to have a fresh black eye and some of the wounds on his arms had reopened. They needed to talk. They all did. But they could wait.

"We've caused enough of a disturbance here. It's only a matter of time before there's an inquiry into tonight's fiasco."

The Wave Mistress shrugged. "Let them come."

She was more cocky than a Fire Dancer, and Jura had to bite her tongue before she said something she would regret. They needed their access to water. "Even if we manage to fight an Inquisition, you open us up to further damage the Tri-Alliance. We want peace not war."

Coral narrowed her eyes but did not disagree.

When she remained silent, Jura plunged forward. "I merely suggested we return to the Republic because I left my father there, alone. Surely you can understand my need to see to the safety of my house?"

Coral nodded. "And your powers? How is it you are able to breathe water?"

"I can't br . . ." She trailed off, unable to argue that the idea was ridiculous as it was. But she had breathed water. At least it had seemed that way.

"What are you?" Coral pressed further, but Jura shook her head in response. If only she knew the answer to that question.

"I'm still figuring that part out," Jura said. And she would, just as soon as they cleaned up the Republic and stopped the Queen of Shadows. She cleared her throat and addressed the rest of the group. "Everyone, gather your supplies. We head out now. We'll leave the city immediately." She turned toward Coral, "I assume we'll need to make a stop at the ports?" She received a crisp nod from the Wave Mistress.

"Excellent, we'll meet there." Dismissed, the Wave Mistress and her man turned and trotted off toward the docks.

She turned toward Tylak, suddenly remembering an old conversation they'd once had. "You'll get to see the ocean after all." He grinned in response.

"Jura, can we talk?" Markhim had grabbed a gentle hold of her elbow. She nodded and Tylak walked off to join Peppik and the Samur.

"Some night, huh?" She tried to find that easy way between them, the communication that stretched across his easy smile, but his smile was forced and his dark eyes were too serious.

"You'll never understand the torment it was, watching myself perform all those evil deeds . . . it was you who kept my sanity. Thoughts of you, of coming back to you."

"Markhim I—"

"No, don't say it. I see the way you two look at each other. I know there's something there. All I'm asking is just for a chance. A chance to remind you what was between us. A chance to show you I still care. I always have. Can you give me that chance?"

Jura squeezed her fingers into fists, noting the way her nails bit into her palm. It wasn't fair for him to bring this up here, not now. She didn't even know what she wanted. His dark eyes captured her own, their expression pleading. She turned away from him to find Tylak watching them, his gray eyes questioning. He took a step forward but stopped short. He would give her the space to make her own decisions.

She forced herself to look back at Markhim. She had loved him once, she—

Strong talons dug into her shoulder blades and she cried out in pain as she was jerked into the air.

"Jura!" Tylak screamed her name and sprinted forward, but he was too far away.

Markhim lunged at her and caught her by the ankle, jerking her leg painfully. She felt as she if she was being torn in half. Markhim clung on tight, good thing because she was being carried high into the air. The earth pulled away from her and she swallowed down a rush of bile and blinked away the sudden fierce wind.

"Markhim, don't let go!" she screamed as they rose higher and higher into the air.

The air rushed around her as she was swallowed by the night sky.

END OF BOOK TWO

Epilogue

The bed was incredibly soft. This must be what it's like sleeping on a cloud, *Jura thought.*

She bolted upright.

Where am I?

The four-poster bed was in the middle of a large chamber. The room was decorated in soft whites and pale blues with gray marble pillars supporting the circular design. One wall was entirely open and a gentle breeze rippled the gauze curtain. Fresh fruit and water sat on the bedside table. She ignored the offering despite the protests from her stomach.

It was then that she noticed she wasn't alone. A guard with wings stood in the corner watching her. He yelled out that she had awakened, and then announced the Speaker of the Winds as another winged individual entered the room.

Jura blinked at them both.

"Greetings, Jura, Daughter of the First."

"Where am I? Where is Markhim?" She kicked at the comforter, but there were yards of the heavy stuff. She'd managed to twist it all around her in her slumber.

"Be at ease, child." The being identified as the Speaker of the Winds said in a beautifully melodic voice that was very nearly a song. He had an ageless face, unmarred by wrinkles, but appeared older than her father despite that fact. His eyes were as light as the blue in a cloudless sky. "Your friend is safe and so are you. More safe than you have ever been in your life, I'd wager. My name is Danos, and I have brought you here to prevent a war."

"Prevent a war?" Jura demanded, finally succeeding in shoving the covers off her. She blushed when she realized someone had changed her into a heavy sleeping gown. "You can't prevent a war. We're already at war and my people need me," she growled.

"Yes, your people need you to win this war. But also to start this war. We have had Dreams."

Jura leapt off the bed and started forward, but with a quick flick of his wrist her captor sent her sprawling back to bed with a heavy gust of wind.

"So I'm a prisoner then?" Jura gave another quick glance around. There was a third person in the room with them. This one, unlike his companions, did not have wings. He appeared just slightly older than Jura and gave her a sympathetic smile.

"A prisoner? No, my lady. You are our honored guest until such a time when it is deemed safe for you to return home."

"I see. And when will that be?"

The Speaker shrugged. "Only the Dreams will tell us. Please make yourself comfortable during your stay."

He left without another word. Jura jumped out of the bed to hurry after him.

"I can help you get a message to your friends," the young man said. He stepped forward, shoulders hunched forward as if he tried to make himself invisible. He came to a stop beside her and held up his left hand, cupping his right over it and creating a little bowl.

"Speak the message here."

Jura raised her eyebrow, skeptical.

"I promise, speak the words and the winds will carry them to your friends."

"I need to get back home," Jura said stubbornly.

The man nodded, raising his cupped hands toward her. "And you will, after the Dreams. Please, I will send your words."

Jura leaned forward and whispered into his hands.

Hundreds of miles away, Tylak walked north, determined to bring Jura back. He didn't understand what force had allowed her to be taken from him, but he would not stop until she was safe and back where she belonged. He kept a harried pace and still he called for his group to push themselves harder. A gentle breeze stirred his hair. In the caress of the breeze, he smelled jasmine. Tylak stopped short as the whispered words reached out to him, her words.

I'm safe. I will come back to you.

ACKNOWLEDGMENTS

Once again, the first shout out goes to my awesome husband who has to put up with so much more than he ever bargained for when he agreed to become mine. Thank you, Robert, for giving me the freedom to pursue my dreams. I also need to acknowledge my wonderful family, in particular my father and sister who have both spent countless hours on the phone discussing magic theory and plot holes. You two are the best and I'm so lucky to have you in my life. I'd also like to thank Melody Greene, my awesome critique partner for checking me on consistency. Melody, you may have read this series as many times as I have and for that, I can't thank you enough. I also need to give huge creative props to Cari Jehlik and Chelsea Herre. Thank you, ladies, for providing so much creativity when my own failed me! Thank-you to the team at Kingsman Editing for the lovely format and assistance on the relaunch. And finally, to my readers: I can't thank you enough. I still can't believe I have readers! Thank you so much for allowing me to share my story with you, I hope you enjoyed it.

About the Author

Alexis Marrero Deese is an avid reader of young adult and fantasy. Her favorite authors include Brandon Sanderson and Jaqueline Carey. She graduated from the University of South Florida with a Bachelor's Degree in Creative Writing and a sun tan she misses dearly since her move to north Georgia. She has a passion for cooking, spends entirely too much time on Pinterest, and is a self-proclaimed dog training expert for her family's legion of dogs. For more information, visit www.amdeese.com or follow her on Instagram at Instagram.com/authoramdeese.

THE WORLD OF JANGBAHAR

•

THE THIRTEEN

Justir

Velder

Amira

Denir

Geedar

Jabir

Kader

Nasir

Beshar

Tamir

Fatima

Ishani

◆

Cobachon
Leaders of Unburdened

Master of Knowledge—Ferrin Neorar

Master of Faith—Amin Leal

Master of Agriculture—Wadi Xola

Master of Health—Ruqayyah Tarub

Master of Peace—Abro Azaha

Master of Economics—Ortuna Nomero

Master of Judgement—Hadiya Nazahah

Master of Histories—Aja Nizboth

Master of Arts—Iona Notsfar

Master of War—Ishani Azaha

SUBMERGED

Dance of the Elements

Book II

Learn more about A.M. Deese
and explore her other titles at
www.amdeese.com